Jackie Watson was born in Newcas
partner and their adored Miniature
village, close to the banks of the Tyn
Bay trilogy which was born out of a recurring dream.
second instalment.

From the reviews of *Apokeri Bay:*

'As temperatures dropped at home, I found sunshine in this page-turner which transports readers to glorious Greece. … This feel-good debut is perfect for all lovers of women's contemporary fiction, or anyone seeking sunshine.' *Living North Magazine*

'I would defy anyone to resist visiting [Lefkada] after reading this gorgeous novel. Evocative, engaging and the perfect advert for this stunning setting, I enjoyed every word of this delightful story.' *Bookaholic Bex*

'A Fantastic Holiday Read!!! … The writer transported me to Greece from the first page with all the beautifully vivid descriptions, then when you add to this the vibrant characters and a story that does not go where you expect it to, each twist giving me an oh or ah moment along with some unknown Geordie facts!' *Goodreads review*

'My favourite book so far this year … It's all too easy to pick big authors whose work I know and trust or well publicised books. I was recommended this by a friend … I am so pleased I bought this. It's definitely an 'unputdownable' book and reading it was very much time well spent. It's beautifully written with great characters & storyline and so much more than just a 'love story'. Thank goodness there's the second instalment on its way, I can't wait.' *Amazon review*

BY JACKIE WATSON

Apokeri Bay
Saving Elora

SAVING ELORA

THERE'S MORE THAN ONE
LIFE AT STAKE

Jackie Watson

First published in Great Britain in 2024 by Hawthorn Wren
This paperback edition published by Hawthorn Wren

Copyright © Jackie Watson 2024

The right of Jackie Watson to be identified as the author of this work has been asserted in accordance with the Copyright, Designs and Patents Act 1988.

All rights reserved. No part of this publication may be reproduced, stored in or transmitted into any retrieval system, in any form, or by any means (electronic, mechanical, photocopying, recording or otherwise) without the prior written permission of the publisher. Any person who does any unauthorised act in relation to this publication may be liable to criminal prosecution and civil claims for damages.

NO AI TRAINING: Without in any way limiting the author's [and publisher's] exclusive rights under copyright, any use of this publication to "train" generative artificial intelligence (AI) technologies to generate text is expressly prohibited. The author reserves all rights to license uses of this work for generative AI training and development of machine learning language models.

A CIP catalogue record for this book is available from the British Library

ISBN: 978 1 7393404 1 4

This is a work of fiction. Names, characters, businesses, places, events and incidents are either the products of the author's imagination or used in a fictitious manner. Any resemblance to actual persons, living or dead, or actual events is purely coincidental.

In memory of Rose Watson, forever missed

Prologue

The exclusive eco-tourist resort nestled jewel-like in an ancient Thai rainforest, but for the only resident languishing in the bar, the opulent lifestyle was losing its sheen. The man stretched out his six-foot-three frame on a comfy rattan sofa and obligingly flashed the quietly spoken receptionist his best smile. A smile that melted hearts. A smile that loosened knicker-elastic and emptied bank accounts.

He casually signalled for another drink and yawned. God, he was bored. It would be so easy to seduce the pretty Thai employee. She was smitten and believed him to be the cash-strapped and downtrodden partner of an uber-rich, uber-bitch who held the purse strings tighter than Ebenezer Scrooge. And the best bit, his fiancée unwittingly helped in the charade as she sneered down her privately educated and privileged nose at the whole world.

Yes, bedding the hired help might be fun but he just couldn't be arsed. His fiancée should have been a winning lottery ticket – easy on the eye, adventurous between the sheets (and everywhere else) and more than happy to rattle through daddy's money. The banking tycoon was delighted his daughter was off globetrotting (undoubtedly glad to be shot of her). The man had barely raised an eyebrow at their engagement after three months. It made Javier wonder if her father gave a toss. He certainly wouldn't be so calm if his only child announced plans to marry a seemingly penniless stranger double her age. In his experience, those that saw themselves as a cut above were often the easiest to deceive. And in a grungy Bangkok hostel, Suzy had been the easiest of them all. He'd immediately clocked her and, over a drink, she'd spouted claims of being a hard-up American traveller, forced to work menial jobs to get by. Heaven knows how anyone fell for that claptrap. Everything about her screamed wealth. And in turn, he spun his fictitious tale of woe, hesitantly confiding how it was such a comfort to find somebody so understanding and easy to talk to. As the drinks continued to flow, he'd fearfully taken her hand and, with guilty embarrassment, admitted to being confused. He felt such a strong connection (surely, she did too?), which made his broken heart sing. But how could it be right so soon after the tragic death of his wife? He'd abruptly pulled away and hurriedly requested that she allow him to go. He should leave, he'd said too much. She'd expected a pleasant evening and not to be burdened by his hardships when hers were far worse.

She'd implored him to stay, persuaded him to put aside guilt and accept that fate had brought them together. And through his honesty, she wanted to do likewise and tearfully admitted to the (obvious) truth of being an heiress. She'd wanted to be liked for herself, not her father's vast wealth. He enveloped her in his arms, sympathised and soothed away her apologies before they tenderly kissed and returned to the backpackers long enough to gather their belongings. He then watched as she flounced up to the reception desk of the city's most luxurious hotel and demanded the best suite – where they feasted on room service for a week. After that, it was five-star living all the way as each place became more luxurious than the last, and they crammed their days with once-in-a-lifetime experiences. It would and should have been easy to carry on, but the novelty had worn off. And for the simple reason – it had become far too easy. Suzy was the culmination of three years swindling a never-ending line of naïve women All he needed to do was turn on the charm, say what they wanted to hear, and bingo. In an attempt to refocus, he withdrew a crumpled handwritten note from his wallet.

Gone to fry me the biggest fish ever! No hard feelings. It was good while it lasted. Thanks for the memories. Cx

His wife's betrayal still festered like a cankerous sore. With Claris, their European scams had been complicated and thrilling. High risk. High reward. He missed that. It was the only thing he had missed apart from their ill-gotten gains. As the ultimate con artist, she'd passed on all her skills and expertise, and they'd been the perfect team for twelve years, right until she walked out, taking all the money. God only knew where the current Mrs Owens was residing, but she would be hustling. It was in her DNA.

Forced to start again, Javier had headed east. South East Asia, to be precise. A perfect location with many unsuspecting fools looking for adventure, a new start or a way to disappear. Having honed his skills, he was now a high-calibre con artist, clever, level-headed, and calculating. With multiple aliases and a master of accents (the soft Irish brogue always went down well), he could justify to himself and anyone else whatever needed doing.

At forty-three with a trim physique and brooding charismatic looks courtesy of Welsh and Spanish heritage, there was never any problem in bedding and then extracting exorbitant amounts of money from any sane woman between twenty and seventy. Javier was flexible regarding age, nationality, ethnicity, religion, and beauty. That was one thing he prided himself on – inclusivity. And that liberal open-mindedness paid dividends.

He caught himself repeatedly flicking his left ring finger and thumb together – a rare tell. Thinking about Claris led to impatience and irritation. It still grated, that he'd never caught a whiff of her double-dealing. He should have seen it coming, but the con man had been well and truly conned. So, he kept the tattered bit of paper in his wallet as a reminder to stay sharp and trust no one. At least the wedding ring came in useful for the heartbroken husband act.

Javier withdrew a second wedding ring from his wallet. This one seldom saw the light. He'd even managed to keep it secret from Claris, who'd lovingly referred to his first wife as 'that pathetic little pipsqueak'. He knocked back his cocktail, signalled

3

the waiter for another and stared at the dull gold band resting in his palm. She'd saved so hard to buy it. After all these years, why couldn't he part with it? Before the waiter arrived, he stuffed it back into its hiding place.

Javier leaned back and glanced across the empty open-air lounge. All the other guests were probably off in stifling temperatures on tailored excursions. Even after he'd spent three years flitting around Southeast Asia, the heat was a killer. Underneath his pristine white shirt and linen trousers, sweat coated his skin. It was mid-March and the dry season. Great for viewing wildlife but not much else. Above him, the ceiling fan barely moved the air. Suzy was ensconced in their lavish bungalow, undoubtedly pondering over which of a dozen outfits to wear for their night safari. That was fine by him. The longer, the better. His third sabai sabai was going down rather too well, best switch to water. With nothing better to do, his coal-black eyes strayed to a selection of glossy eco-magazines on the coffee table. He managed to work up enough enthusiasm to grab one. It promised to reveal the best-kept holiday escapes. Javier snorted cynically but flicked to the article anyway. Unsurprisingly, his current corner of paradise took pride of place. His eyes skimmed down the list and paused at a luxurious eco-spa hotel on a tiny island called Tharesseti.

Why did that name ring a bell? His usually pin-sharp memory drew a blank, so he continued to listlessly turn the pages and almost dropped his glass. A double-page spread waxed lyrical about the best bike tours available on planet Earth, but that wasn't what had snapped his spine straight. It was the four business owners, proudly posing in front of their upmarket establishment. One of whom was the first Mrs Owens.

He punched in *Round the Bend Lefkada*, and Google delivered page after page of hits. A cunning smile played across his lips as he scrolled through the impressive website. Why not go back to the very start? Almost fifteen years had passed. Did she still think of him? Her first true love. Back then, he rarely veered off the straight and narrow, but nevertheless, she was smart. A thrill of excitement ran through him at the prospect of the ultimate high-risk, high-reward hustle. A frosty reception was the least he could expect after what he'd done. But that was the challenge after all. Alert now, Javier studied the picture and article closely. She remained beautiful, clearly kept herself fit and had the same smile that lit up a room. The woman appeared to be doing extraordinarily well for herself but would be on her guard. However, he had no doubt her personality would still be hardwired to see the very best in people, combined with that unwavering compulsion to help.

Javier drained his cocktail.

It was high time to pay Mrs Anna Makris a visit.

Chapter One

Anna Makris exited the gates into the pretty village square and inhaled the cool afternoon air. The rain had ceased but water dripped steadily from bare branches that stretched skeleton-like into an overcast sky. The domino club wouldn't do battle under those boughs until the leaves returned. Behind the plane trees, worn steps ascended to the centuries-old church. The unlocked doors would be thrown open in summer to let in a refreshing breeze, but for now remained closed. Ten years earlier as a British tourist (who'd arrived for a five-day Greek island getaway and never left), she'd married one of Apokeri's most eligible bachelors – the culmination of a five-month whirlwind romance. And nobody had been surprised when less than nine months later the villagers welcomed another new arrival. And it was the behaviour of that new arrival which had seen Anna summoned to appear at a post-school meeting.

As the church bell chimed four, Anna lightly jumped over a puddle and grinned. The meeting had gone well. That is, well for her. The same couldn't be said for the other two attendees. In her usual friendly and polite way, she'd wiped the floor with them in under an hour. To celebrate she decided to walk the longer route home. This early in March, Apokeri was ghostly quiet. Off-season for the quaint seaside village meant only vital businesses opened mid-week. Day-trippers did pass through twelve months of the year but they were mostly from other parts of Lefkada. Some hardened individuals rocked up in the shoulder season but, typically, the trickle of tourists started around Easter and steadily built to a flood. By June all village outlets were flat out seven days a week. Until October when the village began to wind down again. Or for some, collapse into an exhausted heap.

Turning right, Anna passed the Makris commercial bakery and this time inhaled the intoxicating scent of bread, lingering in the damp air. Next door, Aphrodite Café was lifeless. At this time of year, her mother-in-law's business only opened at the weekend. Straight ahead, across the beachfront road, lay the picturesque curved promenade with palm trees and planters packed with early flowering shrubs and bulbs. And hemmed in by towering chalky cliffs lay the turbulent sea. Instead of the chatter of tourists, there was only the relentless crashing of dark stormy waves against wind-wiped sand and the scream of seabirds overhead. Another band of wet weather was passing through and it remained unseasonably cold. But Anna didn't care. She loved Apokeri any time of the year.

Turning left, she waved to a couple of residents popping into the supermarket, and – striding past Odyssey Travel – she knocked on the glass and startled her friend Dania who sat tinkering on a computer. The roadside path continued, leaving behind the horseshoe bay with its boarded-up pedalo hire business, beachside tavernas and, a mile out to sea, Tharesseti island. On her right, the land rose sharply. And on the left, scrub and rocks replaced the higgledy-piggledy mix of whitewashed and terracotta-topped stone-built houses. In five minutes, her family home appeared. Even this early in the year its trellis was smothered with greenery and hid the courtyard from prying eyes. The six-bedroomed house hunkered at the bottom of the torturously steep road out of the village. And next to that sat Round the Bend.

The business was completely unrecognisable from the first time she'd viewed it over a decade ago. Then it was a typical Greek whitewashed building with a first storey featuring bright blue shutters and a vibrant bougainvillaea vine scrambling up and over the roof. In its place was a glass and steel three-storey building with clean, modern lines and eco-credentials that still welcomed those wishing to hire a push bike or take a cycling tour. But the business had since expanded. The ground floor was now a bustling bistro-gallery-bike enterprise and the upper storeys provided guest accommodation.

Anna pushed open the door and her glasses immediately fogged up in the warmth. The regulars were still in attendance. The Apokeri domino club hunkered down in the bistro until the weather warmed up enough for village square combat. In the other corner (as if there was some sort of battle of the sexes going on) was the unofficial village knitting club who would decamp to Aphrodite Café later in the year. Until then, both groups turned up every day to exchange light-hearted banter with one another.

Round the Bend was jointly owned by Anna, her husband Filip, his best mate and secret lover Alex and – for the last five years – Anna's friend, fellow Geordie (and now brother-in-law) Andrew. All of them had unanimously agreed to keep the doors open all year. People needed a place to escape to and it had become a community hub, with a steady flow of patrons keeping the business ticking over.

Amongst the regulars sat two Makris family members. With schoolbooks, a sketching pad, coloured pencils and a laptop strewn across a table was Anna's nine-year-old daughter, Evie. And at her feet with head resting on enormous paws lay Cleo. The half Molossus of Epirus/half probably German Shepherd (but we're not sure because your mother slunk off one day and nine weeks later produced an unexpected litter of six pups) was Evie's shadow. Given half the chance, the hound would have also attended the village primary school.

There was no doubting who Evie's mother was. She was a mini-version of Anna in many ways with studious hazel eyes, fine dark hair and skin that tanned easily. Both were stubborn and academic and steered away from being the centre of attention.

Demisting her glasses, Anna kissed her daughter's head. 'How's it going, kiddo?'

Evie looked up nervously. 'Did you get in trouble because of me?'

'Don't be silly,' Anna replied and was again struck by how her daughter always put the welfare of others first. It probably stemmed from all the intensive hospital treatment Evie coped with as a toddler during her cancer treatment. Thank God, she'd made a full recovery. 'There's nothing to worry about, sweetheart.'

Her daughter bent over and ruffled Cleo's fur. 'See I told you, girl. Mam always sorts everything out, doesn't she? It's because she's the best.' Cleo raised her large head as the kitchen door swung open but immediately settled back down when she saw an empty-handed Alex.

He gave Anna a tight smile. She grinned back but inwardly sighed. She recognised that look and it probably meant he and Pip (her nickname for Filip) had been arguing again. Undoubtedly, the same topic which continued to rumble on for the last four years and showed no signs of disappearing. The door opened, and in walked Pip. He and Alex glowered at each other and, as usual, her friend broke eye contact first and vanished into the kitchen.

'Dad.' Evie bounced on her chair. 'Come and see what I did at school today.'

After kissing her husband, Anna chatted with her regulars and then busied herself behind the counter. Pip and Evie huddled together, giggling. The pair were as thick as thieves and, for Anna, it proved the adage that people see what they want to see. Evie was slim, tall for her age, funny and mischievous – like Pip. People always commented on the similarities. But Pip wasn't Evie's biological father. That title belonged to Daniel Eckvardsson. The former owner of Round the Bend and Anna's secret lover for a few short weeks. He had departed Apokeri before Anna knew she was pregnant. Only three people on the planet knew the truth – Anna, Pip and Alex. For over ten years, the trio had been bound by two secrets. And Anna could see no reason why anything should change, because no matter how badly Pip and Alex argued, Anna knew neither would ever betray her trust. And she would never betray theirs.

Chapter Two

Dominique appraised her gorgeous new kitchen and prepared supper for one. She placed the sharp knife on the granite worktop and massaged tense shoulders. Another tough week, but as always, everything got done. Time to enjoy the weekend. As usual, breakfasting tomorrow down at Brindisi harbourside, a bracing walk before her husband went to the gym and (fingers crossed) a leisurely lunch with her mother.

She stretched her neck, and a satisfying click released days of tension spent analysing data lines. Out of habit, she studied the clock. Twenty hundred hours. Sergio and Hector would be halfway to the location. She could recite their operation word for word, having spent hours double- and then triple-checking everything. Two things drove her obsession: to keep both men safe, and her lack of trust in Hector the impeccably loyal but psychopathic employee. His outward demeanour suggested a conservative mamma's boy dressed in brown and beige cardigans and pleated polyester trousers, combined with a monotonous nasal voice. But underneath, he was a sadist and favourite of the infrequently seen boss. Only Sergio would work with him. She endured his frequent visits for meals or to watch the footie. Her skin crawled in his company, but she kept up the welcoming hostess act to keep him sweet and ensure Sergio got home in one piece. Many of Hector's former partners hadn't been so lucky.

It was early April and dark outside the vast expanse of unadorned glass – company policy. An easy concession to make as the building's clever design kept prying eyes out. She loved the spacious two-bedroom apartment handily located a few miles outside the southern Italian city. Each block contained four units built on Passivhaus principles with relaxing communal gardens. It was a company street and a peaceful sanctuary from highly specialised and sometimes deadly professions. There'd initially been objections to the new development, grumblings about wetland destruction – soon silenced after a quiet word in the right ear. The move a year ago marked an unofficial promotion for an ambitious couple ahead on their career plan. It would take time, considerable talent, and significant guile to reach the same position as her beloved father. But Dominique was determined to do it in his memory.

Her bright reflection in an emerald-green silk blouse and a fuchsia pencil skirt stood out against grey matt units. She adored colour and fondly remembered her father saying it matched an upbeat personality. Despite leaving the gym an hour ago, she'd remain in her work outfit and full make-up until bedtime. And then silk pyjamas or satin chemise. *One must always look one's best* was her mother's motto – neither woman did loungewear. Dominique's only concession was to remove stilettos at the door to protect the oak-engineered floor. She wiggled newly painted toenails and laughed as her playful four-year-old cockapoo pounced on them.

'Pesce.' Dominique drew out her beloved fur baby's name. He instantly stopped and inquisitively tilted his head. 'Look what I've got.'

Eyes tracked the red ball as Dominique slowly moved it from side to side and then a tan blur hurtled across the open-plan room to assail a prized and misshapen toy. She returned to the soothing and rhythmic chopping of vegetables with a backdrop of relaxing jazz. It was usually just Pesce and her at night; Sergio worked most evenings. He always laughed and said the graveyard shift was murder – literally. It'd been that way all their married life, and (just like her mother had), she accepted the arrangement. But eating alone was no excuse to skimp on good food, and cooking kept her mind occupied. She glanced at the calendar. Another month had slipped by with yet another negative pregnancy test.

A single tear slid down her cheek and she hastily dried her face as Pesce leapt onto the sofa. His whole body was rigid, snout twitching at the blackness. Seconds later, headlights flooded the private driveway. Dominique frowned. She wasn't expecting anyone, and people didn't arrive unannounced on this street. Everyone made an appointment. Even family. Not that her mother ever came around. Sergio wouldn't return until the early hours. She studied the surveillance monitor (all employee houses came equipped with one). The knife shook in her hand, and the half-chopped onion skittered across the countertop and bounced onto the floor. Pesce failed to notice as he remained on high alert. The onion's brown skin crackled in her hand as she placed it back on the chopping board.

She watched with mounting fear as the bulletproof Bentley came to a dignified stop. A minute later, burly Vincent opened the passenger door to reveal her boss. Dominique swallowed as the next camera picked up the two men walking to her front door. The infamous chauffeur/bodyguard/anything else required carried a bulging black tote bag. There were only three reasons Francis Del Ambro Contino Junior made unexpected visits:

To reward the employee with a promotion on a job well done.

To offer condolences on the death whilst in the line of duty of a spouse or close family member.

To regretfully announce the employee's services were terminated due to an unsuccessful mission or a perceived breach of trust.

Dominique confidently disregarded the first two. Although she was exceptional at her job (the best in her division), she'd done nothing outstanding in the last few weeks. And while her mother was out of it on a cocktail of booze most of the time, she was unlikely to enter through the pearly gates anytime soon. And meticulous planning meant Sergio and Hector always came home safe.

That left the final reason.

Running through her operations, Dominique failed to see how she could have possibly signed her own death warrant, and she was no informer. Complete company loyalty had been drummed in from birth. Rumour had it that if the boss kissed your forehead, a few seconds later Vincent put a bullet through it. But nobody knew because nobody lived to say otherwise.

When the doorbell chimed, it sounded sombre – her funeral toll, perhaps?

A consummate professional, Dominique pushed back her shoulders. At least the face in the hallway mirror appeared calmly confident with flawless make-up framed by long black glossy hair. Plastering on a smile, she turned the handle.

'What an unexpected surprise, sir,' she uttered before descending into a coughing fit. After an eternity, she gulped down enough air to continue. 'Please come in. I hope all's well.'

Her boss turned and nodded to his accomplice. Dominique froze until Vincent was dismissed. She clung to the door, fearing her legs might give way with relief. He wasn't here to kill her. Not yet, anyway. Instead, he stepped over the threshold to appraise her home.

'I'm pleased the boys did a good job with the kitchen fitting.'

'Oh yes, I had no hesitation in leaving them unattended. Thank you. We love it.' She winced on hearing herself sound like a hyperactive cheerleader, but he waved away her gratitude with a manicured hand.

'Think nothing of it. One is always happy to bestow gifts on those who deserve praise,' he replied and circled the kitchen island before placing the bag next to the chopping board with its gleaming knife. Nonchalantly picking it up, he pressed the deadly sharp blade against his thumb. 'I'm glad you keep this in tip-top condition.'

He gave her a dazzling smile and reached into the bag. Dominique braced herself and hoped the end would be painlessly quick. Instead, he pulled out a bottle of expensive wine. 'I remember seeing you drink red at last month's party.'

The event had been a no-expense-spared masked ball to celebrate Mr and Mrs Del Ambro Contino Junior's golden wedding anniversary. Married at eighteen, they were still going strong. Francis had gone as Beelzebub and his wife as Mother

Theresa, and as he'd been the centre of attention, Dominique was surprised he'd noticed her preference. It gave her a buzz. She'd suggested the party's castle location as it held a special place in her heart, having gone there aged eight to one of the company's New Year's Eve parties. As the daughter of a senior employee, she had slept princess-like in a four-poster bed. Four months later, her father was dead.

'Come, Dominique, let's not stand on ceremony,' he said and opened a drawer to produce a corkscrew. 'Can I not drop in to see one of my most trusted employees? But to call you that is a gross disservice. You're so much more. Guided by your father' – he made the sign of the cross – 'you've equalled his loyalty to my father with your loyalty to me. As has your husband.'

She accepted a generous glass of wine and raised it in salute. 'Thank you, sir. That's very kind.'

'Please, call me Francis.' He smiled indulgently, his crows' feet deepening around soulful eyes that rested on half-chopped ingredients. 'It appears I'm intruding on your preparations.'

To fortify her nerves, Dominique took a swig of wine. It tasted wonderful, and he swiftly refilled her glass. 'Would you like to stay for supper? I was in the middle of preparing a pasta bake.'

'That would be delightful. Milena is out at some fundraising event. I don't like eating alone, and one tires of the fawning attentions from restaurant proprietors.' He shrugged off his Saville Row jacket and rolled up his crisp white shirt sleeves. 'However, I insist on helping.'

Dominique laughed. 'Fantastic, Sergio is more of a liability in the kitchen than a help.'

For the next hour, they chatted like old friends, which Dominique found remarkable as their paths seldom crossed. She was merely a tiny cog in the company wheel and not part of his world, but she soon discovered they had so much in common. Surely this couldn't be the same man people spoke about in fearful whisperings. He was interested in her childhood, her dreams, and what she hoped for in the future. In turn, he hinted at the realities of running a multi-billion-euro organisation and the need to constantly be on his guard, never entirely sure who to trust. His wife and children threaded through the conversation, and he clearly loved them deeply. By the time the meal was ready, one wine bottle stood empty, and Dominique reached up to the wine rack for a second.

'Let me,' he said, and his hand brushed against hers. She caught the scent of Bleu de Chanel. The same aftershave Sergio wore.

She quickly stepped away and mumbled an apology. 'Sorry, I always seem to be in the wrong place.'

His eyes held hers. 'I can't imagine you ever being in the wrong place.'

She hastily dished up. As the alcohol flowed, the conversation moved on to favourite holidays and days out. Francis was a good listener, and Dominique relaxed again to happily recount family trips to Rome, Florence, Pompeii, Venice and countless others. In turn, he talked about sailing around the Med and his favourite pastime – scuba diving. They were opening a third bottle in no time, and he spoke about the joy of being a parent. Was it something she hoped for? Dominique glanced at the hateful calendar. Each month it mocked her inability to produce life. Silence descended for the first time that night, and even the music had stopped.

She sat at the dining-room table and swivelled her wine glass backwards and forwards. Her boss was mortified at his crass question and kept apologising. It opened the floodgates and out poured five years of failing hope, growing despair and her mounting obsession with having a baby. All the tests showed a clean bill of health, and all the specialists said it was simply a matter of patience. But time was ticking. She was thirty-two, and Sergio was thirty-eight, and both being only children, they wanted a big family. Francis nodded to Pesce, who obediently sat waiting for titbits. Yes, he was their surrogate child and a much pampered and adored one at that. Taking her hand, Francis kissed it and implored her to have faith. The doctors were right; she must relax and give it time. He had every confidence and could see her as a fantastic mother.

After a deliciously wicked chocolate mousse, Dominique returned to the kitchen and stood in front of the monstrous chrome coffee machine with its myriad of dials. It was Sergio's pride and joy. He'd boasted employees of their ranking didn't receive this model but a notable exception had been made due to their unfailing dedication to go above and beyond. She still had no clue how it worked and half-heartedly pressed a few buttons for nothing to happen. She hadn't heard Francis's approach until he whispered in her ear.

'There's always instant.' She jumped, and he playfully asked, 'Do I frighten you, Dominique?'

His voice was velvet, a lover's caress. And those intense brown eyes reached into her soul. She laughed nervously but this time plucked up enough courage to hold his gaze for a few seconds. 'You're a powerful man and frighten lots of people.'

***

The coffee cups were almost empty when Francis cleared his throat. 'I wasn't entirely honest with you earlier, Dominique. I didn't just pop around on a social visit.'

She instinctively grasped her throat. It'd all been an elaborate ploy to drop her defences. A last supper before the curtain came down on her pitifully short existence. On the counter sat the bag with something large inside. She suppressed a fearful cry as he reached inside but then squeaked with relief when he brought out a bottle of Disaronno, an A4 brown envelope and a beautiful bouquet. He filled the glasses with ice and then a generous slug.

'I think you might need this.' He sighed and slid a glass across the kitchen counter with the envelope.

She cautiously withdrew three pages of text and flicked through a raft of date-stamped surveillance photos, all at the same villa location. She necked her drink, and Francis swiftly refilled it.

The images slid out of her hand, and she grabbed the report. Another three fingers of Disaronno vanished, and she motioned for more and read out loud.

'Monika Gallante, aged thirty-four. Italian national. No criminal record. No outstanding debts. Bank accounts totalling EUR127,438. A freelance fitness instructor clearly pays well. Owner-occupier of a substantial villa outside Ostuni.' Dominique hissed and took another gulp. Rising above the Murgia plain, the white city was her and Sergio's favourite haunt. They spent hours exploring its medieval streets before tucking themselves away in a cute bistro. It was on the steps of the cathedral Sergio dropped down on bended knee nine years ago. 'It cannot be established when the relationship began, but a reliable estimate would be over twelve months based on the age of …'

She snatched up the photos and rifled through Sergio enjoying the company of a stunning blonde – eating and drinking on the terrace, frolicking in the pool, laughing on sun loungers – and past more intimate ones taken through a bedroom window. The woman certainly had curves in all the right places. And then she came to them – a full glass of Italian liqueur burned her throat – a newly furnished nursery and unconditional love in the couple's eyes. It confirmed her worse fears. Sergio had fathered a child. Hot, angry tears splashed onto the evidence of his betrayal. This couldn't be happening to her. This only happened to stupid wives, too dense to notice their unsatisfied husbands chose to screw around. Plenty of company employees did. So much so that it seemed a prerequisite. Laughing bitterly at past fidelity conversations with Sergio, she dropped her head for a curtain of hair to hide her shame and despair.

'I thought you had a right to know,' Francis said with sadness and blotted her tears away with a handkerchief. It was no longer white but streaked with mascara. 'I hope I did the right thing?'

'I'm sorry.' She went to take the stained cloth. 'I've ruined it.'

'There are more important things in life than a piece of cotton. What will you do?'

'I-I don't know.'

He traced the line of her cheekbone. 'Sergio is a halfwit for taking up with some insipid blonde nobody behind the back of a captivatingly clever wife. You're beautiful, Dominique. A young Sandra Bullock, I hasten to say. Now, if I was thirty years younger…'

When his fingers brushed her lips, she made no movement and in his eyes she saw unsuppressed desire. Her stomach did a slow somersault. His fingers slowly caressed her neck, and she still didn't pull away. When he reached her collarbone, she raised an eyebrow. The whisper in her ear was delightful.

'Am I a fool, Dominique, to believe there's a mutual attraction? After all, I'm old, and you're a tantalising young enigma. Why—'

She didn't know who made the first move, but she found herself up against the fridge, ripping open his shirt. Her fingers raked over his bare flesh, as did her tongue and lips. He was in amazing shape, with a carpet of grey chest hair contrasting against taught, tanned skin. He wrenched up her tight skirt and clawed open her blouse. The fridge magnets dug into her back, and she pushed against them because it needed to hurt. Physical pain needed to replace searing emotional despair. She desperately tugged at his belt and yanked open his fly. He was hard. And both their eyes shone with lust.

'This is what you do to me,' he murmured, tearing at her underwear. She cried out as elastic cut into her skin and then snapped. He hurled her onto the kitchen counter and clambered on top, sending dirty crockery, cutlery and glasses spinning and smashing onto the floor before thrusting himself inside her. She clawed, bit, swore and ordered him on. The whole time his eyes greedily devoured her flesh as he called her his whore. His Domore.

The sex mirrored her emotions – highly charged, aggressive and raw. She expected it to be short-lived, but his staying power was incredible. He fed off her rage, grabbing her hair, yanking it back so her swan-like neck was inches from his mouth, and then sunk perfect white teeth into her flesh. He drew blood and, in heightened excitement, slurped at the red droplets. His other hand groped her breasts and he bit down till she screamed in pain and ecstasy. It was what she wanted – anything but tenderness. Again and again, he drove into her, lost in a power-crazed frenzy and when she finally had absolutely nothing left to give, he came inside her with the bellowing roar of a rutting stag. 'You're mine now. Forever!' he shouted, triumphantly.

She flopped down on the warm floor with a self-satisfied smile. 'I know.'

He tenderly kissed her lips and gathered his things. He needed to go. His ripped shirt was beyond repair, only an odd button remained and it hung open underneath his expensive jacket. She kissed the red welts already appearing on his chest, and in response he cupped her buttocks, pulling her naked frame against him, and then pushed her backwards. His hand slid down to her flat stomach, and a wicked smile licked the corners of his mouth.

'Imagine if our union has produced life. Everyone would think it was Sergio's. Wouldn't that be the ultimate revenge? To pass off another man's child as your husband's.' In return, she kissed him hard on the mouth. 'Enjoy your shower, Domore. It's something we can do together next time.'

After the door clicked shut, she allowed herself a smug grin and began the task of cleaning up a devastated kitchen.

Chapter Three

Dominique carefully shifted her weight on the leather kitchen stool. Her whole body ached. She tugged down the sleeve of her black polo-neck jumper to hide a particularly nasty scratch and picked off a stray dog hair from smartly tailored black trousers. A tan dog and dark clothing were a bad combination, but the outfit was a deliberate choice. It hid a myriad of bites, bruises and cuts from last night and mourned the passing of her happy marriage and, to a greater extent, her common sense.

Sergio had slid in beside her just after two, and she'd gritted her teeth in discomfort and anger as he kept to the usual script of cuddling up and whispering that she'd kept him and Hector safe before rolling over to crash out. She slipped out from under the duvet only a few hours later. He'd be confronted later but on her terms.

Everything hurt, and she wanted to scream at her gross stupidity, despite a splitting headache. She closed her eyes and focused on her breathing until calmness was restored (for the moment). A helpful technique from a weekend yoga retreat that had been the perfect cover for an intel operation. She cast her mind back to the previous evening. The smug grin had remained as she swept up and bagged the debris, loaded the dishwasher with the few undamaged items and wiped down all the counters. It also continued as she enjoyed a blissfully hot shower. Afterwards, she'd even appraised her reflection and congratulated herself for remaining in shape. The athletic figure was a perfect specimen from years spent at the company's gym, pool and football pitch. Climbing into bed, she'd been proud of her conquest and his wanting more. But even as she drifted off to sleep with the scent of fresh soap, her analytical brain subconsciously started to go over the evening's events. Even if her husband's infidelity had spectacularly gone unnoticed, there was a reason Dominique was a valued employee, rising swiftly through the ranks. She had a gift for spotting subtle inconsistencies that others missed. It started with the Sandra Bullock comment and niggled away. Thirty minutes later, she lay wide awake in the pitch-black silence. Only Sergio ever called her that in the privacy of their own home, often in those tender moments between the sheets. She loved how he believed it, but Dominique was no fool. She resembled Sandra Bullock as much as a mule did to a thoroughbred racehorse. Slowly, she broke down the sequence of events, how Francis had brought her favourite red wine, her favourite liqueur, her favourite flowers. How he'd worn Sergio's aftershave, knew how Pesce loved to be scratched in a particular spot between his ears and he'd even used an infrequently used term of endearment for her fur baby – fluffball monster. And with a sickening feeling, Dominique realised Francis had known his way around the kitchen without asking. How did he know where everything was? She'd reordered the kitchen after the workers left. She saw the whole night for what it was – a seduction, an elaborate game. She'd been too nervous, awestruck and blinded by anger at Sergio's betrayal to notice. Looking back, she realised Francis had only sipped his wine and left the liqueur untouched. It meant she'd consumed almost three bottles of potent red wine and a bottle of Disaronno. No wonder she'd readily succumbed to his charms.

Although many employees had affairs, Dominique was willing to bet her boss didn't pop around to console them. So why her? It didn't make any sense. In the end, she'd sneaked into the spare room, gone to her surveillance bag of tricks and carefully swept the house under cover of darkness. And sure enough, the whole place was bugged. She couldn't determine if it was audio or audio and visual. Either way, she'd returned to bed with an appalling sense of violation. Everything she and Sergio did and said was being recorded and scrutinised.

And then the words of Francis floated into her head. 'You're mine now.'

What had she done? Nothing would ever be the same again. Being an employee of a powerful, ruthless man was one thing, but being his mistress would open her up to him in a terrifyingly emotional way. Lying as part of her job was easy enough, but would she be able to play the Domore role? Not that well, she feared. And then what? Despite what Sergio had done and her obsession with wanting a baby, she didn't want to carry another man's child and pass it off as her husband's. The idea was repulsive. For the rest of the night she'd pretended to be asleep, before rising at first light just after six.

And now she sat waiting, exhausted but maintaining the illusion of a content wife to anyone who might be watching or listening. Beside her, a mug of black coffee remained untouched because it refused to go down. All she needed to do was get her husband out of the house. Itchy eyes watched the slow progress of time. It was still early, only seven, but Sergio was moving around. He needed little sleep and would be ravenous. On the day of an operation, he ate little – said it kept him sharp. But the next day, he made up for it. On the counter, her mobile vibrated. A message from an unknown number flashed up, and her heart faltered.

My Domore. I still feel your body against mine. I've barely slept. You consume my entire being. I feel virile, strong and young again. Some business needs my urgent attention today, but then I'm yours: body and soul. I'll arrive on Sunday at one precisely and will arrange for Sergio to be out of your hair. Fx

She plastered on a smile and sent an immediate response; he'd expect nothing less.

It still feels like a dream. I cannot believe I've captured your attention. Last night changed my life forever. You've left me speechless. My heart pounds at the thought of being with you on Sunday.

She pressed send and bile rose in her throat. Pesce watched from the sofa as she threw his red ball. It bounced along the floor and came to rest under the dining table. He jumped down and trotted into the bedroom. Great, a guilt trip from the dog who Sergio was tickling for simply being so incredibly cute.

Dominique narrowed her eyes and wanted to scream at the little dog, 'You wouldn't be in there if you knew the truth!'

The ten-minute car journey and breakfast were torturous. The whole time, Dominique gripped the edge of her seat and envisioned delivering a killer right hook to her husband's temple. The rage was back, and no mindfulness techniques were working. She'd already excused herself twice in the café to silently scream in the privacy of a toilet cubicle. Eventually, it was over, and they were back in the fresh air. An overcast sky with a northerly wind whipping up the sea, it felt much colder than twelve degrees. She pulled down her hat, thankful for a thick fleece-lined ski jacket and gloves. Along the promenade, its row of palm trees swayed as Sergio wittered on that a falling coconut being more likely to kill you than a shark was an urban myth. Every time, the same anecdote. She opened her mouth to tell him so when his mobile rang. He cursed and wandered off, pulling Pesce behind him. She knew what it was about and dragged her sorry carcass over to a bench.

'I don't believe it. That was Hector with an urgent all-day job tomorrow in some godforsaken backwater. That's another training slot down.' He kicked a crumpled drink can across the boardwalk and parked himself beside her. 'It's all fine and well the company signing us up to do the Elba Island marathon, but we need training time and miles in our legs. Gym work isn't the same thing. And it's next month.'

A couple in their eighties tottered past, arm in arm. The gentleman tipped his hat and she smiled. 'Will you go to the gym today after dropping me off?'

'Of course,' he snapped. 'You saw me put my stuff in the trunk because it gave you another opportunity to lecture me on not taking the damned dog food into the house. Why can't you get it delivered like everyone else? I don't have the time to lug kilogram bags down the drive. Or is it because you enjoy teetering into the pet shop in your high heels to play the damsel in distress and get a young buck to carry it to the car?'

The sheer nerve of the bloke. 'It's like that, is it? You cannot spare five minutes to take Pesce's food into our marital home. However, you can drive the thirty minutes it takes to reach a beautiful villa outside Ostuni to screw your mistress in every conceivable position, which I might add you've been doing for the best part of a year.'

He shot away. 'H-how do you know?'

Dominique shuffled to the edge of the bench and looped her arm through his. 'I'm so glad you asked me that, darling. It all started with an unexpected visitor last night.'

For the next ten minutes, she recounted the evening's event with clinical detachment, until the point Francis showed her the surveillance photos and the report. Her voice broke, and the tears started again at how Sergio had cast aside everything for carnal pleasure. She wrenched off a glove and relentlessly twisted her wedding ring from side to side. Did he know what it was like to be utterly betrayed? The devastating pain it caused? And the crippling shame of having her boss, of all people, disclose how little she was valued? To realise her husband would rather be with a flexible blonde than her?

The older couple tottered back in their direction; Dominique deliberately dropped her glove as an excuse to scramble under the bench and hide. After they passed, she sat back up to find a remarkable change in Sergio. He was death-like with grey, clammy skin, and his breathing came in wheezing gasps. He seemed to be having a heart attack as he rocked backwards and forwards.

'What have I done? What have I done?'

His piteous state re-energised Dominique, and she rummaged in her handbag, withdrew a compact mirror and snapped it open. After studying her reflection, she unfurled a monogrammed mascara-stained handkerchief and set to work drying her eyes.

'That's much better. Don't you think?' But Sergio could only sit and stare. 'Well, as I was saying …'

She recounted the physical section of the evening with relish and left nothing out – how Francis could pleasure a woman, was better and could go for longer than her husband. Despite hating the cold, she pushed up a sleeve to reveal nasty scratches and unwrapped her scarf to display an unsightly love bite. His terror-filled eyes stared as a triumphant Dominique declared Francis saw her as his. But even to her ears, the victory sounded hollow as she stammered out that this was only the beginning, and she was eager for more. The wind chilled her to the bone, and the sky darkened. Sergio gently squeezed her hand before she disclosed their home was bugged. Her shoulders drooped with defeat as she sadly concluded it had been a carefully choreographed seduction. She'd been duped twice. Firstly by her husband and secondly by a much more dangerous man – for kicks.

There wasn't any anger in his voice. 'Why did you have to sleep with him? Why did you have to leave him wanting more?'

'Because I'd discovered that the only man I've ever loved has betrayed me.' She spat. 'Because I'd found out my husband has fathered a child with another woman. After all the years we've been trying. You fucking bastard. And finally, because I saw your devotion to your baby in those photos. It ripped my heart out. How do I compete with that? I can't. And that's when I knew I'd lost you.'

She took his silence as confirmation. 'I didn't think I could do it, but what the hell? Perhaps I can carve out a niche as Francis's whore? Although he'll not get his wish of fathering a child and me passing it off as yours because you can pack your bags and leave. Go to your ready-made family. I'm sure they'll be delighted to have you. But I'm keeping Pesce.'

He frantically unzipped his pocket and pulled out an unfamiliar mobile. 'Why didn't you mention the baby earlier?'

'What?' she asked, staring at the simple handset. Where had that come from?

'Why didn't you tell me he knew?' Sergio screamed in her face. 'Please don't let me be too late. Pick up, pick up.'

He walked away and began talking rapidly. Dominique felt strangely removed as Sergio gesticulated wildly. It sounded as if he was begging, and a few passers-by sniggered. He did look funny, storming backwards and forwards in a wind-inflated raincoat. Did Monika not want him either? How weird. Her mind kept slipping away (it must be the lack of food and sleep), and random thoughts popped into her head. How long had Francis been spying on her? Her mundane life must have made for tedious viewing as she chatted to Pesce in Sergio's absence or cajoled her mother over the phone into leaving the house. Hopefully, Sergio would move his stuff out quickly so she needn't see him again. Pesce spent the whole time whining and running backwards and forward between them. Her husband was back but he was no longer her concern.

'Why are you still here?' she asked. 'Just go. You're upsetting my dog.'

He grabbed hold of her shoulders and shook them roughly. 'You have to listen to me. I need your help.'

Pesce let out a sharp bark.

'After what you've done?' She stroked Pesce, and he jumped up on her knee for a cuddle. 'I don't think so.'

'You don't understand. I need to make this right. And I can't do it by myself. Francis didn't seduce you for kicks. He did it for revenge. As soon as he saw those photos, you were on his radar. He's played the seduction card so many times that you never stood a chance. I'm so sorry, Dominique. For what it's worth, I don't love Monika, I love you. I want to be with you. Not her. But my daughter. We must save my daughter.'

'What the hell are you talking about?'

Sergio joined her on the bench and kissed Pesce. 'Sorry, boy. Monika Gallante is not the insipid blonde nobody Francis would have you believe. For the last eight years, she's been his prized mistress. And for the last five, she's lived in fear of him and even more so of leaving. He bought her the villa and set her up as a fitness instructor, and until ten minutes ago, we believed Francis thought Elora was his.'

Dominique inhaled sharply. The last piece of the jigsaw clicked into place. That's why he'd chosen her – seduce the wife of the man who was bedding his woman. She brought up that morning's message and showed it to Sergio.

'That unpleasant business … he means Monika and Elora, doesn't he?' Dominique whispered and reanalysed the text. 'I thought he meant you would only be working tomorrow. B-but that job with Hector tomorrow—'

'It's my execution,' he said calmly. 'And it certainly won't be quick and painless but agonisingly slow. I've worked with Hector long enough to hear about his past exploits.'

Dominique's eyes widened in comprehension as she held her stomach. 'I know why Francis is desperate to be with me again. So I can provide him with a child he knows is his. I told him how we've been trying, how there's no reason I can't fall pregnant. Hell, I probably didn't even need to tell him. We went to a company doctor after all. I might as well have marched up to his front door and handed the results over myself.'

'This is all my fault.' Sergio groaned.

Dominique held up her hand. 'Shut up. I'm trying to think. Francis knows he's got a narrow window of opportunity. Impregnate me in the next few weeks, and I'll be poor Dominique – the unfortunate widow with a child on the way. How sad, Sergio didn't get to see his child. So I can look forward to being pleasured by the man who murdered my husband, his mistress and their child. What joy. Let's hope I'm up the duff soon, or I'll be of little use to him. What did Monika say?'

'Francis told her Hector is popping in later this afternoon to reassess her security arrangements.'

Dominique looked at her watch. 'It's almost ten. You must go, get them both and disappear before it's too late.'

Sergio shook his head. 'That's not going to happen. Monika is exhausted from living in fear and knows she's not up to life on the run. I've promised to take Elora.'

'What about Monika?'

Her husband stared out to sea. 'She will put herself beyond reach when Elora is safe.'

Dominique gasped. The woman was talking about killing herself. It was incomprehensible, but there was no time to quibble. 'Okay, then you need to get Elora and disappear.'

He snorted. 'Really? Come off it, hon. I'd last five minutes tops. We both know you're the brains of this outfit. You bring me home safe. I need you with me. And not just to keep Elora and me alive. I love you and want you with me. Even if you hate me, which I totally understand. And I couldn't live with the thought of you eking out a terrifying existence as Francis's mistress, even if you did manage to fall pregnant. I know what he does to Monika, and he's happily told her what happened to all those other women who went before and failed to satisfy him. The man's a monster.'

Fantastic. Dominique looked out over Brindisi's harbour. Her life had played out a stone's throw from the busy port. There'd been happy and desperately sad times, but now things looked utterly bleak. To stay or go. Both options had a high probability of death, and she wasn't too keen on dying just yet. Sergio deserved to rot in hell, but the baby? And that clinched it. Elora was innocent. She didn't deserve death just because her mother and father were idiots. And maybe, just maybe, if Elora was saved, it might undo some of Dominique and Sergio's past sins.

'I'll come.' She sighed.

His face lit up, and he kissed her. 'That's fantastic. I cannot tell you what this means to me.'

'Don't push your luck,' she spat. 'I hate your guts at the moment.'

'Okay. I'm going to get Elora but won't take our car. I don't usually …' He stopped and nervously coughed.

She refused to make it easy for him. 'Arrive at the villa to screw Monika until at least one. Yes, stealing a car is a good idea as ours will have a tracking device. We don't want to draw any unnecessary attention to ourselves.'

He swallowed. 'Once I get Elora, I'll ring you three times on your mobile from this unregistered one. Then you cross the road to the bank machine and pull out as much cash as possible. That's what we'll use to start with. As of now, we can't go home. We can't use our car or phones. And I'm sorry, no contact with Toni. It's too dangerous for all of us.'

It was asking a lot to flee without saying goodbye to her mother. However, it made sense. Light rain began to fall, and they agreed Dominique should wait in a nearby café. He kissed her again and, out of habit, she responded. Sergio walked off smiling, but Dominique barely registered the exchange. She was looking towards the city. Her mamma was only a short walk away.

Chapter Four

Francis had returned home just after one, pumped up from his evening with Dominique. What rage. What passion. Her reaction shouldn't have come as a surprise and presented an exciting opportunity. Before showering, he'd undressed and folded the shredded shirt as a keepsake. The hot water stung delightfully. At times the woman resembled one of the neighbourhood cats he'd played with as a child. They hissed, spat and clawed for survival as he slowly drowned them in the family swimming pool. His mother had always got upset, but his father laughed and said it served as a warning to the others. Thinking of Dominique as he towelled off filled him with desire, forcing him to enter his wife's bedroom. Milena had barely woken as he hitched up her nightgown. It was better in the dark, it hid a body that was sagging in some places and artificially tight in others. She served him well, but he longed for younger flesh. Not too young, of course. With age came experience, and he liked a woman who knew her way around a man. Too young, and they just squirmed about beneath him. Too old, and they lacked flexibility. Late twenties to mid-thirties seemed to be the sweet spot. There would always be exceptions. But in general, that age bracket delivered the most satisfying results.

He'd risen at five and showered again before selecting a fresh white shirt and a Dior suit before retiring to his study. The temperature in the dark room was cool, but his skin burned. It was always the same afterwards. He'd pulled up last night's footage and his pulse quickened to see her so scared at the start. His fingers stroked the screen until she finally closed the door with a satisfied smile. In the end, he watched the footage three times. He'd never done that before and took it as a sign. He even slowed down the action in some parts and enhanced the screen in others. And when he declared full ownership of her, what a rush. The kitchen fit-out had been a perfect cover to upgrade the surveillance software. Technology moved so fast. And to have visual and audio. What a treat.

He rang for breakfast, and his efficient housekeeper bustled in. He deliberately paused the footage at a particularly raunchy part and waited for a reaction. There was none, as always. The woman never mirrored any emotion, like her nephew Hector. It was a credit to her. As usual, she stood and waited impassively whilst he took a sip of his coffee and cut into a poached egg. It was a little after nine. Domore would either be finishing breakfast at some Brindisi café or strolling hand in hand with her unfaithful husband. Maintaining the dutiful wife act but secretly awaiting Francis's arrival tomorrow lunchtime. He'd already watched today's footage and turned the air conditioning to the max when Domore smiled at his message and instantly replied. Soon she would be his. Sergio would be arriving at the villa in a few hours.

In a rare display of generosity, Francis had decided to let the man have one last afternoon with his mistress and their child. Both Hector and himself would arrive at five. Francis never got his hands dirty but did intend to enjoy Monika first before handing her over to his finest employee. To reward good service, he was allowing Hector to dispose of the woman and child in any way he wished. With the usual caveat that their remains must never surface. And then Sunday. Francis rubbed his hands together at his beautiful plan. Instead of attending to company business, Sergio would discover he *was* the intended business. After being tied to a chair, he'd be forced to watch a live feed of his apartment and witness Francis ravish Domore repeatedly as Hector set to work on him. There were strict instructions for the torture to last the exact time it took Francis to pleasure his new mistress. And based on last night, that would take some time.

Whilst addressing his hired help, he kept his eyes on the image of Domore lying naked and exhausted on the floor. 'Excellent as always.'

'Yes, sir,' she replied and collected his empty jug of water, glass and a brown banana skin from his desk. He studied the electronic tracker log and saw the car was still parked in Brindisi. Sunday was far too long to wait. What if …? His white teeth glinted. Yes, there was ample time. By leaving now, he could arrive ahead of Domore. Imagine her surprise at finding him sitting on her mother's couch, sipping Earl Grey.

He held out his hand. 'Angela, I require your car keys.'

She immediately handed him a key fob, and her eyes lingered on the video screen. Francis was sure he saw the twitch of her lips. 'Enjoy your day, sir.'

He really must give that woman a raise.

Chapter Five

Dominique impatiently tugged at the lead. It should have taken ten minutes tops, but Pesce was determined to sniff every single lamp post along the route, roll around in the wet, kick all four legs in the air or take offence at any individual who dared to walk along the same street as them. She hated doing it but pulled on the harness harder this time. Pesce cocked his leg to dribble out three drops worth before trotting merrily onwards with a nose snuffling and snorting the ground. Dominique seethed as her boots splashed through ever-increasing puddles. Sweat beaded underneath too many layers and she tossed her useless umbrella into somebody's wheelie bin after it repeatedly blew inside out. She was a sodden mess and still needed to go to the cashpoint. They were almost there. She turned into the cul-de-sac that had changed little since her childhood.

Each substantial family residence sat on a generous plot, enclosed in thick perimeter hedging. Back in the day, the broad street had housed five of the seven most powerful company employees. And they all lived a comfortable existence, feeling protected by a network built on fear and respect. Or so they thought. But one night had changed everything. The underboss, the right-hand man and three of the four captains were gunned down. Shockwaves ripped through the organisation and led to a seismic shakeup. The company was radically streamlined and dragged kicking and screaming into the twentieth century. Plenty fell by the wayside, and only the most loyal remained. Even now, any employee who dropped below the exacting standards vanished. Occasionally, Dominique would receive an automated email that a person no longer worked for the company, or found a phone number reassigned. It served as a reminder to all.

But the restructuring had worked wonders. The company was once grossly disorganised, haemorrhaging money through an appalling lack of systems and processes, and diabolical communications. But not now. The company was slick and efficient, and the money poured in. Four of the five widows departed the street shortly after the debacle. They were placed in smaller, more sustainable (and easier to monitor) houses, allowing the company to sell off the properties. Only her mother refused to go, arguing that a familiar setting was essential for a grieving eight-year-old. And out of respect, the company had indulged her.

At last, Pesce recognised where they were and strained at the lead. It was now Dominique's turn to be dragged along. The once-elegant house was long gone. The ageing seventeenth-century property lingered behind an unkempt hedge in an overgrown garden with tangled trees and a never-ending list of repairs which Dominique attempted to resolve. Unfortunately, Toni Bianchi refused all visitors except her daughter, so any non-essential repairs or cosmetic maintenance fell to the non-DIY Dominique or were invariably left until they became essential. Urgent work was then tightly choreographed as Dominique kept her mother out of the house long enough for professionals to get in and out unnoticed. She couldn't even call on her husband to help as Sergio and Toni didn't get along. This time she almost made it to the paint-frayed front door before tripping over an uneven flagstone and falling heavily against the wall, bringing away another lump of plaster. For twenty-four years, the grand villa had gradually fallen apart. Whereas her mother had crumbled overnight.

All the curtains were still closed – usually a bad sign – but she was over two hours early, to be fair. Dominique rang the bell and heard it echo in the foyer beyond. The length of wait varied enormously, but she never complained. It gave her mother time to dispose of empty vodka bottles and hide half-drunk ones. Today the door opened almost instantly.

Fifty-two-year-old Toni Bianchi looked stunning as ever. 'Darling, how wonderful to see you both. Come out of that dreadful weather. My, you do look a state. And you're early. I haven't even started lunch yet.'

She ushered them inside and, as always, Pesce waited patiently for a treat.

'Mamma, I love the haircut. And is that dress new?'

Toni spun around perfectly in high heels. Her eyes were bright, and pirouetting in those shoes meant she couldn't have drunk an enormous amount last night. Thank heavens for small mercies.

'I'm so glad you like the style. I wasn't sure, but Alfonso said the sandy blonde tone and choppy layers would flatter my face. And afterwards, I went for lunch with the girls and an impromptu shopping spree. I was good and only got this dress, unlike Paula, who bought stacks and had to get a handsome chap to take the bags to her car. She took his number; can you imagine that? What fun.' Her mother squealed with delight. 'Anyway, Paula spotted this sexy little number and said I must try it. I'm so glad I did as it sits so well, don't you think?'

She nodded. 'You look gorgeous, Mamma.'

Dominique pushed her mother to leave the house – to the gym, meet up with the four widows, get a manicure, take a painting class, and volunteer. Anything and everything to keep her away from temptation. Because Toni Bianchi never drank in public. But once the front door closed, her mother could crash and go on multiple-day-long benders. Sometimes there was a trigger, and sometimes not. Last week had been horrific – the anniversary of her father's, Alesso Bianchi's, death. But yesterday must have been a good day. However, it meant her mother's need must be unbearable, and she would hit the bottle as soon as Dominique left. Staying dry for over twenty-four hours was an accomplishment rarely achieved. But even without the drink, once her mother was inside the house, she believed her husband was still alive. Dominique had long given up explaining past events. It only got them both upset and led to even greater binge drinking.

'Sweetheart, we must get you tidied up. What will your father think when he gets back? And baby, you look peaky. Are you eating properly? I keep waiting for this long-promised grandchild, which will only happen if you are in tip-top condition. Let me make you a sandwich and a decaf coffee.'

Dominique was pulled along the corridor and into the dated kitchen. Her mother could keep up a one-sided conversation for hours, and time was running out. Her mobile was buzzing, and Sergio was on his way. She had thirty minutes to get back.

'Mamma.' Dominique wrenched her hand free. 'You must listen to me. I came to tell you that I'm going away. That's why I'm early.'

'Oh well, you must eat something before the journey. I'll make a nice packed lunch and a flask. Now, where did I last see that?'

Her mother started pulling decades-old pots and pans out of the cupboards. Dominique slammed her fists down on the table in frustration and screamed, 'Listen to me!'

The hurt expression was quickly replaced by happiness. 'Angel, you're emotional. It'll be the changing hormones because you're pregnant. How exciting.'

Playing along was the best tactic to get out the door. Dominique cupped her stomach and beamed. 'Yes, that's right. It's early days, so please don't say anything. And to celebrate, we're going to the lake for a short break.'

'Your father will be ecstatic. I can't wait to tell him when he gets home. How wonderful. And there are so many walking trails for you to do. I know how much you love it up there.' Her mother gleefully clapped her hands. 'I've got a fantastic idea.'

Dominique was dragged back along the corridor but this time into her father's musty office. A time warp unchanged for twenty-four years. Everything was exactly as she remembered, right down to the desk pad with his hexagonal doodles. When she was a child, the room was strictly off-limits. Which made it the place to be. Dominique would sneak in to carefully perch on his leather swivel chair and pretend to rule the world.

On a bitter February afternoon, with rain lashing the windows, she'd sneaked inside the forbidden vault and issued imaginary orders to Francis Del Ambro Contino Senior from the mahogany desk. Suddenly, the door had flown open to reveal her granite-hard, flint-sharp father with glowering eyes and a hard-set mouth. She was in big trouble. He didn't shout. This man didn't need to. He commanded utter respect and fear from his troops, where any disobedience was instantly quashed. And here was his four-year-old daughter daring to defy his orders. Dominique braced herself for the hiding of a lifetime. 'You know the rules; why have you ignored them? Do you think yourself superior to me?' The words stung. She worshipped her father – a shadowy figure who flitted in and out of her life. Despite being petrified, she summoned up the courage to tell the truth. 'I'm being you, Papa. I'm telling your boss what he should do to run the company better, that he must move with the times.' Alesso Bianchi was across the room in four strides, but instead of punishing Dominique, he'd plonked a cowering daughter on his knee and asked if she really wanted to be the boss.

Her answer was instantaneous. 'Of course I do, and I'll be the best one ever.' In response, he fired up the computer and began her company education. She was a willing pupil, cherished their precious time together and studied hard not to disappoint. The lessons continued every day for the next three and a half years, including the day her father left for work and never came back. After that, grief-stricken Dominique couldn't bear to enter his study, but her education continued as she ran errands and unofficially helped at various offices. And when she left school to take up a junior position, her company knowledge exceeded many senior employees.

Standing in the study, Dominique attributed all her professional successes to that first lesson on her father's knee. She was now willingly throwing everything away. What would her father think? She knew he would say go and stay safe, save the child's life. The half-closed curtains illuminated a room covered in dust – like the many unused rooms in the house. There was only one clean item which her mother hurried over to and lifted the well-oiled lid to reveal an antique ottoman packed with neat bundles of money.

'Would you prefer tens, twenties, fifties, hundreds or two hundreds?' her mother calmly asked as she pulled out handfuls of cash. 'What do you think? Take whatever you need. I thought you could go shopping on the way back and stock up with baby supplies. Your father keeps holdalls in the wardrobe by the window.'

'Where the hell did this come from?' Dominique asked, staring dumfounded at what amounted to a small fortune.

'I don't know exactly,' her mother replied and giggled. 'It's been turning up in the post for years, so I pop it in here. I think it must be your father; you know he doesn't trust banks. Well, I'll leave you to it and go make that sandwich and coffee.'

Dominique was gobsmacked and barely registered a red hatchback slowly driving past the gates. She grabbed a holdall and frantically threw in as much currency as her shaking hands could manage. Who needed a cashpoint with all this loot? Pesce trotted in and launched himself into the trunk. Despite everything, she laughed. 'Nana not giving you any more treats, is she? Well, there's nothing in there.'

She pressed down on the bag to make more room, but it was no good. She tested the handles – cold-hard cash weighed a ton. It was going to be tough to lug it back with Pesce on the lead. She threw a bundle across the room, and he jumped out of the trunk to joyfully shake it before stiffening. He pushed through the curtains and started growling through a wedge of five euros. Dominique peered outside and grabbed a chair to steady herself. Low-level whimpering started, and she realised it was coming from her. Walking up the weed-strewn path with an enormous bouquet was Francis. Oh my God, he'd caught up with her already. Very carefully, she zipped up the bag, bent down and placed a finger to her lips. Pesce dropped his new toy and immediately fell silent. She threw the packet in the trunk and eased the lid shut. She pulled Pesce close and he licked her nose. Five light-hearted doorbell rings sounded.

She stole to the study door to hear dull thuds from the kitchen – the sound of pans being thrown back into cupboards. Her mother hurried along the corridor the next instant, smoothing down her dress. She quickly fluffed her hair in the hall mirror, checked her teeth and straightened a pendant necklace with a satisfied smile. She next turned to the study, and Dominique ducked back inside.

'Mr Del Ambro Contino Junior has arrived earlier than expected for our meeting. You are to wait until the coast is clear and then leave. Make no sound. And under no circumstances are you to join us,' her mother instructed in a business-like manner and vanished.

Dominique was left holding Pesce. She crept back across the room to listen.

'What a surprise!' her mother trilled.

His voice was equally friendly and playful. 'Aren't you going to let me in?'

'Sorry. How silly of me. I'd forget my head if it weren't screwed on. Please come through.' Dominique pulled back as they passed, and then retook her position. 'Thank you for the flowers,' her mother called over her shoulder. 'You really shouldn't have.'

'Don't be silly. I couldn't very well turn up empty-handed. Has Dominique arrived yet?'

The tapping of stiletto heels on tiles faltered for a split second as the pair rounded the corner and disappeared. Dominique could have sworn Francis smirked whilst leering at her mother's ass. A minute later, she fled.

Chapter Six

The local bus had barely shuddered to a halt before everyone stampeded for the exits. The hour-long journey to quaint Apokeri had been torturous, with screaming kids, the incessant barking of a rat-like handbag dog and a heating system on the blink five minutes after leaving Lefkada Town. With the temperature continually swinging between an oven and a freezer, Javier had repeatedly flicked his left ring finger and thumb together. At least the gorgeous scenery was a slight distraction. But now he needed to find his accommodation.

Ten minutes later a petite redhead handed over his keys as he apologised again. She smiled, making a quick getaway. What a first impression. A foul, overpowering stench clung to him from a two-day, umpteen-thousand-mile trip. What a relief to strip off sweat-soaked clothes and lather up in a refreshing shower. He could easily afford a luxurious hotel, but the simple studio suited him. In fact, it was an essential part of the plan. In early April, with only a few tourists kicking about, it was easy to find somewhere. He'd booked a few nights, confident more satisfactory accommodation would be secured, but still slung his battered rucksack on the bed and pulled out its contents – mainly new clothes purchased by Suzy as a farewell gift. She'd taken his departure surprisingly well. He even scored brownie points for what she believed to be frank honesty. He'd always cherish their time together, but it was unfair to continue with a heart still belonging to his deceased wife. Nobody broke up with Suzy. She was always forced to extract unwanted leeches from her life, so his admission was a refreshing change. The deluded woman even bought his plane ticket, although he insisted on a standard seat to be safe. He was a cautious chap – one never knew who might run future checks on his movements. He was glad to get shot of her but maintained the grateful lover to the bitter end. There was never any need to be nasty.

Suitably refreshed, and wearing his faithful white shirt and cargo pants, he studied himself in the mirror. Time had been kind. Flecks of grey in jet-black, closely-cropped hair lent a distinguished air of seeming respectability. He was careful in the sun, so after years abroad only the faintest lines radiated out from intense dark eyes. Anna's obsessive sun lotion policy had rubbed off. He even spouted the same advice. Patting a washboard stomach, he smiled at his impressive physique – maintained via a strict exercise regime, healthy eating and scuba diving whenever possible. She should recognise him.

***

The bus had driven past Round the Bend, affording a fleeting glimpse. But now, standing outside, he was impressed by the contemporary building that sat happily next to a substantial and traditional stone-built house. He pushed open the door and glanced around. A couple were leaving, and he gratefully nabbed their window table. Even its outdoor seating was quickly filling up. The place was a bustling hybrid of a restaurant-cum-art-gallery with one side given over to hiring bikes, scooters, motorbikes, booking lessons and tours. Javier failed to see her, so picked up a colourful brochure and thumbed through an enticing selection of excursions. The kitchen door opened, and there she was. He inhaled sharply. Even from that distance, it was easy to see the magazine photo hadn't captured her true beauty. She glided over to a group of red-faced cyclists and fell into easy conversation. Whilst taking their order, she was aware of a new customer by the window and raised her hand in acknowledgement. All he needed to do was wait.

'Hello, can I help you?'

There was no indication she recognised him. 'What would you recommend for a light vegetarian meal?'

'Our Greek Salad receives rave reviews. However, my personal favourite is the spicy halloumi wrap with couscous.'

'That sounds perfect. I'll order both.'

She laughed, and her eyes crinkled in the same endearing way. If time had been kind to Javier, it had hardly touched Anna. He found it difficult to believe the woman was thirty-six. Her hair was longer than before but she still had that understated style, more French-chic than a lass from the Toon. A slight frown appeared but quickly vanished.

'No worries. And to drink?'

'I'd love a cup of tea,' he replied. 'You're a Geordie, aren't you? I'd recognise that accent a mile off.'

She laughed again, but this time it sounded slightly forced – as if memories were being dredged up. Give it a few more minutes.

'I certainly am. How about you? I'm usually good at dialects, but I'm baffled by yours.'

He adopted a serious face and nodded. 'I'm not surprised. I've lived all over – the benefit of a Forces upbringing. I once lived in Northumberland, but that was a lifetime ago.'

She retreated into the kitchen. The woman was smart, and there'd been enough clues. Time ticked by, was she ever coming back? But then she reappeared with his order and, weaving her way between the tables, exchanged pleasantries with the customers. Javier was disappointed, with no visible change in her demeanour it appeared the penny hadn't dropped. He hadn't changed much, so why didn't she recognise him? Or was she choosing not to?

She placed his dishes down, and with nobody looking, the smile vanished. 'I know it's you, Javier. You unscrupulous, cold-hearted bastard. If I weren't in my own restaurant with paying guests, I'd grind your smug face into this plate of food. Before smashing the other one over your head. What the hell do you want, you worthless shit?'

Okay, so she did recognise him. His eyes flicked sideways; life continued as normal. He tried to grab her hand, but she was too quick.

'Anna, you know I wouldn't have turned up unless I was absolutely desperate. I know I put you through hell, and I'm sorry.' Her eyes narrowed. She didn't believe him, which he expected, but she hadn't thrown him out either.

'Araf, Javier.'

She was allowing him to proceed with caution. It was a code, dating back to their frequent trips to see his family in Wales. Araf meant slow in Welsh and featured on many roads. She'd thought it sounded funny and started using it when he pushed his luck.

He swallowed hard and adopted a desperate tone. 'I'm on the bones of my arse. Catrin left me and took all the money.' She gave a nasty, triumphant grin but before she had the chance to retaliate, he ploughed on. 'Yes, I'm well aware of the irony and it serves me right. but I've got less than fifty euros to my name, and then I'm screwed.'

'You've got one hell of a nerve. But you always did have barefaced cheek,' she snapped and tucked hair behind her ear. He recognised the sign; she was highly agitated. 'Why me? What about your family? Bobby always thought the sun shone out your backside. Why can't he help?'

'Bobby ... Bobby's dead,' he said, and it still didn't sound real after all this time.

He'd known she adored his cheeky kid brother, only a few years younger than her but was still surprised as the colour drained from her face. 'No! Jav, I'm so sorry; what happened? He was brilliant.'

'Do you want to sit down?'

She hesitated for a second but then drew out a chair. 'Make it quick.'

'Thanks, I appreciate it. Bobby joined the army like my dad. He was on a training exercise on an unexpectedly scorching hot day. The stress on his body triggered a fatal heart attack. They reckon he was dead before he hit the ground, aged twenty-four.'

'Oh my God,' she sobbed. 'That's awful.'

'And it gets worse. Bobby's death drove a wedge down the family. Mum and Bethan blamed the military and became obsessed with bringing them to justice. My dad and Celeste refused to back them and said it was a terrible accident. And I was caught in the middle, playing peacekeeper. I really thought my parents were heading for a divorce but then Dad started behaving weirdly.' His breathing was fast and shallow and his voice kept faltering but he needed to let the hurt out because it was the only way to hook her. 'I'm still convinced the shock of Bobby dying triggered his dementia. He's now in private care and barely knows us. Mum's consumed by guilt and is up a height most of the time waiting for the phone to ring.' It was working. She almost reached for his hand but stopped short and he continued. 'Because I could make more money overseas, I decided not to return and instead send money across to cover the exorbitant fees. Catrin has taken all that. Bethan thought I was shirking my responsibilities by staying away and hasn't spoken to me since. Although I've no idea what else I'm supposed to do because she doesn't have any money. At least Celeste and Mum supported my decision. All of Celeste's nursing income goes on bills, propping up her husband's struggling business and covering the cost of three kids in uni. I'm the only one who can help my dad and I'm sure as hell not going to add to my family's stress by saying I've got no job, home or money. I can't do that to them.'

'And there's nobody else you can turn to? No friends who can help?'

'I don't have any,' he replied and realised it was true. 'You're my last hope.'

'Good grief, Jav. How did you get to such a place in your life where I'm the only one who can help you?' He nodded at the question. It was a valid point but it didn't require a response. And then a switch flicked in Anna's face. Both hands on the table, arms rigid, voice tight, low, failing to mask years of hate and rage, she spoke. 'The person, I will remind you, who you promised to love until death do us part. The person you abandoned in a Cusco hostel, taking all their belongings, emptying the joint bank account and didn't even have the decency to leave a note. Do you have any idea what that was like? You almost destroyed me and I will never forgive you for that. Thank God for the kindness of strangers.'

This was not going well. With her voice barely a whisper, nobody around suspected anything but any minute he expected her to hurl the food into his face and bar him from her premises. But instead, she sunk into the chair and repeated, 'For the kindness of strangers.' The silence stretched on but he waited because whoever spoke first was the loser and it wasn't going to be him.

And at last, she gave a resigned look. 'I need to get back to work, but I'll make a few calls. Come back in two days. I'm not promising anything, so don't get your hopes up.'

'Thanks, you're a superstar.' This time she didn't pull away when he grasped her hand. 'I know I don't deserve your help.'

'No, you don't,' she fired back and, standing up, retied her apron. 'I'm warning you now, Jav, dick me around and I will kill you. Do I make myself clear?'

'Yes, I understand,' he replied with false sincerity. 'I'm not here to cause trouble.'

'You'd better not be,' she snapped. 'Don't worry about the bill.' She sighed. 'Pay me back once you've got some more money.'

She left abruptly, and Javier hastily tucked into his free meal (he had no intention of paying her back). The food was amazing and the first meeting had gone better than expected. She'd called him Jav – her name for him. The thaw was underway.

***

Four tables across sat another man who also had a strong interest in Mrs Makris. His name was Inspector Jace Marinos, and for the last ten years, he'd seen himself as her unofficial protector. Any man who interacted with Anna was someone of interest. And the stranger by the window was certainly one of those. Jace watched the intense exchange. They clearly knew one another and, judging by her distraught face when she disappeared into the back office, the conversation had thrown her – and the woman was rarely rattled.

Fifteen minutes ticked by and still no sign. That was highly unusual. During the lunchtime rush, Anna always made a point of being available. The guy was still savouring his meal. He was big, at least six foot three, fit, mid-forties and had a few days' worth of stubble. His healthy tanned complexion suggested an outdoor enthusiast or a life in a warm climate. Jace guessed Spanish, but if he knew Anna, maybe a Brit.

After twenty minutes, she reappeared but wasn't her usual bright and breezy self. Her smile failed to reach those beautiful eyes and she was so tense a light breeze might snap her in half. She made straight for his table.

'Are we going for the healthy option today, Inspector? You know the rules – eat healthily and eat for free.'

'But of course. I'll have poached eggs with avocado on wholegrain bread, a side salad and—'

'Nuclear grade black coffee,' she finished his sentence.

He smiled at her always remembering. 'Have you time for a quick word?'

Her megawatt smile was back, making him happy. 'Inspector, I always have time for you. Let me place this order, and I'll be right back.'

For years he'd begged her to accept payment, but she always refused, said it was continual thanks for saving her not once but twice. Jace had pointed out he'd only been partly responsible for the first. The second was entirely down to her and she'd merely let him take all the credit (which he still didn't understand). What he did know was Anna Makris was one tough cookie beneath her cheerful disposition and no longer a damsel in distress. She had been vulnerable ten years ago and therefore was the type he became embroiled with. But he'd never been more than a friend. Filip Makris had always been her man, and as they remained blissfully happy, Jace pined from afar.

The stranger eased out from his seat and left. He moved with fluidity and power. A Bengal tiger, stalking its prey, heading towards the village and grinning the whole way. And with him gone, Anna appeared more relaxed when she sat down.

'What would you like to ask me, Inspector?'

'I noticed you chatting to the man who left a few minutes ago. Is everything okay? It appeared somewhat confrontational.'

'Everything's fine,' she hastily replied and fiddled with her hair. 'He's somebody I haven't seen in a very long time, and it threw me, I guess.'

'Is he here for long?' Jace casually asked. 'It'll be nice for you both to catch up if it's been a while.'

'I think his plans are a bit fluid at the moment.' She looked out the window and frowned. 'Why do you ask?'

He paused as Sebasti Andino delivered his order, and then ground a generous amount of pepper over his eggs. 'It's my job to notice the little things.'

'You're a good man,' she said and squeezed his hand. 'I'll leave you in peace to put salt on your lunch when you think I'm not looking.'

As he watched her disappear into the kitchen, he sighed. Filip Makris was one lucky guy.

Chapter Seven

The assassin stood impassively as a coffee cup sailed past his head and smashed against the study wall. The older man continued to rant.

'They're not fucking there. They're not fucking anywhere. I want them found, and I want them found now,' Francis bellowed and pointed to his desk phone. 'Get that bitch Toni on the line.'

Hector calmly hit speed dial and waited precisely one minute before disconnecting. 'There's no response, boss.'

Of course there wasn't. Francis sighed. The woman was a pisshead and probably crashed out in bed; how she hadn't managed to kill herself by now amazed him. An alcoholic for twenty-four years but still with a body and looks to die for. He stretched out in his study chair and breathed deeply. Toni wasn't capable of lying after being plied with alcohol. So that meant Domore had deliberately deceived her mother. Because she knew her mother would blab. He groaned. Christ, they could be anywhere by now. He was still furious with Domore. More so than Monika or Sergio. His now-dead mistress had been on borrowed time anyway. Even before getting pregnant, she'd become tedious and uninventive. Falling back, as they always did, on fawning behaviour – like pathetic puppies, desperate to please.

But he'd kept her on, believing the child was his and hoping his protege would be a damn sight better than the ones he already had. In a way, it was a blessing the kid wasn't his so he could wipe the slate clean and start again – with Domore. Their connection had been intoxicating and electrifying; he wouldn't and couldn't rest until he had her again. Could she not see they would be invincible together, and their yet-to-be-conceived child would eventually run his empire? Six legitimate kids and all a bunch of clueless, self-centred lackeys. He'd had to appoint a subordinate for each one to discreetly mop up their continual mistakes. It was all Milena's fault with her softly, softly approach to parenting, where everyone had to discuss their feelings. If only he could cut them loose, but it was a step too far – even for him. He rocked backwards in his leather chair. Sergio had obviously tricked Domore into believing him a monster. But that wasn't true, there was always a reason for his actions. He just needed to make her understand that. His Domore was clever, but Toni was her Achilles heel. He smiled. So that's where he needed to focus his attention.

'Hector, I want to be informed the instant the tracker on Toni Bianchi's car flickers into life. And check all her ingoing and outgoing calls.'

'Yes, sir.'

Francis didn't allow surveillance cameras inside his home, so he didn't see Hector pull a face at his aunt. Or the housekeeper's returning smirk.

Chapter Eight

A starfish under a warm duvet. It was liberating to spread out instead of being smothered by clingy losers. An insistent horn blared – inconsiderate gits. Javier jammed a pillow over his head, but it was no use. He was awake now and might as well continue investigating Apokeri and Anna. The first had begun by getting wonderfully lost in a maze of narrow backstreets. It would take time to get a handle on the twisting lanes that sometimes led to the main road, a public bench tucked next to a flower bed, a postage stamp of green space with a gnarled tree or (more often than not) a dead end.

The village lanes must be a child's hide-and-seek paradise with its many compact fishing houses opening straight onto tiled pavements. Still, each resident proudly personalised their little foothold with pots of flowers perched precariously on steep steps and window troughs crammed with herbs. There were colourful shutters, ornate iron window bars, neatly maintained stonework, or subtly rendered brickwork topped with rustic terracotta tiles. The larger properties sat behind thick walls with solid carved doors or intricate metal gates. And everywhere, nature staked its claim with overspilling foliage, scrambling vines, trees and flowers. It really was quite endearing – a homely village where everyday life ticked along as it had for hundreds of years.

However, investigations into Anna required tact and remained on the back burner.

A patio-sized patch of sun illuminated the studio's white floor tiles – that couldn't be right. He fumbled for his mobile and cursed jetlag. Wasn't travelling westwards supposedly less disruptive? It was four o'clock in the afternoon, and he'd slept eighteen hours straight – apart from a brief interruption when his neighbour returned in the small hours and ran a shower. So with less than twenty-four hours before he was due to meet up with Anna, it was time to get back out there.

The beach was empty. Dipping in a toe, Javier winced, but it triggered a long-forgotten memory at Longsands, Tynemouth. She'd stood laughing with rolled-up jeans in calf-deep freezing water. 'You've got to at least come in for a plodge.' It had been a glorious autumnal day and their first date.

Driven by recollections of a much younger Anna, he waded into the water.

'Bit different to Thailand, I expect.' Javier turned to find the Greek-accented voice belonged to a woman in her mid-twenties. A rock chick in leathers. 'My landlady said the latest guest was easy on the eye, and Dania was right. Are you coming out now?'

He was intrigued by this forthright individual. 'I'm Javier Owens. Pleased to meet …?'

'Mia Tovier,' she replied with a firm handshake, zipped up her jacket and patiently waited for him to dry his feet. He was soon towering above her. She was only slightly taller than Dania. 'Come on, I'll buy you a coffee to warm up. Aphrodite does the best, and their cakes are to die for.'

She casually linked arms, and they walked across the promenade to a pretty café. Javier had passed it yesterday and – like now – it was busy. But they weren't going inside. Mia pulled out a metal seat and sat down. Even with the sun's warmth, he was glad for a thick jumper and jacket. Over their lattes and vanilla slices began the strangest conversation – a carefully choreographed dance with each partner unwilling to reveal any personal information, whilst maintaining a friendly footing. So far, the scores remained level and Javier admired her evasion skills.

He tried a different tack and nodded at her Master Scuba Instructor cap. 'Is that an aspiration or an advertisement?'

He'd found the right key to open the lock and her guarded expression turned to passion and enthusiasm. She was a professional and technical diver with hundreds of dives under her belt and reeled off countless sites and a bucket list of many more. Javier could chip in and although he was no expert, they traded stories. Mia was also a goldmine of Apokeri information and provided amusing stories about its residents. He was enjoying himself enormously. It was refreshing to find someone who spoke as they found.

She removed her sunglasses and leaned forward. 'I like you, Javier. We could have fun together. I like men who break the rules and put self-interest above everything else. I believe you are one of those.'

'I would hardly admit it if I was!' He laughed. She arched her eyebrow, and then the words were out of his mouth before he knew it. 'I think I'm a bit old for you.'

What the hell had he said that for? But before he could backtrack, her eyes slid past him. 'Now, talking about self-interest, here comes a prime example – my boss, Giannis Andino.'

It was a brief introduction as Mia was required on the dive boat earlier than expected. But it didn't stop her from kissing Javier on the cheek and telling him to give her a knock if he was ever lonely. After she dropped some euros on the table, the colleagues set off towards the harbour, with Mia tossing back her long black mane and laughing at an agitated Giannis. So far, the afternoon was paying dividends and was set to get even more interesting as Filip Makris headed his way.

He wasted no time and walked straight up to the table. 'Let's go inside. It's bloody freezing out here.'

Javier cheered inwardly; he could no longer feel his toes. It was like stepping into a warm bath as they squeezed into seats by the bright blue window frames. Both men studied one another. Anna clearly had a marrying type – over six-foot, muscular, healthy Mediterranean complexions, dark hair and dark eyes. But the similarities ended there. Filip was three years younger than Anna and had an open, friendly and mischievous countenance. In contrast, Javier was eight years older than his first wife, serious-minded and reflective.

'Can I buy you a drink?' Javier asked. Confrontational wasn't his style, and he needed Filip on his side. 'It's the least I can do.'

'That's very kind, but there's no need.' Filip replied with the air of someone who knew a secret. 'In less than ten seconds, the charming owner will be over to take our order and won't require payment.'

Javier counted to six before discovering the reason.

A lady bustled towards them. 'My darling boy, who is this fine gentleman?'

'Mama, this is Javier Owens, an old friend of Anna's.'

'Welcome, Mr Owens. I trust you're enjoying Apokeri?' Filip's mother enquired, patting thick black hair.

'I certainly am, Mrs Makris. And please call me Javier.'

'Oh well, if you're sure.' She tittered. 'And you must call me Sofia. A friend of Anna's is a friend of mine.'

Filip rolled his eyes. 'Can we get two beers, Mama.'

In less than two minutes the two men tapped bottles. 'Anna tells me you've fallen on hard times?'

'Does she know you're here?' Javier replied, neatly sidestepping the question.

Filip flashed a wolfish grin. 'I promised to be nice.'

'Like I told your wife, I'm not here to cause trouble. I took a massive risk coming here. I knew Anna was well within her rights to bar me on sight, but thankfully she didn't. All I want to do is get my life back on track. I just need a little help to get there.' Javier finished what he reckoned was a convincing opener.

Filip sipped his beer. 'I'll come straight to the point. You chose to walk out on Anna, which I simply don't understand. However, your loss is my gain. I love my wife and will do anything to keep her safe. If I get even the slightest whiff that you're up to no good – and that extends to everybody I care about – your life will not be worth living. Make no mistake, Javier, this is a close-knit community. We protect our own.'

'I would expect nothing less.' Javier extended his hand. 'You have my word that I'll behave impeccably to everyone in Apokeri.'

After shaking on it, Filip excused himself and left Javier to digest his latest conversation. He smiled and looked across the bay – Tharesseti sat in dark choppy water with a fiery sun dropping behind. Promises and handshakes meant nothing, and neither did warnings. He'd received plenty over the years from loving spouses, partners, family members or friends; all he did was dupe them too. He couldn't recall being threatened with retribution from an entire village before, but it was nothing to worry about. It would never amount to anything, and Filip would be cheering him on in no time.

The husbands always did.

Chapter Nine

Every surface, unit and appliance sparkled – the kitchen had never been so clean. After a comedy of errors at breakfast, Anna had been barred from her own establishment. Okay, she might have put her mug of tea in the fridge, restacked the dishwasher with clean plates, poured orange juice over her cereal and made coffee for Pip, even knowing he never drank hot drinks. Anyone could make those types of mistakes. And hadn't Evie found it hilarious when her dad's plate of scrambled eggs on toast was given to Cleo, and he got a bowl of dog food? Confined to barracks for her customers' safety, Anna resorted to scrubbing, rubbing, polishing and mopping for three hours straight. She'd barely finished when the back door burst open, and in clattered Evie, clutching this week's baking project.

'Have I missed him? Am I too late?'

'No, he won't be here for another few minutes.' Anna glared at the mud trail. She hated housework because everything remained clean for a maximum of three seconds.

Evie looked down sheepishly. 'I'm sorry, Mam, but if Nana Sofi hadn't hung around so long after footie practice chatting to everyone and then if Granda Vas-Vas hadn't forgotten he'd eaten the cheese meant for my quiche so we had to go and get some more I would have been home much earlier and had the time to take off my football boots and not dirty the clean floor – so you see it isn't really my fault at all.'

'Would you like to take a breath now?' Anna instructed as the doorbell rang and Cleo's bark boomed out.

'He's here. He's here!' Evie squealed and jumped around the room, flinging extra mud everywhere and hyping the dog up even more.

Anna rolled her eyes. 'Good grief, anyone would think you'd never met one of my friends before. Cleo sit.'

'I know, but this is somebody different,' Evie whispered, her eyes gleaming in anticipation. 'He'll have lots of new stories to tell me.'

'Evangelina Alice Makris, what have I told you?' Anna was in no mood to mess around.

'Not to pester him with loads of questions.' Evie pulled a face. 'As if I ever do that anyway!'

Anna gritted her teeth and opened the door. 'Come in, Javier. Ignore the recent dirt-fest.'

He skirted around the mess and smiled at Evie. 'Well, hello there, and who would this fine footballer be?'

'My name is Evangelina Makris, but you can call me Evie,' Anna's daughter said politely and handed over her package. 'I made this for you to say welcome to Apokeri.'

Javier glanced at Anna, and she shrugged to show the idea wasn't hers. From an early age, Evie had never been selfish; sharing (and often giving away) toys came easily, and she seemed to have been born with an innate sense of kindness, leading to impromptu gestures.

'Thank you. That's very kind,' he said, peeking inside. 'It looks and smells wonderful. You're an excellent baker.'

Evie swelled with pride. 'Just like my Granda Vas-Vas.'

'Come on, missy,' Anna interrupted. 'You need to head over to the café.'

Javier stuck out his hand. 'Very nice to meet you, Evie.'

'Very nice to meet you, Mr Owens.'

***

Two days ago, it had taken Javier ten minutes to walk from Round the Bend to the harbour, but then he was alone. This time he was with Anna. At first, their progress was fairly steady, and they only chatted with a few people, but once they reached Odyssey Travel, progress virtually stopped. Every few steps, they bumped into somebody – local business owners, Evie's brusque headteacher (providing other parents with the chance to quickly slip by), the local priest, Filip's extended family, customers and a collection of randoms. No matter how busy they claimed to be, everyone stopped for a friendly chat, a joke, an observation, gossip, or a whinge. It was all conducted in Greek, leaving Javier to base his assumptions on body language, facial expressions and tone of voice. However, Anna was a good stick and made the necessary introductions – his orderly brain filed away the names as everyone welcomed him.

They crawled past Thalia Supermarket, Aphrodite Café and halted again at Epione Pharmacy to chat, this time with Tharesetti's Scottish owner. The conversation – fortunately in English this time – lasted longer than most as Jeremy and Anna were clearly good friends, talking business and joking about a recent spat between Jeremy's stepdaughter and Evie. After bidding farewell to the jovial chap in his seventies, Javier hoped it was the last conversation. Their destination must be close as they were fast running out of buildings and would soon be in the harbour – currently devoid of its fishing fleet and excursion boats but still showcasing an impressive selection of yachts moored up at three pontoons.

'Do you know every single person who lives here?' Javier exclaimed as his patience waned. 'How the hell do you ever get anything done?'

'It's a small village, and I've lived here for ten years, what do you expect?' Anna replied in a tone suggesting he needed things spelled out very clearly.

'I suppose … I can see why you settled here – it is gorgeous, and the people are friendly.' He looked back along the road with its palm-lined promenade and pretty shopfronts with competing hanging baskets. 'And thank you for introducing me to everyone.'

They passed the squat whitewashed post office, and she dropped her voice even though nobody was around. 'I'm giving you a clean slate. Apart from Pip' – and a few other people Anna chose not to mention – 'nobody knows you're my unscrupulous ex. As far as everyone is concerned, we're good mates. So when you revert to type and start being a dick, you've got nobody to blame but yourself.'

'You really don't trust me, do you?' he asked and was interested to see if she would keep an old promise of never lying.

Anna didn't even bother to look at him. 'No. I don't.'

Okay, she was going with brutal honesty. Hardly surprising given his past actions. But strangely, he didn't expect her to be that blunt or the accompanying needling sensation – it was only brief, and Javier decided it was best not to identify the emotion. Instead, he frowned and asked if that was the case, then why offer to help?

'Because I'm an idiot, that's why!' she snapped.

'You're many things, Anna. But that's not one of them.'

'Whatever.' She stopped at the entrance to Apokeri's grandest building. It was a beautiful Venetian-style townhouse and reminded him of those on the Venice Grand Canal with its golden sand hue, high-arched windows and detailed stone surrounds. 'You are about to meet one of my closest friends, Kristina. The electrics in the office, apartment block, gallery and house need upgrading, and unless things are radically different, you were always an excellent electrician.'

'I bet that hurt to say,' he teased.

'Shut up. You might think you're a smart-arse, but the casting vote rests with Kristina. Get the thumbs-up, and you're in – the job includes a decent wage, board and lodging.'

Javier grinned widely. 'Of course she'll like me. Who wouldn't?'

'Anyone with half a brain,' Anna countered.

'Ouch, anybody would think you didn't like me.'

'You really are a prat, aren't you? What the hell did I ever see in you anyway?'

'My devastating good looks, wit, charm, intelligence,' he reeled off quickly.

'Yes, but I was a naïve teenager then,' Anna pointed out. 'No wonder my dad pitched a fit after you rocked up for dinner.'

'That's unfair!'

Javier had only met Robert Jenkinson twice, and both had been nerve-wracking. The first time he was invited to Sunday dinner, he was determined to make a good impression. He arrived bang on time, smartly dressed, with wine and flowers. Anna's sister, Julia, and her student boyfriend, Tom, were already there, which helped enormously as the two couples had double-dated on several occasions. The meal went well (he did the dishes with Tom), and then the board games came out. The four Jenkinsons were ultra-competitive. He was paired with Anna's lovely, if scatty, grandma, and his team spectacularly lost every time. Javier took it good-naturedly and, after tea, left with a warm glow.

However, the next day Anna rang in floods of tears, and it taught Javier a painful lesson – what people say and do can be at complete odds with what they think. Javier had certainly made an impression on Robert Jenkinson, but not in the way he wanted. The man saw the confident, good-looking boyfriend as a malevolent threat to be stamped out and forbade his daughter from ever seeing him again. Anna, a daddy's girl, couldn't believe her father could do such a thing and begged him to change his mind. He refused. There was no help from her mother either – who stood united with her husband, and even the protestations of Julia did nothing.

However, Javier was undaunted, leading to the second and final meeting. Unbeknownst to Anna, he tracked her father to his allotment. It was a bitterly cold January morning, and as Robert Jenkinson repaired his raised beds, Javier begged him to change his mind. Yes, Anna was only sixteen, and he was twenty-three, but they loved each other, and it was killing them being apart. He offered up countless solutions and tried every possible logical argument. He would have got more response out of the timber struts Robert Jenkinson was sawing. Javier became increasingly desperate and tried to explain that prohibiting the relationship was counterproductive. Javier had been a perfect gentleman and could be trusted. Furthermore, did Mr Jenkinson not trust his own daughter's judgement? Should she not be allowed to follow her heart? It was entirely the wrong thing to say. Her father rounded on Javier and called him a predator and a sexual deviant who prayed on young girls. What right did Javier have to come to his allotment and tell him how to be a father? What did he know about raising a child? What did he know about protecting a loved one from evil? He then threatened to call the police if Javier went anywhere near Anna again.

Stunned, distraught and tearful, Javier had stumbled back to his car and rung Anna. He didn't know what to do; he didn't know how to make it right. She'd been furious with her father. Her voice hardened and stated they had better not get caught then. And so, their relationship blossomed and (with the help of Julia and Anna's best friend, Annalise) it remained a secret until Anna became an adult. But Anna's relationship with her parents deteriorated. They put it down to a difficult teenage phase. There was no more laughter, afternoon board games, or family holidays. If Anna wasn't working two jobs or studying, she sneaked in time with Javier. It continued for two long years as Anna and Javier held out for the day they would eventually be together. On her eighteenth birthday, she finished work early, packed a few belongings, left a note explaining everything and said she'd see them at the restaurant that night as planned and to expect Javier. Her parents never showed, and the first night under his roof he'd held her in his arms as she cried all night. And if it was at all possible, Javier hated her father even more.

'Do you talk to the cantankerous old git, now?' Javier bitterly asked.

'That would be hard,' she replied and turned to open the door. 'As he's dead.'

Chapter Ten

The gallery door was halfway open before he grabbed her hand and pulled her back.

'Wait! I-I ... didn't know, okay,' he stammered and scrambled to collect his thoughts, but there were only countless questions – what had happened and when? Had Anna made up with her parents beforehand? How much had she been affected by his death? Her face remained impassive and offered no clues.

'My father unjustly judged you to begin with, and because of that, it set off a chain of events that nobody can change,' she stated in a detached manner which did her credit. Javier knew how much her parents had meant to Anna, and their relationship breakdown had deeply affected her. It was why she'd bonded so closely with his family. 'He didn't trust you; perhaps it could be argued he was right because of what you did to me. However, I'm willing to give you a second chance, Javier. You claim to have turned over a new leaf – I want you to prove it by doing me a favour.'

He liked the sound of this; it was an easy way to score much-needed brownie points. 'You're on. What do I need to do?'

'Kristina is a sprightly and proud nonagenarian who doesn't take kindly to being mollycoddled. But over the last few years, I've noticed her becoming more and more fixated on the past and, coupled with that, she's had a couple of falls which, thankfully, weren't serious. Apart from one a decade ago that nearly killed her. I need you to report back anything of concern. I'll warn you now; she's extremely independent and will try to fob you off.' They were standing side by side at the door now. 'All Kristina knows is that you're an old friend going through a rough patch.'

They stepped inside a gallery that reminded Javier of Round the Bend with its upmarket, contemporary Scandi feel. The walls and displays featured work by a range of Lefkada artists from paintings and photography to pottery, jewellery and metalwork. Kristina's portfolio mainly consisted of uplifting Apokeri seascapes, but there were also beautiful bowls, vases and plates reflecting the everchanging sea. Behind the counter, a woman chatted on the telephone but pointed to the rear. They walked through the gallery, a welcoming lounge, and a homely kitchen as Anna explained that Kristina spent her time pottering in the garden, delivering local art classes and artists' retreats at Tharesseti Spa resort. And it was at the bottom of the substantial walled garden they found Kristina collecting hens' eggs.

Javier conceded he was guilty of ageism. On hearing Kristina was in her nineties, he'd imagined a doddery Greek hunched spinster, dressed in black with thinning grey hair. Instead, the woman was a tall aristocrat in slim-legged tartan trousers, a blue polo-neck, and a red beret jauntily sitting on short, choppy silver hair. But it was the eyes that made the strongest impression. Javier firmly believed they were windows into the soul. Kristina's piercing blue eyes reached inside him, probing and seeking the truth. Fearful she could read his mind, he broke the connection.

'My darling Anna. How wonderful to see you.'

There was a slight Scandinavian inflexion to the cheerful voice and her eyes were now welcoming and mischievous.

'Kristina, I'd like you to meet Javier Owens.'

A broad smile spread over her face, and she nodded towards Javier's hands. 'And what do we have here?'

'Oh yes, it's a feta and spinach quiche,' he proudly stated and presented it for inspection. 'Evie made it for me, and I thought you'd like it for lunch?'

He hadn't planned on giving away his gift and was experiencing an unfamiliar sensation – he wanted Kristina to like him. It was as if he was meeting a long-held hero and desperately wanted their approval. But that was a ridiculous notion – she was just an old woman, not some all-knowing deity. The penetrating eyes were back, and he hastily looked away again.

'How delightful, thank you,' she replied light-heartedly – was she laughing at him? 'I have the patio table all set. Let's head that way.'

And she was off, moving at a steady pace. He grimaced. What was it about people wanting to eat outdoors? It wasn't that warm yet, but he dutifully followed.

'Luckily, you're wearing a jumper and coat,' she called over her shoulder. 'Our climate must be far cooler than Thailand.'

'I'm getting used to it,' he replied and shivered. How silly of him – there was no such thing as mind readers.

The quiche took pride of place between fresh bread, salad and boiled potatoes. They were soon tucking in, and he was relaxed with all his answers ready.

'Tell me, Javier, what did you think of Evie?'

'Erm, I only met her briefly, but I would say confident, respectful and selfless.'

Kristina nodded. 'Very much like her mother, wouldn't you say?'

'There's no mistaking the family resemblance,' Javier replied and wondered when the interview was likely to start. 'Evie is a miniature carbon copy.'

Anna snorted. 'Don't let my daughter hear you say that. She hates the comparison.'

'Rubbish,' Kristina responded. 'When I was little, I always complained when anyone likened me to my mother, but secretly I loved it because she was beautiful and graceful. What about you, Javier?'

'As a kid, I idolised my dad, and I wanted to be him.' He watched the bees dutifully buzzing between the borders, going from one flower to the next. His father had done that, going from base to base with his family in tow – dutifully following orders. And for what? To end up stuck in some round-the-clock-care facility with fluctuating mood swings and loss of movement, comprehension and dignity. A life serving others was for suckers. His mind cleared. It was time to bury past attachments. He'd already become too distracted and needed to refocus on the plan. He straightened in his seat and caught Kristina's mournful expression before it vanished.

'I hear you want to come and work for the crazy Swedish lady,' she said and pulled such a ludicrously funny face that he laughed. The interview had started.

'Yes, please.'

'Well, if there are no objections, I should like you to start on Monday.' He could only sit and stare. 'Is there a problem?' Kristina asked and smirked. 'Did you expect a grilling?'

'Well, I thought you might ask me a few more questions,' he admitted and scratched his head. It had been a bizarre job interview.

'Anna vouched for your character and credentials. We've met, and I like you. What more is there?'

'Nothing, I guess. I'm paid up at Odyssey tonight. Is it okay if I move my stuff in tomorrow?'

'Of course,' Kristina replied and studied her watch. 'I think it's time you made a move. I believe you have a second appointment to keep.'

After bidding his new boss adieu, Javier headed towards the kitchen, but a hand stopped him.

'Not that way,' Anna advised. 'Follow me.'

They went through a side gate and disappeared into a maze of empty backstreets he couldn't remember seeing before. The narrow path forced them to walk single file much of the way. And like the previous day, steep steps led up to front doors, seemingly haphazard houses hunkered together, and everywhere there were flowers, shrubs and trees humming and buzzing with pollinators. As Anna powered ahead, he had time to glance down a side street to see the village square and beyond that the main road, promenade and sea. He knew where he was now as they walked between the high walls of the church garden on the right and impressive residences on the left. They were heading into the southern labyrinth of streets from yesterday, and with it came familiar markers – a flowering lilac shrub, a lavender hedge, and a bright green door. However, he couldn't remember noticing a black door with an elegant Benrubi Enterprises sign.

'Okay, where have you brought me?'

After their rapid progress, he was panting and gratefully stripped off his coat – Anna rarely strolled anywhere.

'This is my friend Agnes Benrubi's high-end catering company. She is an exceptional and demanding chef who is always keen to scope out new serving staff. I know you've done silver service and bar work before, so I thought you might be interested.'

Javier could have kissed his ex-wife if not for the prospect of being smacked. This was a dream opportunity – high-end meant affluent clientele. His list of targets was rapidly expanding. The door opened and revealed a tall, thin, stern-looking Greek woman dressed in chef whites. She stood in the middle of an empty commercial kitchen, and immediately a phrase popped into his head: bitch face.

'Take off your jumper,' she barked. He did so, and she grabbed his upper arm. 'Good, very good. Firm biceps, you'll have no problem serving large platters of food and drink.' She circled behind him and made appreciative noises.

He couldn't believe the highly inappropriate behaviour and watched as the giggles bubbled up inside Anna. She was getting a kick out of the degrading spectacle, knowing there was nothing he could do about it. Agnes began pacing backwards and forwards. He was in the presence of a drill sergeant and, like a parade soldier, kept his eyes front and centre.

'In five years, I have built up a successful and award-winning business that provides exceptional cuisine to discerning clients,' she said and spun around. 'All my orders are repeat clients or through word of mouth.' Another turn. 'I create masterpieces here' – she stopped and flung her arms wide – 'in my kitchen, that is my forte.' She stalked towards him, and he fought the urge to step back. 'You provide flawless service.'

She looked him up and down disdainfully. 'It would be too much to suppose you speak any Greek?'

He ground his teeth. 'Not yet.'

'As I thought,' she uttered. And then, with little hope, she asked, 'Are you capable of conversing in any other language apart from English?'

Suzy had nothing on this woman. If he didn't want the job so badly, he would tell her where to stick it. 'Yes. Fluent Welsh and fluent Spanish.'

'That makes sense with a name like Javier Owens,' she replied but managed to sound wholly unimpressed as if merely his name enabled an understanding of languages. In his peripheral vision, Anna's shoulders shook with unsuppressed delight as he stood and took everything Agnes Benrubi continued to dish out. 'I do not tolerate tardiness. I do not tolerate insolence,' she said, and although inches shorter, managed to convey the impression of looking down her hawk nose at him. 'If you agree to a shift and do not turn up, you had better be dead. My word is law. Do you understand?'

For the sheer hell of it, he clicked his heels together, saluted and then winked. 'Yes, ma'am.'

Agnes smirked. 'You've got balls of solid rock, Javier. I like that. You're in.'

He breathed out to see Anna grin. 'Gotcha!'

The two witches cackled. Christ, it had all been a set-up.

Agnes shook his hand. 'Anna vouched for you, so the job was always yours. I'm so relieved you took that all in good fun. Anna said you could take a joke, but at one point, I did think I'd taken it too far, and you were going to punch my lights out.'

'Don't worry. It takes much more than that to wind me up,' Javier replied light-heartedly whilst glowering at Anna as she headed for the door.

'Come on, there are some people I want you to meet,' Agnes said and steered him towards an inner door. 'Thanks, Anna,' she called over her shoulder. 'I'll make sure he gets home safe.'

***

Anna was still chuckling when she arrived back in Kristina's kitchen. She slipped into the understairs seating booth, and gratefully warmed her hands around a mug of hot chocolate. She had insisted on lunch outside (only because Javier would have been freezing), but it meant her fingers were complaining.

'Well, how did your joke go down?' Kristina tucked into a homemade flapjack.

'It was taken in the spirit it was intended,' Anna cryptically replied. She'd loved watching Javier squirm like a worm on a hook. It afforded her a small crumb of comfort. But reporting back on her piece of fun was not why she was there. 'You have met my hard-done-by friend now. What does your intuition tell you?'

There was a reason the residents good-naturedly referred to Kristina as 'the crazy Swedish lady'. She had a seemingly psychic ability to read people. Anna had seen it in action countless times, and ten years ago it had saved her from a violent attack.

Kristina sighed. 'You are right to be concerned. I see many secrets and plots behind those gorgeous brown eyes.' Anna gave her friend a withering look. 'Come on, girl. There's no denying the man is an outstanding specimen.' Kristina wafted herself. 'I might be old, but I'm not dead! Anyway, enough of that. Back to business. He has slipped a long way off the straight and narrow. There is a core of goodness, but it's deeply buried. I nudged his conscience a few times, but he quickly shut me down. At the moment, he doesn't know what to make of me. One minute he's on edge, and the next is dismissing me as a doddery old crone.'

Anna's thumbs held her chin, and index fingers tapped either side of her nose. 'Okay, do you think he can be saved?'

It sounded dramatic, but Anna needed to know if she could justify the unknown risk to her family and friends. She didn't trust him and was floundering in the dark to work out what he might do. One thing she did expect was for him to snoop about the place, but as Kristina had nothing of value and no money, he couldn't rip her off.

'Yes, I believe he can, but it won't be easy. There are years and years of deceit to peel back, which will be painful, at times unbearably so. He'll fight it all the way because it's easier to hide from the past than confront it.' Kristina studied Anna closely. 'You must care for him greatly to go to these lengths.'

Anna clutched her drink. The heat burned her hands, but she didn't let go. 'A long time ago, I did.'

'Is there anything more you want to disclose?' Kristina squeezed Anna's arm, but she slowly shook her head. 'Okay, sweetheart. I understand you don't want to cloud my judgement. I look forward to becoming better acquainted with Mr Owens, and as I work my magic, I'll report back.'

Anna ambled through the back lanes, lost in thought. Could her friend help Javier? Little got past Kristina, but some things did – Pip and Alex for a start.

Chapter Eleven

Life was far easier with alcohol, Toni thought. It numbed the pain, absolved guilt and made you invincible. Unfortunately, it also screwed with your memory. She sat at the kitchen table and rechecked the clock. Another five minutes had passed, and still nothing. Had she forgotten an instruction? Two instructions? Probably.

The past week had slipped by in blissful oblivion and led to the rare event of drinking her supplies dry. She twisted the three rings on her left hand – engagement, wedding and eternity. The diamonds caught the early evening sun, and shafts of sparkles danced around the room. Her tongue licked dry lips. What she wouldn't give for a slug of booze. By now, she was usually well on the way to la-la land – after Francis had left and when the shame and guilt became unbearable. She shuddered, repulsed at her body's desire, and her cravings intensified. But something wasn't right, and working it out required a clear head. She always had two Saturday visits. Both should have happened by now. Think woman. Try to remember.

Toni Bianchi had at one time been both beautiful and intelligent. The former remained, but the latter ebbed and flowed. Nowadays, it took a supreme effort to function without alcohol. Her addiction left little room for anything else, but she still managed to pull it off. Apart from the very early days after the funeral, none of her friends knew what went on behind closed doors. At every Friday lunch, the four other widows raised champagne flutes to toast one another. They'd survived brutal, adulterous husbands and gone on to thrive. None of them had remarried – who would risk going back to that? Toni would raise her mocktail and use the celebration to justify her past actions. It worked for a few hours, but by Saturday afternoon, the guilt and rage were back with the arrival of Francis and his flowers.

Neither visitor was coming, and she slowly stood up to tidy away in her chic outfit, styled hair and perfect make-up. Why hadn't they arrived? Every Saturday for the last ten years, one visit swiftly followed by another. Toni slammed down the anchovy quiche in frustration, and shortcrust pastry scattered across the workbench. Last Saturday remained a fog. Something must have happened. The answer was there; she could almost taste it, licking her lips again. The need was growing. Luckily, she'd driven a massive loop yesterday to click and collect, on edge for fear of a breathalyser test – there'd always be too much alcohol in her system.

Without even realising it, she was in the pantry. Maybe just a sip as she caressed each bottle, selected one, unscrewed the lid and inhaled heady citron. The aroma fired nerve endings in her brain – what a rush. Flavoured vodkas beckoned. Cucumber and mint, blood orange, grapefruit, ginger, peach and a new one – strawberry and lemongrass. Her heart rate spiked. She could happily drown in a lake of them all.

Wham. That one word – lake – and the bottle slipped from her hands to smash on the floor. Grabbing her bag, she tore along the corridor and sprinted for the car. What had she done?

***

The car bumped along the rough track after a four-hour nightmare. All the road-rage idiots were out tonight and multiple diversions had sent her miles out of the most direct route. She clung to the steering wheel, arms rigid, eyes unblinking, and stomach churning. Each siren (and there'd been plenty) had generated waves of adrenaline. Her head pounded from withdrawal, and the countless motorists who'd delighted in cutting her up because she refused to exceed the speed limit. Thank God for satnav; she'd never have found the place otherwise. It had been years since she'd trekked up to their lakeside shack. Alesso and Dominique had loved its simplicity and said they could get away from it all in a space no bigger than a double garage.

It was pitch black now, but she supposed little would have changed beyond the headlights and wire mesh fences. There would still be the narrow agricultural strips with citrus and olive trees and neat rows of vegetables. Many plots had squat concrete huts with roller-shutter doors for storing fishing boats and gardening tools. Others had slightly better buildings with basic living quarters. Their smallholding had been a step above with a two-star option featuring a solar panel, generator, compost toilet, garage and veranda. Fighting the screeching gate, Toni shivered in her thin cardie. She'd forgotten how the temperature plummeted next to southern Italy's largest lake.

Thirty metres away, gentle waves lapped the shoreline of sixty square kilometres of deep water. Lago di Varano stretched into the darkness and had always creeped her out. She quickly shot the bolt home and jumped in the car. Was it a good idea to be warned if any other vehicles arrived? The terrain didn't exactly lend itself to a quick getaway and she shivered again. This was a perfect place for murder. She pulled next to the garage and got out into deathly stillness, but with no light pollution millions of stars enabled her to cautiously head towards the door. And sure enough, under a large plant pot lurked the key. Nice to know security was tight in the middle of nowhere.

Damp had swollen the wood, forcing her to shoulder barge the door. It suddenly yielded and she stumbled inside. With little hope, she flicked on the light switch and was rewarded with a feeble glow. The place still looked homely with its rustic kitchen, pine table and mismatched chairs. All handmade by Alesso, and amazingly his questionable carpentry skills had stood the test of time. She sniffed the air. It wasn't too musty, as if someone had been here recently. Banging on an arm of the sagging sofa bed, only a little dust puffed up. The simple bathroom was clean and smelled fine. Then to the bedroom with its double bed and chest of drawers, but there was no trace of her daughter's perfume on the sheets. If Dominique had ever been here, she was long gone. It was too dark outside, but tomorrow Toni would check for signs of newly disturbed earth. Please God, anything but that.

Chapter Twelve

The early morning sun slanted through the bedroom window and came as a welcome relief. On the point of exhaustion, Toni had crawled into bed fully clothed a little after nine with every blanket piled on top of the duvet, clutching a precious hot-water bottle found stashed in a drawer. Even so, she was amazed to have slept right through. Her nostrils twitched with the unmistakable smell of coffee and bacon. She flung back the covers and excitedly raced into the kitchen. The bench was littered with half-opened groceries, and a dirty frying pan sat on the stove. The table was set, and in its centre, a steaming dish of bacon, scrambled eggs and mushrooms; a plate of buttered buns; a cafetiere of coffee and a jug of milk. Her heart soared. However, it wasn't her daughter and son-in-law sitting on the sofa but a bleary-eyed individual in an expensive but crumpled suit.

'Hello, Toni,' Francis said pleasantly with a yawn and scratched his beard. 'This sofa's unbelievably uncomfortable to sleep on.'

She propelled herself across the room with manicured nails outstretched to claw his eyes out and almost succeeded. In the nick of time, he got a leg up and kicked out hard. It catapulted her against the armchair, but she instantly righted herself and came again. He managed to untangle himself from the blanket and staggered to his feet, warding off an onslaught of blows that threatened to break through his defences. She feigned a right hook to his head and instead drove her fist hard into his gut. He doubled over but used his head and shoulders to hurl her backwards. Yet again, she surged forwards, and he desperately put the table between them. She screamed, picked up a chair and launched it over the cooling food. He ducked, and it smashed against the concrete wall.

'You ... killed ... my ... daughter. You bastard,' she screeched with a heaving chest and manic eyes. 'After everything ... I've done. You promised.'

She darted around the table and grabbed him, but he was fractionally too quick.

'I ... haven't ... touched ... her. I haven't seen her,' he panted.

She could do this. She was strong enough to beat him. Her eyes scanned the table and fell on the bread knife. She picked it up and lunged again.

'You liar,' she screamed. 'That's all you do. Lie and cheat – and kill.'

She was going to make him pay but couldn't get close enough. So instead, she gripped the knife and sent it javelin-like to where his heart should be. He dived sideways and the blade clunked harmlessly against the window frame. She ran to the kitchen bench, grabbed a carving knife next and went to throw it.

'If I'd killed your daughter, I would tell you,' he said in an eerily quiet voice. 'Just like I did when I killed your husband.'

With the knife in her hand, she slumped to the floor. The fight was over. He gently steered her to the table and pulled out a seat for her to collapse into. He sat opposite and loaded two plates of food, but she pushed hers away. He shrugged and dolloped tomato sauce over his bacon. He bit into the soft roll, and the red sauce oozed out and clung to his silver moustache and beard. Behold Dracula. She wanted to vomit as he excused himself to get a napkin.

'Although you mightn't be hungry, you must be thirsty,' he said and conjured up a bottle of her favourite vodka.

She licked her lips in anticipation as he ran his fingers up and down its surface. Her skin itched, and her pulse quickened. But no, she had to resist. It was a trick. He'd get her drunk again and extract more information that she didn't even know she possessed.

'I'm not here to trick you,' he replied with a sad smile. 'After all these years, I hoped you'd trust me by now.'

The man had an unnerving habit of reading her mind. But she refused to cave – not this time.

'I know you got me drunk last Saturday to find out about this place,' she hissed, stabbing a finger at him. 'Admit it.'

'Yes, I did. But it was the only way,' he responded in a small voice and took a deep breath. 'That Saturday, I discovered something truly terrible. I was out of my mind with worry and couldn't think of another way.'

She narrowed her eyes. 'Continue.'

'Sergio is a bad husband.'

She snorted. 'Tell me something I don't know.'

'We both tried our hardest to unite Dominique with my Frankie. And I know my eldest was delighted at the prospect.' He shrugged his shoulders. 'But unfortunately, Dominique doesn't always know what's best for her, does she?' It pained Toni to do it, but she nodded in agreement. 'Only think, my love, if everything had gone to plan, we could have had a brood of grandchildren by now.' Toni's heart lurched. Each Friday her friends exchanged stories about their grandchildren's exploits. They were all so proud and happy. She'd smile along with them as they all said it'd be her turn soon, but it never had been. Francis shook his head. 'Sorry, I digress. Anyway, as Dominique seemed happy, I went along with it. But I must admit I kept a close eye on their relationship because I wasn't convinced. Unfortunately, over a year ago, my worse suspicions were confirmed. Sergio was being unfaithful.' Toni inhaled sharply. She'd been right not to trust her son-in-law. With the anger, the itch grew, and her eyes strayed to the bottle. Francis interrupted her train of thought. 'Dominique was suffering the same fate as her mother. Married to an adulterous husband.'

Toni flinched as if burned. She still remembered the night Francis visited with a bottle of wine and photographic evidence of her husband's multiple liaisons. Alesso had always handled her like a china doll with average-at-best lovemaking. She'd expected more from a man of his standing and was left disappointed and frustrated. Along with her parents, she'd been flattered that the much older and more powerful company man could possibly be interested. It had been a swift courtship and a year later Dominique was born. Toni was twenty and decades younger than the other wives in her new social sphere. But they'd all been lovely to her, except for the intimidating Milena. However, Milena's husband, Francis, was always kind and courteous, and it seemed almost natural for them to end up in bed that night. She found him able to tap into her innermost desires, and he fed off her rage. It led to an illicit affair which had endured.

But that was then, and now she needed to refocus. The need for a drink was unbearable, and Francis must have sensed her mind wandering off because he placed the bottle out of sight on the floor.

'Not yet, baby. You need to keep listening.' He had such a lovely soothing voice, and Toni mutely nodded. 'I decided to approach Sergio, and naturally he agreed to call the whole thing off. Excellent I thought, but I was deceived. However, against my better judgement, I decided to try again because Sergio is extremely talented and I was loath to lose one of my most efficient employees if there was another way.'

Toni listened, eyes glued to the spot where the unseen vodka bottle sat, and heard how Francis had next approached the lady in question who knew all about her visitor and had expected the worse but was surprised and relieved when Francis only wanted to talk. Unaware of the original discussions with Sergio, she quickly agreed to end the relationship. But the woman had been clever and saw an opportunity. She offered Francis a drink, and then another, and another. All too soon, things got out of hand.

Francis broke down in front of Toni. He wept at being so easily misled, swore it happened only once and explained how he had quickly left, never to see the woman again. Toni allowed herself a moment of smugness when Francis declared that no woman made him feel the way she did.

It took her a few moments to realise he had restarted the story, and she picked up the thread when a few months later, Francis received a call. The woman was expecting his child – a girl. A precious daughter, something he'd always longed for. After six boys, he and Milena had finally agreed to call it a day.

Francis came around the table and grasped Toni's hands. 'Can you remember all those evenings I sneaked to yours when Alesso was working? How we'd sit in the garden and chat, and hearing Dominique wake with a nightmare, you'd go upstairs to her room. I'd secretly follow and stand out of sight on the landing as you stroked her head, soothed away her worries and watched over her till she drifted back off to sleep.'

Toni gave a start. She'd never known that. And then he returned to the story. He shouldered his responsibilities and ensured the baby and mother were provided for. In the back of his mind, he wondered if the child was his, but the affair was over, so he was content. A healthy baby girl was delivered, and they named her Elora. The first time he held her, his heart soared and he'd do anything for his daughter. But the niggles persisted, and he secretly arranged a DNA test and was horrified to find the baby wasn't his after all. The tears streamed down his face, and Toni couldn't fail to be moved. To be deceived in such a way. Francis cast a collection of surveillance photos onto her uneaten food. She wiped off bits of mushroom and saw nursery scenes. She quickly flicked to more intimate images of a woman with Sergio and her hands began to shake.

'The dates are from last month,' she whispered. 'That means—'

'The affair never ended. It means your son-in-law is the father.'

Toni really needed a drink now. 'I don't want to believe it. My poor Dominique.'

But something was puzzling her. Why would Dominique leave with Sergio? Again, it was as if Francis was psychic.

'I think I might have set off a disastrous chain of events,' he admitted and buried his face in his hands.

Toni was in no mood to play nursemaid. 'What did you do?'

With no other option left, he'd finally shown Dominique the photos because she deserved to know the truth. Naturally, her daughter was distraught and raged about trying for a baby, but she persuaded him to go, insisted she was fine and would deal with Sergio in her own way. It had made Francis determined to confront Monika and Sergio with the truth. No more skulking about in the shadows. He drove to the villa the next day in a towering rage expecting to find Sergio but discovered carnage.

'I-I found Monika shot through the head and Elora gone. I tore back to your daughter's house, terrified Sergio had gone on a crazed shooting spree, but found nobody. Next, I patrolled the harbourside – I remembered Dominique mentioning they went there before she came to yours. I found their car but no sign of them. Next, I raced over to yours – perhaps you knew something.'

Toni sat wide-eyed. 'And you realised I did but wasn't going to tell.'

He kissed her cheek. 'Oh, my love, please forgive me. I didn't know what else to do. Don't you see Sergio has tricked your daughter into believing I'm a monster? Yes, I drove up here like a man possessed to save Dominique and Elora – I would never harm them. Your daughter is so obsessed with wanting a baby that she's willing to go along with anything Sergio tells her to get one. They've gone on the run with a three-month-old child.'

'Francis,' Toni pleaded. 'We must help them.'

'I think the best thing is to get you home and from there we can decide on our course of action,' he replied slowly, staring past her and out the window. But then his voice became strident once more as if a decision had been made. 'Lying on that sofa last night, I had plenty of time to think, and I reckon I might have a plan. Vincent is outside and he'll drive you back – I don't think you're up to it. I'll tidy up and then drive your car. What do you think?'

It was a relief to have a chauffeur, but she sat fiddling with her fork. 'I-I have a confession. I-I thought you were here to—'

'Kill you.' He kissed her mouth this time. 'Do you seriously think I'd drive all the way up here, half-freeze under a paper-thin blanket all night, cook breakfast and then bop you off?'

'I suppose when you put it like that.' She licked her lips. 'I couldn't have one tiny sip?'

He ran a finger down her breastbone, and as always, his caress triggered an unbidden surge of sexual desire. He whispered it was only a short drive home. She nodded and anxiously twisted her watch – the roads should be quiet this early on a Sunday.

Chapter Thirteen

Ten o'clock on a Tuesday morning and Toni hid in the bathroom. It was the only place which afforded a modicum of privacy. For over two weeks, her home had been invaded. No sooner had she agreed to Francis's plan than an army had descended to disturb her peace. They had commandeered her living room with all their electronic listening devices, and a nameless entity sat poised by the telephone. She was no longer allowed to cook in the kitchen as someone else prepared all the meals. But not before Angela, the terrifying housekeeper, had cleaned the house from top to bottom, and then thankfully left. After that, Francis swept into her husband's office and declared it would be his for the duration. Ten minutes later, she'd been dragged inside and an explanation for the open ottoman's remaining contents had been demanded. With everything going on, she'd genuinely forgotten about the money, and he was eventually satisfied. Even the bedroom offered no solace. Francis would slip between the sheets each night and expect a star turn. At least that was one area in which she didn't need to feign interest.

Toni stared at her reflection. How much longer could she walk this tightrope? She allowed herself a quick grin. Up to now, Francis had bought her bullshit loyalty act. She still couldn't believe he'd spent the night shivering under a blanket in the lakeside shack, but who knew the inner workings of a psychopath? And Francis was right up there with them. He was convinced Dominique would make contact, and unfortunately Toni agreed. It was that damned doorbell ring. Francis hadn't just rung it once as a stranger would. No, he'd rung it like he always did. A friendly tring-tring-tring-tring. A 'look it's me, I'm here again' type of a ring. And that would eat away at Dominique and force her to call.

The hardest part of the charade had been managing her alcohol intake. Toni needed enough to keep functioning but not so much that her mind became hazy. And helpful Francis ensured her supply of vodka was always on hand. But those beautiful bottles of vodka had craftily been watered down. The night Francis served up that delicious stew and kept excusing himself, she'd quickly tipped half the contents of each bottle down the sink and replenished them with good old-fashioned tap water. And so far, so good. Because, luckily, Francis loathed the stuff.

There was only so long she could hide. Time to trudge downstairs. She sidled into the kitchen and failed yet again to engage in conversation with the intimidating cook (she was certainly Angela's sister). Pouring a coffee (at least she was permitted to do that), Toni headed outside as the landline rang.

Everyone was in place, and on the fourth ring, Toni hesitantly lifted the receiver and took a deep breath. 'Hello?'

'Mamma, it's me.'

'Thank God, Dominique. Are you all okay?'

The nameless entity gave a thumbs-up sign.

'We're all fine.'

'Sweetheart, I went to the lake, but you weren't there.'

'We had a change of plan.'

'Can you tell me where you are?' Toni asked as Francis wolf-grinned.

'I don't think that would be a good idea, do you?' Came her daughter's deadpan response.

Toni recognised the sign. Dominique's temper was starting to build, and it was her job to stoke it.

'Whatever makes you say that, darling?' she trilled.

'Because you've probably got Francis, Hector and a gaggle of technical bods there desperately trying to trace this call as we speak!' Dominique screamed down the phone.

Toni held the receiver away from her ear, and the whole room listened as her daughter lost it. She hurled abuse down the line. How she'd fed her mother the bullshit story about the lake, knowing fine well she'd blurt it all out once she was sozzled. And how she realised her mother had been lying to her for years – Dominique wasn't the only regular visitor.

'It was the doorbell chimes, wasn't it?' Toni whispered. Goading her daughter was awful, but it was necessary – a matter of life or death.

'Tell me, Mother-dearest, how long has that chirpy ding-dong been playing out?' The hate-filled voice demanded.

'Twenty-eight years.'

There was absolute silence at the other end. Toni couldn't even detect breathing and thought the line was dead. But the technician nodded. Her daughter was still there.

'That's before Papa died,' Dominique whispered. 'You were bedding Francis four years before my father was gunned down in cold blood.' Toni stiffened and looked at Francis, who stared back. Would her daughter put two and two together? 'You bitch. You alcohol-soaked slag. How could you? How could you do that to him? Papa worshipped the ground you walked on.'

Toni relaxed. The hate had clouded her daughter's clever mind, and it was time for Toni to play her ace. 'You don't know what you're talking about, young lady,' she snapped.

'Well, why don't you enlighten me,' Dominique retorted.

'My husband, the man you continue to idolise, was nothing but a worthless shit. Oh yes, he put me on a pedestal whilst he screwed around with countless prostitutes and other gutter-level whores.'

Toni didn't have to pretend. Years of rage exploded down the telephone line, and she ranted and raved about the shame, the humiliation and the anger his betrayal had caused her. Yes, she'd initially bedded Francis out of vengeance but found she enjoyed being with a man who knew how to please a woman. Not like her lacklustre husband. And she had therefore kept up the passionate affair. At the end of her tirade, Toni found her chest heaving, and tears tracked down her cheeks. Everyone in the room stared at her. Nobody had expected that outburst.

'I hate you,' came the bitter response. 'From this point on, you are no longer my mother.'

The phone went dead, and Toni stared at the shaking handset before dropping it with a resounding clunk. Despite the horrific conversation achieving its goal, she felt numb. To deliberately make Dominique not only despise her but to destroy the golden memories of her father was unforgivable. It didn't help that there'd been no other option. She staggered sobbing to the sofa, her whole body shaking, but it wasn't alcohol withdrawal this time – she simply felt sickened to the core. Francis handed her a full tumbler of vodka; she knocked it back and signalled for another. The watered-down drink was vile, but it would do. She blew her nose and waited.

The nameless entity coughed nervously. 'They used a secure VPN, boss. We were unable to trace the call.'

'Francis, what are we going to do?' Toni wailed, wiping away tears of joy, but Francis wasn't listening. He was busy hurling expensive kit across the room.

'Almost three weeks I've waited,' he roared and ripped the telephone cord out of the wall. 'Waste of my fucking time. Why the hell didn't anyone tell me the call was unlikely to be traced.' Nobody spoke. Nobody dared remind the boss that was precisely what he'd been told but he'd refused to listen. 'Out!' Francis bellowed. 'I want everyone gone. Take all your worthless gear and clear off.'

There was a frantic scrambling by the underlings, and they quickly vanished. Hector strolled to the kitchen and nonchalantly re-entered eating an apple. At least somebody appeared unfazed by everything.

'I'll be in touch,' Francis snapped before storming out, with Hector dutifully following.

In less than five minutes, the house was finally hers again. She gratefully sank into the sofa and closed her eyes. Her tightrope walk continued – Dominique, her son-in-law and the baby were safe. And hopefully, Francis would keep away for a little while.

Chapter Fourteen

The CCTV footage finished, and Anna triumphantly turned to Kristina. 'See, I told you. Didn't I tell you he would snoop!' It was a Saturday morning in early May, and the pair crowded around Anna's home computer in the downstairs study. They'd spent the last ten minutes watching evidence of Javier's attempts to access the filing cabinets, desk and computer in the Apokeri Apartments office. With what looked remarkably like a nail kit, he'd picked the locks and speed-searched the contents. Anna had laughed out loud at his mounting frustration. She'd bulked out the dead files to infuriate him and was pleased it had worked. He could search the office during the day but had to undertake his dirty work in the gallery after midnight. The blood pounded in her ears as Anna watched him nervously hide the torchlight whenever he heard a noise outside or the old house creaked.

Kristina sipped her black coffee and playfully rocked backwards and forwards in her chair, appearing to have a whale of a time. 'But of course he snooped, my dear. That's what you expected, wasn't it?'

'Doesn't it bother you that he's sneaking about!' Anna cried. 'He's in your house right now doing lord knows what!'

'Well, technically, it's your house, gallery and apartment block, which is maybe why you're getting so wound up?' Kristina replied, her voice level.

'How can you be so relaxed?' Anna demanded and slammed her mug down. 'I do believe you are enjoying this – admit it.'

'Yes, I am. How often do you get to redeem a fallen angel?' Kristina teased before bringing her chair to the upright position. 'Give the bloke a chance, Anna. It's only been a few weeks. I did tell you the change was going to take time.'

'Fine,' Anna replied sharply. 'I'll do what you say and give him another chance. But that man is on borrowed time. Any more dodgy business and he's out.'

Kristina swallowed the last of her coffee and rose. 'Yes, yes. Whatever you say. Now, if you don't mind, I need to make tracks. A particularly thorny shrub needs my attention, and Javier said he would lend a hand.'

'What? He hates gardening.'

'People change, Anna. That's the whole point of this exercise.'

Her friend was (as usual) making perfect sense as Anna followed her into the kitchen but it couldn't stop that sense of betrayal she'd worked so hard to suppress for years.

'See you later, Kristina,' Filip cheerfully called out as the back door closed, and then caught sight of his wife's face. 'Uh oh, imminent Geordie explosion alert!' He listened as Anna stormed around the kitchen recounting Javier's ongoing betrayal.

'I gave that man a chance, and he doesn't give a toss,' she shouted and slammed a cupboard door shut as Filip sat and ate a slice of toast.

'Are you not maybe a bit jealous of the friendship between Javier and Kristina?'

'Don't be so ridiculous,' she spluttered with rage. 'Don't you get it? He's only being nice because it makes it easier to rip her off!'

'But he isn't able to, is he? She doesn't have any money or property to scam. Isn't that why you gave him the rewiring job in the first place?' he asked with the same infuriating calmness as Kristina. 'I thought he seemed okay when I chatted with him. Perhaps after all these years, you don't want him to change – maybe it's easier for you to keep hating him.'

Her mouth dropped open, and she stood statue-like beside the fridge as Evie waltzed into the kitchen clutching a tin.

'Are you trying to catch flies, Mam?' Evie asked as she tickled a highly excited Cleo. 'Good girl, have you missed me?' The dog barked twice and shot off after her rubber chicken.

'Your mam is struggling to find inner peace this morning,' Filip said and winked at his daughter. 'So we need to be on our best behaviour.'

'I think I'll just return to Granda Vas-Vas to do some more baking,' Evie whispered as she crept backwards pantomime-style towards the door.

'Will you two pack it in,' Anna snapped and glowered at the co-conspirators who loved to wind her up. 'I am not in a bad mood.'

'Yeah, right, grumpy bum,' Evie replied and skipped over to the table. 'Don't you want to see what I made?' She triumphantly prised off the lid to reveal ten perfectly rounded pink macaroons.

Anna grinned, despite her anger. 'Wow, they look amazing!'

'I know. Granda Vas-Vas was dead impressed. He said they were better than his. And everyone knows Granda is the world's best baker, isn't that right, Dad?'

'He certainly is, kiddo. And now he's passing his skills on to you.'

'And we went down to the bakery to show Viktor and Nikki, who both gave me full marks,' Evie exclaimed in wonderment. 'They each had one, well, Nikki had two, and I also gave Viktor another three to take home.'

'I'm sure Agnes and the twins will love them,' Filip replied. 'Are you going to follow in Granda's footsteps and become a baker then?'

Evie frowned and gave the matter serious thought before shaking her head. 'No, I don't think so. I love baking with Granda once a week, but I don't think I could do it as a full-time job.'

'How about a world-famous footballer then?' Anna asked and winked at Filip.

'Maybe. Javier says I've got potential.' Evie offered up the macaroons. Her dad lobbed one into his mouth and bit down appreciatively.

'Javier?' Anna replied dully as Filip shot her a warning look. She declined a biscuit – her appetite had vanished.

'Yes,' Evie replied, eyes wide as if Javier's approval was front-page news. 'He came along to training with Agnes and the twins as he used to coach a kids' team and wondered if he might lend a hand, even though he can't speak much Greek yet. But he did try out a few phrases he'd been practising and was quite good. And he told all the kids to call him Javier, not Mr Owens because he wasn't a proper teacher. We all thought that was pretty cool.'

'And is he a good coach?' Filip asked whilst watching Anna's face harden.

'Definitely, I reckon he's better than our proper coach. Javier showed me this new trick to fool your opponent, and I tried it out and scored two goals! All the pitches were full, so tons of people I knew saw.' Without pausing for breath, she proceeded to list everyone there. 'It was great. I hope he goes next week.'

Anna opened her mouth but Filip shook his head.

'That's … really … good,' she managed, resulting in Filip giving her a sly thumbs-up, which made her want to slap him.

'Oh, and I almost forgot.' Evie dug around in her pocket. 'Javier said to give you this. It's the money for the meal when he first arrived – he apologised for taking so long to pay it back.'

'I see … thank you.' Anna fingered the notes as Filip raised his eyebrows. Her head pounded. Any minute now, she was going to blow a gasket. The man was manipulating everyone, and nobody else could see it. She needed to get out of the house. 'I'm taking Cleo for a long walk, and I don't know when I'll be back.'

'You had better take your keys,' Filip said with amusement. 'I'm running Evie up to Steffi's soon and will undoubtedly get waylaid.'

Anna's mood failed to improve as she stropped around the house for the next twenty minutes tracking down her missing keys, listening as Evie pointed out to her dad that it had been rather silly of her mam to leave them in a coat pocket and not on the hook like everyone was told. Didn't she remember that one of Cleo's favourite games was pickpocketing?

'Yes, sweetheart,' Anna managed through gritted teeth before kissing her family and storming along the cliffs for the next two hours.

Chapter Fifteen

It was an unassuming little restaurant tucked up one of Brindisi's side streets. The rustic two-storey stone building was centuries old with its arched doorway, and Toni suspected the entrance troughs with their tightly clipped shrubs were of a similar age. There was no seating outside this establishment; everything went on behind closed doors. Unsuspecting tourists occasionally wandered in, ate, praised the food and left satisfied. Little knowing it was a front for the Company to launder money.

The five widows had frequented the cute bistro with its private wooden booths, windowless walls, and wax-covered carafe candleholders for decades and saw no reason to change their Friday routine. The food was excellent, the service first-class and the champagne (so Toni was informed) was to die for. The quintet cackled away as usual, and Toni revelled in their friendship – especially with Dominique gone. Her daughter's absence left a cavernous void in an aching heart. Toni tried to get out of the house each day but rarely did now that her daughter's prodding presence was gone. She filled her days with thumbing through family albums, baking for nobody and attempting to keep the house tidy, but usually resorted to opening a bottle to fill the hours and forget. Francis still popped around each Saturday but always seemed distracted.

Five glasses clinked the usual life-affirming celebration.

'Mrs Bianchi,' Luigi, their favourite waiter and the formidable owner's grandson interrupted. 'Your hairdresser is on the telephone.'

Toni patted her newly blow-dried hair. 'Excuse me, ladies, I must have left something.'

They all laughed. Toni's abysmal memory was legendary. She wound her way through the crowded tables to a phone in the back. There were no customers, but the shouting and clattering from the kitchen meant Toni had to press a finger against her ear to hear.

'Hello, Alfonso? Can you speak up? It's always noisy here.'

'Mamma, it's me.'

Toni's heart soared before plummeting. 'Darling, are you out of your mind?'

'It was the only way I could think to contact you,' Dominique spoke clearly and quickly as if every second might be the last. And indeed, Toni furtively glanced around, fearful of eavesdroppers. 'Mamma, I'm so sorry about all the terrible things I said. Please forgive me.'

Toni could hear her daughter sobbing. 'Sweetheart, of course. It broke my heart to say those hurtful words, but I needed to—'

'Make me hate you,' Dominique finished, and Toni could hear the smile down the phone. 'It worked ... to start with – but then I started to think about everything you'd said.'

'And?'

There was a deep sigh. 'I idolise Papa, maybe too much, but he was a shit to you. And I can understand why you did what you—'

'Dominique, listen very carefully. Alesso had his faults but don't let that cloud your memories of him. He was a fantastic father and, for the most part, a wonderful husband. We did love each other very much, and I would never have done anything to hurt him.'

'Thanks, Mamma,' her daughter replied, but Toni could hear a question forming.

'What is it?'

'I know there's more to the story,' Dominique stated and then stopped. The silence stretched out, and the phone receiver became clammy in Toni's vice-like grip. Even with time of the essence, she held her breath – please, please don't let her daughter ask about Alesso's death. 'But I don't need to know, Mamma. The important thing is that you're safe. And I had to ring to tell you that I love you and think you're the most amazing person.'

Toni sent up a silent prayer of thanks. 'Oh, angel. Don't worry about me. I can take care of myself. I'm so proud of you … and … and I know your father would be too. Not many women could do what you're doing.'

'I need to keep Elora, Sergio, and Pesce safe, Mamma,' Dominique said, but the strident, confident voice wavered ever so slightly.

Toni picked up on it instantly. 'Baby, what's wrong? How are things between the two of you? How are you coping with unexpected motherhood?'

'I-I won't lie; my gorgeous Pesce has kept me sane. Things were unbearable to start with, but … but we're slowly getting there – it doesn't help being exhausted all the time.'

Toni could hear the smile again and knew the couple were looking at each other. 'Sergio's there, isn't he?'

'Yes, along with Elora and Pesce.'

'Can you please put me on speaker, darling?'

'Why?'

Toni laughed at her daughter's nervousness. 'Don't worry; I'm going to be nice.'

There was a click and then the voice of her son-in-law. 'Hi, Toni.'

His voice held a note of trepidation and with good reason.

'Hey, Sergio. Firstly, I'm still furious at what you did and what you have put my daughter through. I won't lie; I wanted to kill you when I heard about your betrayal,' Toni seethed but took a breath and tempered her tone. 'However, based on my own behaviour, I'm in no position to cast judgement. What is done is done, and it's time to move on.' There was only his breathing down the line. 'Anyway, that's not why I wanted a quick word. I-I wanted to apologise.'

'Oh,' he exclaimed in a mixture of surprise and curiosity.

'I never gave you a chance, Sergio. All I wanted was to keep Dominique safe, and I believed the only way was for her to marry another. And because of that, I couldn't accept you. It didn't matter to me that you made her happy. And except for very recent events, you excelled at that. I love my daughter more than my own life, and it was unforgivable that I didn't welcome you into our little family the same way she did.' Toni pressed a thumb and index finger to her forehead. 'You lost both your parents when you were just eight, the same age Dominique lost her father. His death devastated my daughter, but selfishly I never gave a second thought to what you must have suffered – even though Dominique told me in great detail. I'm so very sorry and am deeply ashamed of my past behaviour. I should have been there for you as well. We are in a little bit of a pickle at the moment, and I don't know what will happen. But I hope if we meet again, you will allow me to be the mother-in-law I should have always been. Can you forgive me?'

There was a long pause, and Toni heard Dominique sniffling.

'I-I wasn't expecting that … but yes – I forgive you,' he replied, and his voice became more confident. 'And I would love it if we could start again. I can see where my wife gets her strength. A little bit of a pickle must be the greatest understatement ever.' A cry started up in the background, and Toni heard quiet murmurings. 'I need to go, Toni, and see to Elora. I'll hand you back to Dominique. Stay safe, and we'll see you when this is all over.'

There was another click, and then Dominique's voice, thick with emotion, was back. 'Mamma, thank you. That can't have been easy.'

'Sweetheart, there's no time left to leave things unsaid. I-I love you so much.' She choked on the words and fought back the tears, knowing it was probably the last time she would ever speak to her daughter. 'My gorgeous girl, you must never ring me again. It's far too dangerous. I can cope if I know you're all safe – that's all I ask.'

She could hear Dominique sobbing; all Toni wanted was to hug her child, soothe away the fear and say everything would be alright. It was heartbreaking.

'I love you too, Mamma. And I won't take any more risks, and you shouldn't either. So it would be best if you told Francis about this call. The guy's a paranoid, obsessive psychopath and seems able to second-guess people. Please, don't get on the wrong side of him. God knows who's listening to this call.'

Although her daughter was unable to see, Toni nodded. 'Good thinking, I'll do that. Stay safe.'

She carefully replaced the receiver and glanced around. The tyrannical chef was still barking out orders, the waiting staff shuttled backwards and forwards, and she could hear her friends' laughter rise above the low hum of customers' conversations. Nobody was any the wiser. She needed to sort herself out and slipped into the toilets to dry her eyes as a debt-ridden Luigi stepped outside to make a call.

Chapter Sixteen

Weeks had passed, and for all his sneaking about, there was nothing Javier could use. The office drew a blank, as did the gallery's computer. He'd have loved to access Round the Bend's back office, but it was never left unlocked.

Over that time, he'd wheedled information out about Anna and her burgeoning business empire. In fact, everyone in Apokeri was happy to sing her praises once they knew he was an old friend. It left him wondering if there was anybody who disliked her. She was sitting on a goldmine that tormentingly remained out of reach. There was Round the Bend, Apokeri Apartments, Apokeri Gallery and the highly profitable online Geordie Lass company. Anna had tapped into a lucrative market of Brits thriving abroad and had an army of social media followers that brought lucrative advertising revenue alongside guest speaking. And on top of that, she was a tour guide, ran a free self-defence class in the local school and raised money for her sister-in-law's domestic abuse charity. Oh yes, and she was happily married with a daughter. Was there anything the woman couldn't do?

She'd always been a grafter, slogging her guts out to save money for their adventures together. A smile crept over his face at the memory of a proud sixteen-year-old Anna handing him half the money for their first long weekend away. He'd dismissed the offer to his cost as she refused to back down until he finally relented. It had always been like that. So he'd started fibbing about the price of days out, weekends away and the occasional holiday they managed to wangle. He was eight years older and on a good electrician's wage, there was no way she was paying half from her apprenticeship and a part-time job. But when she'd moved in (and appointed herself their finance manager), she discovered how he'd misled her. She well and truly hit the roof. How dare he lecture her on deceit and extract a promise that she'd never lie to him again when he was lying to her all the time. His explanations and justifications were ignored. She was a sight to behold in a towering rage. And as she ranted away, he knew with utter certainty he always wanted to be with her. He remembered his proposal and her response as if it was yesterday. 'My, you're magnificent when you're angry. Will you marry me?' 'Yes, you infuriating arsehole,' she'd snapped. 'And don't think this means I'm not still mad at you because I am.' She'd then flung herself into his arms, shouting, 'Together forever, I've never been so happy.' And neither had he.

In mid-May, the apartments and gallery were rewired, and he moved on to the main house. It was a big job. But it gave him plenty of time to work on Kristina, who was nice, trusting and, at ninety-two, a far easier target than his ex-wife. On her house tour, they'd cautiously proceeded down worn stone steps to the musty cellar, where he immediately clocked the safe – or, more accurately, the vault – and almost salivated. He made it his mission to break in. By night, he tried to crack the combination, and during the day he continued to snoop through the rest of the house.

Javier paused as he rifled through Kristina's personal effects. His grain of a conscience vibrated but was shoved back into its box. He was in Kristina's bedroom whilst she was on Tharesseti, taking her twice-weekly art class for the hotel's discerning guests. Penelope was downstairs managing the shop and diligently never left her post. The woman must have an iron-clad bladder, judging by the amount of coffee she drank. He worked through the chest of drawers with its neatly folded clothes, then moved to the wardrobe and extracted a box hidden behind folded blankets. It was full of paperwork which looked promising. Sitting cross-legged in the sun, he eagerly worked his way through the contents. He shook a brown A4 envelope, and weighty correspondence tumbled out. It was from somebody called Daniel. The bloke was in Australia nursing a terminally ill father, and in the next letter (dated ten months later), the father had pegged it, but not before his son was married and expecting to be a father. The last letter was full of parental slush (our daughter is so beautiful, blah, blah, blah) and a move to be near his wife's family in Brisbane. After that, there were several return-to-sender letters from Brisbane and Adelaide. However, there were annual postcards from far-flung destinations with the usual content – having a great time, little Simone enjoying the beach, etc. Javier rolled his eyes and bundled everything back inside before noticing an unsealed, small, white A5 envelope on the rug. He unfolded a single sheet and recognised Kristina's flowing script.

> Hello Javier,
> I wondered how long it would take you to get here.
> I don't think Anna would be very impressed, do you? She already knows you've been poking around in the office and gallery. Why don't you put everything back and return to rewiring the house?
> See you later.
> Your friend
> Kristina

He dropped the note as if burned. His heart pounded, and an unfamiliar sensation washed over him – shame. He quickly returned everything and scuttled back to work.

Chapter Seventeen

All the bags were inside, and Dominique unpacked again. All they did was repack and unpack every few days. It was exhausting, and she yawned loudly.

'Take a seat. I can sort everything out,' Sergio said quickly as he jigged Elora up and down. He was so eager to please, to gain her affection once more. 'Why don't you have a rest? I can pop to the shops and get a few bits and bobs. I could murder a coffee.'

She gave him a tight smile and reined in her immediate response to snap back and point out there was no way she could relax as Elora needed a bath, feeding and a nap, Pesce required a walk, and she had to assess their new surroundings. And then find something to eat that preferably wasn't full of fat and sugar. Healthy eating had gone out the window recently, as had any chance to exercise, and it was badly affecting her mood.

'It's okay; I want to get some fresh air. I'll take Pesce out and nip to the shop by Reception which will give me a chance to get a lay of the land. And you can get Elora settled and unpack.'

'That sounds a plan, sweetheart,' he happily replied and tentatively kissed her on the cheek, which she had the good humour to accept.

'Come on, Pesce. Walkies,' she called to her obedient cockapoo. At the magic W word, he launched off the bed, hurtled into the kitchen and beat his tail against the units. At least somebody was pleased with the constantly changing surroundings.

Dominique stepped out of the static caravan and surveyed her surroundings. The latest place had been an instinctive choice. Driving along the northern side of Lake Lucerne with no clear plan of where to go, a pretty sign advertised secluded wooded accommodation and she immediately made the turn. The narrow road carved its way between the rocks with glimpses of the lake between a canopy of trees. As promised, lodges, static caravans, hardstanding and grassed pitches were available. She breathed in deeply; mixed in with resin was the tantalising scent of barbeques in the early evening air, and her stomach rumbled. Food would have to wait, and she set off to explore. Strolling through the trees and well-tended grounds, she found the site was surprisingly large and well-designed.

The lodges and static caravans sat higher up, nestled amongst the trees and were far enough apart to provide privacy. Further down, there were various pockets of mown grass with rectangles of hardcore for caravans, campervans and motorhomes to hook up. There were so many different vehicles, each with an assortment of canoes, paddleboards, dinghies, bikes, mopeds and some even towed cars. And then further on were the grassed areas with a myriad of tents – one-person expedition options right up to eight-berth air-beam creations. And everywhere families, couples and groups enjoyed the Swiss countryside and conversed with their neighbours. Dominique had been surprised that the longer their flight lasted, the more she gravitated towards campsites. Motels or apartments were too confining and isolating, with only Sergio and, more often than not, Pesce and Elora to converse with. On campsites, people were friendlier in an unobtrusive way. And if she talked to strangers, she could avoid talking to Sergio. Her feelings towards him still swung wildly from tolerance to barely suppressed rage. On a campsite, her little family was simply one of many, and nobody paid them much attention other than to coo over Elora and Pesce.

The cockapoo snuffled in the grass and, in an instant, swallowed something. Dominique immediately prised open his jaws to extract a half-eaten sausage and chucked it in the bin. Her dog was a sod for vacuuming up discarded food. She continued on her way past various buildings – toilet and shower blocks, drying rooms, indoor kitchens, washing-up areas – and headed down towards the entrance with its reception, café and well-stocked shop. She bought a few supplies and two takeaway coffees whilst the young lad behind the till came around to tickle Pesce and give him a treat. After dragging her dog away from his new best friend, she stopped to chat with various people, and by the time she returned, the sun was dropping, and Sergio and Elora were flat out. She tiptoed out of the bedroom and set about making tea. The sizzling of onions, garlic, ginger and chilli soon enticed her husband out of his den. Rubbing tired eyes, he thanked her for his coffee and popped it in the microwave. After wolfing down their stir-fry and with one ear open for Elora, they reclined back and, swaddled in blankets, star-gazed.

'You made a good choice, babe,' Sergio murmured into the still night. 'Let's stay here for a bit.'

There was no response from Dominique; she was already asleep.

Chapter Eighteen

It was glorious late May, and Javier worked away at the bottom of the garden. The sun rebounded off the stone wall, and he relished the heat as he took a bite of his sandwich. The rewiring was going well, but to get some fresh air (and help Kristina), he ventured outside at lunchtime to do some gardening under her tutelage. Today he was battling a particularly stubborn patch of dandelions and was determined to get all the tap roots up. Once done, they would get fed to the chickens, who were contentedly clucking away as Kristina collected their eggs. He stood up and admired his handiwork. A pile of weeds sat to one side, and the flowerbed once again looked pristine. He understood why Kristina spent so much time pottering about – it definitely kept her young, and with an army of helpers, it was a beautiful space. Once a week, kids from the village school arrived for their Gardening Club and – guided by Kristina – planted, weeded and harvested produce. It had proved so popular that some still popped in to help once they moved to high school.

Two months had slipped by as Javier discovered his landlady was both savvy and inquisitive. She still unnerved him with her seemingly psychic abilities, but he genuinely liked the clever and witty woman, so he helped with the garden. He'd not forgotten Anna's request, but as Kristina rarely talked about her past, she was certainly not fixated.

Slim arms snaked around his waist and unfastened his shorts. He firmly did them back up before turning around. 'This is an unexpected visit, Mia.'

The young woman stood in skin-tight leggings and a vest top. She dropped her eyes and ran a finger down his chest. 'Come on, Owens. You know you want to.'

'For the hundredth time – I'm very flattered, but the answer remains no,' he politely replied and gently removed her hand.

She crossed her arms and nodded. 'I understand, you're gay.'

'Naturally, what other explanation could there be?' he replied with a smile. It amused him to see her failing to get what she wanted.

'It's the only answer,' she replied and grinned. 'Nobody, and I mean nobody, turns me down.'

'I cannot imagine you sneaked in here just to try your luck again,' he observed. 'What's the real reason?'

Yesterday he'd decided to be a tourist. He'd taken up Mia's offer of a free place on Giannis' dive boat, and saw a side of her he'd never seen. She was no longer a temptress but a consummate professional who was friendly but firm. The group's safety was paramount, and she'd taken a young couple to task for messing about during pre-dive checks. Over the weeks, Javier had frequently noticed the boat out at night on what he thought were organised trips. However, he discovered that wasn't the case as the company didn't offer them. But what had piqued his interest was the entire crew spinning the same word-perfect story about Giannis taking his mates fishing. His bullshit antenna immediately spiked – something was going on, and his casual enquiries had clearly sent up a red flag.

'That's why I'm attracted to you, Owens; there's no boring small talk,' she replied, happy to get right to the point. 'I have a business proposition – something lucrative. I believe you appreciate an opportunity to make easy money. Even if it is ... shall we say ... slightly dubious.'

He waved her over to a bench whilst his mind ticked over. It appeared he was being asked to join, not warned off. However, he remained cautious. 'What makes you say that?'

She flashed him a knowing smile and leaned over to seductively whisper in his ear. 'You're just like me. Loyal to no one but yourself – irresistibly drawn to making money off other people. Those who choose the legitimate way are fools. Think what we could—'

'Oh, I-I'm sorry. I-I didn't mean to disturb you.'

He looked up to see his flustered ex-wife with a face mirroring embarrassment, shock and something else he couldn't place.

'Anna,' he yelled, but the gate slammed shut. Shit, how could he forget she always arrived early for everything. He didn't want her to think ...

Mia raised her eyebrows and smirked. 'No, not gay after all.'

'It's not what ... I mean, you shouldn't—'

'You're wasting your time there, Owens,' she calmly replied and patted his knee. 'Anna's devoted to Filip.'

Javier eyed Mia. Like a cat, she sat motionless, waiting. The woman knew him for what he was – a hardened, unscrupulous individual. A twinned soul. There was no risk of a set-up. The day was turning out to be better than expected.

He grinned with anticipation. 'Tell me, what's the job?'

Chapter Nineteen

A sharp breeze rattled the open door and jerked Dominique awake. From behind the caravan, a twig snapped, and she stiffened. Where was Pesce? No sooner had the thought popped into her head, he wandered outside.

'You're looking decidedly pleased with yourself,' she responded to a lick around the chops. 'Woah, what have you been eating, Pesce? Your breath smells of cheese.' He wagged his tail, then scampered to the gate and sat, ears straining. A few seconds later came the crunch of gravel, the car door was flung open, and her husband bounded up the steps with his daughter, eyes shining.

'Come on, sleepy-head, rise and shine. I've got a wonderful surprise for you.'

His enthusiasm was infectious, and Dominique laughed. 'What is it?'

'Look at these,' he proudly replied and withdrew two tickets. 'We're going on a free paddleboat cruise. It departs in thirty minutes, so we need to be quick.'

'What? How did you score these?' Dominique scrambled to her feet.

'I had to stop in a lay-by to change Elora in the boot,' he explained and followed her inside. 'A black people-carrier pulled up, and the lady from the next door's caravan got out. She said they had spare non-refundable tickets because their friends had dropped out, and I could have them as you mentioned wanting to go on one. How amazing is that!'

In five minutes, they were pulling away, and thirty seconds later, Elora started screaming. Dominique frantically searched in the bag. 'I can't find her dummy!'

The screams reverberated inside the car, and Sergio hit the steering wheel in frustration. 'Crap. It's on the kitchen bench. I forgot to pick it up.'

'No worries. Pull up at the shop, and I'll jump out and get one. I'll also grab a thank-you bottle of wine.'

With three minutes to spare, their party breathlessly raced up the gangplank and sunk into seats next to their bemused campsite neighbours.

***

The hour-long serene cruise was delightful, with good company, gorgeous scenery, entertaining commentary and a sleeping Elora. Having given their word to pop around for a drink and meal that night, the Castellas parted company from their new friends and strolled along the lakeshore. With nothing more than a coffee all morning, Dominique was thinking about what to do for lunch when two dogs kicked off up ahead.

'Oh, that reminds me,' Sergio said as they watched both owners drag their pets apart and furiously scold them. 'Pesce went berserk in the car earlier when you ran into the shop.'

Dominique froze. 'Who was he going mad at?'

'Well, that was the weird thing,' he replied and steered the pushchair between rollerbladers and cyclists. 'It was that young bloke who works at the campsite. The one Pesce adores.'

As Sergio talked, Dominique picked up the pace and headed for the car. His steps were in time with hers, and the claws of Pesce rapidly clicked on the pavement. Her heartbeat was increasing, matching her rapid strides.

He grabbed hold of her arm. 'What's wrong, Dom? You're freaking me out.'

They reached the car, and she speedily unclipped Elora, gently lifted the sleeping child into her car seat, and then Pesce onto his cushion and clipped in the lead.

'Pesce only barks when there's something wrong. We have to go back to the caravan. I think … no, I don't want to say anything yet. It might not come true if I don't say it aloud.'

She refused to say anything more, and for the seemingly never-ending return car journey, she sat in silence, eyes forward. She was out of the car, up the steps in seconds, and threw open the bedroom door. Pesce bounded in behind her and began to growl. How hadn't she noticed earlier – there on the carpet lay a ten euro note and a dog treat. She picked it up and sniffed – cheese. And there, underneath the window – a very faint footprint. How bad was it going to be? She dropped to her knees and slid open the wardrobe door. Sergio walked into the bedroom with a giggling Elora and stopped dead.

His wife rocked gently backwards and forwards on the carpet. 'The money – our safety net – is nearly all gone. We've been robbed.'

She hurled the bag across the room, stuck the duvet in her mouth and screamed. Elora shuffled in her father's arms and let out a whimper, and Pesce crawled across the carpet to paw his mistress.

'Sorry about that,' Dominique said calmly and retrieved the holdall. 'Okay, we need to leave immediately.'

'Do we need to go this instant?' Sergio implored as his face crumpled. He already knew the answer.

'Unfortunately, we do. There is no telling what our burglar is doing with that money. If the bloke is a greedy, brainless worthless individual, he'll lead the police right to our door. He's already had two hours to go on a spending spree. Grab everything of Elora's and Pesce's. Leave anything of ours that's not essential. We don't have the time.'

Dominique maintained her composure as she hastily packed away yet again, but inside her brain spooled wildly. She wanted to scream, rage against the injustice of the world and collapse in a defeated heap. In her mind's eye, the thief walked into a high-end store and tried to purchase goods far beyond his means. It aroused suspicion; he was unable to prove the money was his, and when the police arrived, he blurted out the truth. They were on their way, and it terrified her. Not as terrifying as seeing Francis walk up her mother's driveway but a close second.

In no time, their stolen car trundled towards the exit; the needle sat bang on the five-mph site limit whilst tempers continued to fray inside the vehicle. Elora was crying, Pesce was whining, and Sergio was grumbling. Dominique had refused to allow him to change and feed his daughter. He argued she was being unreasonable, and she replied if he didn't stop badgering her, she would reach inside his throat and rip out his voice box – it did the trick. Campers and caravaners all about them went about their business, enjoying the spring sunshine with not a care in the world. Dominique gripped the steering wheel, willing the entrance to appear. And there it was. She turned the car onto the quiet lane and let the needle climb.

There was barely room for two vehicles to squeeze by as the road dropped steeply. She held her breath as the road vanished into the trees, and the sun shining on the windscreen wasn't helping matters – she could hardly see. Suddenly, the undergrowth rustled and something big shot out in front of them. Dominique slammed on the anchors and waited for her heart to drop back into her chest cavity. A majestic stag proudly eyeballed them for a few seconds before casually vanishing. Finally, the main road appeared. It was a still afternoon, and Dominique sat with the window down. She shut off the engine and debated whether to turn left or right. She strained to hear any approaching traffic, but there was too much passenger noise.

'Pesce, be quiet for Mamma.'

The dog fell silent, as did Elora. Sergio continued to grumble. She firmly placed a palm over his mouth and closed her eyes. A gentle breeze rustled the leaves, birds tweeted in the branches, and Dominique heard the low hum of tyres on tarmac to the right. Her mind was made up, and the car turned left. She eased the accelerator to the floor, and slowly the old engine groaned into life – they were never going to outrun anything in this heap of metal. Her eyes constantly flicked between the road curving away to the left and the rear-view mirror. Only a few seconds more and they would be out of sight, and they almost were when she caught sight of the distinctive bonnet of a marked police car taking the turn up to the campsite – Sergio saw it too.

'Babe, I'll never disagree with you for as long as I live,' he said, breathing out and reaching back to stroke his daughter's leg. 'It won't be long, baby. We'll soon have you changed and fed.'

But Dominique continued to push the car – they weren't out of the woods yet. In more ways than one. The trees hemmed them in, the lake glinted below them to the right, and there were few exits off the road. Claustrophobia washed over her; it wouldn't take the police long to figure out they'd fled, and to learn their car details. It was not only the law Dominique feared but corrupt cops who passed on information. She'd dealt with plenty in her time, and Francis had a long arm. She needed a miracle, and up ahead might just be one.

A black people-carrier with a distinctive diagonal green strip across the bonnet was driving towards them. Dominique repeatedly flashed the vehicle, hit the indicator and pulled into the lakeside lay-by. The approaching car did likewise.

'If there were ever a time to pray, it would be now,' Dominique suggested and released her seatbelt. 'I'm about to gamble all our lives on a brief friendship based on two free boat tickets, a bottle of wine, an hour chat on a paddle steamer and a dinner invitation.'

Sergio stared horror-stricken at his wife, discreetly pointed and talked out the side of his mouth as if he feared their campsite neighbours could lip read. 'I know I just said I wasn't going to disagree with you, babe. But those two individuals in that car are former Italian police detectives. You know as well as I do cops never retire, and we would be a dream collar. People like us are their sworn enemies.'

'And that's why I'm hoping they'll help us,' Dominique replied and eased the door open.

Sergio grabbed her arm. 'Are you absolutely sure about this?'

'Not at all,' Dominique conceded and gave him a brave smile. 'But I'm counting on the fact they know exactly what we're up against ... and Elora reminds them of their granddaughter.' On jelly legs, she confidently strode towards the car. Both doors opened, and the couple hurried towards her with concerned expressions, asking what was wrong. With fingers crossed, Dominique flashed her best smile. 'Have you ever fancied being superheroes?'

Chapter Twenty

The contract killer stood at the solid oak door and knocked.
'Enter.'
It was the same curt instruction year after year from a boss who sat behind an enormous mahogany desk in a dark room. The glow from various computer screens was the only light source and revealed a half-eaten pastrami and feta bagel, alongside a bottle of water. The room had a slightly sour smell as if his boss had spent more hours than he should scrolling through information – maps, CCTV and other surveillance data – in his obsession to trace the missing Castellas family. And it was starting to impact the business. Not good.

Hector studied Francis's haggard face – the beard and moustache were no longer perfectly groomed, the cold eyes looked tired, and his boss still wore the same wrinkled shirt and mustard-stained tie from yesterday. For thirty years, the paid assassin had undertaken every unsanctioned activity for Francis. And for generations, Hector's family had loyally served the Del Ambro Contino clan. Embedded in the household, his mother and aunt knew first-hand the cruelty and ambition of Francis Jnr from a young age, and made sure to profit from it. Hector fondly remembered his first assignment. As a fresh-faced eighteen-year-old, he silenced a mistress who was getting a bit too presumptuous, and there had been plenty since then. As soon as his boss tired of them, Hector moved in. But the most satisfying job had been twenty-four years ago when he single-handedly wiped out four old-guard members, set up the fifth and paved the way for his boss to take control of the Company and turn it around. But even his ruthless employer appeared to have an Achilles heel and remained infatuated with Toni Bianchi and now her daughter, Dominique. However, the hunt was not going well.

'What is it, Hector?'

'I've got good news and bad news, boss.'

Francis dragged his nail-bitten fingers through his hair. 'What's the good news?'

'An idiotic campsite employee walked into a Lucerne car dealership yesterday and attempted to buy a Porsche 911 Sports Classic.'

Francis nodded like a wise old professor. 'I knew that stolen cash would serve me well.'

'Yes, you were right, boss. God knows how the kid thought he could pass off two-hundred and fifty thousand as his own.'

'And the bad news?'

'The Castellas obviously realised the money had gone missing pretty sharpish and cleared out before the police arrived. They left some belongings, but our sources said the couple prioritised the baby and the dog because their stuff was gone. A car, confirmed by the campsite as theirs, was found abandoned a few miles away. However, there have been no reports of any other vehicles stolen from that area, and we have been unable to trace them on any CCTV. We have no idea as to their direction of travel or even how they are moving about. Unfortunately, they've vanished again.'

Hector waited for the usual explosion on being told another lead had come to nothing but was pleased to see his boss adopting the usually thoughtful pose – hands behind the head and leaning back in his leather chair. It made a pleasant change from items being hurled across a room, even if it was mildly entertaining to watch. Hopefully, it signalled a return to more rational thinking.

'How much did our light-fingered friend take?'

'Four hundred thousand.'

'Thank heavens for greedy morons,' Francis mused as he continued to slowly rock backwards and forwards, thinking out loud. 'Okay, so we know Dominique managed to escape with half a million and has less than one hundred grand. She can make that stretch, but this woman isn't used to roughing it. And being constantly on the move with an unfaithful husband and his child – the strain will be taking its toll. You've seen Dominique; when is she anything other than immaculately presented?'

Hector nodded – so as not to break his employer's train of thought – he could almost hear the cogs in Francis's devious mind moving up the gears. Francis returned his chair to the upright position, and signalled for the door to be closed – a sure sign of an illicit assignment. Hector's pulse quickened with excitement.

'We need to force Dominique into making a mistake; she's been far too clever,' Francis said, tapping his fountain pen on the desk for a few minutes. His face broke into rapturous delight. 'I was touched that Mrs Bianchi admitted to receiving that call from Dominique; it did her credit – but I'm sure you'll agree her usefulness is … waning.'

'Yes, boss,' Hector replied and grinned. Francis Del Ambro Contino was back in the game. And finally, the longest-serving mistress was about to go the way of all the others.

Chapter Twenty-One

A quiet family life.

Only four everyday words that meant so much but were now unattainable for the dark-haired woman and her partner in crime.

Her partner in crime.

Another four words, partners and lovers for a decade, and two of the most successful foot soldiers in the Del Ambro Contino crime family. Unwavering loyalty to a charismatic and ruthless boss had brought rich rewards and seen the married couple want for nothing – except a quiet family life.

The cherished long-term goal was unattainable now, spectacularly blown out of the water by her adulterous husband. What the hell did he think would happen, cuckolding their boss with his mistress? But therein lay the problem – Sergio didn't think. Ever. Instead, he completed orders with cold-blooded precision, and it had never mattered before as his unassuming wife had brains enough for both.

Less than three months ago, her life had spiralled out of control (was that all it'd been?). Sitting on the metal café seat, Dominique fought all-consuming tiredness. How did any parent cope with more than one child? Her former colleagues had compared exhaustion levels at work, she'd suspected they exaggerated for comic effect – they hadn't. No wonder sleep deprivation was a form of torture. All she wanted to do was lay her head on the table and slip into a forgetful slumber. Even when she managed to snatch any sleep, it was only to be plunged into a repeated nightmare of Monika's heart-rending plea. An electronic voice begging them to flee and keep Elora safe so she could grow up happily, away from hate, fear and violence. And then the sound of Hector and Francis inside the house as the call ended with an eerily calm Monika stating she hoped to see Elora in the next life before pulling the trigger on her own. In her waking hours, Dominique juggled caring for Elora and Pesce whilst living on tenterhooks as they kept moving from place to place to stay safe.

How many times had Sergio apologised? His words were cheap – another four words – but actions spoke far louder. And over the preceding twelve months, his had bordered on lunacy. However, hers were hardly angelical.

A quiet family life. There was no chance. Francis and his army were coming for them. Dominique, Sergio, Elora and Pesce – four little foxes flying ahead of a relentless hunt. Their haphazard route had taken them from southeast Italy into France, Switzerland, Germany, Austria, Slovenia, Croatia, Hungary, Romania, Bulgaria and now Greece. So many places and Dominique no longer cared or had a clue where they were half the time. All in a desperate attempt to throw the pursuing pack off their scent. Had it worked? It was difficult to tell. Every time Pesce barked, her heart faltered. He'd definitely saved them three times after spotting somebody from the Company twice, and the Castellas melted into the crowd. And the final one at the campsite, the closest yet and still made her blood run cold. If Pesce was marginally ill-at-ease, they now walked away – out of cafes, restaurants, parks, beaches, and campsites. Their cockapoo was better than any alarm.

On the flip side, Dominique continued to be amazed by the generosity of strangers. Be it kind words of parental guidance, heating bottles of milk, singing lullabies, and the last and greatest act of kindness. Two former police detectives drove them over a hundred miles to safety, where Dominique finally broke down and sobbed with relief knowing their lives had been saved – for now. It had given the Castellas a glimmer of hope that there was goodness in the world, but Dominique knew there would be a next time, and they mightn't be so lucky. It was a game of diminishing odds, and sooner or later, they'd lose. But holding Elora, her protective instinct flared again. She would fulfil her pledge and ensure the child got a new start, whatever the cost.

This tiny innocent, who was rapidly destroying her life, continued to cast a powerful enchantment.

Sitting in the early morning sunshine, her frazzled brain could only come to one conclusion – they were flailing and rapidly sinking. But in a matter of hours, they'd be with Sergio's long-lost childhood friend, who was completely unaware of their predicament and only too delighted to catch up after so long. And Dominique needed a sanctuary. She was running on empty; they were on borrowed time and as hope ebbed away, exhaustion and paranoia gave her a haunted and gaunt appearance. Nobody could run forever. It was impossible. To evade capture, you needed a network of support, a secure place of safety and funds – they had precious little of those.

At first, killing to protect Elora had seemed the most likely scenario, but as time ticked by, Dominique slowly started to understand Monika. It wasn't a case of killing to protect, but dying. The Castellas were too identifiable, but until Elora was safe and with somebody Dominique trusted everyone needed to stay alive

Thankfully, she'd passed the stage where the sight of Sergio made her want to smash his face in with a hammer. The awful call with her mother and those revelations about her parents' infidelities had left her reeling and made her question everything, including her own behaviour. In the end, if she could forgive her beloved father and mother, she must do the same with her husband. People might think she was crazy, but when Sergio pulled her close, she didn't recoil and instead clung to him for strength, safety, and support. How she needed that. And knowing her amazing mother was okay.

It was early June, and the sunshine warmed her aching bones. Customers bustled backwards and forwards, many wearing tight cycling outfits – an act of immense bravery for some. Lycra could only stretch so far. The spikes clicking on the pavement were strangely soothing, and Dominique fought to keep her eyes open. Sergio was off, swapping their latest stolen vehicle for another and acquiring more supplies. He'd promised to be quick, but she still needed to stay alert. Elora and Pesce came first, and everything they needed was neatly packed in a bag with its handle wrapped around the table leg. She inserted a forefinger into Elora's hand and tiny fingers latched on. Nothing else mattered, but she was powerless to stop her dry, itchy eyes from closing. Only for a minute while Pesce stood guard.

***

Two voices – male and female – spoke Greek which she didn't understand, but they sounded nice. After a few moments, Dominique realised they were speaking to her. She opened her eyes to see kind and concerned faces. The woman was speaking English now. And the man was tickling Pesce's tummy. The words buzzed about for a bit before her groggy mind made sense of them. They were asking if she was okay, and Dominique managed a nod.

But the woman shook her head in a nice way and smiled. 'The last thing you are is okay, pet. Good sleep and a decent meal are what you need, and that's what I'm going to provide.'

Dominique shook her head. 'I-I c-can't. Y-you mustn't.' But the friendly woman wouldn't take no for an answer. 'Come on, love. I've got a lovely room for you and your beautiful family to relax in.' Dominique shrank away; eyes saucer wide. But she was too tired to fight, and besides, Pesce liked them. The woman placed a cool hand over hers and gave a reassuring squeeze. 'There's nothing to worry about, sweetheart. We're not going to hurt any of you.'

She let herself be led away, clutching the baby carrier. The man unwound her bag and followed with Pesce trotting merrily beside him. Their little party trooped past tables and chairs brimming with happy people, through an archway, into a pretty courtyard, and through a set of patio doors. The homely bedroom was the sanctuary she craved with its flowery bedspread and worn pine furniture. She sank onto the bed and her fingers remained vice-tight around Elora's chair. The cool air soothed her skin, sleep whispered and Pesce curled up.

The woman's voice was soft. 'You don't need to fight the fear anymore, pet. You're safe here.'

'My ... husband,' Dominique murmured; she hardly had the energy to talk as the mattress beckoned. 'He'll return in a few hours and be worried.'

The lady smiled. 'Alex will keep an eye out for him. What's his name, and what car is he driving?'

The panic bubbled up as she fumbled for her phone. 'Here's a photo of Sergio. I-I don't know the vehicle. Sorry, I-I'm just so very tired.'

Alex looked at the screen, nodded and left.

'It's not easy having a little one, is it?' said the woman in a singsong sort of voice and Dominique let it wash over her. 'My name is Anna, and I'll stay here to watch over your baby.'

'Thank ...'

Dominique was asleep before she finished the sentence, and as her fingers relaxed, the baby carrier was placed on the floor, and Anna took a seat in the corner to watch the sleeping strangers.

***

It was mid-afternoon when Dominique became aware of noises. The ensuite door was open, and beyond, Anna changed Elora's nappy and chatted with a young girl. They all looked happy – even if the girl was wrinkling her nose. Anna nodded outside, and as the girl took the nappy bag, Dominique quickly closed her eyes. If only she could stay like this. There was a waft of cool air as Anna moved past and sat down to feed Elora. She was chatting to the baby and Pesce, keeping her voice low. It was calm and friendly, and before she knew it, Dominique fell asleep again.

The second time she woke, the courtyard was in shadows, and outside, Anna was cradling Elora and chatting in Italian with Sergio. She could smell garlic, and her stomach sent up a howl so loud everyone looked. Slowly she sat up and came across on rather wobbly legs to join them. There was a large pot of tomato-based stew, salad and homemade bread.

Anna nodded to the second plate. 'Help yourself. There's plenty.' It tasted so good, and three helpings later, she sighed with contentment. Anna laughed. 'That appetite rivals mine.'

Dominique stroked Pesce, who hovered under the table. 'Why are you being so nice?' The words were out before she could stop them.

'Because you need it,' came the simple reply.

Sergio and Dominique exchanged a glance. They had been involved in violence and deceit for so long that it was incomprehensible to them that a perfect stranger would provide kindness and ask nothing in return. In their world, everything had a price.

***

Dominique didn't want to leave and leaned into the hug. The two women held each other tightly.

'You know where I am. Don't hesitate to contact me,' Anna said earnestly and handed over a bag full of nappies, cartons of formula milk powder, baby grows, bibs, a fluffy teddy donated by her daughter Evie, and dog supplies. She smiled as Dominique fumbled for a response. 'Us mams have to stick together.'

Being a mother was an obsession unexpectedly thrust upon her and over the past few weeks, Elora had stolen her heart. She looked across at Sergio, holding his sleeping daughter and her throat tightened.

'Sì,' she whispered before gripping Anna's hand. 'Grazie, arrivederci.'

Her guardian angel waved farewell as they drove away up the steep bank, and Sergio gently wiped the tears away from his wife's cheek. 'What a lovely woman.'

'Yes, and she didn't even ask our names,' Dominique replied distractedly. She stared out the window but didn't see the rocky hillside with its gnarled olive trees slide by. Her mind was elsewhere.

It was little more than a thirty-minute drive, and in the setting sun, the old car struggled up the steep hills. Dominique paid little attention to where they were going but was happy that the higher they climbed, the quieter it got. They passed through a small village – a charming hotchpotch of stone buildings with tiled roofs and paint-flaked doors and shutters. The headlights illuminated washing strung across tiny gardens, and a canopy of trees overhung a narrow road sandwiched between old stone walls. A few minutes later, Sergio swung the car off the road, and she was relieved to be buzzed through tall and sturdy gates. A well-maintained driveway guided them to a beautiful, impressively lit neo-classical mansion. In front of the heavyset front doors stood a forty-year-old, tanned, athletic-looking man – Tinto Zagrokis.

The two men hugged each other before Dominique, Elora and Pesce were introduced.

'Come in, come in.' Their host beckoned them through a grand foyer and into a huge lounge. 'Make yourself comfortable, and I'll get us some drinks before we eat.'

Although the structure was old, the inside was contemporary with clean lines and vast expanses of glass which Dominique wandered over to, clutching Elora. There was a warmly lit infinity pool and terraced gardens and, in the distance, pinpricks of lights twinkled from far off Agios Nikitas but Apokeri remained hidden. Before long, Tinto was back, and Dominique curled up on the sofa as the childhood friends caught up. It had been almost thirty years since the pair last met – the reason Dominique agreed to come. Nobody could tie the squeaky-clean logistics boss to them. Sergio assured her the man had no connections to organised crime, had no clue they did and was only too delighted to welcome them.

Chapter Twenty-Two

For the last two days, the Castellas had relaxed in Tinto's secluded guest cottage. Dominique had explored the substantial gardens, taking care to keep out of sight of the main house, but not many people came and went – the gardener, housekeeper, Tinto and his moody younger brother, Petre. Their host frequently dropped in, preferring their cosy accommodation to rattling around a mansion. In the warm evening sun, they sat drinking on the terrace as Tinto described buying the property ten years ago.

'It was a wreck,' he informed them and savoured his red wine. 'Since then, I've spent countless hours and a small fortune renovating and landscaping the property. No sooner was it finished to my wife's exacting standards than she up and left, taking my daughter and saying the property was too remote and she needed to be by the sea.' He waved in its general direction. 'She certainly got that by marrying the multi-millionaire owner of Tharesseti island, and now she runs its exclusive hotel.'

'You must miss your daughter?' Dominique replied.

'Yes.' He sighed. 'Narella has no interest in coming here because the hotel is far more interesting. I see her at Saturday morning football practice or by arranging to meet in Apokeri.'

Sergio was splashing in the pool with Elora (it ensured the little girl slept right through), providing a perfect opportunity for what Dominique hoped was a casual enquiry. 'Do you spend much time in Apokeri?'

'A bit. Not as much as Petre. His girlfriend's from there. Although for how much longer, I can't be sure.'

'Why's that?'

Tinto gave a knowing smile. 'Even in your short time here. I'm sure you've worked out my younger brother is a spoilt, selfish and arrogant tosser.' Dominique wisely kept quiet. 'Don't get me wrong, I love him, but my parents indulged their longed-for second child beyond belief. And the results speak for themselves. To be honest, I hope he does finish it. The kid is far too good for him, but unfortunately, she is absolutely besotted – they always are.'

Dominique chewed her lip, debating how much to say. 'Before coming here, we ate at Round the Bend and chatted to the owner, Anna. She seemed nice.' Tinto chuckled. 'Isn't she?'

'Anna Makris is one of those people you'd love to hate – friendly, a smart businesswoman, and does stacks for the community. Plus, she always remembers little things about you. When I see her, she asks how my violin practising is going, which is usually the kick up the butt I need.' He rolled his eyes. 'And my ex-wife has got the biggest girl crush on her. Our daughters have been in the same class since pre-school, and Eris is now married to Jeremy, one of Anna's old friends. And by that, I mean he's seventy-three! Heaven knows why he decided to lumber himself with my ex-wife and daughter – he's got grandkids older than Narella. But I can't complain; he's a good bloke, treats them right, and I get on better with him than Eris. Anyway, my ex-wife is in seventh heaven. For years, anytime I ever complained about anything, it'd be, "But Anna Makris works umpteen jobs even when her daughter had cancer." "But Anna Makris can speak four languages fluently" – English, Greek, Italian and French if you're wondering. "But Anna Makris negotiated the safe release of three hostages whilst held at gunpoint." Do you know—'

'Back up a minute.' Dominique interrupted. 'What do you mean, hostages at gunpoint?'

Tinto refilled her glass. 'Let me tell you a story,' he said, and began the tale.

'For the past ten years, Anna's sister-in-law has operated a domestic abuse charity that gives women sanctuary and protection. Four years ago, a crazed husband decided to wreak revenge on who he saw as responsible for providing his wife with the opportunity to escape a violent marriage and start a new life. He tracked that person to their home in Apokeri and burst into the living room, expecting his victim to be alone. However, Steffi Makris was with her seven-year-old daughter, Leyla, and her sister-in-law Anna Makris with her five-year-old, Evie. He started taking pot-shots at the furniture and said Steffi had ruined his life by turning his wife against him. After an hour, Anna talked the stranger into releasing both children. By this time, the police were outside. After five hours, Anna had negotiated the release of Steffi, and she walked out physically unscathed. Another six hours later, Anna walked out with the husband, who voluntarily gave himself up to the police.'

'That's amazing,' Dominique replied, mulling over the information. 'Anna took a massive risk.'

'I know; I've got a mate in the police who said the guy was a total nut job. He'd ripped the phone out the wall and smashed all the mobiles, so the police had no idea what was happening inside. And do you know something? Anna refused to take any credit and demanded the police take all the recognition.'

Dominique watched Sergio and Elora bobbing in the pool. 'The woman must be made of strong stuff.'

'Oh, she is. The incident freaked Steffi out. How a total stranger could so easily track her down, walk into her home and threaten those she loved. It's why her now husband, Andrew, built a fortress above Apokeri for his new family. Anna refused to move and, with her husband Filip, bought the old property.' Tinto looked a little sheepish. 'I've also been on the receiving end of Anna in action. Narella came home with a black eye a few weeks back, courtesy of Evie. And the parents were summoned to school. As Eris refused to cross swords with her idol, she demanded I go instead. And I was up for it. Nobody hits my daughter and gets away with it. And if truth be told, I wanted to take Anna Makris down a peg or two.'

Dominique peered over the rim of her glass and raised an eyebrow. 'But?'

Tinto began to squirm. 'It didn't quite turn out that way.'

No sooner had the meeting convened than Anna launched into a scathing attack regarding the teacher's ineptitude in failing to notice Evie had been the victim of bullying. Anna was polite and never once raised her voice, but the teacher didn't know what had hit her as Anna drew out a notepad to catalogue a three-month intimidation campaign. How Anna had initially had a quiet word with the teacher about Evie's withdrawn behaviour but received reassurances that there was nothing to worry about. The teacher even promised to keep a close eye on things. It'd all started with a local newspaper article about Round the Bend which incorrectly stated Evie was eight not nine.

Narella and her group of friends started a systematic campaign of name-calling – 'baby bunting', 'nappy pants' and 'nursery-girl' to name a few. It also involved jibes about Anna being stupid, a non-Greek and she'd better get back to where she came from. Evie was repeatedly tripped up in the yard, accidentally bumped into, and had her school things go missing, only to reappear days later. But for three months, Anna's daughter kept quiet and ignored it all. Finally, the group encircled her in the playground, taking turns to push her. Even then, Evie warned Narella to call them off but she'd laughed and ordered them on. Evie calmly stated Narella deserved what was coming and punched her in the face before confronting the others.

With their ringleader floored, they fled – but Evie stayed. She took Narella to the school nurse and explained everything. Anna went on to say the girls had resolved their differences, so there was nothing further to do. And neither Evie nor herself would be apologising as her daughter was completely justified in her actions. She expected the teacher to be more observant in the future to stamp out bullying and xenophobic behaviour. Anna had been taught if someone hits you, hit them back twice as hard, and she had passed the same advice on to her daughter. She then shook hands, said there were no hard feelings, and recommended Tinto keep practising his violin or he'd never be as good as his parents.

Dominique placed her empty glass on the table. She liked Anna's style. 'Did you question your daughter? Was it true?'

'Oh yes, Narella immediately admitted the whole thing. As soon as Anna said "baby bunting" my heart sank as I'd pulled her up about that before. I was so ashamed of my daughter and myself for not noticing. Narella even told me she liked Evie, but Uncle Petre had said it was important to find out how far you could push someone.' Tinto shook his head in disgust. 'Can you imagine a grown man telling his niece that? Eris went ballistic and blamed me for inviting Petre to live with me, and I kicked off with Petre for being an arse. He wasn't even sorry, said it was better his niece found out early that it was a dog-eat-dog world.'

Unfortunately, Dominique knew that was true. But it didn't stop her from thinking Petre was even more of a git than she'd realised.

Chapter Twenty-Three

It was there again, the screech of tyres or maybe nails on a blackboard. Dominique peeled open lead-heavy eyelids, but this time the noise was followed by muffled laughter.

The thick stone cottage walls regulated the bedroom's temperature – not too hot, not too cold, but just right. It was similar to the king-size bed – not too hard, not too soft, but obscenely comfortable and why she'd unexpectedly fallen asleep in the early morning sun. She stretched out, Goldilocks-style – the character featured in one of Elora's favourite nursery rhymes in a battered storybook lying next to an empty crib. Luckily, there were no fearsome bears to contend with as she opened the bedroom door, only a relaxed domestic scene. Elora lay in the lounge on her interactive playmat, energetically kicking little legs skywards and chuntering away, Pesce chased his red ball around the kitchen, and – sitting around the dining-room table – Sergio and Tinto persevered with violin practice. To her untrained ears, there were fewer dud notes.

Their wonderful host was happy for them to stay indefinitely, and Dominique suspected it was because of loneliness. He had a beautiful big house and nobody to share it with – a self-indulgent brother didn't count for much, it seemed. The rest and relaxation were terrific, but the Castellas knew it was a temporary measure. There was going to be a big shindig next week, and Tinto had begged them to join in celebrating his twenty years in the business. The house would be packed – as it should be – but it was too dangerous for them and served as a reminder to move on again. However, Tinto was determined to play his violin to the assembled guests and had roped Sergio into helping. First thing in the morning before work, and in the evening, they relentlessly practised, and slowly but surely, the pair improved.

'What do you think?' Sergio asked.

Dominique kissed him. 'You're both really good.'

Tinto nodded. 'Sergio could be great. He's a phenomenal talent – like his parents.'

'Thanks, mate, but I've got a long way to go till then.' He nodded at the clock. 'Don't you need to make tracks?'

'Damn, I'm going to be late for work. See you later.' Tinto paused at the door. 'I'm so happy you're all here. It's refreshing to be around people who like me.'

Dominique watched him go. 'What a sad thing to say. He's such a great guy and would make somebody a wonderful husband.'

Sergio stretched and packed away his violin. 'I feel sorry for the bloke – all that success and for what? He said it gave him hope to be around a couple who were clearly in love with one another.' Dominique refused to reply as Sergio cautiously approached and gingerly took her hand. 'Is he right? Do you still love me? Can you still love me after what I've done?'

She led him into the bedroom, not because it was the best time to conceive but because it felt right – like it did before she became fixated on having a child. And it was as if they found themselves again. Dominique allowed herself to hope. Perhaps they could all get through this nightmare and have a nice quiet family life.

***

She woke to a silent house, a note, and a flower on the bedside table.

> *To my own beautiful rose. Thank you. Enjoy the peace and quiet. I've gone for a stroll around the estate with the munchkins. Sx*

Dominique smiled and, pulling on a robe, she glided into the kitchen and sat by the open window with a steaming mug of coffee. The view rose up towards the main house, screened by trees and bushes, but from her vantage point there was a small clearing. She watched a few little birds on the grass enthusiastically pecking for worms but they took flight when the bushes rustled. She expected Sergio to appear, but instead, it was the ever-moody but undeniably attractive Petre, closely followed by a rather plain-looking girl in her late teens. He was angry, and she tried to appease him by stroking his arm. The conversation continued for a few minutes and whatever she said worked. Petre smiled, kissed her and pointed back towards the house.

The girl disappeared, and so did his smile. No love lost there. Petre was grumbling to himself and then drew out a vial and grinned. Dominique suddenly felt uneasy for the girl. And then a dark-haired female wearing a dive-master baseball cap stepped out from the bushes. She took the vial, laughed and slipped it into her jeans pocket. Now, these two looked like a couple. In their mid-twenties, with a shared casual, arrogant confidence. They compared phone messages. Petre grinned, and then the woman passionately kissed him. He pushed her away, shook his head and looked towards the mansion. The woman laughed, perhaps baiting him because the next instant, he yanked her towards him and viciously returned the kiss. As they groped and fumbled on the grass, Dominique turned away. She'd seen enough.

Chapter Twenty-Four

Elissa Andino was halfway through tidying the house in an attempt to calm her mounting anxiety. She didn't want to go to Stelios with her concerns but was running out of options. The stock at the pharmacy refused to tally. It appeared prescription drugs were going missing – again. The duster circled around and around on the dining-room table. She'd strip the veneer off at this rate, so she flung the cloth across the room. God damn it. She should have listened to Stelios and sacked Colin after he was caught red-handed. He'd tearfully admitted thieving because, like many others in the downturn, he had been in dire straits and desperate to support his family. She'd almost lost the pharmacy.

Elissa laughed bitterly as she retrieved the duster. What should have taken months to sort out with the authorities was quickly and quietly resolved when Mrs Dubois stepped in. How that'd stuck in her throat – accepting help from the beautiful and adulterous Irina. Did the woman still feel guilty for bedding Stelios, back when she was only nineteen? Twenty years ago, Irina had been staying with Daniel and his father while grieving the death of her brother but had made a sharp exit from Apokeri after being confronted by Elissa. And on top of that, Stelios couldn't understand why Elissa pleaded with the judge to pardon her Deputy Manager. And that came on the back of Nereus almost going under. It was a miracle they'd clung on until the tourists returned.

She opened Sebasti's room, even though her eldest had moved out five years ago and rarely returned. The family had been so close when the children were young, but it felt like everything was falling apart. And now, Rika. Ever since that Petre Zagrokis came on the scene, she'd changed – her schoolwork was suffering, and now she was talking about giving up on her university dream because she claimed to be in love. Her youngest was clever but green – the first serious boyfriend and she was willing to throw everything away. Elissa didn't trust him, and it had nothing to do with him being twenty-five. The bloke was smooth-talking (like her husband) but also manipulative and arrogant. However, she appeared to be the only one who could see it. Stelios loved him (but of course he did), failed to see the harm and acknowledged the bloke brought plenty of business into the restaurant. And that was what it always boiled down to with the Andino brothers – money.

The cord was too short to reach the far corners of Rika's room and as Elissa angrily shut off the vacuum, her foot kicked a suitcase under the bed. From it came the unmistakable rattle of pills. She stopped dead. No, it couldn't be true – Rika wouldn't do that to her. Gingerly she tapped the side with her shoe, and there was no doubt. Grabbing the handle, Elissa heaved the case out and, with shaking hands, unzipped the lid. It fell back with a thud, and inside, hundreds of bottles of pills, packets and vials – all printed with Epione Pharmacy. Here was the missing stock. Elissa gagged before dragging it along the corridor and slamming her wardrobe door shut.

Sitting at the kitchen counter, she stared at her severe reflection in cold coffee. She should be back at the pharmacy but had rung in, claiming a migraine. It was almost true – her head was banging. What was Rika messed up with? She'd rung her daughter countless times, but they all went to voicemail. Elissa didn't trust herself to leave a message and instead sat waiting with only her anger for company.

Chapter Twenty-Five

Sergio tidied the cottage before Tinto arrived, and Dominique tiptoed out of the bedroom, quietly closed the door and leaned against it. At long last, Elora had given in to sleep. The open front door let in a waft of air and provided a clear view of the sunny terrace. The gate slowly opened. Being too early for their regular visitor, Dominique froze. Sergio was immediately alert, but his wife shook her head. There was nothing to worry about; it was only the plain girl she'd seen out the window. However, Dominique realised something was amiss. The girl drunkenly stumbled forwards – an outstretched arm wafting away imagined cobwebs – before being transfixed by shimmering water. She smiled serenely and staggered towards it. Like an arrow from a longbow, Dominique shot through the doorway, across the paving and hooked her left arm around the girl's waist in the nick of time. Although Dominique was strong, she was off balance and ended up clumsily waltzing/quick-stepping with her partner towards the shrubbery and they both plonked down on a bench. The girl now wore a floaty summer dress, with carefully applied make-up and pin-straight long hair. And at these close quarters, Dominique realised the girl was actually pretty, but it was masked by a naturally stern expression. However, her eyes or, more accurately, the pupils were tiny pinpricks – the kid was high. She happily snuggled into her rescuer and zonked out. Listening to gentle snoring, Dominique leaned back and stroked the girl's head.

   The scene reminded Dominique of the first time she'd ever got drunk, aged sixteen. One of the kids from school had foolishly decided to hold a house party while his parents were away. Hordes of teenagers turned up, and with no supervising adults, it had been a wild night. One drink turned into two and then another, and soon Dominique was knocking them back and having a great time – until she threw up in the downstairs toilet. Unable to find her friends, she staggered home and, too drunk to find her house keys, hammered on the door to be let in. She was found slumped on the doorstep, giggling as the garden and house spun wildly before throwing up again. For the next hour, she'd clung to the toilet for dear life before cuddling into her mother and steadfastly refusing to drink to excess again. And unlike her mother, Dominique rarely had. The memory of soothing words and a comforting hug cut deep.

Sitting with her arm around a stranger in the garden of somebody's house in a country where she neither belong nor spoke the language, Dominique was overwhelmingly homesick and desperately needed reassurance that everything would be okay. She'd chatted with her mother daily and cherished the Saturday afternoon visits, so keeping her promise to sever all contact was unbearable. Lost in thought, she failed to see Sergio in the doorway until he coughed. He looked concerned, but she gave him a thumbs-up. The movement was enough to rouse the girl, who groggily sat up.

Dominique didn't imagine the girl spoke Italian but hoped English might suffice. 'Are you okay?' The girl slumped forwards. Dominique brought her back to sitting, but worryingly the girl's head lolled to one side. 'Sweetheart, can you hear me?'

This time there was a reaction, and the girl rushed over to the bushes and threw up. She then staggered back to the bench and started to cry, accompanied by the wailing of Elora in the background.

'It's okay.' Dominique handed her a hanky – the benefit of having a baby.

The girl blew her nose and then focused on Dominique and her surroundings for the first time. She looked around wildly. 'H-how did I end up here?' she asked in a terrified voice. 'P-please don't tell on me.'

Dominique winked. 'Don't worry, your secret's safe with me. But I should take you back up to the house.'

'Would you?' the girl begged and grasped Dominique's hands. She was like a little lost kid. 'I don't know the way.'

'Of course, let's get you back to where you belong.' As Dominique steered the girl past the pool, she heard Sergio singing and his daughter laughing.

The ten-minute journey took forever, with numerous stops to rest or wretch, and the steep uphill terrain with its narrow steps didn't help. Dominique walked behind most of the way and kept her hands around the girl's waist, and gradually the intoxicating effects were wearing off. By the time they climbed the last few steps, the girl had reassured Dominique everything was fine and blamed it on a dodgy glass of orange juice. Dominique was loath to abandon the girl, but then she heard the voices of Tinto and Petre above. In an instant, the girl sprinted up the steps to the pool terrace.

'Ah, there you are, Rika,' Tinto exclaimed. 'Let's get something to eat before my violin practice.'

'Sorry, Mr Zagrokis, I'm needed back home.'

'Oh, okay then, if you're sure. Thank you for all your help, the house looks wonderfully tidy.'

Relieved Rika was heading home, Dominique retreated to the cottage.

Chapter Twenty-Six

The car could practically drive itself, Jace thought as he swung off the main road and into the swanky development. Each of the ten houses commanded stunning views high above the Ionian Sea and a price tag to match. During the day, his sister was one of the few people at home as most other properties were second homes or holiday lets. It was a sign of the times, Jace supposed, but it always saddened him. He didn't like the thought of his big sister stuck up on the hillside by herself and made the eight-minute drive every day because he was passing (or so he told her). Not that Olivia believed him or needed a babysitter; being five years older, she had always protected him, and he'd been secretly distraught when she took off for America aged twenty-three.

Jace walked down the block-paved driveway to the beautiful one-storey dwelling. It was light, bright and spacious and at total odds with his Apokeri cubbyhole. But he'd never move because it held too many cherished memories – the first place he'd ever felt safe. Olivia said he clung to the past and needed to move on. But he wouldn't. Couldn't. The past defined him, whereas the present and the future gave his sister strength. She refused to dwell on what had gone before and with good reason.

He pressed the intercom, and the image of his sister popped up with her usual wry smile. She buzzed him in, and he made his way to the large conservatory where she worked. As always, he stopped and drank in the view – double doors led out onto a furnished veranda with a pool that appeared to merge into the big blue beyond and a cloudless cobalt sky. No wonder people paid over the odds to live here. He leaned down and hugged her.

'Heaven knows why you don't use your key,' she exclaimed, rolling over to her workbench and picking up a pair of secateurs.

'I'd never presume to walk in. I respect your privacy,' he replied and dropped down on a stool.

Olivia laughed, and the sound lightened his mood. 'The most exciting thing you'll find me doing is arranging flowers, swimming in the pool and maybe doing stunts in my wheelchair. I can't even barge into your house unannounced even if I wanted to – navigating your outside stairs is a nightmare. Unfortunately, it means I'll never be able to catch you with your latest married damsel in distress. Who's it this time?'

'No one,' he replied miserably.

'Still lusting after Anna Makris?' Olivia set about twisting branches into a gravity-defying display.

'No,' he shot back a bit too quickly.

'Liar.'

'Okay, I'll admit it but only to you – anyway, she's out of my league.' He unrolled a ball of twine.

'Well, for one thing, she's happily married, and we both know that isn't your type,' Olivia said with a grin as she grabbed the twine and rewound it. 'I thought your libido only operated around women in desperate need of saving?'

The corners of his mouth turned down. 'There's always an exception to the rule,' he said. 'Anyway, enough about my sad singleton status. What's keeping you busy?'

His sister brightened as she interwove bay leaves between the twigs. 'This week is all about weddings, and next week I have dozens of floral arrangements for Tinto Zagrokis' big shindig.'

'Oh yes, the twentieth anniversary of his haulage company. Are you going?'

'But of course, as stuntwoman turned best high-end florist in Lefkada, it'll be the ideal networking opportunity.'

'Subtle as always, sis!' He poured her a coffee, which she gratefully accepted.

'No one ever got anywhere by being shy and retiring. I bet you got an invite, Inspector Marinos but will you be there?' His silence spoke volumes and Olivia rolled her eyes. 'Of course you won't, unless there's a sniff of something dodgy. Isn't that right?'

'You know those pretentious parties aren't for me, Ol,' he replied in a placatory tone. 'I'm not like you. I don't do small talk while sipping an expensive glass of fizz and holding a plate of crumbly canapes. If I'm not working, I like to withdraw to my nest and brood.' He was only half-joking. Being surrounded by people was not his thing. It was stillness and solitude he craved.

'I know! But sometimes you need to switch off,' she replied earnestly. 'I worry about you alone with your thoughts – it's not healthy. You need to kick back and embrace life. I don't think you've been to a social occasion without your policeman's hat on since I moved back five years ago.'

'Actually, smart-arse, I think you'll find I went to Steffi and Andrew's wedding three years ago.'

'Yes, and as I recall, that ended with you breaking up a fight between Stelios and his brother.'

He shrugged and drained his cup. 'It's what I do, Ol. Anyway, I'll not keep you.'

'See you tomorrow, little brother, when you come to check up on your big sis.'

Jace shook his head and left. Straightaway his good mood evaporated as he drove off and mulled over the growing drug presence on the island. It had been steadily rising for the last few years, and they didn't seem to be able to get a handle on it. Sure, there were the small-time players they knew about, but this was something else – more organised. His usual sources maintained they knew nothing and, unfortunately, he believed them. And with drugs came petty crime. He was getting it in the ear from his superiors. Was he not aware that it was bad for Lefkada every time a tourist got robbed? Especially with everything shared, tweeted and whatever else five seconds after it happened. He was tempted to say that most tourists brought it on themselves. What was it about people on holiday switching their brains off? Would they leave their front door and car unlocked at home? Or go for a walk and leave all their belongings in plain sight, unguarded on a beach? Of course they wouldn't.

He was so engrossed in his rantings that he almost hit the scooter as it shot out of a side street only millimetres from his bonnet. He slammed on the brakes and blared the horn with no effect on the erratic driving. Judging by their physique, it looked like a young female, but a crash helmet hid her face – that probably meant it was a tourist. No matter how many fatal or life-changing accidents, locals refused to wear them. His fellow Greeks could be incredibly stupid at times. The scooter pulled out into oncoming traffic and, at the last second, swerved back in to avoid a head-on with the local Lefkada Town bus. Did they have a death wish? After continuing to weave about, they screeched in front of a lorry to take the steep twisting road down to Apokeri. Jace had seen enough and hit the siren, half-expecting them to take off. It was a relief when they came to an abrupt halt in a dusty lay-by. As he walked towards the scooter, the person kicked down the stand and wrenched off their helmet, ready for a fight.

Almost twenty years on the job, and it sometimes surprised him. He would never have expected to see a teary-eyed Rika Andino – Stelios and Elissa's quiet, academic youngest daughter. However, the usual respectful and polite eighteen-year-old was currently auditioning for the role of an aggressive screaming banshee. How dare he pull her over? Who the hell did he think he was? She knew her rights. He let her continue until she ran out of steam. He would have said she was high on drugs, except the idea was preposterous. What to do? He was loath to press charges. Rika was a good kid, a straight-A student off to university later that year – something he knew her hardworking parents were immensely proud of. And if truth be told, he had a soft spot for the serious-minded Elissa.

'Get in the car, Rika.'

'No,' she snapped and crossed her arms tightly across her chest (just like her mother). 'You can't make me.'

Good grief, did the girl want to get arrested? 'Don't be a fool, Rika. You know I'm entirely within my rights.' He softened his tone. 'What if you'd killed somebody back there? What would that do to their family, to your family?'

Her thin lips started to tremble as the fight left her, and fresh tears rolled down her cheeks. 'I-I promise I wasn't trying to hurt anyone … I just need to get home.'

'Rika, I need you to answer me truthfully. Have you taken any drugs?'

'No,' she said, hiccupping. 'I-I don't do drugs.'

'Have you been drinking?'

'I had an orange juice, but it tasted funny and made me throw up. P-please, can you take me home, Inspector Marinos? I want to go home.'

Wherever Rika had come from, she'd made an effort, wearing a pretty short-sleeved dress, make-up and straightened hair. But now, with mascara halfway down her face, the kid looked like her world had ended. He didn't think she was lying about the drink and drugs. She was so unlike her gregarious father and older sister, Jace thought. In looks and temperament she definitely took after her mother.

'You're in luck, young lady, because that's exactly where we're going.'

***

'Do you want me to go first?' Jace asked.

Rika shook her head. The girl had failed to utter a single word since shrinking into the passenger seat, clutching her bag like it was a surrogate teddy bear. She fumbled with the door key, shaking so badly he was on the point of helping when it eventually hit the mark.

'Hello?' Rika called out tentatively, undoubtedly hoping nobody would answer and she could be left in peace.

But Jace wouldn't allow that. The girl was a mess and needed company. He would ring her parents and make sure at least one of them came home. But thankfully, he heard movement at the back of the house and saw Rika bracing herself.

'I want a word with you. What the hell—'

As soon as Elissa spied him, her mouth clamped shut. Well, that was interesting. 'Can I have a word, Mrs Andino?'

Fifteen minutes later, he was back in the car. Elissa Andino had sat stony-faced whilst he recounted her daughter's escapade. She'd been polite and grateful to him for bringing Rika home with nothing more than a ticking off, but it was obvious she wanted shot of him. There had been no offer of a coffee, no friendly chit-chat, no volunteering of information but only a 'thank you and if that's all' before being firmly shown the front door. Jace felt his spider-sense twitch. Something was going on – maybe Rika Andino wasn't as innocent as she seemed.

His stomach rumbled as he sat in the car pondering what to do next. It seemed forever since breakfast, and he was only around the corner from Round the Bend. As long as he chose something healthy, he always ate for free – it was a no-brainer. He was just about to start the engine when his phone rang. It was his sister, and she wasn't in the mood for small talk.

'Jace, get here immediately. I've already called the paramedics, but this is also a matter for the police.'

He was already pulling away. 'What's going on?'

His sister never flapped. She took everything life threw at her (and there'd been plenty) and soldiered on regardless. He was relying on that stoicism.

'I'll update you when you arrive. All you need to know is I found an unconscious woman dumped on my driveway five minutes ago.'

Lunch would have to wait.

Chapter Twenty-Seven

He arrived moments before the ambulance did. Just as well, because there was a fresh set of tyre tracks on the road. He jumped out of the car and waved the paramedics past what might be potential evidence. They barely acknowledged him. Mia Tovier was their focus.

At least she was breathing when the ambulance left. Jace had taken photos of the tyre tracks and called it in before turning to his sister, who recounted the events since he'd left.

At twelve fifteen, the postman sounded the buzzer. It was something he always did. Drop the post off and buzz three times. She'd looked at the clock because it felt earlier than expected (usually one on the dot). Twenty minutes later, she finished the floral arrangement and decided to grab the post before making lunch, and that was when she found Mia and immediately rang for help. Olivia had wisely not touched anything for fear of compromising a crime scene and hurting Mia and, unfortunately, hadn't heard anything after the postman's buzzer. Working in the conservatory with the radio on, she didn't hear anything on the road.

Leaving the tech team to do their thing, and with a heavy heart, Jace retraced his steps to Apokeri. The hospital had confirmed Mia went into cardiac arrest in the ambulance and was yet to regain consciousness. With no intensive care beds available in Lefkada, she was being transferred to a neighbouring island. The initial assessment pointed to a drug overdose, and they were currently unsure about her chances of recovery, but the signs weren't hopeful.

His first port of call had been Apokeri Dive Centre to question Giannis Andino about his employee. The man appeared genuinely upset and collapsed into a chair when Jace broke the news, but did answer all the questions.

Mia had arrived in Apokeri four years ago and came in asking for a job. She was a highly qualified technical scuba diver and all her references checked out. Giannis was delighted and Mia had never given him any bother. She was a nice girl, liked to drink but never on duty, and he'd never seen any signs of drug taking. Jace had asked why Giannis was listed as the next of kin, and the answer was simple – Mia had none. Giannis could shine very little light on Mia's personal life, except she refused to talk about it. She was glad to have no family and frequently stated families were for losers. The only area Mia talked about passionately was diving, and she was working through the world's top fifty dive sites. Giannis remembered how Mia was particularly proud of having gone under the arch of the Blue Hole in Egypt, reputedly one of the most dangerous dive sites in the world. He didn't know where she went in the winter, except it was to have fun. She always turned up at the start of each season, raring to go and was a favourite with the guests. She always took a room above Odyssey Travel and seemed most friendly with his niece Rika Andino since they worked together at Nereus a few years back. Today was Mia's day off, and he hadn't known her plans but Jace left with the distinct impression there was more to the story because the man was clearly holding back.

The next logical place was Mia's accommodation, and a shocked Dania unlocked the room. The diminutive redhead also happily answered his questions. Like Giannis, she had no problems with the girl who lived quietly, but she did know Mia liked to party. The only person Dania noticed coming around was Rika (but as the entrance was out the back, it would be easy to miss someone), and the pair appeared good friends despite the six-year age difference. Mia rented a studio each season and always paid on time in cash. She never talked about family, only diving and seemed obsessed with it. The emergency contact was Giannis, and Dania also had no idea where Mia went in the winter. Jace jotted down Mia's passport number as Dania explained that she had no sense there was anyone special in Mia's life, but her cleaner Violet Iardanou might know more.

'That's Stelios and Giannis' aunt, isn't it?' Jace asked as he glanced around the simply furnished room.

'Yep, can you believe she's in her eighties now and shows no signs of slowing down? She's a first-rate cleaner and says the work keeps her young and sharp.'

'I bet, and she still cleans with her sister Thelma over at Apokeri Apartments?'

Dania nodded. 'Yes, she's part of the furniture over there. Anna wouldn't be without them as they keep the place immaculate and provide valuable feedback on the first hint of any guest's grumblings.'

To be thorough, Jace took the details of the guests in Dania's other two rooms but didn't expect them to be of any use. With Dania keen to return to the office, Jace was left alone in an extremely tidy room. He got the impression Mia Tovier was a person who travelled light – no framed photos. In fact, no photos at all. They were probably on her mobile, yet to be recovered. There were only a few garments in the wardrobe, along with a rucksack that was well-worn but had no baggage tags. The neatly folded clothes in the drawers were mainly casual, and there were only a few personal effects on the bedside table – bits of inexpensive fashion jewellery, some loose change, her passport and two diving books (*Dive Atlas of the World* and *100 Dives of a Lifetime*). Flicking through them, Jace saw ticks and stars next to various places. Out of curiosity, he flicked through her passport and confirmed her full name was Mia Tovier, Greek national, and twenty-five in February. He cross-referenced a few passport stamps – Egypt, Costa Rica, Bahamas, Philippines, Indonesia, and Australia – with the dive sites. Mia had packed plenty into the last few years, tallying with what Giannis said and again, the emergency contact was Giannis Andino. Jace frowned at his name on an official document – was there something going on between Mia and Giannis? It was an avenue worth pursuing and might account for Giannis not telling the whole truth earlier. Giannis and Sarah Andino seemed a tight couple, married for over a decade, but Jace never ruled anything out in his line of work.

It was time to go and break the news to Rika and see if she could help with his enquiries. However, there was no response to his knock at her door. Jace turned to find the helpful next-door neighbour (always happy to help the police) approaching. Nosy neighbours often came in useful, and Jace heard how Rika had left twenty minutes earlier on foot heading towards the beach and appeared upset. Ten minutes later, Elissa stormed out, and the neighbour (who happened to be trimming the adjoining rose bushes) tried to exchange a few words.

'The woman was abrupt as usual and could only curtly respond to my friendly enquiries. She claimed to be running errands and couldn't stop to chat.' The neighbour snorted, clearly believing nothing of the kind but unable to come up with a suitable alternative.

Jace wasn't surprised at Elissa's response; even without her daughter's shenanigans, he'd hate a neighbour constantly prying for information. However, he kindly thanked the man for his time. Then he also struck out at Violet Iardanou's house – neither of the formidable sisters were home. His stomach fiercely growled, and it wouldn't be put off this time. That was fine, he needed cheering up, and a visit to Round the Bend always did the trick.

Chapter Twenty-Eight

'What will it be today, Inspector? Something healthy?' Anna Makris prompted, standing next to him with an electronic device.

'Why not?' He flicked open the menu. 'I see Evie is getting along with your friend – they look as thick as thieves.'

Anna glanced over to where Javier was laughing as he showed Evie a sketching pad. 'My daughter has a gift for seeing the best in people, Inspector.'

Jace hesitated; it was unusual for Anna to ever comment negatively about anyone, especially a friend. 'Isn't that a good thing?'

'I'm sorry, Inspector.' She chuckled, maybe realising her response was out of character. 'I guess I'm still smarting on behalf of Pip, who now has another person to spectacularly lose against at poker. I did warn him that Javier was an excellent card player.'

Jace nodded. 'Yes, Mr Owens does have an uncanny knack for scooping up all our money.' Anna's clear laugh rang out across the café, and Jace felt his heart swell.

'I bet you hate that, Inspector Marinos. You and Alex always win.' She grinned at him, her eyes shining, and looked back to her daughter, who was earnestly talking. 'Evie adores Javier for helping her become a better footballer; in turn, she's decided to teach him how to draw. Anyway, down to the serious business of what you'd like to eat?'

'I'll have the roasted vegetable ciabatta and a black coffee, please.' He placed the menu back in its holder. 'And have you time for a chat?'

As she keyed in his order, her megawatt smile lit up what Jace thought was the most beautiful face. 'I've always got time for a chat with you, Inspector, but first, I'll grab your coffee.' She returned a few minutes later with his drink, a jug of iced water and two glasses.

'Will Violet be at Apokeri Apartments tomorrow?'
'Yes, she'll be there from twelve onwards.'
'Excellent. I need to have a word.'
'Not a problem. Take as much time as you need. And?'
'How well do you know Mia Tovier?'

Anna contemplated the question as she sipped her water. 'Not very much, really. I've seen her about over the last … what is it? Four seasons?' Jace nodded. 'Our paths don't tend to cross that much. She's been here a few times when Rika drops in to see her sister. That's when I ask how everything's going. She's always happy to chat about diving, where she wants to dive and where she's been, but nothing else – it seems to be her life. Why do you ask?'

Jace hesitated. The Apokeri grapevine would soon be humming, and he knew Anna was discreet, but at this stage in the investigations it was best not to reveal too much. 'She was found unconscious earlier today, and we're trying to trace her next of kin.'

The news had evidently yet to reach Anna as her eyes widened. 'Oh no, is she going to be okay? The poor lass.'

'At this stage, the doctors don't know.'

Anna remained motionless, and he could almost see her replaying past conversations. 'I don't know if it might help, but she made one comment a couple of years back that stuck because it was both sad and strange. Mia saw my sister and me together and mentioned how similar we looked. I remember asking if she had any siblings she resembled. The woman was utterly appalled. "I don't have any family, thank God. Nothing but a hassle, it seems to me. Better to be by yourself." I never brought the topic up again, so I've no idea if it's true or if she'd had a massive falling out with them.' Jace's order was deposited in front of him. There was a generous slice of chocolate cake in addition to the ciabatta. His eyebrows lifted as he looked up at Anna. 'It looks like you could do with cheering up, and I thought that might help,' she answered his unspoken question and stood up smiling. 'But don't get used to it. That's your one and only free bit of naughtiness.'

Jace watched as Anna took a seat with Javier and Evie, and he digested the latest bit of news. Mia Tovier was turning into quite an enigma.

***

He could tell she'd been crying, which was hardly surprising after today's events, but she was a proud woman, so he didn't comment on it. This time Mrs Elissa Andino did offer him a coffee and fruit cake but made no move to tidy away a depleted wine bottle and an empty glass. They sat at the kitchen counter, and he listened as she repeatedly thanked him for his kindness but watched as gratitude turned to concern when he asked to speak with Rika.

'B-but I thought you weren't going to press charges?'

'I'm not,' Jace explained and passed her a cotton handkerchief. He had a strong desire to rock the distressed mother in his arms. 'I'm trying to tell Rika some upsetting news before anyone else does. Do you know where she's gone?'

'For a walk to clear her head and will be back soon, I expect.' Jace glanced at his watch. He needed to get on and tackle a mounting pile of tasks. 'Can you tell me, and I can pass the message on?' she gently asked and dabbed her eyes.

That would probably be best, Jace thought. He relayed the information about Mia and explained how he urgently needed to trace her next of kin.

'I need Rika's help. I understand Rika and Mia are very close, and your daughter might have vital information.' Elissa sat dumbstruck. 'Mrs Andino, are you okay?'

'I'm sorry, Inspector. That's shocking news, the poor girl.' She fidgeted with her blouse buttons, checked her gold earrings, straightened the coffee cups and placed the remaining cake inside a tin. Her movements were sharp and jarring but she eventually refocused. 'Yes, the pair are very close, and I understand why you need to talk to Rika. But Mia doesn't have any relatives. She told me she's never had a family and never wanted one because of what they do to each other – you were better off without them.'

And there it was again. Mia was consistent with her family history at any rate.

The front door slammed. 'Sweetheart, is that you?' Elissa called out.

'Yes,' came Rika's curt and tearful response.

'Can you come here for a minute, please? Inspector Marinos has something he needs to tell you.'

With bloodshot eyes and a blotchy complexion, Rika absorbed the news and then broke into a nasty self-satisfied smirk. 'Serves the bitch right. She's no friend of mine. I've got nothing more to say on the matter. But thank you for everything you did for me today, Inspector Marinos. I'm extremely sorry I was rude earlier, but if you'll excuse me, I have a great deal of last-minute revision to get the grades I need for university.'

Rika then walked swiftly out of the room to leave her bewildered mother mumbling an apology. Things were getting more and more interesting.

Chapter Twenty-Nine

The next morning, Jace worked from home until it was time to question Violet Iardanou. He tracked her down in the Apokeri Apartments store cupboard as she manoeuvred in the vacuum cleaner and locked the door.

'Hello, Inspector,' Violet's gravelly voice greeted him. 'Anna said you'd be dropping by to ask about Mia, and said to use the office unless you prefer to sit outside?' The woman extracted a packet of cigarettes and a lighter from her skirt. The inference was clear.

'Outside, don't you think, Ms Iardanou?' Jace replied.

'I think we can forgo the titles, Jace. After all, I've known you as a boy and man. No disrespect intended,' she said and held Kristina's garden gate open for him.

While on duty, Jace wasn't one for first names, too intimate. Titles and surnames provided boundaries and professional courtesy. He believed Violet knew this. He took the spare seat, which he realised was facing the sun and repositioned it. She sat opposite, smirking. The woman was a wily fox.

'What can you tell me about Mia Tovier?' She raised her eyebrows and waited. Inwardly, he sighed. 'Violet.'

To her credit, she refused to answer until receiving a full update on Mia's condition. Unfortunately, it remained fifty-fifty at best.

Violet sadly shook her head and lit up. 'I'm very surprised Mia miscalculated.'

'What do you mean?'

'Mia is a party girl – a regular drug taker and binge drinker.' She took a long, satisfying drag on her cigarette before blowing out the smoke. 'I wish these things were good for you. But enough about my vice. Mia never lets hers interfere with diving. That's her passion – her first and only love. She repeatedly told me you don't mess around when diving; it's too dangerous. The safety of her guests is paramount.'

'Giannis said Mia is clean living.'

Violet scoffed. 'A word to the wise – don't believe everything my nephew says.'

'Don't you like him?'

'It's not that I don't like him or his three older brothers.' She took another drag. 'But those boys would have you accept anything if it suited their purposes.'

'Like what?'

Violet cackled. 'Come now, you're a clever bloke. I'm sure you can work it out.'

Jace stared at the weed-free flower beds. 'Okay, is there something going on between Giannis and Mia? She lists him as her next of kin, which I find odd.'

Violet smiled and raised her left eyebrow. 'Now you're getting there. All I'll say is Giannis is a great deal like his eldest brother.'

'Do you think Mia and Stelios are involved?' Jace recalled the brothers' wedding fight, which neither had explained. He'd put it down to booze, but had they been rutting stags fighting over Mia?

Violet shrugged. 'I don't know anything about that, but it wouldn't surprise me. Mia likes men and has no scruples if they're attached.'

'How do you know this?' This was the downside of opinion – he could never really know how much was truth or only imagined, and added to that, people always had their own agendas.

'Because she told me. If a man played away, it was because he wasn't satisfied at home, so it was hardly her fault.'

'Interesting.' Jace shuffled his chair into the shade. 'So, she might have made enemies?'

Violet remained in the sun as smoke wreathed around her short grey Brillo-pad hair. 'She never gives any indication of being worried about anyone or anything. She says life is for the taking, and people need to stop being so precious about relationships because you always get let down in the end.'

'Is there anyone special in her life?'

'No,' Violet replied with certainty. 'Mia looks after herself.'

Jace had met Mia on several occasions over the years, and the woman had never made much of an impression because she was neither rude nor overtly friendly. She was one of those people you nodded hello to in the street and moved on. But he was discovering she was not a straightforward character, and those were the most fascinating.

'Do you like her?'

'I actually do, which I know might sound surprising after everything I've said. But it's because she's so very open about her views and says what she thinks. Titles and status don't bother her, and not many people are like that. Mia is always happy to chat with me – a lowly cleaner.' Jace frowned, and Violet caught his expression and nodded. 'Don't you know, we're second-class citizens that you mustn't make eye contact with or even acknowledge? We can't be trusted or we're too stupid to bother with because we do mundane jobs.'

He glanced up at all the balconies of Apokeri Apartments and wondered how many of its occupants over the years had thought that. 'You don't sound bitter.'

'Oh no, I find it amusing,' she replied and grinned wickedly. 'Us cleaners are the eyes and ears and can tell you a thing or two.'

Jace fed out the line to pick up a bite. 'What else would you like to share?'

Violet held his eyes. 'Ask specific questions, Jace. This isn't a fishing expedition.'

Begrudgingly he admired her refusal to gossip. 'Alright, do you think Mia could be involved in anything illegal?'

'Mia is a high-adrenaline risk-taker, so it's possible.' Jace sat forward excitedly, waiting for more. 'But I saw no evidence or suspicious behaviour.'

Another door closed, but he was sure there must be something Violet could tell him. 'Does she have many visitors?'

'If you mean lovers, I've never got a hint of them, so they must go elsewhere. The only person who comes over is Rika Andino.'

'The pair are close?'

Violet paused as if she was struggling to put the relationship into words. 'Mia does care for Rika in her own way, but I cannot imagine she confides in the girl. Mia jokes that Rika is too strait-laced and says those types are easy to sucker.'

Finally, he was getting somewhere. 'Is Mia tricking Rika, then?'

'I don't know. As I said, Mia looks after herself and doesn't appear to have a strong concept of loyalty. I don't think she feels guilty about much. In four years, I've never seen her upset or affected by anyone, which maybe tells you something.'

It was a case of one step forward and two steps back. 'Did Mia ever mention my sister?'

'No.' Violet lit up a second cigarette.

He was running out of questions. 'Is there anyone else she talks about?'

Violet paused. 'The only other person she mentions is Javier Owens.'

'In what context?'

The older lady grinned. 'Mia says he's the only bloke to turn down her advances. She repeatedly offers it to him on a plate, and every time he politely declines. And she likes him all the more because of it.'

Wasn't it always the case – we want what we cannot have. He was unsure how valuable the information was, but at least it gave him an insight into the man. 'And one final question. Do you know anything about Mia's family? We urgently need to trace them.'

'There isn't any. Mia grew up in care, decided to run away at fourteen and never looked back.'

'Do you believe that?'

'Yes, I do.'

Jace left Violet enjoying her cigarette. At least he was now confident that Mia didn't have a family, but it was the only point he was sure about. In the interests of thoroughness, he questioned Javier Owens next. Which was handy as he was only a few dozen metres away, rewiring Kristina's house. The man appeared genuinely upset and answered every enquiry in a friendly and straightforward manner. He'd known Mia for two months after she'd tracked him down on Apokeri beach and introduced herself as his Odyssey neighbour. He also confirmed Violet's account of respectfully refusing Mia's repeated attempts to bed him. Jace was satisfied he was being told the truth. However, he kept thinking back to the looks and comments Anna Makris had dropped. And the fact that Javier Owens was an exceptional poker player. There was definitely more to the man. But then again, everyone has secrets, and if they weren't illegal or connected to Mia Tovier, they weren't his concern.

Chapter Thirty

Dominique double-checked the connection and the computer – everything was set. Beside her on the bed, Pesce snoozed, curled up in a tight ball of fluff. It was easier with him in the room, he would only scratch at the door to be let in and potentially arouse Sergio's suspicions. She glanced at her watch – five to ten in the morning – a few minutes more, and she'd make the call.

The muffled sound of two violins drifted in from next door – last-minute preparations for the party that night. And having listened to them practice over the previous couple of weeks, she was beginning to understand the men's obsession with classical music. Yesterday, Sergio brought up a YouTube video of Tinto's parents in concert and they'd watched as they entered the auditorium with their walking sticks to a rapturous reception. Their aids were the evidence of a horrific coach crash that had killed fourteen members of a touring orchestra – Sergio's parents being two – and scores more were injured. Tinto's mother had needed one leg amputated, and his father lost a foot. But when they picked up their bows, all that was forgotten. Afterwards, Tinto plugged in his phone and through the speakers came the most uplifting piece of classical music Dominique had ever heard. The harmony of four violins filled the room. It was as if the music was inside her and her spirit soared to believe anything was possible. When it ended, there were tears in her eyes, and both men were unashamedly crying. It was the last recording of their parents playing together over thirty years ago.

It was ten precisely, and she donned headphones, took a deep breath and entered the number for an efficient young man to answer.

'Good morning, Hair by Alfonso. How can I help you?'

Dominique activated the voice manipulation software. 'Could I speak to Mrs Toni Bianchi, please?'

'Who's calling?'

'A friend,' she replied and anxiously fiddled with the headset wire. Dominique had finally given in to a child's desperate need to hear their mother's voice but promised herself it had to be the last time. And because of that, she was going to record the call this time and was annoyed at not having done so before.

'One moment, please,' came the courteous response.

***

Dominique slowly opened the bedroom door and walked into the lounge. Everything looked the same, and she wanted to freeze-frame the scene of her husband and his friend sitting with closed eyes swaying backwards and forwards in time to the movement of their bows across violin strings. And by their side, Elora was on her playmat, pushing upwards off her tummy to stare intently at her father. It was something Dominique wanted to remember forever – because nothing would ever be the same again. Sensing her distress, Pesce clung limpet-like to her side. The two men came to the end of the piece, and Dominique clapped appreciatively.

'Thanks,' Sergio said brightly before he saw her face. 'What's wrong?'

'It's Mamma. She's ... dead.'

Tinto immediately hugged her, offered his condolences and respectfully left as Sergio steered his shell-shocked wife to the sofa. She was shaking so severely that it took her five minutes to form a sentence.

'I-I rang her hairdressers ... they said ... they said last month ... an overdose at home. Her funeral was t-two weeks ago.'

Their eyes met, and neither needed to say it – an overdose was a classic company method. Dominique gripped her head with both hands as a juggernaut of searing emotional pain overwhelmed her. The only outlet was a drawn-out anguished cry that emptied her lungs. She fought for air as sobs wracked her body, and still, that unbearable pain. A poker had slammed through her ribcage and plunged straight into her heart. Never again would she hear her mother's chatterbox voice, see her mother spin around in stilettos to show off the latest outfit and hairdo, cosy up in the kitchen with a coffee to trade stories, or hug her wonderful mother and say 'I love you'.

Dominique had hero-worshipped her father but only over the last few months had she realised her mother was the stronger of the two. And now she was gone, and Dominique was to blame. Everything Toni Bianchi had done since the death of her husband had been to protect her daughter.

Sergio was talking, urging her to listen, saying she was blameless in all of this. But smiling sadly, she cupped his face. 'No, not this time. This is down to me – I killed my mother.'

The chisel of guilt hammered into her body, seeking out any weak spots, and found them – in one fell stroke, her heart, mind, and soul broke apart, and, like her mother, all hope died.

The tears started again as Dominique grieved for them all. 'Sorry, Mamma. Sorry, I couldn't keep you safe.'

The cottage had been a haven of peace and safety for a few weeks, but not anymore. Francis was winning. He could worm his way into whatever corner of the world she cowered in. And wherever they went, he would be a malevolent presence. Sergio wrapped his protective arms around her shoulders and rocked her backwards and forwards for how long, she didn't know. But eventually, the all-consuming darkness lifted. Elora desperately tried to reach her father, but, unable to crawl, she became increasingly distressed. Sergio scooped her up and returned to the sofa, but not before Pesce seized the chance to jump onto Dominique's knee to nibble her left ear affectionately.

'You did not kill your mother,' Sergio admonished as he bounced Elora up and down and desperately tried to make his wife see reason, but she was having none of it.

'Mamma kept herself safe for over two decades.' Her hands shook against Pesce's fur. 'I told her to tell Francis about the restaurant call, and a couple of days later, she was dead. That's too much of a coincidence. My call was the catalyst, so I'm to blame.'

Sergio sighed as Elora nuzzled into him. 'No, my actions were the catalyst. None of this would have happened if it hadn't been for my selfish behaviour. I'm so sorry, Dominique, for ruining your life and ending Toni's.'

'If I'm not to blame,' she pointed out, tickling Pesce under the chin. 'Then neither are you.' And she meant it. Despite everything, Dominique understood that Sergio was not accountable for the actions of the deranged and psychopathic Francis. The man was a destroyer of worlds.

Sergio enveloped Elora. A tear slid down his cheek as her little hand grasped his finger. 'For my entire adult life, I've been a contract killer who efficiently dealt out death in exchange for money. And then, unexpectedly, I produce a tiny piece of life that I must protect at all costs. My daughter will not pay for my sins.'

Even as hope died, the smouldering embers of determination flared once more in Dominique, enabling her to see clearly. She kissed each member of her little family in turn, leaving Sergio till last. 'Our part in this story is drawing to a close, sweetheart. But I believe I've figured out a way for our two munchkins to go on to thrive. Do you trust me?'

He smiled and returned the kiss. 'Always.'

Chapter Thirty-One

The house on the hill looked magnificent, Javier thought as he wandered around the assorted guests handing out drinks and canapes. Tinto Zagrokis was pulling out all the stops for his twenty-year celebration. And why not. The bloke was a self-made millionaire. From one truck aged twenty-two, he'd built up a transport empire – legitimately. Javier was impressed. He himself had made plenty of money but very little was above board. It was hardly his fault he had an uncanny knack for sniffing out dubious ways to make money – such as his new night-time job. For the last few weeks, he'd steered the boat to wherever they told him and then the crew set to work. Although he was not yet privy to goings on, if what they were doing was kosher, he'd eat the snazzy tuxedo he was wearing.

Javier replenished his tray, walked past the piano player and weaved his way through the packed lounge. Einaudi music blended with countless conversations, bursts of laughter and clinking glasses. As well as the canapes, a staffed poolside buffet dispensed hot and cold food. Amongst the throng were plenty of people he recognised from Apokeri.

He nodded to his younger boss, dive-boat owner Giannis Andino and his wife, Sarah. They looked happy together, but the reality was somewhat different. Mia had openly told him about shagging Giannis for years – and plenty more men besides. Whereas Javier was precise, organised and risk-averse, she was the complete opposite (apart from her diving), and it had cost her dearly. He hoped Mia could pull through – the girl had spirit. She was certainly persistent even though he'd repeatedly knocked back her indecent proposals. A few months ago, he wouldn't have thought twice, but now things were different. He easily explained away his reticence with a host of half-hearted excuses, not wanting to face the obvious truth – he was going soft. Of course, that was the only reason.

Away to his left, he caught sight of his first wife and sighed. It was just as well he had the dive-boat side-line, his waiter and rewiring jobs because he still hadn't figured a way to access her money. She was chatting with the host and undoubtedly praising him for a fantastic violin performance. All night Javier had surreptitiously tracked her movements as she glided through the room, looking radiant in a simple calf-length brown dress. Anna was head and shoulders the most beautiful woman in the room as she chatted and laughed with fellow guests before moving off. But all the time, she gravitated back to Filip, who always broke off from whoever he was with to smile or kiss his wife. The pair were still very much in love, and Javier frowned as an uncomfortable emotion needled away. He needed to stop this. It was his iron-clad rule. Stay detached.

And then there was Evie. A whole other mess he'd unintentionally landed himself in. How he had ended up volunteering to run a girls' Saturday football coaching session through the school holidays remained a mystery. His eyes flitted around the room as he picked out the team's parents. They were all thrilled with him – that might come in handy. The usual coach ceased practice during the summer. Javier had thought that was madness and refused to let the girls lose out. There was some natural talent in the team, with the standout players being the two forwards – Evie, and Tinto's daughter Narella.

The more time he spent with Evie, the more he recognised the characteristics of both Anna and Filip. She was a great kid, not that she couldn't be a stubborn so-and-so at times, and he had no qualms in pulling her up during coaching sessions. But she always listened (at the same time as putting up an excellent defence) and respected his decision. And now he found himself being her art pupil. She took her teaching role very seriously, so he didn't have the heart (because he actually enjoyed it) to refuse. Javier sighed again as he smoothed down his jacket and continued his rounds.

It was just as well he didn't care for Evie or have any feelings for Anna because that would be really stupid. But as she moved away again, his eyes followed her – and he wasn't the only person.

***

'As I live and breathe,' Olivia Marinos declared. 'Is my baby brother having fun on a Friday night?'

Jace kissed her on the cheek. 'How's everything going? The flowers look stunning.'

She did a mock curtsey. 'Why, thank you. I've had lots of compliments and enquiries – so this looks to be a very profitable evening for yours truly. But enough about me. Are you here on business or pleasure, Inspector Marinos?'

Jace took a sip of water and swept his surroundings. 'A little of both.'

She prodded him in the stomach. 'I knew it. You think this is dodgy dealings central. But surely not our host? He seems as clean as freshly washed laundry.'

Jace continued to scan the room. 'You're right there. No, I'm keeping an open mind about Mia Tovier as we are no further forward in our investigations, and I don't think the poor thing will be waking up anytime soon – if at all.'

'Well, I've been setting up since this afternoon,' his sister confided and gratefully accepted a glass of champagne from a passing waiter. 'So, do you want to hear my observations?'

'Yes, please,' Jace replied, knowing that Olivia often provided unexpected and valuable information.

'Well, first thing, you've got serious competition for your beloved Mrs Makris – and I'm not talking about her husband.'

'Will you keep your voice down!' Jace hissed.

Olivia waved away his concern. 'Don't worry, nobody's paying any attention to us. Your competition is the drop-dead waiter in the corner.'

Jace looked over to see four waiters standing in two corners.

'You're going to have to be a bit more specific, sis?'

'Come on.' Olivia whacked her brother on the arm. 'The best-looking bloke in the room – present company excepted! The six-foot-three Spanish stud with come-to-bed eyes. The man I'd crawl over red hot coals to get to, like most women in this room. And a lot have tried this evening, but he isn't interested in them.'

'Okay, I get the picture.' The man was handing out champagne. 'That's Javier Owens. He's the one that keeps beating me at poker. He's an old friend of Anna's.'

Olivia snorted. 'He wants to be a hell of a lot more than friends by the way he follows her every movement.'

'Interesting. Anything else?'

'There's something up between the elder Andino and his wife. Elissa is all smiles till Stelios turns away, and then she looks like she could happily kill him.'

'Yes, I noticed that.' He smiled at the thought of being with Elissa again.

His sister's interest spiked. 'I knew there was somebody! EA is your current damsel in distress, is she?'

'Shut up, Ol,' Jace snapped. He hated how his sister picked up on any woman he was interested in or involved with. 'What else?'

'Touchy, touchy, Inspector,' she joked. 'I caught the tail end of Filip Makris and Alex Panagos arguing in the garden. Alex was demanding an answer to something.'

Jace dismissed it. 'Probably something to do with the business. Have you seen Rika Andino?'

'No, why?'

'Her boyfriend isn't exactly being subtle with that blonde over there.' He nodded to the terrace where a scantily clad young woman was laughing and trying to get Petre into the pool.

'Oh, didn't you know? They've split up. Rika dumped him last week.'

'How do you know that?'

'I overheard Tinto and Elissa. Tinto said it sounded harsh, but he was relieved Rika had ended it and hoped she got into uni.' The siblings watched as Petre accompanied the giggling blonde down the terrace steps and into dark shrubbery. 'It sounds like Tinto has got the measure of his brother. Anyway, he asked how Rika was coping with Mia's condition. Apparently the two women visited his house a few times.'

Jace's antenna hummed. 'Did he say when?'

'No.' Olivia pursed her lips. 'But I imagine you're going to ask him. I mean, it's only the man's party – why would that small matter stop you?'

'Good grief, you make me sound such an unfeeling, cold-hearted git!'

His sister gripped his hand and kissed it. 'You know I don't believe that, and the complete opposite is true. That's why you're so good at your job – and have no life. It's why I worry about you.'

'Look, Ol.' Jace cleared his throat. 'There's the Mayor and Deputy Regional Governor. Why don't you go over and do some schmoozing while I talk to Mr Zagrokis?'

'Fine,' she replied with a gentle smile and deliberately rolled her wheels over his feet – he needed to watch out for that more.

'Mr Zagrokis.' Jace raised his voice enough to intercept the haulage boss as he made his way towards the back of the house. 'I just wanted to thank you for the invitation. You have a beautiful home.'

Tinto smiled and shook the outstretched hand. 'You're most welcome. And I must say your sister has surpassed herself. The flowers are stunning. I hope you're both having a good time?'

'Yes, but I wondered if I might have a quick word?'

'Certainly.' Tinto motioned for him to follow. 'I'm off to the kitchen to thank Agnes. And we can have a catch-up after that. How does that sound?'

'Perfect.'

Jace followed the man down a flight of marble stairs and into a kitchen larger than his house. It was a hive of orderly activity with sharp-eyed Agnes Benrubi at the helm. Everyone knew what to do, and Jace watched as her team dished up, cleared away and replenished platters, trays, glasses and everything else besides. After swiping a slice of baklava and coffee, Jace followed Tinto into a snug office.

'May I tempt you with a brandy?'

Jace held up his coffee. 'Thank you, but not whilst I'm on duty.'

Tinto settled in behind his desk and motioned Jace to sit. 'I suspect you're always on duty, as this request demonstrates.'

It was an observation, not an accusation. 'I was wondering how well you know Mia Tovier? I understand she's visited your house a few times.'

Tinto swilled the golden liquid around his glass. 'I don't, really. She came here with Rika, but it was usually when I was working.'

'Do you know the last time she was here?'

The answer was instant. 'Over a month ago. There was a pool party to celebrate Petre's twenty-fifth.'

'And you didn't see her on the day she was hospitalised?'

'No. I came home from work. Rika and Petre were here. I invited Rika to stay for dinner, but she was in a rush to get home and seemed upset. It was only afterwards I presumed that must have been when she ended things with my brother.'

Jace nodded. 'Did Mia and Petre get on well?'

Tinto's mouth hardened. 'My brother always gets on well with attractive young women, as you may have observed this evening. But if you want to know if something is going on between the pair, you need to ask him.'

Jace mulled over the information. 'Are the front gates the only way to access your property, sir?'

'No, there's a dirt track at the bottom of the hill. If the gate was left open, you could get in that way.'

'And does your perimeter fence run the full length of your grounds?'

Tinto finished his brandy and laughed. 'I'm only a haulier, Inspector. I don't take my security too seriously. If someone wanted to get in, it wouldn't be that difficult. But as far as I know, the fence is sound.'

'Do your gardener and housekeeper live on-site?'

'No.'

'And do they come in every day?'

'No, they usually work five days a week. But that fluctuates, depending on the time of year.'

'Were they at work the day Mia was found?'

'No, they were off.' Both men sipped their drinks as Jace processed the information and Tinto cleared his throat. 'Inspector, in your line of work, I can imagine you need to adopt a range of interview techniques depending on how cooperative people are being. In my line of work, I find being direct is the best course of action.' He placed his glass on the desk and leaned forward. 'By that, I mean ask me what's really on your mind, and I'll answer if I can.'

Jace appreciated the man's candour. If only everyone were like that. 'Could Mia have been at your house on the day she was dumped on my sister's driveway?'

Silence enveloped the room, and Jace became aware of the caterers in the kitchen. The smell of roast lamb was amazing. As the silence lengthened, Jace heard a noise behind him and turned, but the doorway was empty. A second later, there was a gentle knock on the door.

'Sorry to interrupt, gentlemen. Mrs Benrubi asked me to remind you the cake-cutting ceremony is scheduled to start in five minutes.'

'In other words, I need to get my backside upstairs. Thank you, Javier. I'll be there shortly.' He waited until the footsteps faded. 'I've been wondering that, and the truthful answer is yes, quite easily. However, I cannot understand why.' The man placed his fingers together as if praying and slowly began tapping. 'From the little I knew of Mia, she didn't seem the type to volunteer to clean somebody's house. Would you agree?'

'I would say that is a fair observation, sir.'

'So why else would she be here?' Tinto pondered. 'And even if she was, I cannot see Rika being involved in anything untoward. She's a good kid.'

Jace nodded. He'd left Olivia's and a few minutes later saw Rika zig-zagging through traffic on a scooter. The girl couldn't have shoved Mia out of a car because the timing didn't work. So that left Petre.

'What about your brother, Mr Zagrokis?' Jace probed.

'Now you come to it, Inspector. Do I think my brother got Mia high on drugs and then tossed her out the car like a bag of rubbish?' He jabbed the desk with a finger. 'No, I cannot believe that. My brother is a great many things, but to willingly abandon a person who is clearly in need of hospital treatment? He wouldn't do that.'

Tinto spoke passionately and believed what he was saying, but that didn't mean it was true. Petre was arrogant, and Jace suspected he was also manipulative and self-serving. But would he deliberately harm somebody? In a police career spanning two decades, Jace had seen it all, from the seedy underworld of Athens to the sleepy villages of Lefkada, and he knew people would do anything if they felt threatened or needed to save their own skin.

He stood and handed over his card. 'Thank you, Mr Zagrokis. You've been most kind. Please don't hesitate to contact me if you think of anything else.'

Walking back upstairs, Jace heard a door further down the corridor close quietly. He chewed on his syrupy cake and watched Javier standing in the corner. The man's face was expressionless, but he couldn't shake the feeling that somebody had been lingering outside the office door. Had it been Javier or someone entirely different? Perhaps he needed to dig deeper into the poker-player's past. His mobile vibrated with two missed calls and three messages. He was officially back on duty again and made his way to the front door but not before seeing a friendly face.

'Escaping so soon, Inspector?' Anna asked.

'Needs must. I don't suppose you've seen Giannis Andino recently?' he asked. He might as well kill two birds with one stone.

'I saw him leave about twenty minutes ago with Stelios,' she replied. 'Sorry, I don't know why. Sarah and Elissa are still here, though, if that helps?'

He decided the younger brother could wait until tomorrow.

'Thanks. Could you do me a favour and apologise to Mr Zagrokis for my early departure?'

'Certainly … and try not to work too late – it's not good for your health.'

He nodded and went to move, but she remained in place with an enigmatic smile. 'Is there something wrong, Mrs Makris?'

She handed him a napkin. 'You might want to wipe your mouth, Inspector. If I'm not mistaken, that's baklava pastry clinging to your lips.'

He watched Anna walk away. He couldn't even have a sly treat without getting caught.

***

Dominique slipped into the shrubbery and breathed a sigh of relief. Entering the house had been a huge gamble, but it had paid off. The garden door was open. She'd stolen up the stairs and watched a man eavesdropping at the office door before making his presence known. She'd been intrigued to know what this Javier Owens was doing and waited until all the serving staff filed past before creeping along the corridor to listen. It did little to improve her opinion of Petre. Dominique would bet her life that the younger brother had thrown that unfortunate woman out of the car even though it sounded like the same woman he'd fornicated with outside the cottage window. And tonight, she'd almost tripped over him in the shrubbery bonking a compliant blonde – he was certainly a virile young man.

This time, Dominique was alone amongst the dense foliage, notwithstanding countless creepy crawlies and other creatures which took grim satisfaction in biting, dropping on her head or brushing past her in the dark. She shimmied back up the rope ladder and into the abandoned treehouse. She wondered if Narella had ever used it. There were no signs of a child ever camping out amongst the branches of the vast Turkey oak. Its only occupants appeared to be spiders patiently hanging in their webs, awaiting unsuspecting insects. At the open window, Dominique retook her reconnaissance position and peered through military-grade binoculars. The vantage point provided ideal viewing into the house, the pool terrace, and the terraced gardens. Small pedestal lights branched out from the house into the grounds and uplights cast intricate shadows in trees and shrubs. A great deal of thought had gone into the lighting scheme. The estate was one giant stage and Dominique waited for the next act to start.

The lights dimmed, and a glow appeared in the open-plan lounge as a cake in the shape of a gigantic Zagrokis Enterprises lorry was wheeled in. Twenty sparkling candles fizzed, and through her long-range listening device, Dominique heard Tinto give a short thank-you speech before blowing out the candles to rapturous applause and the chinking of glasses. A dramatic piece of classical music started to build, and fireworks exploded into the sky at its crescendo. The spectacle lasted ten minutes and marked the end of a glorious event. The guests slowly vanished, and the catering staff packed away. Finally, Dominique watched the solitary figure of Tinto Zagrokis stand on his poolside terrace and raise a glass to the night before going inside. With a flick of a switch, the house, terrace and gardens plunged into darkness.

Alone beneath a star-filled sky, Dominique was satisfied with her plan. She unrolled the rope ladder and stole back to the cottage.

Chapter Thirty-Two

A butterfly fluttered past his head as Kristina wiped away tears of laughter. 'I don't believe you. She actually did that?'

'No word of a lie,' he exclaimed and held his hands up. 'I'm asking Agnes for danger money on the next assignment. I don't know if it's Greek women in general or those who live in Lefkada, but they are unbelievably persistent.'

It was the morning after Tinto's party and as they sat in the garden eating breakfast Javier recounted stories about fending off unwanted female attention. He could have easily got laid twenty times if the mood had taken him.

'There must be somebody special if you kept knocking back all those advances?' Kristina enquired but he shook his head and she smiled enigmatically. 'There's always someone for everyone.'

'Why should there be?' he retorted. 'What about you?'

Kristina tapped her heart. 'There is, it was a long time ago but he lives here. If you're very lucky I might tell you about him one day.' He apologised for snapping but she waved it away with a slice of buttered toast. 'Don't worry, it's nothing a good night's sleep won't solve.'

And there was that smile again. He froze. Did she know he was in the cellar night after night, trying and failing to crack the vault's combination? Of course she didn't. He'd be out on his ear, but he remained her lodger. The rewiring job would've been much further on if she didn't keep wandering into whichever room he was in, declaring he'd done enough for that day or that week. On top of that, he got every weekend off. She must simply like the company. And it was just as well, because the woman refused to accept her age and he'd caught her up stepladders on numerous occasions washing windows, dusting, rearranging cupboards or pruning trellises. Each time he'd demanded she get down at once, stop being so ridiculous and he would do any at-height jobs. The final time he caught her up a ladder dusting a crystal chandelier in what he called the French chateau bedroom. It was beautiful with its hand-painted mural of flowers and an eclectic mix of antique furniture, but he hadn't been in the mood to admire her interior design skills and declared if she so much as glanced at a stepladder again he'd tell Anna. Kristina had mischievously laughed and called him a snitch but the threat had worked. Living with Kristina for over two months he was only now gaining a sense of his landlady's personality and there were definite signs of her retreating into the past. However, Javier didn't share Anna's concerns. Kristina wasn't obsessed with events gone by, she merely liked to reminisce. And everyone did that, hankering for a time when things seemed better. He was on the verge of asking about her sweetheart when Giannis Andino appeared from the kitchen. He looked appalling. His eyes were red, his hair dishevelled and his skin was sallow and unshaven. The cocksure swagger was gone and he looked bereft.

Kristina rose to greet him. 'My boy, you look dreadful. Come join us and have some breakfast.'

He shook his head. 'Thank you but no. I don't have the stomach for food right now. I wondered if I might have a word with Javier, please?'

'Of course you can,' Kristina said kindly and kissed him on the cheek. 'And please accept my condolences for Mia. I know how close the two of you were and she'll leave a void in your life.'

Giannis plonked himself down and watched her go. 'She really is the psychic crazy Swedish lady.'

'Hey!' Javier growled. 'Less of the name-calling. Kristina's fantastic. She can mentally run rings around most people in this village.'

'I'm sorry, mate,' his young boss apologised, absent-mindedly tinkering with the cafetiere. 'You're right. I've no qualms with Kristina; she's always been good to me, and I know Sarah adores her as the school kids love their weekly garden club.'

He fell silent and began to shred a discarded napkin. Javier firmly took it off him, poured out a cup of coffee and handed him a Danish pastry. 'For God's sake eat something, man. You look like hell.'

Giannis nibbled a corner of the sweet pastry and sniffed. 'I wanted to come around first thing to tell you that Mia died last night – she never regained consciousness.'

The young man broke down in tears as he explained receiving an anonymous call at the party. The robotic voice on the other end said the funeral arrangements were sorted, and when he'd asked where it was to take place, the clipped voice informed him that was not his concern. All he needed to know was Mia's temporary replacement was now permanent.

'Y-you should have heard the voice,' he tried to explain as his shoulders shook. 'So utterly cold-hearted as if Mia meant nothing at all. As if her whole life was only an entry on some spreadsheet, erased with a keystroke. Unlike the hospital, which rang me next and was heartily sorry for my loss. And I'm sure I'll have Inspector Marinos dropping by to pass on his condolences – I don't envy him that job.'

'Did you love Mia?' Javier asked.

'I don't know,' Giannis admitted. 'She was unlike anybody I've ever met. She lived every day as if it was her last. And in one way, she didn't care about people's opinions so she was brutally honest. But then again, she was always discreet and didn't want to break up my marriage. If I wanted to fool around that was down to me and it was not for her to go blabbing or be a bitch. She was the same with Sarah as she was with everyone else. I think I was only ever a bit of fun for her and I know she didn't love me. Her only love was diving. And I guess that's what I'm struggling to cope with. She was so full of life that I assumed she would easily pull through and be back to work in no time. It seems incomprehensible that she's gone.'

Javier studied the younger man and was trying to muster some compassion. 'Do you love your wife?'

'Yes,' he instantly replied. 'Sarah's the best thing that's ever happened to me.'

Javier leaned forward and his face hardened. 'Then get your shit together, sunshine. If you love your wife as much as you claim, you have a funny way of showing it. You might not like what I have to say but you came here and I'm telling you what I know – don't throw away the love of a good woman because when it's gone it's gone for good. Marinos is a good copper and will keep going until he solves Mia's death. And as part of that, he'll work out what went on between you and Mia. Will Sarah stand by you if she finds out?'

Javier knew he was being harsh, but the bloke needed to hear it straight. Mia had turned his head, and it was easy to see how. But with her death, Giannis had a chance to start again. And if he was very lucky his wife would be none the wiser.

'You're right.' Giannis anxiously pulled at his sleeves. 'But it doesn't seem right that we can't pay our respects.'

'I agree, and my suggestion would be to go to Father Katechis and say that as Mia's employer, you'd like to hold a memorial service in her memory,' Javier explained. 'Nobody will think the request is strange, and I can help if you need me to. At the very least I'd like to do a reading. For all her faults, Mia was a big part of this village and an exceptional dive master.'

Giannis brightened. 'Yes, that sounds ideal. I'll be able to sort everything out, but I'll hold you to the reading, it'd be lovely to hear from someone else who cared about her. I don't know if you knew this, but she rated you, and that was rare.'

'Well, if there's nothing else?' Javier began clearing away. He had football coaching and wanted to arrive early.

'Actually, there is,' Giannis whispered. 'The voice also instructed me to say you're promoted to a junior diver as of today. My employer is impressed, based on Mia's feedback.'

***

Javier dumped the breakfast dishes on the bench when Giannis left. At last, his suspicions were confirmed. He now knew what the divers brought up from the depths. The washing-up bowl filled with hot sudsy water. The Andino brothers were playing a dangerous game, but that wasn't his concern. All he cared about was the money, which would come in handy until he hit the jackpot.

Kristina wandered in from the lounge and began drying up. 'I was right about Mia, wasn't I?'

Lost in his own world, Javier took a while to answer. 'Unfortunately, yes.'

'How are you feeling?' Kristina asked. The affection and concern in her voice was like a hug that held him safe and warm. 'I know you were good friends, and I don't think she had many.'

Javier stared out the window. Only a few weeks ago Mia had been in Kristina's beautiful garden, offering him a job. And now she was gone. It didn't seem real. 'Incredibly sad. She was only twenty-four, with her whole life stretching out ahead. What a total waste.'

Kristina continued to dry. 'It's an old adage but very true – if you play with fire, you'll get burned.'

'That's a bit harsh, isn't it?' Javier exclaimed. He was still unable to get the measure of the enigmatic nonagenarian. One minute she was kindness and compassion personified, and the next, brutally honest.

'Perhaps,' she replied but failed to sound apologetic. 'Thank you for defending my honour earlier.'

He was still thinking, and it took a second to work out what she meant. 'Oh yes, the crazy-lady insult. Well, I didn't like it. Out of interest, how long have you lived in Apokeri?'

She peered up at the ceiling, wiping a glass. 'Let me think … it must be seventy-four years. How time flies.'

'And do you still think of yourself as Swedish?'

'Yes, it's funny having spent so little of my life there. But what about you? Your childhood was spent moving about and you've lived in lots of countries. How would you define yourself?'

'Welsh.' He didn't have to think twice.

Kristina nodded. 'Now take Anna. She identifies herself as a Geordie first and foremost. Not English or British. Our roots make us who we are, and I suppose we look back at those before us and want to emulate them, make them proud or be a better version of them. Wouldn't you say?' Javier kept quiet. He didn't want to compare himself to his parents or even his siblings because he fell far short. Kristina placed the clean cafetiere on the windowsill. 'Anyway, talking of ancestors, I thought tonight I'd make us a lovely meal before your dive-boat duties and give you a glimpse into my own.'

Chapter Thirty-Three

Dawn crept over the land, casting shadows across an unofficial Apokeri parking area. It was sometimes used by those keen to torture themselves on the dirt track up to the southern Apokeri cliffs and then upwards to the mountainous villages of Vafkeri, Egklouvi and Karya. But more often than not, it was a handy overflow for Round the Bend patrons. The engine of their gifted four-by-four cooled as the Castellas waited. Now that they'd come to the crunch, neither wanted to make the first move. With the windows down, Dominique closed her eyes. The dawn chorus was in full swing, and a light breeze rustled the leaves overhead. In the distance, a cockerel repeatedly crowed, telling her to get on with it.

Her hand was on the door handle when there was movement over the road. Filip Makris and Alex Panagos appeared on two gleaming road bikes. During the party, she'd caught the tail end of a heated debate between the pair on her listening device. But without understanding Greek she was none the wiser, and for the rest of the party they appeared fine. And now they were smiling, laughing and seemed ready to tackle anything in their tight-fitting Lycra outfits. Despite everything, Dominique murmured in appreciation, resulting in a shove from Sergio.

'Hey, less of that, missy!' her husband joked. 'I'm sitting right here!'

She leaned over and kissed him. 'You're still my number one, babe. I reckon we wait ten minutes to be safe.'

It was just as well because five minutes later, Filip reappeared pushing his bike with two shredded tyres, and he was furious. The pair watched as he disappeared from sight.

'It's now or never,' Dominique advised. 'I have no idea how long it takes to change bike tyres which is what I reckon he's doing.'

The pair clicked open the doors and slid out. On one side, Dominique lifted a drowsy Pesce who murmured and nuzzled up to her – driving another spike into her heart. On the other side, Sergio unclipped Elora's baby seat, and he was fairing far worse. Luckily, his daughter slept peacefully. Unaware of what was about to happen.

The previous day, Tinto had arrived early doors, laden down with leftover party food and a massive slab of cake. He was in high spirits until he heard his guests would be leaving obscenely early the following day. The Castellas had remained tight-lipped about their lives, and Tinto had asked no questions, but the man was no fool and asked if there was anything he could do to help. Not wanting to put their friend in danger, the couple had only requested that he forget they were ever there. He happily agreed and said Petre would do likewise. His brother had only gained a fleeting glimpse of the visitors on two occasions and was so self-absorbed he'd probably failed to notice them. As far as his housekeeper and gardener were concerned, there was nothing to worry about; they had never met the Castellas.

For the rest of the day, Dominique and Sergio had fussed over Elora and Pesce to make their final day together a happy one. In the evening, Tinto had returned with a set of keys as a parting gift to the couple. Unfortunately, the bag of rust they'd arrived in had somehow vanished and in its place was a powerful four-wheel-drive all-terrain vehicle. He was unable to account for the mystery or explain how it was currently sitting by the bottom gates that would be left unlocked. In a tearful farewell, Dominique wished her extraordinary new friend everlasting happiness. Nobody mentioned a future visit. And as the couple had lain in each other's arms for the final time, Sergio cried all night as the realisation struck home – he would never see his daughter grow up.

In a monumental effort, Dominique had clamped an iron lid over her emotions. She adored Elora but loved Pesce. He was her fur baby, and she dare not allow space to contemplate being separated from him, because if the tears started, there'd be no let-up. She was barely holding it together after losing her mother, but soon they would be together again, which was the only thing that gave Dominique enough strength to carry on.

The pair tiptoed under the rose arch into the deathly quiet courtyard and sneaked up to the back door. There were no signs of life from within the house but was it only her imagination or could she hear cursing from the workshop? Sergio placed his sleeping daughter next to her baby bag on the doorstep. Elora's peaceful breathing carried in the quiet air as her father hung his head and tears slid from bloodshot eyes.

Dominique steeled herself and deposited Pesce on a blue mat next to Elora and tucked in his favourite cuddly toy. He sleepily opened his eyes and protectively placed a front paw over the blue-and-white striped cow. She set down his bag of supplies and, although it was torture, she couldn't resist bending down to say she loved him, and he must be a good boy and always keep Elora safe. She gave him one last kiss on the top of his head, and in response, he lifted his back leg for a tickle. After stroking the downy fur of his inside leg for the final time, she retreated as a sob threatened to burst forth. The couple stumbled back to the car with Sergio in floods of tears, and Dominique's throat burned with the effort of maintaining the dam that held back her emotions.

'I'm sorry, sweetheart,' Sergio sobbed as he closed the door. 'I thought I could hold it together.'

She passed him two tablets and a bottle of water. He gratefully swallowed them, settled back, and waited for the powerful sedatives to kick in. Dominique was going to drive. Sergio didn't trust himself, and it was why he'd insisted on being knocked out. Otherwise, he would fight to save himself. To save them both. When ultimately, they weren't the ones who needed saving.

They said their last goodbyes and kissed before the drugs enveloped Sergio in blissful sleep. At least he wouldn't feel a thing at the utmost end. Dominique clicked her seatbelt in and started the engine. The huge car glided up the steep bank with horrifying ease as time ticked down on her inconsequential existence. Would anyone miss her when she was gone? Dominique thought not as she turned onto the empty highway and stepped on the accelerator. The needle surged past eighty as she decided Pesce would, but the thought of her faithful pooch waking up to find her gone forever sent hairline cracks through the dam. She gripped the steering wheel and focused on the task at hand. There were jagged cliffs on one side and, on the other, the cliff-edge safety barrier whipped past. It would only take a few minutes to reach the roadside viewpoint, and at its far end was a gap into the big blue yonder. All she needed to do was line the bonnet up with that and keep her foot flat to the floor – gravity would do the rest.

The road snaked around the cliffs. Not long now, and it would all be over. The sky was getting lighter, and it was going to be another beautiful day. She crested a ridge and screamed. There, in the middle of the road, was Alex Panagos on his bike. He was moving too slowly, and she was going too fast. In sickening slow motion, she saw him desperately try to generate enough speed to clear the car, but he didn't have enough momentum and his horrified face registered the fact. In a frantic attempt to save him, she yanked the steering wheel hard right and watched as the front edge of the bonnet missed him by millimetres. But with a sickening crunch, the back left corner made contact and the man who'd offered her nothing but kindness at the café ricocheted across the carriageway. He slammed against the cliff like a rag doll, and his lifeless body crumpled onto the tarmac.

The dam broke on her emotions as she fought to gain control of the car. It swerved across the carriageway and shot past a water delivery truck. The contents were apt as she sobbed at the horrifying mess she'd made of everything. In a split second, she'd sealed the fate of yet another individual. First, her mother, then Alex, and in a matter of seconds, she would erase Sergio and her own life. The deserted lay-by opened up on her right; she eyeballed the gap and stamped on the accelerator again. The car surged forwards, and the vast sky and sea welcomed her.

In the end, Dominique was there to ensure the task got done – like she always did.

Chapter Thirty-Four

The irritating buzz on the bedside table woke him. Jace groggily looked at his clock. Who the hell was ringing him at this time on a Sunday? He staggered to his feet and tiptoed past the sleeping form. Five minutes later, he was back, all traces of sleep erased. Today was gearing up to be another busy one.

He got ready as quickly and quietly as possible, but she sat up rubbing sleepy eyes. 'What time is it?'

He wanted nothing more than to crawl back under the sheets and curl up against her warm body. A little more than a week since she'd turned up at his door, and every day she found a way to slip away to be with him.

His fingers traced a line down her backbone, and he drew her close. 'Too early, sweetheart. I think I might be some time.'

She stretched and kissed him. 'No worries. I'll see you later.'

Despite the phone call, there was a spring in his step, and Jace couldn't help grinning. Elissa made no demands on him, and he relished her company.

Ten minutes later he knocked and heard a familiar bark. Evie opened the door, holding back Cleo who immediately wriggled her way free and jumped up to greet him. She was a robust dog, like her mother, Cassie, and he always braced himself for the friendly onslaught.

'Come on, girl,' he instructed between enthusiastic licks. 'Let's get you inside.'

He was in a regular family kitchen. Post-it notes covered the fridge, a blackboard listed to-dos, the dishwasher was half-empty, kids' toys and chewed dog ones littered the floor – and he was relieved to see and smell percolating coffee and toast. However, the reason for his call was on the table in a baby carrier, energetically kicking her legs while giggling at Evie. And another small creature was insistently pawing his trouser legs, demanding to be tickled. Once done, the cute dog happily trotted off and curled up with Cleo.

'I see you've had an early morning delivery,' Jace observed. His voice was deliberately light in front of Evie but inside, a lead weight settled in his stomach.

Filip placed a plate of scrambled eggs on toast and a black coffee in front of him. 'Yes, it's not what you expect to find on your doorstep after changing two bike tyres. I'd like to present Elora and Pesce.'

He studied the baby carrier. 'We'll need to dust for prints.'

'That mightn't be necessary, Inspector.' Anna handed him an unsealed envelope. 'We know who deposited our new guests – and I've even met them.'

Jace raised his eyebrows and started to read the typed note.

> Dearest Anna,
> You said if there was anything I ever needed to get in touch. And in our darkest and most desperate hour of need, I beseech you to please help us.
> We have not taken this decision lightly, knowing that our actions will change your family's life forever. But be under no illusions. This is a matter of life and death.
> Despite what you might have thought (and what I've longed for), Elora is not my daughter. She is the product of a union between my husband, Sergio, and his mistress Monika Gallante. The lady in question was also the mistress of Francis Del Ambro Contino Junior, Head of the Del Ambro Contino crime family. I'm sure by now you have a sinking feeling and a terrible inkling of what's coming next.
> I will lay out the facts.
> At the end of March, Francis discovered he wasn't Elora's father and sought revenge. Monika begged us to take Elora into our safekeeping. She then made the ultimate sacrifice to keep her daughter safe and

ended her life moments before Francis brutally intended to. Since then, he's been hunting us down in order to destroy Sergio and Elora. My fate is little better. I am to be his whore and produce an heir. I'll then be kept around until he tires of me, and I'll go the same way as all of his other countless mistresses. My mother (Toni Bianchi) was killed last month on the orders of Francis. I also believe he organised the execution of my father (Alesso Bianchi) and four other leading members of the Del Ambro Contino hierarchy twenty-four years ago to clear his way to the top.

The man is a cold-hearted, calculating, obsessive and paranoid psychopath. However, I would not place Elora in your care if I did not believe you could keep her safe. It is Sergio and myself who will lead Francis to Elora. After learning of my beloved mamma's death, we realised that we must follow in Monika's footsteps to ensure the safety of Elora and Pesce.

I will never forget the kindness you showed my family and especially me. And because of this (and my own investigations), I know that you (along with Filip, Evie and Cleo) can be the family that Elora and Pesce desperately require.

As one (surrogate) mother to another, I hope you can accept this mammoth burden we have placed on you.

With eternal thanks and love,

Dominique (and Sergio) Castellas

Jace placed the letter back in the envelope and wished he could re-write its contents. The letter's author was right – this would change the Makris family forever. It was an immense responsibility to thrust upon complete strangers.

Anna gave him a brave smile and turned to Evie. 'Sweetheart, why don't you go and show Pesce your room and play quietly until it's time to go to Aunt Steffi's.'

Evie scrutinised her mother. 'What you mean is I need to go upstairs so I can't hear what's being discussed.'

'That would be right,' Anna replied in a no-nonsense tone. 'Off you go.'

'I never get to hear any of the good stuff,' Evie whined and marched out of the room with the cockapoo.

Jace opened his mouth, but Anna shook her head and pointed to the kitchen door. 'Evangelina Alice Makris, if you are not up those stairs in five seconds flat, there will be big trouble.'

'Fine!' came the angry retort. 'I can't wait to be a grown-up.'

The clatter of footsteps and the slamming of a bedroom door signalled the coast was clear.

'She's got a bit of a temper that one,' Jace observed.

Filip replenished the empty coffee cup. 'Just like her mother, Inspector.'

'Very droll, Mr Cool Calm and Collected,' Anna retorted.

Jace listened to the light-hearted banter and felt a pang of jealousy, but it quickly vanished. He wouldn't want to be in this family's shoes right now.

'Tell us the worst,' Anna asked casually as if enquiring about the weather. 'Do you know anything about the Del Ambro Contino crime family, and what are our chances of pulling this off?'

Jace pushed his empty plate away. 'Are you seriously considering this request?'

Anna gripped the table. 'Inspector Marinos, you didn't meet that woman. But you've seen the women Steffi's charity helps. Each one has the same haunted look – full of fear and a sense of nothingness. Well, take that and multiply it a hundredfold. When I looked into the eyes of Dominique Castellas, I was staring into the soul of somebody who had seen hell … who knew death stalked her every move, who knew she couldn't turn aside, and she couldn't be saved. Have you ever seen that? Because I hadn't, and it was terrifying. I wanted to put my arms around them all and provide a wall of protection that nothing could break. And that was before her mother was killed. No wonder Elora and Pesce ended up on our doorstep. The Castellas are out of options. And now that I know what they were fleeing from, Pip and me want to help them more than ever. Don't you see, we could never forgive ourselves otherwise?'

There were goosebumps under his shirt. He'd seen what Anna had witnessed – abject fear in his mother's eyes at his father's explosive rage. He'd been too young to stop the escalating violence. Instead, he could only cower behind his sister, who tried and failed to stop it. And years later, he still lived with the nightmares of hearing his mother's screams and then silence. It was the past that drove him on in the hopes of changing the future, of preventing it from happening to others. And it was why he couldn't switch off from his job, why he relentlessly took on extra work, helped and supported Steffi's charity and ultimately why he remained single. There was no room left in his life for somebody to truly love.

'I understand,' he said, knowing he would go above and beyond to help the Makris family should they need it. 'This is what we're going to do.'

Chapter Thirty-Five

After an hour with Anna and Filip, it wasn't even eight o'clock when Jace left. For the last fifteen minutes, his silent mobile had been going berserk in his pocket. He was ready to hurl the stupid thing across the road but began scanning the increasingly irate messages instead. He climbed into his car. It didn't seem possible, but things were about to get even worse.

In less than ten minutes, he pulled into the enormous lay-by on the edge of the white cliffs. Jace made sure the handbrake was on. It was a two-hundred-foot drop straight into the sea and a favourite spot for coach tours with magnificent views along the twisting coastline. But there'd be no tourists for the foreseeable future. They'd been forced to close the road and divert traffic on an enormous loop. As it was the main island highway and the quickest route, tempers were already fraying on both sides. He could still hear horns blaring and the raised voices of those idiotic drivers who (for reasons unknown) decided the detour didn't apply to them and were determined to force their way through. Jace left instructions to arrest anyone who refused to cooperate and didn't give a rat's ass if his superiors had a fit.

He strode over to the fateful spot. 'What can you tell me, Henri?'

His deputy hitched up his trousers and gave Jace a withering look. 'Nice to see you finally decided to join us, sir.'

'Less of the attitude,' Jace barked. 'I've been up with the larks because of work, so I'm not in the mood.'

'Well, excuse me for trying to inject some humour,' Henri groused. 'Anyway, it looks to be a classic hit-and-run. The delivery guy over there found the bloke unconscious on the road and a tangled bike ten metres away. He rang emergency services and wisely didn't touch anything. The ambulance has already left with the victim, who is banged up pretty bad with suspected multiple fractures and head trauma. The helmet undoubtedly saved his life when he was flung against the rock face.'

Jace grimaced at the jagged cliffs that overhung this particular section of the road. He looked at the tyre marks. 'It looks like our cyclist stopped at the lay-by, maybe to take a photo—'

'Probably a selfie.' Henri interrupted.

Jace nodded as he visualised the scene. 'And when he crossed the carriageway, he was struck by the vehicle which promptly took off – lowlife scum. Do we have any info about the vehicle or drivers?'

'Delivery bloke states a vehicle hurtled past him less than five seconds before he found our man. But he cannot give us a description because, at that precise moment, he was looking down—'

'At his mobile, no doubt,' Jace fumed.

'Probably, but he claims otherwise,' his deputy explained. 'I can easily check, but I don't reckon he'll be using a mobile at the wheel again. Look at the skid marks, boss. That cyclist is one lucky bloke. He not only survived a hit-and-run, but our delivery driver stopped within centimetres of squashing his head like a melon.'

'You're right, Henri.' Jace stood above two thick black tyre skids. 'There's no need to waste time with the mobile. We've got plenty to deal with as it is.'

'Do you want me to notify his next of kin? It shouldn't take too long to discover who they are.'

'No. I'll do that,' Jace replied with a shake of his head. 'I've actually met his parents, and they're a lovely couple. I also know who has their details.'

Jace pointed his car towards Round the Bend for the second time that day. Only this time, it was to inform Mr and Mrs Makris that their business partner, Alex Panagos, was fighting for his life.

Chapter Thirty-Six

She was ten minutes early for Mia's memorial service, but in Anna's book that was late because Elora chose to throw up over her just as they were about to leave. A week on since that fateful morning, Elora had settled in far quicker than Pesce. Anna supposed it was because the little girl had spent her short life being shuttled about. However, the little dog was suffering severe abandonment issues and couldn't be left alone (even with Cleo) because he would howl, whimper, wretch up and desperately claw the furniture. This gave Pip the perfect excuse not to attend. Anna knew the real reason: Pip couldn't deal with attending the service of someone younger than Alex. His lover was currently in an induced coma, having been airlifted off Lefkada the day of the hit-and-run.

Walking into church, Anna was always struck by its calming atmosphere. Today it looked and smelled gorgeous, with a white and green floral spray behind the altar and vases of freshly cut flowers dotted on windowsills beneath beautiful stained-glass windows. The church was already half full with those wanting to pay their respects, and Anna recognised everyone except a couple of serious suits. She judged the man and woman to be in their mid-thirties and they sat on the back left away from everyone else. On the other side were the eagle-eyed Iardanou sisters, Thelma and Violet, then in front the domino club, the knitting club, the church volunteers and many members of the village committee.

As Anna made her way further forward with Evie, she nodded to Tinto Zagrokis and noticed his brother had a face that would curdle milk. Inspector Marinos and his sister were across the aisle. As the leading officer on the unsolved case, he saw it as his duty to attend and undoubtedly use it as the perfect opportunity to observe – the man was never truly off-duty. On the front row there was Giannis Andino and his wife Sarah, and the Andino dive-boat crew. Stelios, Elissa and Sebasti sat behind them but notably, no Rika. Mia's landlady, Dania, was there with her husband Max. Afterwards, food and drink would be served at the couple's taverna in the village square. Anna was one of the few not going as she wanted to get back to Pip. He was struggling to cope with Alex's accident, consumed with guilt at having argued with his lover at the party. He was also terrified that Alex would die, or Alex would survive but not remember him, or Alex would survive, would remember him but disclose their thirteen-year relationship.

The week was one of the worst of Anna's life – Elora and Pesce arrived, the Castellas killed themselves, Alex became a hit-and-run victim and the ongoing presence of her ex-husband. Then the unexpected news Mia had died and Evie's insistence on doing a reading. Added to that the hurt and anger of being informed she was not required to help her daughter with the speech because Evie had asked Javier. The pair had locked heads for hours in the café or at Kristina's, going through the closely guarded reading that Anna wasn't allowed to see.

Evie slid into the pew first next to Javier and gripped his hand, and on his right sat Kristina. Anna had been left confused and conflicted upon discovering Javier was also doing a reading. There'd been surprise, begrudging admission that maybe he had a sense of decency, a stubborn refusal to accept he could possibly change and finally what she could only describe as jealousy – and it was that emotion that unsettled her the most. Why was she bothered about Javier and Mia? What if they had been friends with benefits? The man was entitled to a life, and she had no feelings towards him anymore. Plus, there was Kristina and Javier's blossoming friendship. How could Kristina be so trusting? She was usually so good at reading people. And finally, Javier and Evie's closeness caused the most pain. Her daughter idolised him and who was she to dash Evie's trusting view of humanity when, to all appearances, Javier genuinely cared?

Everyone settled down as Father Katechis took to the front. He was halfway through welcoming the mourners when the church doors slammed shut. Everyone turned to see a red-eyed Rika Andino. The agitated teenager looked around wildly, horrified to see how far away her immediate family sat. However, relief flooded her face when Violet and Thelma motioned for their great-niece to sit beside them. And then Anna understood why the pair had positioned themselves right at the back – they'd expected Rika to appear. The sisters really were experts on human behaviour.

After the brief interruption, Father Katechis seamlessly continued. With a nod and a smile, he explained everyone was gathered to mark the life of Mia Tovier, cut tragically short. The dive master had always been polite, respectful and friendly on those occasions he'd found her sitting at the back of the church with her head bent in quiet contemplation. After the first hymn, Giannis Andino was welcomed to the podium. It was strange to see the usually self-assured man cautiously take the microphone. At first, his words were halting, but as he spoke about Mia's passion for diving, his voice gained in confidence. Mia never had an off day, and she never arrived down in the mouth. Giannis grinned and said even the serene Father Katechis probably had frustrating days with wayward members of his flock. The priest knowingly smiled, and a chuckle ripped through the congregation. However, Mia was never like that and had so much positive energy that it lifted everyone. In four years, he never saw her unhappy at work as she chatted to the guests and put them at ease; she never flapped but demanded utmost respect for the rules, and she wouldn't tolerate people mucking about during safety checks. Mia had been a consummate professional, and Giannis remembered a honeymooning couple two years ago. The pair were confident PADI-certified divers, but on the first dive of the day, something spooked the husband, and he couldn't catch his breath and that in turn panicked his wife. Mia was there immediately and calmly brought both up to the surface. The couple were highly emotional, upset and embarrassed and wanted to hide in a corner for the rest of the trip. However, Mia patiently sat with them, passed no judgement, and built their confidence back up so that the pair again took to the water in the afternoon. The example demonstrated Mia's passion and professionalism. The confident voice broke as Giannis stumbled over his last few words. He'd always felt humbled and privileged when Mia arrived at the start of each season when any number of companies would have snapped her up. Her death had devastated him and the crew.

The congregation clapped as Giannis returned to his seat to be comforted by Sarah, and singing voices filled the church. As nobody knew what Mia liked, Father Katechis had selected a range of appropriate hymns. Evie started taking deep breaths, Anna kissed her and said she'd be amazing. The priest then welcomed Javier and Evie. Watching her daughter walk up the aisle holding hands with her ex-husband was surreal.

'Now we are going to do something a bit different,' Father Katechis explained. 'Whilst Javier's Greek is coming on leaps and bounds, he's asked Evie to translate his words. I'm sure you'll all agree Javier needs to speak. And for those who understand Greek and English, you have the benefit of hearing his fine words twice.'

Javier took to the podium, and Anna was pleased to see him adjust the microphone for Evie, not himself. 'Thank you, Father Katechis and Giannis, for kindly allowing me to say a few words. I'm sure some of you might be thinking, what is this Welshman doing up here talking about someone he hardly knew? Well, the answer is simple. I wanted everyone to know how fond Mia was of you all. I know she tended to keep people at arm's length, but she always spoke with such warmth about life in Apokeri.'

Anna closed her eyes and listened as the authoritative voice of Javier alternated with Evie's quieter and higher pitch. He was an excellent orator, and his reading was a perfect blend of respect peppered with humour. It was like listening to a long-distance telephone call as some of the congregation laughed at his words, and then a few seconds later, the rest laughed at Evie's translation. Each day Mia would leave her studio and deliberately take the long route through the backstreets so she could pass the domino players and wish them a good morning, and joke about the previous day's scores. They would always doff their hats in greeting, and one gentleman, in particular, would always proposition Mia and tell her she didn't know what she was missing – and every day, she would laugh and say maybe tomorrow. A chorus of cheers and heckles erupted from the club members. Mia would then pop into Aphrodite Café for a coffee and ask the knitting club how their latest creations were coming along. There would always be one lady who proudly showed off her knitting and happily pointed to all the dropped stitches and another beckoned Mia over to prod her in the ribs with a bony finger and say she was too skinny and needed fattening up. Another collective cheer went up in agreement. There were other heart-warming examples of Mia enjoying chats with Dania and tidying up before Violet arrived so they had time for a catch-up over a cup of tea. And then Javier spoke about the fondness Mia had for Rika, how she admired her friend's healthy outlook on life, which was so different from hers. A sob echoed off the stone walls; nobody needed to turn to see where it came from.

'Mia was a great mimic and storyteller and reminded me very much of someone I was very close to many years ago—'

Anna snapped her eyes open to find him speaking directly to her. He'd always loved her stories about the day's events or if they were out and about the elaborate tales she concocted about strangers. In that moment, it was only the two of them facing each other. Heat flamed her cheeks, and she was unable to breathe. And then the connection was lost as he looked down at his notes. The discomfort increased as Kristina patted her knee.

'That amazing ability to bring people and events to life enabled me to feel part of this community long before I was known to you all,' he continued and grinned. 'Well, I say not known to you all. I've quickly realised that the Apokeri grapevine rivals the speed of light, and my presence was quickly noted.' At this, everyone burst out laughing. It was an undeniable fact news whipped around the village. 'I'd like to conclude by saying I hope I've enabled you to see how much everyone here meant to Mia. And if I haven't, I've done my departed friend a great disservice.'

There was a round of applause as Javier stepped off the podium. Anna felt strangely proud of her ex-husband for having acquitted himself so well. He had indeed done Mia a great service. As Evie shuffled her notes, Anna grasped Kristina's hand.

'Thank you, Father Katechis and Mr Andino, for letting me speak today. I didn't know Mia other than to say hello to, but I wanted you to know that she made a massive difference to everyone in my class. Each year our teacher Mrs Andino arranges for people to come and do talks or demonstrations and they're really interesting,' Evie earnestly explained. 'But Mia was always the best. She showed us life beneath the waves from dive sites in Australia, New Zealand, Thailand, the Caribbean, Egypt and Scotland. And not just the superstars like whales, sharks and dolphins that everyone knows about. But the tiny ones like little crabs that burrow away in the sand to stay safe, fish that clean other fish and little creatures that live in coral. She showed us that everything has its place and it all needs to be there to work, that just because we can't see what goes on under the waves doesn't mean we should take it for granted. And because of Mia, me and my classmates know we need to care for what lives in the water just as much as what lives on the land or flies in the sky because everything is connected to everything else.'

There wasn't a whisper in the church as Evie continued. 'In *The Little Mermaid*, Ariel was born underwater but wanted to live on dry land, and I think because Mia loved the sea so much, she was really a mermaid who was born up here by mistake. But now she doesn't need to wear a mask, flippers and air tanks anymore. With her long black hair streaming behind her and a beautiful shimmering tail she's now swimming in all the connecting oceans, making friends with all the underwater creatures and keeping them safe. She's finally free to go wherever she wants and be who she wants to be. That makes me happy and I hope it makes you all happy too.'

The church was absolutely silent until Evie finished and then there was rapturous applause. All around Anna, from Evie's classmates to weather-beaten grizzly fishermen, was the sound of sniffing and noses being blown.

'Everyone's crying, Mam,' a stricken Evie whispered when she sat back down. 'Does that mean I was really bad?'

Anna wrapped her wonderful, selfless daughter in a hug and blinked back tears. 'No angel. Those are happy-sad tears. You were awesome. I'm so proud of you.' After one final hymn, the service was over, and everyone filed out. Anna's pew was the last one to stand. 'Evie, I need to get back home. But would you like to go to Apollo with Kristina and Javier to hear stories about Mia?'

Her daughter's eyes lit up. 'Yes, please.'

'Come on, then,' Kristina instructed and held out her hand. 'Let's get going before we miss out on a comfy seat.'

Anna watched her friend and Evie walk hand in hand down the aisle and felt incredibly moved. Javier was also watching the pair as she cleared her throat. 'Thank you so much for helping Evie with her speech; it was beautiful.'

He stood silently for a few seconds and then smiled in a bemused fashion. 'Anna, all those words were Evie's own. All she wanted me to do was listen to her practise them. She told me she didn't want to bother you or her dad because you both had plenty on your plate with Elora and Pesce arriving, working all hours and coping with Uncle Alex being poorly.'

Anna slumped back into a pew. She was a terrible parent. Jealous of Javier and Evie when all along her daughter had only been trying to help.

Javier bent down. 'Evie's a great kid because she has such a fantastic mum.' And after giving her a quick peck on the cheek, he was gone. She was more confused than ever.

Chapter Thirty-Seven

The confusion cleared on her walk back home, allowing Anna to see Javier for what he was – a manipulator. She touched the cheek he had dared to kiss and the anger built. He was messing with her mind. He might have successfully wheedled his way into everyone's hearts, but she refused to let him into hers again. Her pace quickened as the obvious questions rose up to taunt her. So why did you give him a chance? Why do you continue to give him chances? She refused to answer and the welcoming licks, whimpers and tail wagging from Cleo lifted her mood. Tiptoeing upstairs she discovered Pip flat out with Elora and Pesce. It was such a peaceful scene but by some sense, Elora awoke and stretched out her arms. Anna lifted her and inhaled that intoxicating baby smell. She protectively hugged the little girl and was joined by Pesce as they crept downstairs and into the lounge.

Anna sat cross-legged on the floor as Elora chuntered away on her playmat, pushing herself up on chubby little arms. 'You're getting good at tummy-time, sweetheart, you'll be crawling in no time.'

Pip wandered in with dishevelled hair and dramatically yawned. 'How did Evie do?'

'She was amazing.' Anna beamed but noticed how drawn Pip looked. 'Why don't you go back to bed? You look wrecked.'

He tickled Elora's waist, and she rolled over giggling. He swooped down to fly her around the room to squeals of laughter. 'I don't want to miss out on this. Did everything else go as planned?'

'Yes,' Anna stated calmly as Pip placed Elora back on her mat.

'Giannis and Javier both spoke well.' He gave her a knowing look.

'I know what you're going to say.'

'Well listen then! The man is trying to turn his life around and from what I can see he's doing a good job.'

'I don't trust him.' Anna defiantly crossed her arms.

'Babe,' his response bordered on a growl and Anna knew she was on dangerous ground but couldn't stop herself.

'It's what he does,' she snapped. 'He smiles, he charms and wheedles his way into people's affections before betraying them.'

'Enough.' His slow simmering anger had eventually boiled over. 'I'm sick of this, Anna. I'm sick and tired of listening to your venom about the bloke and his past sins. If I knew you were going to be like this, I'd never have let you offer him a job interview with Kristina.'

'Let me! As if you could prevent it. You have no say in what I do to that building. It's my decision, it's my property and I'll do what I deem is for the best.'

'No,' he snapped. 'Kristina had the final say and she trusts Javier. And that property was gifted to you and it's in trust to Evie. Lest you forget.'

Her hackles were up like an enraged porcupine. 'Yes, and that's why I'm getting it rewired. Face it, Pip. You don't understand, you'll never understand.'

He drew himself up to his full height. 'I don't understand? Is that what you think?' She wanted to take the words back but it was too late. She started to speak but he held up his hand. 'What I understand is that you claim to be worried about Kristina being fixated on the past. When it's you that is! You're obsessed by it! And it would be nice if you thought about someone other than yourself for once.' She gasped as if he'd slapped her. She always put others first and was just about to tell him when he ploughed on. 'Alex is currently in an induced coma and I don't think you give a shit about that. I don't think you care what I'm going through, that I'm terrified of all the outcomes whether he lives or dies. That whatever happens I could very well lose the man I love. But you're too wrapped up in your own personal vendetta to notice.'

His chest heaved and there were tears on his cheeks. Anna stepped back, mortified. He was partly right. She'd let her emotions for Javier cloud what was really important.

'I'm so sorry, Pip,' she sobbed and rushed over to hug him. 'I've acted like a selfish cow. I'm worried sick about Alex and I'm really worried about you. I promise to keep my mouth shut about Javier from now on.' How was she going to accomplish that? Pip was right, she was fixated on proving Javier's deceit but must keep it secret. She raised herself on tiptoes and kissed his nose. 'Still friends?'

He gave her a watery grin. 'Of course.'

'Does this mean you're not going to argue anymore?' In the doorway stood Evie, stroking Pesce. Filip and Anna had been so focused on their argument that they'd failed to notice the cockapoo trot past them to the kitchen door and welcome their daughter home. 'I really hope so because it's like living with a pair of crocodiles snapping at each other.'

Anna and Filip dropped their heads. 'Sorry, Evie.'

Out the corner of her eye, Anna saw Pip clutch his hands together and swivel his left foot backwards and forwards like a naughty schoolboy. The side of her mouth twitched.

'Dad,' Evie snapped. 'You never take anything I say seriously.'

He grinned. 'That's not true and you know it.'

'Okay, I'll give you that.' She gave a dramatic eye-roll. 'Why do parents think their kids are stupid? I told Kristina that you'd be up here having a row, waiting till I was out the house so you think I wouldn't know. As if! I said if you didn't pack it in, I was going to move in with Nana and Granda.'

'We're so sorry, Evie,' Anna apologised again. 'Your dad and me have been having a bit of a hard time recently with worrying about Uncle Alex and the arrival of Elora and Pesce and unfortunately we've been taking it out on each other, which is wrong. There's nothing to worry about. It's just a blip in the road and everything's fine.'

'Come here and give your dad a hug.' Filip knelt with arms outstretched for Evie to rush over and be swung around the living room with a whoop. 'And we certainly don't think you're stupid, sweetheart. Far from it. You're easily smarter than both your parents.'

Evie beamed with pride and took her dad's hand. 'As proof of my superior intelligence, you'll be delighted to hear that I've brought home a doggy bag full of treats for tea.'

Anna threw back her head and laughed. 'You are your mother's daughter. Lead on.'

Chapter Thirty-Eight

It was two a.m., and the old house was as silent as the grave. Javier shivered in the cellar, although it wasn't that cold. His conscience whispered: *why not go back to bed, there's still time for redemption*. But his darker side instantly responded: *this is why you've come; this is why you continue to worm your way into people's affections to steal and cheat and increase your bloated bank balance.*

His demon always wanted more.

He remained motionless in front of the vault and recalled yesterday's memorial. A perfect platform to work his magic. He was a wordsmith and only required an audience to pour honey into their ears. And the best part – every word was true. With Evie's help, the congregation lapped up the touching stories of Mia. And it had been nice for the villagers to understand Mia a bit better. Locking eyes with Anna had been a nice touch, he thought – the woman still refused to accept him but that fleeting connection might tip the balance in his favour. He repeatedly flicked his left ring finger and thumb together when he remembered the kiss. That hadn't been part of the plan. She was a terrific mum, and Evie was a great kid. In Apollo, he'd enjoyed being part of a community, having a laugh and reminiscing about Mia. He'd even insisted on walking Evie back to make sure she got home safe (even if she'd needed to take his hand to steer him through the myriad of baffling backstreets).

His annoying grain of conscience was mushrooming, gaining strength and trying to unseat its alter-ego, which refused to go down without a fight. A war of good and evil continued unabated in his head, driving him to distraction. He'd worked so hard to gain the approval of Anna's nearest and dearest, and she would go the same way soon enough. So why was he contemplating throwing that all away for the affection of a woman he'd betrayed? His demon mocked him, taunted him. What sort of man was he? A weak loser? A good little boy, like all the other fools who would never amount to anything? And like a boxing ring, his angel roared out of its corner to deliver a right hook: *don't listen, don't be seduced. Be strong, be better than what you've been – return to the man Anna once loved. It's the right thing to do. This isn't about Anna. It's about you.*

The battle raged on as Javier was irresistibly drawn forwards to the vault. His demon crowed as a hand rested on the bulky dial. His angel screamed *no*. His fingers nimbly twisted the combination and with a click, the safe finally opened. His demon cheered. *Let the good times roll.* Carefully, very carefully, he swung open the door, wincing at the high-pitched screech. He paused and listened but the house remained silent above. He stepped inside, to find one metal bookcase containing stacks of black hardback journals. Javier switched on his headtorch to find each embossed with a year, but he refused to be disheartened (there might still be something he could use) and flicked through the top one. Bitter disappointment welled up – the language wasn't English; it wasn't even Greek but he recognised Kristina's handwriting. On the front page was her name, dated over seventy years ago. He gingerly turned brittle, yellowed pages and imagined Kristina in her youth – celebrating milestones with friends, laying out the garden and setting up her easel in the rooftop studio. He reached for a second diary and froze, for sitting underneath was another white A5 envelope.

> Hello Javier,
> Well done. You certainly are a most determined individual, spending hours huddled in a damp cellar in the dead of night when you think I'm asleep. Think of all that precious time wasted to access a pile of my memories. And you don't even know Swedish – how frustrating. Why don't you apply your talents in a more positive way?
> It was lovely of you to suggest Giannis arrange Mia's Service of Remembrance. I know how fond of her

you were. Is that because you recognised a kindred spirit? Another lost soul? Mia never had the chance to find her way back to the light, but you still do.
By the way, Anna still doesn't trust you. Why not call it quits before it's too late?
As ever, your loving friend,
Kristina

He was falling into quicksand. It eagerly sucked at his calves, his thighs, his waist. Shame was dragging him down. He had to fight to break free so he clawed and clambered and finally hauled himself out. He continued to underestimate his landlady. With trembling hands, he quickly put everything back, carefully closed the safe and stole back to bed. Hours later, he heard the rhythmic chugging of the fishing fleet putting out to sea and finally fell asleep.

Chapter Thirty-Nine

A few days later, Javier and his demon regrouped. Kristina was too crafty, and after the cellar fiasco it was time to sack off snooping in the house. He needed to mine a different seam. Anna wasn't in the café, and the ever-cheerful Sebasti pointed him towards the house. The dogs were barking before he even knocked on the kitchen door, and as Evie welcomed him in, Cleo and Pesce tried to outcompete one another for attention.

'Howay, man. Give the bloke some space,' Evie instructed, and both dogs dropped back. 'Mam's upstairs. I can go and get her if you want?'

'No, it's fine, I can wait,' Javier responded as Evie entertained Elora in her baby seat.

'Mam and Dad help kids, you know, and Elora needs their help for a bit.'

'Have they helped lots of babies?' Javier threw a red ball and watched Pesce outstrip Cleo to retrieve it. He knew about the emergency foster parent role and grudgingly admired the couple. He didn't know how they juggled everything. It couldn't be easy at the moment, being a man down with Alex still unresponsive in the hospital.

'They aren't usually this young, but whatever their ages, they stay here until their mams get better,' she replied and tickled Elora. 'I prefer babies.'

Javier glanced around at the ordered chaos of the kitchen. It had a homely atmosphere, a nice place to grow up. 'Why?'

'Because they're cute,' Evie replied as Elora giggled and gripped the girl's finger. 'See.'

'Yes, she is sweet,' he conceded and remembered his nieces and nephews at that age. He hardly knew them now, having spent so many years abroad. Something else he'd missed out on and something else his eldest sister had berated him about before ceasing all contact.

Evie continued to play with the baby. 'I know who you really are.'

Javier smirked. 'And who would that be?'

'Mam's first husband.' She delivered it as a fact that was neither particularly shocking nor interesting, and he wondered why she was telling him. 'I listened at the kitchen door; the parentals thought I was in bed.'

He wondered what else she might have overheard. 'Do you do that often?'

Evie shrugged. 'Sometimes. It's the only way you get to know what's going on.'

The little girl was so much like Anna, it was scary.

'What else do you know?' Javier asked because you never knew what useful information kids would blab.

Evie stopped shaking a teething ring and considered the question with utmost seriousness. 'Mam's still furious with you. She doesn't trust you.'

So, Anna's anger hadn't diminished, which was disappointing but valuable information. It just meant he'd need to work that bit harder.

'I know,' he tried to sound apologetic.

'Did you do something bad?' Evie whispered fearfully.

He hesitated and thought about the best way to phrase his response. 'I made your mam sad a long time ago.'

'And are you sorry?'

It was a straightforward question, but he paused long enough for Evie to repeat it.

'Yes.'

'Then why's Mam still mad?'

'She doesn't believe me,' he said truthfully.

The little girl turned to him and placed her arms on the table as if she was about to read the evening news. 'I'll give you some advice, Javier. If you apologise to Mam, you'd better be soul-sorry. As in, you must mean it. Believe me, I've learned that lesson the hard way.'

Wise words issued from such a young mouth was comical. How could he have forgotten about soul-sorry? How many times had she kicked off for his half-hearted apologies, saying not to bother because it was just as bad as lying? And after she'd stormed off, he'd track her down and apologise properly.

'You're right.' He tapped the table with both hands. 'I'll remember that next time. Do you like me, Evie?' Like a ventriloquist's dummy, the question popped out as if someone else was talking.

'Of course, why do you even need to ask?' she responded as if he was asking a pointless question. 'But if you ever did anything to upset Mam again or me, I'd tell Dad, and he'd sort you out. He'd never let anyone hurt us.'

He loved the straightforward childhood innocence and logic. If only everything were that simple. 'Yes, your dad said something like that to me when I first arrived.'

Evie lifted Elora with practised ease and started to bounce her up and down to squeals of delight. 'Did you know Mam saved Dad's life?'

Javier was sceptical, although Evie wasn't a deceitful child it sounded too fanciful. 'Really? How did she do that?'

'Well, this wasn't long after Mam arrived in Apokeri. There was this massive electrical storm one October afternoon and Dad got caught in it up at the huge southern Apokeri cliffs viewpoint. He turned to come home, but the ground gave way, and he slipped over the edge. Luckily, a tiny ledge broke his fall, but he was all alone and clung to tree roots for over an hour as the rain lashed down. When he didn't come home, Mam knew something was wrong because she's clever like that. And with Uncle Alex, a friend called Daniel who I've never met because he moved away before I was born and Cleo's mam, Cassie, they mounted a rescue operation. Mam abseiled down the cliffs to Dad, and the others hauled him back up first and then Mam. How cool is that!'

'Pretty cool,' he replied. 'I don't know many people who would be brave enough to do that.'

Evie gazed at Elora and then Javier with a faraway look. 'Mam saved me, Auntie Steffi and my cousin Leyla as well from a bad man. But I don't want to talk about that, because it was really scary.'

Javier felt the need to reassure the young girl. Something about her made him want to help. 'But he's not here,' he said. 'So, there's nothing to be scared about anymore.'

'Yes, you're right. Mam is always so brave. I'd like to think I'll be like that when I grow up. That I'd save my loved ones if they were in trouble.' She returned to entertain Elora as Javier threw the ball for two tireless dogs. 'I'm sorry your brother died.'

It was the last thing he expected to hear, and it floored him. He appraised the girl and wondered what went on inside her head.

'It's not always good to listen in on private conversations,' Javier pointed out, knowing he was a fine one to lecture about ethics and morals. Her eyes narrowed and a pout formed. 'I'm not telling you off,' he quickly replied and held up his hands in a sign of peace. 'But your parents' job is to protect you. They don't want to tell you sad things if they don't need to.'

Evie frowned and then nodded. 'That makes sense.' He appeared to be back in the good books again. 'Your brother will be watching over you, won't he? He'll be making sure you're safe and being good. That's what my Granda Robert does. It's nice to know that, isn't it?'

He muttered a non-committal response and fidgeted. Bobby had idolised him. What would his baby brother think of him now? Javier stood up so quickly that a startled Pesce shot into his basket and snuggled beside his blue-and-white striped toy cow.

'Aren't you waiting for Mam?'

'No … I-I best be going. But tell … tell your mam to drop me a line. I want to invite you all for paella one night. A thank-you for all your kindness.'

Evie clapped her hands. 'Thank you very much. How exciting, I can't wait to tell her.'

Chapter Forty

Javier took a sip of wine and put the finishing touches to his signature paella dish. He needed to re-establish trust with his guests – or at least the appearance. A week since he'd found Kristina's note and she still showed no outward signs of placing it there. And it was time to redouble his efforts with the Makris family. It was his grandmother's recipe. Anna had loved it and she knew that he always made it when he'd been in the wrong. Hopefully, she'd accept it as an admission of guilt for years gone by. There was going to be Kristina, Anna, Filip, himself and, the clincher, he'd insisted they bring the kids. Pay the little cherubs some attention, and parents lapped it up.

It was early July and a perfect evening to dine outdoors. With the patio garden in deep shade, Javier had opted to eat up on the rooftop terrace with its fantastic sea view and, hopefully, an amazing sunset. It was where he and Kristina gravitated to in the evenings. As darkness fell and the stars appeared, she transported him back in time with tales about her childhood.

He leaned against the kitchen worktop to wait and ridiculously had butterflies nervously flitting inside his stomach. It was almost seven when he heard Evie's rapid-fire chatter coming up the garden path and then the kitchen was packed with voices, laughter and dogs' claws tapping on tiles.

Anna retrieved Pesce from the larder, handed Javier a bottle of wine and kissed Kristina. 'I'm sorry, we've brought the dogs as well. Pesce is still grieving and can't be left, and it seemed cruel to bring him without Cleo.'

With multiple conversations going on, he needed to shout. 'Everything's set. Why don't you all head to the roof, and I'll bring everything up.'

Evie shot off with the dogs, keen to nab the best seats for her and Kristina. Filip handed Anna the baby carrier, and she disappeared.

The two husbands were left alone, but Javier had no concerns. He'd played poker with Filip for weeks and liked the guy's laid-back attitude and amusing take on life. However, the bloke looked tense with bags under his eyes, and Javier was sure he'd lost weight.

'How's Alex doing?'

Filip rubbed his face and gave a rueful smile. 'They successfully brought him out of his induced coma yesterday.'

'That's great news,' Javier replied brightly, attempting to inject positivity into the room.

'I know, that's what Anna said … I guess I'm just worried about what the specialists will discover. Alex always said he'd rather be dead than left a drooling vegetable. And that's what I'm worrying myself sick about. I don't know how Alex will cope if he's left with life-changing head injuries.'

Javier gave the paella one final prod. 'I don't know what to say except worrying won't change anything. Unfortunately, you can only be patient and let him know you're there for him. There's nothing else you can do.'

Filip picked up the tray containing bread and salad and nodded. 'You're right. Sorry to be a whinge. Anyway, enough sadness. Let's enjoy tonight. I can't wait to try that paella – it smells divine.'

***

The sun was slowly sinking, casting long shadows, and Javier extracted the last crispy grains of rice from the enormous pan and popped them in his mouth. 'Judging by the lack of leftovers, I'd say that was a success.'

'Hear hear,' everyone chorused and raised their glasses in appreciation.

The two dogs were curled in a patch of fast-vanishing sun, and Elora dozed peacefully in her baby seat. However, Evie was wide awake and demanding to hear stories about her mam.

Javier grinned at Anna, who narrowed her eyes in mock defiance. She was giving him the green light, and he leaned over to Evie. 'Do you know the first time I met your mum, she lied to me!'

'No!' Evie stared at her mother with utter shock. 'But, that's naughty, isn't it?'

Javier nodded solemnly. 'It most certainly is. Your mum told me she was eighteen when in fact she was only fifteen! Imagine that?'

Evie swung her head backwards and forwards between Javier and Anna, weighing up this new fact before reaching a decision. 'There must have been a good reason for Mam to lie because she's usually very honest.'

Anna kissed Evie and stuck her tongue out at Javier. 'Thank you, sweetheart. And there was a good reason. I didn't want to get your Aunt Julia into trouble.'

'Another one, another one,' Evie cried out.

Javier scratched his head for a few seconds. 'Okay, I've got one. I bet your mum has never told you about learning to drive?' Anna groaned and hid her face as Evie bounced about on her seat, waiting to hear the juicy details. 'It was a nightmare!' he began dramatically. 'Let's face it, your mother doesn't exactly like being told what to do—'

'Well said, that man!' Filip banged the table with his empty wine glass.

'Don't we know it!' Kristina butted in and drained her glass.

'Excuse me,' Anna interrupted. 'I'd like to defend my honour here. Evie, why don't you ask Javier about the Cornish surf school? When he refused to pay attention to the instructors because he thought he knew best and spent all lesson falling off the board. While I did listen and was catching waves by the end.'

'I think we should get back to the other story,' he responded, but his eyes had a mischievous glint.

'Ha!' Anna declared triumphantly. 'He doesn't like it when the shoe is on the other foot.'

Evie giggled at the verbal ping-pong, Filip smiled and Kristina deftly changed the subject. 'If you will indulge me, Javier. I might ask you to make that exceptional meal next month when Irina and Hugo visit. As great foodies, I'm willing to bet they've never tasted a better paella.'

'Oh yes,' Evie exclaimed. 'That'd be great. Will you, will you, Javier? In return, Aunt Rini can teach you how to punch properly – she's brilliant.'

Javier laughed. 'How could I refuse an offer like that? Irina sounds like an interesting character.'

'You'd better believe it,' Filip responded cryptically.

'Come on, Little Miss,' Kristina interrupted. 'Let's go down to the kitchen, and you can help me bring up that fantastic chocolate cake you've baked.'

***

The rooftop fairy lights flickered, the candles burned low and now and again Javier caught the scent of what little remained of the chocolate cake. Muffled chatter drifted up from the village below and in the background was a lullaby of gently lapping waves. Elora snuggled up to Anna, the dogs and Evie slept in a tangle of arms and legs on a sofa and Filip and Kristina snoozed in two chairs. Only Anna and Javier remained awake, reclining on respective sun loungers, looking up at a star-studded sky. They'd been chatting about life in Apokeri for the last thirty minutes. A nice safe topic.

Anna carefully stood and gently shushed Elora. 'I think it's time for us to make a move. Thank you for a wonderful evening. I haven't laughed that much in ages, and it's done Pip the world of good.'

'My pleasure.' He glanced over at her sleeping family. He didn't want her to go. 'Are you okay getting home?'

'Never fear,' she replied with a grin. 'Watch this. Cleo, Pesce – walkies.'

Both dogs leapt up, enthusiastically wagging their tails. She eased Elora into a baby harness, clipped it to her front, and then the baby's rucksack was slung over her back. With one hand she picked up the cot and with the other nudged her husband awake.

'Let's go, Sleeping Beauty. You need to piggyback Evie home.'

Javier held the rooftop door open and the Makris family trooped past. 'See you later.'

'Sleep tight,' Anna's voice drifted up from the stairwell. He closed the door and a few minutes later heard the garden gate click shut. It was late, he'd better wake Kristina up.

'Did you have a nice chat with Anna?' Kristina asked. She sat bright-eyed with the remaining slice of cake. The woman had never been asleep.

Chapter Forty-One

The laptop sat open on the dining-room table. The image of him at twenty-one and his ten-year-old brother mucking about on Llandudno beach stared back.

Kristina kissed him on the cheek. 'He looked like you.' She took a seat opposite with two mugs of coffee. 'Do you want to hear the next instalment?'

He slowly closed the lid. He needed cheering up. 'Yes please.'

She stirred her coffee. 'Now where were we?'

'You're seventeen and on the annual family holiday to that posh Greek island resort,' he immediately responded.

'Oh, yes.' Kristina straightened in her chair. 'Now, the year before, my childhood friendship with Adrian Andino had blossomed into something more.'

'Andino?' Javier interrupted.

'Yes, Stelios and Giannis' great-uncle. He was two years older than me. Oh my, I can still remember that firm, muscular tanned body. I'd run my fingers—'

'Kristina,' Javier exclaimed. 'You're making me blush.'

She laughed and the clear sound lifted his heart. The pair were secret lovers and in the intervening year, a steady stream of letters flowed between them with plans to marry and emigrate to Australia. For Kristina, it would be a new start and freedom from stifling upper-class constraints, parental pressures and expectations. From previous stories, Javier knew her father was a shrewd businessman from a family empire and had organised the marriages of his other two daughters to incredibly wealthy American and Swiss industrialists. But in this story, Javier discovered his youngest was earmarked for a different union – an old money marriage to access the upper echelons of society. Kristina was to marry the eldest son of an Italian duke. The very duke who owned the island they holidayed on. Kristina point-blank refused. Her first-class education had instilled self-confidence and an independent streak. She was going to marry for love. In response, her parents imprisoned Kristina in her hotel room. But in the dead of night, she fled. She climbed barefoot out the window of her third-floor prison, scrambled down an ivy-clad trellis and ran to a small rowing boat where Adrian awaited. It meant disownment, but she didn't care.

Javier gulped his coffee. 'Good for you, Kristina.'

However, Lars Nilssen wasn't giving up so easily. He ordered Adrian's father to return Kristina at once. She was to have a life with Italian nobility, not an inferior Greek fisherman. Of course, that only insulted Dimitri. His youngest son could marry whoever he wanted. The next tactic was to cut off the Andino family's source of income. The duke refused to do business with the family and would ensure nobody else on Lefkada did. But the tight-knit community stood united, forcing the duke to backtrack, and Kristina's family returned empty-handed to Sweden. Kristina moved in with Adrian's aunt and uncle and worked on their farm while he continued fishing. She was desperate to marry as soon as possible and offered to sell her gold necklace. But Adrian was proud and refused. Eventually, he had enough for the wedding and their passage to Australia and on a beautiful June evening, Adrian proposed with a ring of straw. He promised the proper ring would be on her finger by the end of the week but until then it was their delicious secret.

'Hooray, love won out!' Javier cheered but there was no returning smile.

The following morning, Adrian sailed out from Apokeri and was never seen alive again.

'No! What happened? Did the boat sink? Was there a storm out at sea?'

When Adrian failed to return, a search party went out and quickly located the anchored and undamaged boat bobbing about in one of his regular coves. But the wheelhouse was full of blood, evidence of a violent attack, and two days later, his body washed up on a beach south of Apokeri. He'd been bludgeoned to death. Kristina was inconsolable, convinced her father was behind it. Three days later a short telegram arrived. It expressed sorrow at Adrian's passing but her father expected Kristina to return home. She was to forget the unfortunate incident and make a far more suitable match.

Javier reached across the table and squeezed the hand of his tearful landlady. He was shell-shocked and unable to fathom how Kristina had found the strength to continue. 'How did you cope with your grief? How aren't you bitter and twisted?'

'Vengeance,' she whispered and winced at the word. 'I did something which at the time I deemed to be my right, but I wish with all my heart I could take it back.'

'What could possibly be worse than what happened to Adrian and you?'

'Probably this,' Kristina replied mournfully. 'I instructed Dimitri to dictate a response to my father. The letter stated that Lars Nilssen was held entirely responsible for the death of Adrian by his daughter, Kristina, and the Andino family. They never expected justice but knew Lars Nilssen had conspired with the duke to commit the horrific crime with the sole purpose of returning Kristina to Sweden, where she would be forced into the original arranged marriage. It then went on to say that on receipt of her father's telegram, his grief-stricken daughter sneaked to the beach and took her own life on the exact spot Adrian's battered body had washed ashore. Lars Nilssen had united both families in grieving the loss of their youngest child.'

'It serves him right!' Javier blustered. 'The man was a monster.'

Kristina stared off into the distance. 'What my father did was unforgivable. But I should never have claimed to be dead. Imagine what my sisters must have felt. I lobbed a hand grenade into my family hundreds of miles away with no consideration as to the consequences. That is also unforgivable.'

'You're a good woman, Kristina Nilssen.'

She squeezed his hand in response. 'And you can be a good man again. Good night, Javier. Rest well.'

He reopened the laptop and took one last look at the picture of Bobby and himself in a time when life made sense. He opened his emails to find one from Celeste. His dad continued to deteriorate. Javier dropped his head into his hands. Maybe he should go home. Perhaps it was time to make up with Bethan, and finally put things to bed. But then again, he opened up his bank accounts and experienced the familiar thrill of seeing all those digits. Money equalled power; it made the world turn, and – as his demon proudly declared – it felt so good, fleecing unsuspecting fools.

Chapter Forty-Two

Anna closed the kitchen door, cut through the car park and hit the steep track behind the house. It was before nine and, tightening the baby harness, she chatted away to Elora who recognised her name. There were no words yet but each day the little girl was finding her voice and chuntered away merrily. Anna was happy with Elora's progress even if they'd needed to take her to the doctor for slight wheezing which luckily had cleared up. After she'd laboured uphill, the track levelled off to reveal sweeping views of the sea and Tharesseti. The pleasant breeze ruffled her hair and two seabirds glided by. The track ran close to the edge and she peered down on a warren of back streets and everywhere there were flowers and greenery. She loved the village, her home. A proud Geordie still but she had no desire to move back.

The local bus was leaving, early beach lovers set up their sun loungers, charter boats geared up for another day, sleek yachts remained in no hurry to go anywhere, and a few people picked up early morning supplies. And on the air, a slight trace of freshly made bread from her father-in-law's bakery. The dirt track continued along the ridge, and she could spy into the gardens of the larger houses behind the church, view her own Apokeri Apartments and the tiny figure of Kristina setting up an easel on the rooftop terrace. And that was Anna's destination. But she was in no hurry as Pip, Evie and the dogs would be gone for hours.

***

After Penelope cooed over Elora, Anna climbed up to the rooftop with two mugs of coffee. Kristina never refused one and Anna desperately needed caffeine. For months, sleep had been a distant memory. Javier's appearance heralded the return of her realistic dreams, which materialised in times of stress. Night after night she'd frantically shout, jump out of bed or sleepwalk. Luckily, she hadn't got any further than the bedroom door. Elora's arrival had reduced the number of night terrors but only because Anna was often up tending to the little girl.

'Good grief,' Kristina exclaimed when she saw Anna. 'You look rough. Another bad night by any chance?'

'Don't worry. I feel much worse. I could sleep for a year.' She dutifully slathered more suntan lotion on Elora before plopping her on the playmat to roll about gleefully.

'I thought you might turn up this morning,' Kristina said as she sketched the outline of the horizon. 'To check up on Javier.'

Anna gratefully took a sip of coffee. 'Nice to know I'm so transparent.'

'Not all the time, my dear. You'll be pleased to hear that we made a breakthrough last night. He's definitely finding his conscience. I'm confident he'll get there soon.' Anna snorted. 'I thought you had a lovely evening?' Kristina probed.

'I-I did, but—'

'And didn't you agree to give him a second chance?' her friend persisted.

'I did give him a second chance,' Anna snapped. 'While he happily snooped in the office, the gallery and – although I've got no proof – in your house.'

'Yes, but you agreed to overlook that because any change in him is going to take time.'

'That's not the point,' Anna said with mounting frustration. She'd promised not to vent to Pip but had made no such promise to Kristina. 'Everyone thinks he's great. I'm the only one who knows what he's really like. Even Agnes thinks he's wonderful because he's tall, dark and handsome and bears more than a passing resemblance to her husband.'

'That's a rather bitchy thing to say, don't you think?' Kristina calmly responded. 'Do you honestly believe Agnes can be fooled so easily?'

'No, of course I don't!' Anna battled to get her anger under control. 'It's just Javier still pushes my buttons after all this time.'

Kristina bent to hand Elora a squidgy building block and then sat next to Anna. 'Well, past lovers tend to do that.'

Anna choked on her coffee. 'I don't know what you mean.' The response was a withering stare that resulted in a mumbled apology.

'I might be in my nineties, but I'm no fool. The level of animosity you have towards him, the way you talk to one another and last night those stories you traded – she jabbed a finger at Anna – that's more than friendship.'

Anna stared off into the distance because it was easier than admitting the truth eye to eye. 'He's my ex-husband and my first love. And I have so much pent-up rage towards him for what he did – I can't control it. I think I've got it contained but then it explodes out of me. And … I don't know what to do. It's driving me up the wall. I'm so angry because everyone loves him and I want to scream out loud that he's a manipulator and a betrayer but then I want to keep quiet and let him be the amazing person I know he was.' Elora called out as she desperately stretched forwards. Dragging a hand under her nose, Anna reached down and cuddled the distressed child. 'I'm sorry, baby. It's okay; everything's going to be okay.'

'Why don't you tell me how you met?' Kristina asked and rubbed Anna's knee.

'I don't want to.'

'It would help me understand.'

Anna looked over the rooftop, over the sea and back to a dreary October evening in Newcastle. Julia was a second-year student at Northumbria University and after months of continually badgering had eventually caved. Anna and Annalise were allowed to tag along to the Students Union with two provisos – no alcohol and no fake IDs. If they got in, great. And if not, they went home. Anna wasn't bothered about drinking. She only wanted to dance. And for an hour that's exactly what she did. But then during a particularly energetic song, her arm connected with a pint glass and emptied the entire contents over the most gorgeous man she had ever seen. She stood gawping as the beer dripped down his face and waited for the explosion. Except, he winked and said it served him right for bringing a drink onto the dancefloor. And by some miracle she'd managed to grin back and said it was if he stood anywhere near her. He'd grabbed her hand and pulled her to the bar and asked what she wanted to drink. On strict orders from Julia, she'd asked for a Diet Coke and for the rest of the night they'd chatted, laughed and danced. At the end of the night, he asked for her number and she reeled it off thinking he'd never ring, not when he could have any girl he wanted. But he did.

'And what happened then?' Kristina probed.

Over the next few weeks, they went out on dates and he was always the gentleman. Up till then she'd never been particularly interested in boys. The ones at school were immature, annoying or mates and the ones at her part-time job were intimidating, pushy or ignored her. But Javier was different. It was a cliché but the moment she saw him it was like being struck by lightning. She counted down the minutes until she saw him again and lit up like a Christmas tree in his presence. On each date, Anna swore she was going to tell him the truth but every time she bottled it, afraid he'd refuse to see her. And then in December her year group attended a careers fair and he was at the final stall her group visited. His face when he clapped eyes on her in a school uniform was a mixture of outrage, shock and fear but he held it together and then vanished. For the rest of the day, she'd frantically rung his mobile and left countless messages with no response. She'd blown it. The school day finished and after a catch-up with a teacher, she trudged home along a deserted, rain-soaked cycle track. Quick footsteps came up behind but instead of overtaking they stopped. She turned and there he was. Her heart was pounding, and she burst out crying and sobbed about how sorry she was. He nodded to his car and told her to get in. They drove in absolute silence to the same beachside car park from their first date. Without the engine running, the rain pounding on the roof was almost deafening and she'd strained to hear his shaking voice. 'Have you any idea what you have done? Have you any idea how much trouble you could have caused? You lied to me. You said you were eighteen and at uni. How old are you really?' The shame and guilt were horrific as she admitted to turning sixteen the week before. He sat with his head in his hands for what seemed like forever before looking up and telling her never to lie to him again.

'And do you know what,' Anna explained. 'I never did. He asked if I cared about him and I said, "Yes, I love you." And he responded, "Good, because I love you too." We were a couple from then on, despite my parents forbidding me from seeing him, despite my dad, God rest his soul, threatening to call the police if Javier came anywhere near me. It forced us to keep our relationship secret until the day I turned eighteen. I moved in with him and my parents broke all contact with me.'

'And then what?' Kristina asked as Anna placed a squirming Elora back on her playmat to rock backwards and forwards on hands and knees before sitting down and sticking a teething ring in her mouth.

'We married a few months later and spent nearly three years travelling until …'

'Until what, Anna?'

Her breathing was fast and shallow. All the pain, hurt, humiliation and anger. It seethed inside. It was building and burst out. 'I went on a day trip. It was in Peru, high up in the Andes. I got back to the hostel. Our room was empty. I thought we'd been robbed. I went to Reception to find a guy there. He'd been on the same trip as me and was reporting he'd been burgled. But neither of us had. His girlfriend had vanished with my husband. They'd taken everything from our rooms and emptied our joint bank accounts. I never thought I'd recover from what he did and I refused to respond when he emailed, so he posted the divorce papers to my parents, who didn't know we were even married.

They got in touch with me pretty fast after that and even though we started talking it caused years of bad blood between my dad and me.'

Kristina interlaced her fingers. 'If I am not mistaken, what you are saying is that if you'd responded to Javier, he could have sent you the divorce papers and your parents would have been none the wiser.'

Anna opened her mouth but nothing came out.

'And by sending those papers he reunited you with your parents. And did your dad not apologise before your wedding to Filip and you then went on to have a great relationship before he passed away last year?'

And still, Anna couldn't find the words.

'And finally, who lied first – you or Javier?'

'I thought you'd be on my side,' Anna shrieked, on the verge of tears.

'I'm not *not* on your side,' Kristina pointed out. 'And you still haven't answered my question.'

'Me, I lied first. Okay, does that make you feel better?'

'And he forgave you.'

'I wish he never had, and none of this would've happened,' Anna retorted. Why was Kristina being so mean?

'You can't undo the past, Anna. All you can do is learn from it.'

'Well, maybe I don't want to!'

Kristina raised her eyebrows. 'Childish and bitchy in one visit! I am honoured.'

'Are you enjoying my misery?' Anna bit back. She couldn't believe how unfeeling her friend was being.

'Sweetheart, I never enjoy watching you suffer. But I'm doing the same to you that I'm doing to Javier. I'm holding up a mirror so you can understand that you must let the past go. I know you don't like what I'm saying, and you think I'm being a bitch, but you cannot bottle all this anger up inside, Anna. It's not healthy.

And believe me I've been around long enough to know what I'm talking about.'

Anna sat quietly for a few minutes. It was true, she didn't like what she'd heard but that didn't mean Kristina was wrong. It also didn't mean she was right either. Reason and emotion strove to gain the upper hand. 'I'm trying.' It was the best she could do for now.

'I know.' Kristina hugged her younger friend. 'But no more checking up on Javier, agreed?'

'Agreed,' Anna responded, and another bit of land crumbled into the sea. She now stood alone on a thin pinnacle of rock, defiantly resisting Javier's charm whilst everyone else she loved patted him on the back as he laughed at their stupidity.

***

She stomped up the hill, angrily swatting away annoying insects and slumped down on Kristina's beautiful oak-carved bench. It had stood proud on the northern Apokeri cliffs for over twelve years, a welcome relief for the less fit.

Anna tickled Elora. 'You believe me, don't you?'

The little girl giggled and tried to grab Anna's prescription sunglasses.

Instead of being angry, Anna laughed at the utter ridiculousness of what she was doing. Was she really that desperate to ask the opinion of a seven-month-old baby who couldn't talk yet? What did she hope to achieve? Elora would stroke her chin, pondering the question and then fix Anna with a knowing look and declare, 'Well, yes, after careful consideration I do believe you make a valid point.' Anna laughed out loud again and when she looked up the sky seemed clearer and the sun shone that bit brighter. She slapped her knees and Elora bounced up and down, kicking her legs with excitement.

'Come on, sweetheart, let's go and have an adventure.'

The track dipped steeply to become a tunnel between thick tangles of scrub, before coming up and out into the sunshine. The crosswind caught them but only for a moment and then the track dropped again into dense vegetation. It blocked all sounds except their breathing. The undulating track passed a thicket of wild olive trees and a long stretch of brambles that eagerly tried to tickle her bare legs. And then she took a left onto a faint goat track that plunged past hawthorn bushes, between pine trees, and under a canopy of flowering wild roses. She breathed in their heady perfume as the track clung to the cliffside. She was forced to unclip Elora and the rucksack to squeeze between two huge boulders hidden by dense foliage. Entering a dry, narrow gully she fished out a head torch before temporarily clipping the harness and rucksack back in place. With hands against the walls, she carefully picked her way over rocks until the torch highlighted a narrow chink on the right. It was a tight shimmy but holding Elora in one hand and the rucksack in the other they were eventually inside her fairy grotto. Beautiful stalactites hung suspended from the ceiling, and dozens upon dozens of elegant stalagmites rose from the smooth floor. In many places, the two met to form elaborate columns and everything was dappled in soft light filtering through a gap in the cave's ceiling. A tiny patch of blue sky poked between gigantic ferns, slick from a narrow waterfall plunging into a crystal-clear thermal spring. To Anna's knowledge it remained a geological anomaly. She knew of no others nearby.

Apart from Elora, Anna had only brought Evie as a baby and nobody else. She'd never even told Pip. It was the only secret she kept from him and for good reason. She'd been shown the wondrous cave by Evie's real father (and remained convinced it was where Evie was conceived) who her husband could no longer abide. It hadn't always been that way. But Daniel went down in Pip's estimation the moment he departed Apokeri with no indication he was ever coming back. When Daniel eventually wrote to Kristina ten months later to say he was married and soon to be a father, Pip's feelings turned to disgust and loathing. Initially, the news of Daniel's marriage and impending fatherhood devastated Anna. She'd refused to contact Daniel in Australia to tell him about her pregnancy because she didn't want to trap him, knowing he didn't want kids and yearned to be free to travel the world. But to find out he'd replaced her so quickly was soul-destroying, and for a time Anna also despised him. However, as time passed her feelings mellowed and despite everything, she loved him, yearned for him and cherished the few passion-filled weeks they'd had together. And that's why she couldn't tell Pip about the cave, because he'd destroy her precious memories. On their very last morning together, Daniel had lit the cave with dozens of tealights and in the flickering light, they'd waltzed together to 'He/She Danced with Me' from her favourite musical *The Slipper and The Rose*. And when she watched the *Cinderella* story and danced around the living room with their daughter, she imagined what might have been if he'd never left.

Anna slid her legs into the warm bubbling water and cuddled Elora. Why could she forgive Daniel far more easily than she could Javier? Her ex-husband had pledged to be with her 'till death do us part' and she'd loved Daniel despite knowing he was always going to leave. And that was the difference. Javier had broken a solemn promise, but Daniel hadn't. And wasn't that the most ironic thing of all? She continued to rant about Javier's deceit while projecting the illusion of a perfect marriage to not only support Pip's web of lies but to hide the identity of her daughter's real father. No wonder Pip was so worried about what would happen if and when Alex recovered. But that was a whole other problem, for another day. For now, Anna was going to enjoy her time alone with Elora. No matter what happened, her main priority was to keep her little family safe, regardless of the emotional cost to herself.

Chapter Forty-Three

While Anna Makris contemplated the state of her life, Javier Owens was doing likewise. He was currently on the deck of a superyacht serving drinks. Agnes Benrubi's team were providing all-day catering for some fabulously wealthy individual. As usual, Javier had already received several X-rated proposals from various guests, both male and female. As he flirted with a very attractive lawyer in her fifties, he wondered if he should go back to his tried and tested technique of slipping between the bedsheets whilst sliding out all the money from their bank accounts – but his heart was no longer in it. As he eavesdropped on the vacuous posturing, pompous conversations and increasingly ludicrous bragging, nausea washed over him. No matter how much money these people had it would never be enough. With a curt nod, he excused himself and undoubtedly offended the successful prosecutor. He went to refill the empty drinks tray. What the hell was he doing with his life? Was this how he wanted to end up? So far up his own backside, he'd need a periscope to see. With replenished champagne glasses he ventured outside and activated his auto-charm button but inside there was nothing. As the multi-million-pound craft slid past Tharesseti, Javier noticed a fishing boat chugging merrily by. And after months of grasping for the memory, it was there. He finally remembered where he'd heard the island's name. It was the bedtime whispering of one of his many conquests retelling a Shakespearean family tragedy. A great-great aunt from Stockholm had escaped an arranged marriage by clambering out a third-floor window on Tharesseti to elope with a local fisherman. But after he was killed, she took her own life aged barely eighteen.

Javier studied Tharesseti's rocky shore. Its dense vegetation blocked prying eyes from glimpsing the sumptuous hotel and its manicured grounds. He imagined a moon-lit night and a young

Kristina scrambling down that rickety trellis to safety, scratching and catching herself on rose thorns, stealing glances up at the windows as she hugged the stone terraces and then making a break across open ground to the cover of trees, picking her way across boulders to reach her lover and the safety of his boat. In all her stories, Kristina had never mentioned the name of the island, but it made perfect sense. And for the first time in as long as he could remember, Javier was excited – and not because he was about to rip someone off but because he was going to help them.

On autopilot, he handed out drinks and engaged in banal small talk while scrolling through his memory bank. His storyteller was from upstate New York. Did that mean Kristina might have living relatives? What if he could trace them? Maybe, just maybe, her two sisters might still be alive? It was a long shot but perhaps if Kristina could meet them or at least talk to them, it would help ease his friend's guilt for misleading her family so many years ago. He could remember the names of the two sisters so that was a start. He grinned from ear to ear, at long last he had a purpose again – to secretly track down Kristina's long-lost family and present her with his results. He stole a glance at his watch as the excitement bubbled up inside. There was a resounding splash as he cast his demon overboard.

As soon as he got off the boat, he would commence Operation Nilssen.

Chapter Forty-Four

With bath and bedtime routines completed, Anna gratefully sank into the sofa to enjoy a cuppa and gloried in the silence of the house. It was broken with the tip-tapping of claws. As if by some sixth sense, Pesce and Cleo knew she was available and both dogs took a flying leap through the air to land on either side. As they spun around and got comfy, her mobile buzzed. She swiped and beamed at Annalise Burn whose Geordie accent was long gone, replaced by what could only be described as posh American. Everyone now thought her childhood friend came from old Boston money and not an everyday street a few miles outside Newcastle.

'Yo-yo girlfriend. You're looking mighty fine as always, bookended by your furry friends.' Annalise tore into a cheese salad sandwich. 'Sorry, it's my lunch break and I'm so hungry I couldn't wait. I've been here since seven and haven't come up for air till now. How's it going with the husbands?'

Anna frowned. 'You work too hard, petal.' The usual comment was waved away as Annalise continued to demolish her food. 'The current one's doing okay. He's currently upstairs talking to Alex's parents. Alex is being transferred to a state-of-the-art rehab facility in Thessaloniki.'

'That's fantastic, and it's where his parents live. That'll be so much easier for them,' Annalise managed between mouthfuls.

'I know, and once Alex is further down the road to recovery, I'll suggest Pip goes to visit him which will help them both.' Anna chewed her lower lip. 'Pip is putting on a brave front but he's so worried. And when it comes to the ex, I'm alone in believing he's up to no good.'

It was meant to sound light-hearted, but the words were laced with bitterness and Annalise straightened. 'Feel free to rant. You've heard me do it often enough.' For the next ten minutes,

Anna railed against everyone to the accompaniment of encouraging nods and murmurings of agreement. 'Hell girl, hold a grudge I say. The guy was an asshole, and what I'm about to say might help your cause.' Annalise threw a crumpled napkin into the bin. 'Yours truly has been given a temporary additional string to the fifteen bows she already has – Historical Customer Delight Facilitator.'

Anna burst out laughing. 'What the hell is that when it's at home?'

'I know. Who comes up with these names?' She grimaced. 'Like I don't already have a mountain of crap to wade through. Anyway, I answer any query about the company's history and you'd be amazed how many we get. The last bloke quit with immediate effect, so I've been drafted in and judging by his backlog I don't think he ever answered a query. But enough of my whingeing. This might be nothing but I had an enquiry into the founding family. It's all public record so nothing they couldn't get from a library. Anyway, it turns out the bloke was some fabulously rich industrialist called Barclay Rodgerson III who married a young wealthy Swedish socialite by the name of Birgitta Nilssen.'

'Okay. Do you know how old Birgitta was when she married?'

'I can do better than that. She was born in Stockholm to Lars and Margareta Nilssen. And was married aged eighteen. She died a few years back aged eighty-one. And it got me thinking, was she a relation of Kristina? According to the web, Nilsson – with the letter "o" – is the fourth most popular surname in Sweden but Nilssen – with an "e" – doesn't appear in the top 100, so perhaps it is unusual?'

'I'm not sure. Maybe.' It was sad that Birgitta was dead. Anna knew she was Kristina's sister, but was unable to admit it. She'd given a promise over ten years ago to Evie's father. She felt awful lying to her best mate. It was another one to add to her list of secrets.

'Anyway, that's not why I'm ringing,' Annalise interrupted her friend's self-recriminations. 'It's about the person who made the email enquiry. What I'm telling you is in the strictest confidence so you didn't hear this from me, but the bloke called himself Patrick O'Donnellan and said he was helping a friend with her family tree. I asked if she was American and he said no, an older Swedish lady. It wasn't till afterwards I started thinking could the bloke be Javier? Maybe it's a coincidence but he turns up in Apokeri, you're worried he's up to no good, he's lodging with Kristina and a few weeks later this query pops through. I'm probably being paranoid and I've no idea why he'd want the information but I thought it best to tell you.'

'Thanks, Annalise you're a star. Out of interest—'

'I know what you're going to ask, and don't worry – all enquiries come through a generic email address. And with it being an alleged temporary role I haven't bothered to update the email signature. Patrick thinks he's been conversing with a Brant Anderson-Smith.'

After promising to inform Annalise of her findings and a general chit-chat, Anna hung up. She scrolled through her contacts whilst alternatively stroking the snoozing dogs. It was time to find out what Irina could uncover. Anna grinned wickedly. This was it, the chance she'd been waiting for. She was about to delve into the murky world of Javier Owens and finally receive the proof that she was right and he was deceiving everyone.

Chapter Forty-Five

The last few weeks hadn't been enjoyable, with a revolving door of partners. He hadn't gelled with any of them – too young, too old, too arrogant, too blasé, too talkative, too messy, the list went on and on. It was like the bad old days when nobody wanted to work with him. Until Sergio. He missed the banter. The guy had been a first-rate killer and knowing that Dominique had triple-checked every assignment was a godsend. For over six years their unit had worked perfectly. But now Hector frowned as he pressed the intercom and the security gates slowly slid open. The last job had almost ended in disaster. The intel was crap, his partner was an idiot and they'd been forced to hastily improvise. Something he hated doing. The job got done in the end, but he'd made his displeasure known. At this rate, he'd be running out of people to work with.

He nodded to his aunt when she opened the door and there was less of a spring in his step as he made his way through the maze of corridors. The person who said crime didn't pay had never been inside this lavish mansion. He knocked and wondered what he'd find on the other side of the door. Happily, the boss was back to his dapper self in a perfectly pressed two-piece suit, crisp white shirt and checked tie.

'Delighted to see you, Hector.' Francis beamed and signalled for him to sit down. 'Good work the other day. Despite everything. And you'll be pleased to know there'll be no more problems when you get back.'

'Back from where, boss?'

Francis settled into his chair and savoured his coffee. 'I know the last few weeks haven't been ideal for you. Therefore, a change of scenery will do you the world of good.'

A key operative in a lucrative four-year operation had managed to have a bit too much fun with the product they were trafficking and ended up dead. Luckily, an additional and more sustainable transport route had been secured. Everything was in place and things were proceeding well. And in the interest of thoroughness, Hector was to go over and ensure the latest operative was made fully aware that failure was not an option.

'And the other business?' Hector asked.

He'd carried out his instructions regarding Toni, but the deed had failed to change anything. Weeks later the Castellas were nowhere to be found. It was as if they'd dropped off the face of the earth. A quiet road outside Lucerne was their last known whereabouts. After that, the trail went cold.

Francis carefully placed his fine china cup on its saucer and spoke in a measured tone. 'I cannot deny this unresolved issue continues to irritate me. However, I believe fate will deliver what I deserve.' Hector nodded and took the envelope containing all the details. He would read it later as his boss was in a rather talkative mood for a change. 'You're heading to a beautiful part of the world, they tell me. A quaint little Greek fishing village on Lefkada, and you'll be staying in nice, low-key accommodation. One of your contacts owns a boat so take the opportunity to mix business with pleasure.'

Hector thanked his boss. He'd heard good things about the island's fishing and was looking forward to the trip. He needed a holiday.

Chapter Forty-Six

Anna was on edge. Her nerves were frayed, her emotions fraught. And the cause – Javier. He'd been in Apokeri for months now and she was no closer to figuring out her ex. She'd initially done some sleuthing when he arrived which confirmed the truth about his family and that he'd been living in South East Asia and flown out of Bangkok. Irina was still digging and had so far reported back that, according to his bank account, Javier was skint. And his history showed he'd sent significant sums through to his mother, sisters and an armed forces bereavement charity.

'Evie,' Anna bellowed up the stairs. 'Why is this kitchen still a pigsty and the washing machine silent?'

Above her the bedroom door slammed, followed by stomping footsteps. Evie stropped into the kitchen with a basket full of dirty clothes and began shoving them into the washing machine.

'Keep your hair on, Mam. What's the rush?'

'What do you think you're doing?' Anna said.

'I'd have thought that was pretty obvious.'

'Less of the sarcasm, young lady. Are you doing it the way you've been shown? Or are you loading red shorts in with white T-shirts and black underwear?'

Evie yanked out all the clothes and tossed them on the floor. 'Some of my friends don't do any housework, they have cleaners,' she muttered angrily.

'But most do help their parents,' Anna retorted. 'Like your cousin, Leyla. And the quicker you complete your chores, the quicker we can have some fun.'

'Yeah right. Like what?'

Anna took a deep breath and counted to three. 'I thought we could walk along the prom with Elora and the dogs and then visit Nana and Granda.'

Evie rolled her eyes and sighed dramatically. 'Boring, snoring. We've done that twice already this week.'

'Fine then. If you don't want an Aphrodite ice cream, it's no skin off my nose.'

In a flash her daughter separated the washing into three neat piles, loaded the darks, started the machine, whipped around the kitchen (tidying as she went), clipped leads on the dogs and grabbed the baby harness from its hook.

'Howay, Mam,' she declared, impatiently tapping her foot. 'What are you waiting for? There's a Knickerbocker Glory with my name on it.'

Anna laughed. Evie had a knack for making things better. 'Come on, Cinderella. Let's go.'

Chapter Forty-Seven

Javier walked out of the gallery and sank onto the bus-stop bench. He closed his eyes and hoped the sun could work some magic. It didn't. His iron-clad calm composure had deserted him. He was no longer certain what he should be doing.

The local bus pulled up and a group of passengers disembarked. He nodded at some of the villagers who gave him a wave or a smile. Everybody had welcomed him with open arms. Except the most important one. At the start, it was expected. But months on and she was still refusing to submit to his charm offensive. It was driving him around the bend. Sometimes he made headway, like at last month's paella meal. She'd been encouraged by Evie to dish the dirt on Javier and entertained them with amusing stories at his expense. He'd forgotten some of them and laughed with everyone else. She was witty and he'd forgotten that as well. Anna, Filip and Kristina bounced off one another. They were close and he'd enjoyed being in their gang.

That night was the closest he'd got to recapturing his Anna. She'd smiled at him the way he remembered. As if she had a secret only he knew. They'd had a lovely evening and chatted long after the kids zonked out. But it had been fleeting and the next day her emotional shutters were back up. It was infuriating because, to the casual observer, she maintained the illusion of an old friend, more than happy to help. But to him, she warily held him at arm's length. He was a squirming, vicious octopus that could strike with a bone-crunching beak at any moment.

He quickly brushed away tears and checked to make sure nobody had seen. It was fine, the world was going about its business. Nobody cared about him. He stretched his long legs and tried to relax. The whole point of coming to Apokeri was to scam his ex-wife and anyone else for that matter before clearing out. But all he'd accomplished was to fall in love with the village and grow attached to its inhabitants. That hadn't been the plan. He fidgeted and sat back up.

What the hell did he want?

It was becoming increasingly difficult to answer that truthfully. He didn't know whether to laugh or continue crying. He'd spent the last fifteen years deceiving others. So much so that he could easily deceive himself.

The rewiring job was almost finished and he'd had plenty of offers for similar work. Steffi's husband, Andrew, had plenty of Lefkada contacts and was keen to discuss a possible partnership. And Agnes had also brought up the idea of bringing him into the business at a senior level. If he wanted to make a decent legitimate living in Apokeri it was there. And if he wanted to make a dubious living that was also possible. He knew what lay on the seabed and how it was moved on. But Giannis said there were other more lucrative avenues opening up and wanted to chat about them later.

And what if he did stay, could that possibly work?

A Greek family walked past him and studied the bus timetable. The father looked to be his age and the wife a few years younger. The son could have been classmates with Evie and gleefully informed his younger sister there was plenty of time to get ice cream before the next bus. They all trooped off happy. Javier sighed. If things had been different that might have been him, Anna and their kids. He abruptly terminated the fantasy. They were occurring with alarming regularity.

Maybe it was time to go home and face reality. But he was making real progress tracing Kristina's family. The person at the bank had been so helpful. He'd almost used his real name but that was a step too far. He didn't want to leave a paper trail. It was enormously satisfying to think after all these years he could bring some closure to his new friend.

Javier sunk lower on the bench. Maybe he could just crawl under a rock and hide from the truth. Before arriving in Apokeri, when was the last time he'd had a true friend? But he knew the pitiful answer. His last true friend had been Anna.

He looked over to the harbour and the pontoons, installed a few years back, with all the fancy boats. The Andino dive boat moored up and its day-trippers disembarked. Another group of satisfied customers it seemed. The new Italian dive master got on well with the rest of the crew and Javier now did some of the less technical dives. The final straggler walked down the gangplank dressed in beige, an unassuming man who reminded Javier of his former geography teacher. He didn't look the type to do anything as adventurous as diving and was standing on the quayside having an in-depth conversation with Giannis and Stelios. The brothers looked nervous, and Javier sat up a bit straighter, his interest piqued. The Andinos were immensely self-assured, often tipping into cocky arrogance.

Petre Zagrokis was with them, a strutting peacock dressed in fine clothes and determined to make a good impression. Even from where he sat, Javier could see the bloke's fawning behaviour. When Mr Beige motioned for Petre to join him, the young man looked fit to burst. As the two men walked along the promenade, Javier found himself irresistibly drawn to follow them.

The early evening sun basked Apokeri in a golden glow as Javier casually stood up. There were plenty of people milling about – strolling along the street, browsing in shops, coming off the beach, heading back to their accommodation or deciding on where to eat for tea. The two men were none the wiser as they crossed in front of Aphrodite Café and headed up towards the pedestrianised square.

Javier spied Anna sitting with her brood at one of the outside tables and doffed his baseball cap to a delighted Evie who gave a royal wave with her long ice-cream-sundae spoon. A dollop of cream sailed through the air, right into the wide-open mouth of Pesce. A cheer and round of applause went up from the table.

Leaving them behind, Javier scanned the square, past the wrinkled men playing dominos, past the loved-up couples sitting under the plane trees and past the large audience enjoying a group of juggling buskers. The two men bypassed the busy Apollo restaurant and the church. Javier hurried to catch up. It would be far too easy to lose them in the baffling maze of backstreets.

Over the years, bars, restaurants and boutique shops had sprung up amongst the narrow alleyways. Javier still got lost in them with their frothy flowers spilling out of window boxes, vines winding their way up and over stone walls and gnarled trees that managed to push their roots down into unimaginably small gaps and stretch branches up to the sky. But he didn't have far to go. The pair chose a cosy tapas restaurant. Javier walked by and then doubled back to take up a position outside the adjoining café. All that separated them was a trellis smothered in roses and clematis.

The men talked over coffee, ouzo and food that had Javier drooling. He'd walked out with only the change in his pockets so had only enough for still water which he sipped slowly. Even though he was close enough to smell Petre's aftershave, the men kept their voices so low it was impossible to hear anything. Through the leaves, Javier determined some sort of deal was being struck. Mr Beige was definitely in charge and Petre was a puppy dog, eager to please his new master. After half an hour, Javier was beginning to wonder how long he could eke out a five hundred millilitre bottle when Petre glanced at his watch, seemed to apologise and signalled for the bill. His companion waved the gesture aside, pulled out a photograph and passed it across. It was done in a resigned fashion, like those who hand out flyers and know they'll be cast aside around the corner. However, the man struck gold as Petre gabbled away excitedly. The other man's face remained impassive. He pointed at the photo and said something. In his excitement, Petre's voice rose enough for Javier to hear him. 'Definitely, one hundred per cent positive it's them.' Only after Petre vanished did the bland geography teacher's mask slip, revealing a sadistic smile as the man cracked his knuckles with relish. Javier shuddered; he didn't fancy being in the shoes of whoever was in the photo when Mr Beige caught up with them.

Chapter Forty-Eight

It was almost lunchtime, but Jace had no stomach for food. The kitchen table was strewn with notes and he stared at his open laptop. What a mess. He was no closer to solving who'd dumped Mia, who'd almost killed Alex or to finding the Castellas. At least Elora and Pesce were safe. Everyone had bought the official story of a young mother dumping the two at Anna's. And the powers that be only remained unhappy at his lack of progress (and not furious) because luckily no tourists were involved.

Jace knocked back his cold coffee in disgust. God forbid it was only the island's workers and a couple of mafiosi who were dead, hospitalised or missing. He brought up the interview notes with Alex Panagos from last week. The man had been transferred at his parents' request to a Thessaloniki facility for brain rehabilitation and had finally been deemed fit enough for questioning.

He rubbed his gritty eyes. He'd been staring at the screen too long. The interview had thankfully been done remotely as it was of little help. All Alex could remember was the gunning of a powerful engine before a dark green four-by-four with tinted windows blasted around the bend. It had been in the middle of the road, as was he. The car had desperately swerved to miss him and almost succeeded. The most interesting piece of information was Alex being convinced the car was deliberately heading for the cliff edge. But no vehicles matching his description had been reported missing. Jace had a hunch the unseen driver and passenger were the Castellas, based on their harrowing note to Anna. He'd requested a Special Forces Diving Unit to search the seabed below the cliffs. His supervisors turned him down flat and said they weren't going to expend time, money and resources to confirm the death of two Italian lowlifes. So Jace was still no further forward.

His mobile began to vibrate. Please let it be good news. It wasn't. In less than three minutes he'd blasted up the steep Apokeri road and had already issued an immediate all-unit response with sirens. He wanted whoever it was to know they were coming.

The message from an unknown number had been short and far from sweet.

Tinto Zagrokis life in danger. At his house. Come now. Do not enter alone. Not a hoax. He will be dead if you fail to arrive.

Jace was taking no chances and floored the accelerator. He was coming from Apokeri and the others from Lefkada Town. The mountainous inland roads were torturous but thankfully quiet. He rounded a bend and slammed on the anchors. This was not happening. Up ahead chugged an ancient tractor driven by Old Father Time. There was no room to get past so Jace brayed on the horn. Eventually, the rickety vehicle pulled into the first available gap and waved him through. Time was slipping away. His mobile kept beeping and messages flashed up.

Where the hell are you?
You're going to be too late
Help him!

As promised, the main gates stood open and Jace did a handbrake turn off the main road, following just metres behind Henri's bumper. Another police car turned into the driveway directly behind him and in the rear-view mirror another shot past, heading for the lower-level gate. All three cars screeched to a halt, but Jace was the first one to lead the charge into the house.

Jace was glad he hadn't eaten as he looked upon Tinto Zagrokis. The face was a bloody pulp – barely recognisable from the smiling one he'd chatted to at the party. Tracks of cigarette burns ran along both arms. His wrists were cut from fighting against thin metal wire tying him to a chair. The same wire had been used to tie his legs. He was a terrible sight and must have endured absolute agony. Jace felt for a pulse. Thank God, he was still alive.

'Mr Zagrokis, can you hear me? This is Inspector Marinos with police backup.'

There was a groan. Jace suspected the man's jaw was broken. In the next moment, two officers bounded up the poolside steps and charged into the lounge.

'All clear, boss. No sign of anyone or any other vehicle down at the cottage.'

'Good. Do a sweep of the house and then the grounds.'

'On it.'

The pair disappeared, to join two other officers.

Henri returned from the lower ground floor. 'There's nothing down there. No signs of forced entry.'

'Thanks. We'll need to do a full search. I'm not expecting to find anything though.'

'We need to find the bastard who did this,' Henri replied. 'Tinto's a good bloke.'

The paramedics arrived and carefully transferred the broken and bloody patient onto a stretcher as a commotion broke out in the foyer. Jace heard the conceited voice of Petre. Brilliant, just what he needed.

The younger brother was demanding entrance when Jace appeared.

'What the fuck's going on?' Petre's arrogant drawl echoed in the hallway.

'I'm afraid there's been—'

Jace didn't have time to finish his sentence. Petre caught sight of his brother's face as he was wheeled past. He blanched and then vomited all over the marble floor.

'I-I need … I need to go with Tinto,' the younger brother's voice was desperate and frightened. 'H-he's not going to die, is he?'

'We hope not, sir,' Jace replied. 'Do you know anyone who would wish to harm your brother?'

Petre looked wildly about as if he expected the perpetrator to come storming in. 'No, everyone likes him. H-he's always been there for me … even when I was trying to push him away.'

'An officer will accompany you to the hospital, Mr Zagrokis. But I will need to speak to you later.'

Petre's terrified eyes watched the paramedics close the ambulance doors. 'Of course, Inspector.'

***

Jace thanked the doctor and headed up the corridor. He was unable to interview Tinto Zagrokis. And at this stage, it was impossible to say if he'd sustained a serious brain injury. The doctor had been hopeful, which was something. However, Jace was taking no chances and posted a uniformed officer outside the room. He might not be able to speak to one Zagrokis but he was sure as hell going to talk to the other one.

The younger Zagrokis was a wreck. His snazzy suit was crumpled from a night spent by his brother's bedside. The usual expensive, coiffured haircut was dishevelled, and the man looked shattered and still terrified. His eyes nervously flitted around the room as he bit his fingernails. He'd readily agreed to help in any way he could as Jace led him to an empty room. Jace asked again if Petre knew of anyone with a grudge against Tinto. And the answer again was a resounding no.

Jace's team had searched the house from top to bottom and there was no sign of a break-in, or of anything being stolen. It appeared whoever was responsible had gone there with the sole intention of beating Tinto to death. But everyone liked the guy. Jace studied Petre. The man was hiding something. He just needed to find the right key to unlock the door.

'Why do you think someone would want to beat up your brother?'

'I-I don't know.'

The kid was a terrible liar. But Jace kept his composure.

'Did your brother know something? Information about something ... or someone?'

And there it was. Petre's eyes widened with fear at the last word. Tinto must have information about somebody. But who? Jace was convinced Dominique and Sergio were linked to Alex's accident but what about Mia? Mia had been Rika's friend and Rika had been Petre's girlfriend. He tried a different route.

'Why did Rika finish with you? From what I hear she was besotted.'

Petre frowned. It was clearly not the question he'd been expecting. 'She said there was no point staying together with her going to university.'

Another lie. Jace could feel his tolerance ebbing fast. 'And Mia? What can you tell me about your relationship with her?'

'I-I don't know what you mean.'

Another lie and the kid was pulsating with fear. The answer was within reach. It was time to push hard.

Jace slammed his palm down on the table and pointed at the door. 'Your brother is fighting for his life and a young woman is dead. But you have the nerve to sit there and lie to my face. I want to know what information your brother knew, and I want to know what happened the day Mia was dumped. And if you don't tell me now, I will drag you down to the police station where you will remain until you do tell me. Do I make myself clear!'

Petre broke down completely. 'I-I can't tell you ... they'll kill me ... they'll kill Tinto.'

Jace knew better than to push that line of enquiry.

'Okay then, tell me about Mia.'

'It was me,' Petre whispered. 'I dumped her on the driveway ... because I had no choice ... because they told me I had to or bad things would happen to those I cared about.'

The kid was undoubtedly an arse, but he was in way over his head. Jace felt sorry for him. 'Tell me what happened that day.'

Rika had decided it would be a nice gesture to help tidy up the house ahead of the party. They'd made a start and then gone for a walk in the grounds. She'd headed back up to the house and he'd stayed behind to meet Mia. He'd chatted briefly with Mia and then he'd joined Rika to do some more cleaning. After sandwiches and orange juice for lunch, the next thing he remembered was waking up naked in bed with Mia passed out beside him.

There was no sign of Rika, and he knew Tinto would be home in a few hours. He freaked out and rang a number he'd been given. They said he needed to dump Mia but not at the hospital because he'd be seen. Petre was terrified but remembered that the florist for the party was Olivia Marinos. Her card was on the foyer table. He grabbed it and carried Mia to the car. Olivia worked from home, she'd find Mia and call emergency services or at least call her brother. And she'd done both.

'I didn't think she'd die,' Petre sobbed. 'I didn't want her to die.'

Jace knew the story had been severely edited. There'd been something more than an affair going on between Mia and Petre.

'Thank you, Mr Zagrokis. You've been most helpful.'

'Y-you aren't going to arrest me?'

'Not at the moment. But don't leave the area.'

'No, Inspector. I'm not going anywhere,' Petre said solemnly. 'I need to stay with Tinto. It's the least I can do. I just hope I get the chance to be a better brother … because I've been a completely shit one so far.'

Chapter Forty-Nine

Anna knelt on the living room floor and laughed as Elora commando-crawled across the carpet to reach Pesce. As soon as the little girl got within millimetres of grabbing the cockapoo's tail, he would set off again and wait till she caught up. It had started last week and cracked up everyone who received the footage. After the second lap, Elora received a round of applause as she sat down and placed hands to her mouth.

'Do you want something to eat?' Anna said and swooped down to swing Elora up into a hug. 'Come on, let's get you some porridge.'

Like a little procession, Anna and Elora were accompanied to the fridge by Pesce and Cleo.

'Now, will you look at that? Naughty daddy promised to get us some milk before he left with Evie this morning but didn't.' She bounced Elora up and down as she walked over to the door. 'Let's go and get some from next door.'

As Anna extracted a milk carton from the fridge, Elora was enthusiastically passed around the kitchen staff for cuddles before regretfully being handed back. Anna turned to leave but a voice called her back. Inspector Marinos was in the café, could he have a quick word? The tone implied a negative response would be extremely unwise. With milk in one hand, Elora perched on her hip, and full of curiosity, Anna pushed open the door. Inspector Marinos stood ramrod straight, impatiently drumming his fingers on the counter with a face that suggested he was going to kill somebody.

Anna instinctively hugged Elora and approached with caution. 'I hope your barely suppressed rage is not directed at me, Inspector?'

The forced smile didn't reach his tired, bloodshot eyes. 'Of course not, Mrs Makris. I was hoping you could advise me where Sebasti might be. I must speak to her.'

'I'm so sorry, she's gone away for a few days with Elissa and Rika but she's back in tomorrow.' On the one hand she was relieved not to be in the firing line, but was also frustrated at being unable to help. 'Sebasti didn't know where they were going as it was a last-minute surprise. To be honest, it was the last thing I needed. Pip and Andrew are away on a three-day trip and with Alex recovering I've had to pull in favours to cover shifts. But Rika's been going through a tough time and then with the shocking news of Tinto, I could hardly say no. I do have Sebasti's mobile if that helps.'

'Thanks, but I've already got it,' he said, clenching his fists. It was one of the few times Anna had seen the man lose his composure. But then he relaxed and this time the smile did reach his eyes as he tickled Elora. 'You might want to take this little cutie and go console your friend in the corner. It looks like he's having an even worse day than me.'

In the hustle and bustle – the laughter, animated conversation and general mirth of holidaymakers relaxing – sat her ex-husband despondently stirring a cup of coffee and staring at his mobile. Aware that the inspector's eyes were on her, Anna had little option but to go over.

'Come on you. Let's go,' she instructed and nodded towards the exit.

'Are you kicking me out?' he replied, sounding utterly dejected.

'No, you're coming with me because you're likely to scare away my customers,' she joked but there was only the slightest upward twitch of his mouth and he obediently followed her out like a lost soul.

***

An enthusiastic welcome from Pesce and Cleo succeeded in getting a lukewarm smile and he half-heartedly threw a rubber chicken across the kitchen floor and watched as the dogs played tug of war before Pesce was allowed to win. Anna handed over Elora and instructed him to entertain the little girl while she boiled the kettle. With his pitiful voice mingled with Elora's giggles, her glacial hard hatred creaked and shifted. She glanced at the calendar and sighed; it was time to be the better person as she rummaged around in a kitchen drawer.

'Happy Birthday to you. Happy Birthday, dear Javier. Happy Birthday to you,' she sang joyously, hoping to lift his mood, and placed a chocolate cupcake with four lit candles in front of him. 'Make a wish but don't tell me or else it won't come true.'

Even though it was a minuscule cake he took a deep breath, closed his eyes and blew out the flames. 'I can't believe you remembered ... after all this time.'

It was a reflex. Her body acted without instruction from her brain. She hugged him and kissed his cheek. 'How could I forget? Now pass me Elora so you can enjoy your cake and a cuppa and tell me why you look like total crap.'

'How do you always know how to do that?' he said tearfully and handed across a squirming Elora who was frantically trying to grab the cake. 'You always say and do the right thing. You're always so kind and selfless in such an effortless way. I think it's amazing ... I think you're amazing. I've always thought that.'

She sat in stunned silence as he quickly looked away and began to eat his cake. It was gone in three bites. Her brain refused to function properly. How was she supposed to respond? In the end, she merely repeated the same question.

'Why do you look like total crap?'

He laughed without humour. 'I'm forty-four years old today and there's nothing more sobering on your birthday than to realise you've squandered away your life, that you've alienated loved ones and through your own selfishness find yourself utterly alone.'

'But ... but that can't be true. What about your family? What about Celeste and your parents?'

'I had a massive row with Celeste the other day. She sent me an email a few weeks ago to say Dad was deteriorating faster than expected and I needed to think about coming home. I pointed out that we'd agreed by working away I could continue to pay for his ongoing care but if I returned, we'd struggle financially. I didn't think anything of it until Celeste rang, demanding to know my whereabouts.'

He looked utterly wretched and, sensing his distress, Pesce trotted over and jumped onto his knee. Javier stroked the dog absentmindedly. 'You know I've never been able to lie to my family when asked a direct question, so I told her I was in Greece and she lost it big style. She made me tell her how much I was earning and pointed out I could easily make the same at home so why hadn't I come back? And then she started asking about you and me and wanted to know exactly how we broke up.'

Internally, Anna squirmed. She'd rung Celeste when Javier first arrived, to check out his story. She hadn't given anything away but must have got the woman thinking.

'I ended up admitting how I'd abandoned you in Peru to shack up with Catrin,' he continued. 'She said I was a disgrace, that Bethan was right that I only ever give a toss about myself and that the best of me died with Bobby. Mum and Dad still believed I was a decent human being and in the little time Dad had left she certainly wasn't going to divulge the truth or burden Mum with the knowledge that her only remaining son was a turd. And then today, I received this.'

He slid over his mobile and Anna winced at the message. Celeste hadn't held back.

Happy Birthday dearest brother. Although I hate your guts right now, the better part of me still has to send you a message to mark your entrance into the world. I expect you'll be living it up in style, no doubt stabbing somebody in the back to achieve your goals. I hope it's all been worth it. Our parents as always send their love. If there is a shred of decency left, you will return home to spend what time is left with our father while he still remembers who you are.

'You need to go home, Jav,' Anna implored and reached for his hand. 'Go see your dad and make up with your sisters. You've already lost a brother. Please don't leave it too late.'

He raked fingers through his hair and spoke to the table. 'I've cocked everything up. They'll never forgive me. Not now. I've done other things, things that only Celeste knows about. Things I-I can't tell you about, Anna. But I'm putting things right. I'm doing something good, something to help someone that'll make you proud of me. But I must finish it first before I can go home and try to set things right with my sisters.'

He spoke with conviction, passion and so earnestly that Anna saw the old Jav struggling to break free. Kristina was right, he'd only ever needed the time to change. And he was almost there.

'I understand,' she replied but then stiffened as Elora's breathing changed. 'My timing is rubbish, but I need to leave and take this little one to A&E. We can talk more when I get back and if it's not too late why don't you and Kristina come around for a birthday tea? Evie's spending the night on Tharesseti. She wanted to go over and comfort Narella, with her dad being in hospital.'

'Like hell, Anna. I'm coming with you. With Filip being away I'm not letting you go to the hospital alone.'

She cupped her hand to his cheek. 'Thank you, that'd be nice.'

In a matter of minutes, they were in the car. It was going to be tight but thankfully as she looked right the Lefkada Town bus sat at the bus stop. Thank God, she wasn't going to get stuck behind that trundling up the switchback road. She put her foot down and sped past the steep, rock-strewn, tree-clad landscape. The morning sun shimmered on the sea as the car zipped along, but Anna failed to notice, with both eyes fixed on the road and ears tuned in to Elora's breathing which fluctuated between normal and wheezing. The main island road climbed again, high above the sea, past gravelled viewpoints lined with motorhomes, cars and buses. The gods remained on her side as the traffic flowed. They were fast approaching a key junction. The left was quicker but on narrower roads, the right was longer but on the main highway – she kept right. For the whole journey, Javier had remained silent but in her peripheral vision, she could see him staring at the speedometer. Did he think she was driving too slow or too fast?

'You doing okay over there?' she asked whilst overtaking a group of erratically driven scooters.

He tightened his seatbelt. 'I can see why you wear one of these. Is it my imagination or do the rules of the highway code not apply in Lefkada?'

'It does sometimes feel that way,' Anna replied. 'It's why I insist that anyone in my car wears a seatbelt or they walk. I also make Pip and Evie use them in whichever car they're in. Evie thought she could get away with it a few years back until I found out and grounded her for a week. She never did it again.'

'A mean mother, eh?' Javier joked.

'Too right. Give them an inch and they'll take a mile.'

'I don't believe that.' He smiled. 'Evie's a terrific kid. You should be very proud.'

Anna laughed. 'Most of the time she is. And Elora will be the same. They can drive you up the wall but at the end of the day I'd go through a brick wall for them.'

'You think of Elora as your daughter, don't you?' he asked and glanced backwards at the baby who was now dozing fitfully.

'Yes, I made a promise to always protect her and I take that very seriously.'

He shifted uneasily in his seat. 'Hang on, what do you mean? Filip told me Elora was dumped on your doorstep but the way you're talking it sounds like something more to me.'

Anna cursed inwardly. She'd forgotten his super spider-sense was more finely tuned than hers. He'd always had a gift for knowing when something was off – although whether he did anything about it was a completely different matter.

'I promised Inspector Marinos I'd take care of Elora,' she replied in a level voice and waited.

There was a slight pause. 'You're not telling me the whole truth, Anna. What's going on? Who is Elora? Who are her parents? What the hell have you got yourself into?'

'Are you worried about me?' she joked. Maybe it would calm him down.

'Too bloody right, I'm worried about you,' he snapped. 'There are some really bad people out there and I don't want you or any of your family getting mixed up with them.'

'Jav, you've been watching too many thrillers.' She patted his leg. 'We live in a sleepy little village where nothing ever happens, so you don't need to be concerned. Everything's fine. Elora's a little girl who's had an unusual start to life and, unfortunately, her parents – for whatever reason – were unable to care for her.'

He only murmured in response, but Anna took that as a good sign. She hadn't exactly lied but skirted around the truth. Anyway, the hospital was in sight which was the most important thing.

Chapter Fifty

Elora was whipped straight in, and Anna was instructed to take a seat in the Waiting Room.

'It'll be alright,' she said, more for her reassurance than his. 'Kids are tough.'

'How are you so calm?' he demanded, repeatedly flicking his left ring finger and thumb together. 'I'm freaking out here.'

She placed her hand over his to stop the twitching. 'Believe me, I've been in hospitals too many times over the years. Me and Pip practically lived in them during Evie's cancer treatment. It's a case of going with the flow or losing the plot.'

'But we don't know anything about Elora's medical background. We don't know if her parents have any medical conditions so we don't know why she's ill!' He started pacing up and down between the rows of crowded seats.

'She's in the best place, Jav,' Anna replied steadily even though he was voicing her exact thoughts. 'Come and sit down and tell me a story about your best-ever birthday.'

He slumped down beside her and recounted a glorious sunny day on Llandudno beach. And as time slid by and people came and went, they both reminisced about other family holidays but slowly the stories became about them. And in doing so they recounted (prompted or disagreed with) their memories of nights and weekends away, short European trips. And then naturally the conversation turned to their worldwide extended honeymoon adventure. And as in the past, they became highly animated, gesticulating wildly, laughing together or defending their interpretation of events.

He wiped a tear of laughter away. 'We had some brilliant times, didn't we?'

She nodded and up bubbled those two questions that had consumed her every breath fifteen years ago, until for her sanity she'd locked them in a vault in the deepest recesses of her mind. By arriving, Javier had ruptured the secure steel box and they'd begun to seep out and – like a poison – had infected her mind, feeding off her hatred and rage to grow strong and consume her again. And now was the time to ask, because the anger was gone. Emotionally she was in control. She needed to know the answers to move forwards even if it terrified her to hear his response.

'Why did you leave me, Jav?' she said quietly. 'What did I do wrong?'

The busy Waiting Room melted away and it was only the two of them sitting side by side. His face was so close, there was only the sound of their breathing. His eyes were unguarded and hers were wide. He was going to tell her the truth.

'You did nothing wrong, Anna. You never did anything wrong. It was me. It was all me. I was an idiot. I was so incredibly stupid. I cast aside your love, the most precious gift I've ever had, for greed.' He extracted his wallet and laid a dull gold band in her palm. 'I kept it, all these years. I kept it.'

She stared at his wedding ring with 'A & J' stamped inside.

'Mrs Makris ... Mrs Makris.'

The crying, whimpering, talking and shouting of the Waiting Room was back and somebody was calling her name. In a daze, Anna stood up and walked trance-like towards a young woman in a white coat.

'Mrs Makris, are you okay?'

Anna mentally face-slapped herself and refocused. 'I do apologise about that. I'm not sure where I went there. What can you tell me, Doctor—?'

'Shah. My name is Doctor Shah,' she replied calmly and reassuringly shook Anna's hand. 'I'm one of the paediatricians here and have been assessing Elora. If I can ask you and your husband to follow me, we can go and see her and I can explain our next steps.'

The woman was already retreating down the corridor before Anna could correct the mistake. She stood for a moment at a loss before Javier grasped her hand and gave her a wink.

'Come on, slowcoach, let's go. I don't think Filip will object this time. After all, I did have the role once before.'

***

The car idled by the kerb in the late afternoon sunshine. In Apokeri Gallery, Penelope bubble-wrapped a painting for a delighted customer and Kristina was showing off a range of pottery.

'Thank you so much for coming with me today,' Anna said and leaned over to peck Javier on the cheek. 'It might not have been a great way to spend your birthday but at least I made you smile and laugh a little bit.'

'Are you sure I can't keep you company?' he probed once more. 'You're going to be all alone in that big house. Will you be alright?'

'Don't worry about me. I've got Pesce and Cleo for company.' She motioned for him to get going. 'But thank you for the offer. And remember not a word to Kristina. They're only keeping Elora in overnight as a precaution, so I'm not telling Pip. He needs to enjoy his getaway with Andrew and Hugo. It's not right to tell anyone else about Elora if Pip doesn't know.'

'You take too much on,' he responded with concern etched around his eyes. 'Pip would want to know. But I'll do as you ask. And remember if you change your mind, I'm happy to come to the hospital first thing tomorrow with you.'

He clambered out and Anna called through the window. 'You're a good man, Javier Owens.'

She waited as he held the door open for the parcel-laden customer, as her friends welcomed him back and as Kristina produced a lit birthday cake from under the counter. Penelope handed him a small present and everyone sang 'Happy Birthday'.

He turned and Anna blew him a kiss before driving off. The little surprise was the least she could do.

Chapter Fifty-One

Anna sat. Five minutes, ten minutes. The kitchen clock ticked on. This morning's hospital visit hadn't gone as planned.

Dr Shah wasn't wholly satisfied; tests were being run.

Anna was told to go home; they'd be in touch.

Good, the medics were thorough, but worryingly Pip was still away. Did she fess up or keep quiet till he returned? Luckily, Evie was none the wiser. She was going straight to football with Narella that morning, baking with Granda and then a sleepover at her cousin's. And Irina was due to land in a few hours.

The mobile in her hand vibrated. Please let it be the hospital with good news. But it was Irina, and panic set in. Why was she ringing? Anna couldn't deal with any more bad news right now. A finger swipe revealed her immaculately dressed friend lounging on a sofa.

'Don't worry, there's nothing wrong with me,' Irina announced abruptly.

'Thank heavens.' Anna breathed out. 'So why the hell are you ringing then?'

'My, my, somebody's having a bad day. I can always stay here if you're going to be a pain in the ass,' she retorted but frowned. 'What's wrong?'

Anna shook her head. 'Sorry, it's a long story. I'll tell you when you arrive. I'm fine, just wired. Please come; I want to see you.'

'Of course I'm coming. Even if you were being a bitch, I'd soon put you right.' Anna had no doubt Irina would do precisely that. The woman didn't take crap from anyone. 'Anyway, your brilliant friend is ringing because she's finally pulled together the dossier on Mr Ex-Anna. Credit to the man, he covers his tracks well,' Irina remarked but patted herself on the back. 'However, not enough to throw yours truly off the scent. I thought it best to send my report now. That way, you might have calmed down a little before picking me up. I don't want to spend my entire visit listening to you ranting and raving. All I am going to say is that you were right. See you later, sweetie.' And she was gone.

Up popped an email notification. After months of waiting, the truth was within her grasp. And Anna realised she didn't want to know. She desperately wanted to believe in him. Believe he couldn't betray her again. What if she simply hit delete and just forgot the whole business of snooping around in his past? Wasn't that where it deserved to be kept? Unfortunately, she knew herself too well and not knowing would nibble and gnaw away. With a heavy heart, she succumbed and double-clicked.

It was worse than bad. It was sickening and just as well she was alone as she stormed into the lounge, the phone shaking in her hand. She didn't trust herself in the kitchen with so many sharp implements and instead stuffed a cushion in her mouth and screamed and screamed. Pesce and Cleo shot along the corridor as she hurled any non-breakable item across the room. And still, the blood pounded in her ears. Her phone buzzed and it took mammoth self-restraint not to smash it against the wall.

Hi babe, how's Elora? Brilliant news! I've finally cracked it and wanted you to be the first to know. You'll be so proud of me. Message back and let me know when I can pop around.
Jx

She gagged but punched in a reply.

Excellent. On my way now.

The dogs fled in her wake as she grabbed her car keys and slammed the kitchen door so hard the reinforced glass reverberated. It was a two-minute drive, but with ever-dithering tourists crawling along looking for that elusive promenade parking spot, delivery trucks double-parked and scooters erratically challenging all known rules of road etiquette, Anna was ready to explode as she slalomed up the beachfront road. There was one precious vacant spot right in front of Apokeri Gallery, and right under the nose of a pristine all-terrain vehicle, Anna shot into the gap and leapt out. The shed-sized driver hurled abuse out the window, calling for her head. She abruptly swung around and stalked towards him, fists clenched and bristling with rage. Seeing his wrathful enemy bearing down on him, the man wisely raised a hand in surrender and swiftly drove off.

It was time to deal with Javier.

***

From upstairs he called down. 'Anna, is that you?'

'Yes, I'll be right up.'

'Wow, you were quick. Did you fly?' he joked and barely registered her rigid stance or fierce glare. He was so excited to explain his fantastic news. 'Do you remember how you asked me to keep an eye on Kristina and let you know if she was fine?'

'Yes, and you said there was nothing to worry about,' her voice was cold and challenging, but he dismissed it.

'Well—'

'You lied, didn't you?' she shrieked.

Anna was technically correct so had a right to be annoyed but he didn't worry. That would soon change once she'd heard what he had to say.

'Kristina does keep returning to the past and wants to reconnect with it. But' – he quickly held up his hands as she bristled – 'not in the way you think. It's not in an obsessive way. Okay, well, maybe it is.' He couldn't get the words out right; she was making him nervous. He tried again. 'What I mean is, she's full of regret and wants to set things right. Over the last few months, she's shared her life story with me, starting from being a little girl in Stockholm through her Bristol boarding school and Swiss Finishing School days and everything in between. Now that's a dysfunctional family if ever there was one.' She was watching him like a cat eyeing a mouse. 'And then all about her true love, Adrian. How she came to arrive in Apokeri and then the tragic tale of his death, how she chose to remain and—'

'Kristina told you all that?' she said quietly. He heard disbelief and something else he couldn't place. But it wasn't anger because that had evaporated. Instead, his ex-wife stood frozen, holding her breath.

He briefly frowned but continued because there was so much to say. 'Kristina's web history is full of links to ancestry sites and companies with Swedish, Greek and American links. In her wardrobe, there's a box full of letters and postcards from some bloke called Daniel, and in the vault, there are piles of diaries. I can't understand them because they're in Swedish, but they go right back to—'

'You went through Kristina's personal effects and broke into the safe?' she demanded, eyes bulging. 'Is that what you're telling me, Javier? Just so I have it right. So that I haven't misunderstood your gross breach of trust.'

Stupidly he realised his mistake as she exploded. He'd never recalled her being this angry. There was no let-up as she screamed at his betrayal – yet again. She was sobbing. Uncontrollably sobbing – something he'd never been able to cope with – and as the tears streamed down her face, Javier knew he'd finally gone too far. He tried to explain, but it was like talking to a brick wall, except this one shouted back. And suddenly, he was back in an allotment in southeast Northumberland as he tried and failed to reason with Robert Jenkinson to be allowed to date his daughter. Javier had been right then, and he was trying to do the right thing now, but – like her father over twenty years earlier – she refused to listen.

'You had me fooled,' she screamed. 'After all these years of hating you. I actually forgave you in the hospital. An electrician? You should be an actor with that award-winning performance. Extracting your wedding ring, confiding you'd never been able to part with it! How many others have fallen for the haunted husband act?' The words hit him like a freight train. 'I'm such an idiot. I so wanted to believe you'd changed. I held out long after everyone else fell for your smooth patter. But like everybody, I crumbled.' She was a religious zealot, holding hands aloft, but instead of praying she was cursing him to hell. 'I thought you were back. I thought you'd returned to be that amazing man I fell in love with at first sight.'

'Anna—'

'Don't you dare,' she bellowed, jabbing a finger in his direction. 'I gave you a second clean slate, Javier. Even after you smashed the first one!'

Out of habit, he went to deny it, but she stopped him dead with hate-filled eyes and, like fruit left too long on the vine, his hope of winning her around withered and died. 'I saw the office and gallery CCTV footage. Kristina and me watched you snoop around, but she persuaded me to let it go, and I stupidly did.' She broke into maniacal laughter. 'And for what? For you to trick and deceive one of my closest friends. I'll never forgive you for that. What has Kristina ever done to you? Except welcome you with open arms.'

It was terrifyingly hypnotic to witness her unravel. She was out of control. Hadn't she told him that his abandonment had almost destroyed her? He'd thought she was exaggerating but the dawning realisation hit. Because of his actions, he was breaking her mind – again. What had he done? He glanced at the open window, fearful people would overhear her falling apart. He couldn't bear that. She was always so strong and hid any weakness.

'Worried what your adoring fans might hear, are you?' she shrieked.

'No, that's not what I was thinking,' he cried. Everything was going horribly wrong.

Her voice dropped to a triumphant whisper. 'Worried that I might tarnish the reputation of the great Javier Owens? Or should I call you Mr Patrick O'Donnellan, Simon Morales or any of the other half a dozen aliases you go by?'

This time he froze in horror. How did she know about them? Because if she knew about those, it meant she knew—

'Everything, Javier. I know everything. I cleverly pieced it together – right back to when you abandoned me in Cusco. How you set up a fake life with your new wife, Catrin – or should I say, Claris Pickering, who is probably still Mrs Owens as I'm sure you haven't got the faintest idea where she vanished off to.'

Why had he chosen to forget how brilliant his first wife was? Why did he ever think coming here to con her was a good idea? He wanted to curl up and die and stop witnessing what he'd done to her, what he was still doing to her. To stop hearing about the sham he called his life and not feel the overwhelming guilt of having destroyed countless lives. But that wasn't going to happen. She kept hurling more and more evidence of his past deceits and was crowing in satisfaction.

'Celeste confronted you because of me. I rang her when you first arrived because I knew you were spinning me a line. And even though I never gave anything away, she figured out you were deceiving her – your own flesh and blood.' Anna spat out her words, and then the unhinged laughter started up again. He wanted to shut his ears to the pain he'd caused his loved ones. 'And do you know the worse of it? Right at the very start, I knew you were lying to me because Celeste proudly told me about you rebuilding your life after Claris walked out with all the money three years ago! And even then, I thought, what if you were in trouble? What if you did have no other option and I was the only one who could help your family? And that's what you were counting on, wasn't it? The fact good old Anna can never turn anyone down. How many people have you conned? I bet you've lost count. Is any money in those bank accounts legal? Tell me. I want to hear you say it.'

He couldn't lie anymore. There wasn't any point. It was over.

'Very little,' he mumbled.

Her eyes narrowed and her body tensed. She revved up for another final explosion. 'You have used and tricked everyone I love, including my husband and even my daughter! You total bastard.'

'No, not Evie. I never lied to her,' he insisted, but even in his ears, he sounded pathetic and ridiculous.

She grabbed a paperweight, raised it above her head and bore down on him. 'I said I'd kill you if you messed me around.'

He didn't call out or raise his hands to ward off the attack, but instead, he cast down his eyes and waited. But the blow never fell. He looked up and Anna stood horrified at what she'd almost done. The glass ball slipped from her fingers and cracked in two on the floor.

'I want you gone, Javier. By the time I get back from the airport, you'll have left Apokeri, never to return,' she spoke with utter contempt. 'And if you ignore my instructions, I'll call the police and have you arrested even though ... even though it'll break my daughter's heart. No more chances. I'm done with you.'

He didn't go after her as she stormed down the stairs. Through the open window, he heard her distraught voice snap at someone before he collapsed on the bed and cried for what he'd lost.

Chapter Fifty-Two

Kristina waved to Jeremy from the quayside as he sped across the water back to Tharesseti and glowing reviews. The art course had been a genius idea, if she did say so. Even at ninety-two she still had it and with an impish grin she set off towards the gallery, keen to tell Javier how it'd gone. The change in the man since he arrived was remarkable. If only Anna could see it ... but her friend was still blinkered by so much pent-up rage and couldn't let go.

The sun beat down on the pavement and the street was fairly quiet with most tourists on the beach or sightseeing. Any local not working was wisely sheltering from the heat. She was almost at the gallery when a distraught Anna came barging out and almost knocked her over.

'What's the matter?' Kristina asked and went to grasp Anna's hand, but it was snatched away.

'Why don't you go and ask your new best friend, Javier?' Anna spat. 'After all, the two of you are bosom buddies and confide your innermost secrets to one another.'

And before Kristina had a chance to respond, Anna turned and strode off. With a brief nod to Penelope, Kristina climbed the stairs to find a tearful Javier hurriedly packing his bag.

'What's going on?' she asked with a gentle smile. He glanced up, dragging the back of his hand across a snotty nose. She handed him a tissue.

'I'm leaving.' He sniffed and dumped the contents of the drawers into his rucksack. 'Anna's told me to go.' His dark brown eyes were filled with remorse and her heart went out to him.

'You still haven't answered my question, Javier.' She kept her voice calm.

He grabbed a shirt from the wardrobe, threw it across the room and yelled, 'What difference does it make? It's over. I've ruined everything.'

Kristina pulled out a chair and slowly sat down. 'And what you do next makes all the difference, wouldn't you say?' He halted and she saw the tiniest flicker of hope. 'Why don't you tell me what happened?'

And for over an hour, he did just that as his crumpled form shook with tears of shame and regret. He didn't hold anything back about his fake life, about coming to Apokeri with the sole intention of conning Anna – and everyone else – by any means possible. How one of those people had been Kristina and he confessed to snooping in her bedroom and cracking open the vault and finding both the white envelopes which temporarily stopped him but then he'd kept going. He told her about using Mia's memorial to tug at people's heartstrings and win them over. But how the people in Apokeri began to make their mark. How he'd decided to change and was trying to fix things but then there'd been the terrible fallout with Celeste and then Anna uncovered everything. With the tears still streaming down his face, he recounted the final terrible confrontation with Anna and even though he'd truly changed, his explanations only inflamed the situation.

'Anna refused to listen, didn't she?' Kristina interrupted.

'Yes. I should've realised how angry she was, but I was too wrapped up in my breakthrough and wanting to share the news. And now she despises me more than ever!' he cried and sank onto the floor. 'She never wants to see me again. And who can blame her?'

Kristina sighed. The past cast a long shadow. 'Did you think it was going to be easy, clambering back onto the straight and narrow?'

'I never intended to, but it sort of happened despite my best or worse intentions,' he admitted and gave a rueful chuckle. 'But yes, I thought it'd be a hell of a lot easier.'

Kristina sat on the bed and placed a hand on his shoulder. 'What you need to understand is Anna is hurt and feels betrayed. And not just by you, but also by me.'

'I-I don't understand.' He frowned and levered himself up to join her. 'You haven't done anything.'

'Oh, but I have,' she replied, lacing elegant fingers together in her lap. 'I chose to confide in you about my past. It was done in good faith to help nudge your conscience and I would like to think it worked. But Anna—'

'Thinks I tricked you.'

Kristina sadly shook her head. 'No, that was a deflection, said in the heat of the moment. Anna doesn't want to believe I'd choose to confide in the one person she's hated for so long, the person who stole her dreams and broke her heart. You said yourself, she froze when you said I'd shared my stories. The poor love, it must have felt like a slap in the face.'

'It's a total disaster.' Javier stared at the two halves of the paperweight sitting in the sun. It had cracked exactly down the centre.

'But don't you see? It means not all's lost. You can fix this. As I said earlier, what you do now makes all the difference.'

He pushed off the bed and reached for his bag. 'It's too late for that with Anna but there's still time to go home and make amends with my family.'

Chapter Fifty-Three

Adrenaline got Anna to the airport, but parked opposite the terminal, the shock kicked in. She stared out the window with hands wrapped around the steering wheel, unable to stop the shaking. Forty-five minutes later, she'd succeeded in throwing up into one of Cleo's poo-sacks and staggered to the bin before collapsing back into the driver's seat. There was no way she could greet Irina in Arrivals and in the rear-view mirror she saw her friend stride across the road in towering stilettos, glittering with her signature diamond jewellery.

The suitcase was thrown into the boot and the passenger door yanked open. 'First you're a cow on the phone and the next you can't even be arsed to greet me at the gate. I have to say—'

'I nearly killed somebody,' Anna blurted out and recounted the horrific confrontation with Javier and then her appalling behaviour towards Kristina.

Despite Irina's best efforts, Anna refused to let her drive. Having already thrown up once she didn't fancy doing so again and that was a strong possibility with Irina's refusal to conform to any open-road speed limit. The twin cannons stood guard on either side of the short swing bridge which separated Lefkada from the mainland. The metal reverberated briefly under the wheels until they were back on the tarmac. And then a left turn and the sea lagoons shimmered on each side of the road to reveal Lefkada. Anna loved that view. The whole island lay before her – Lefkada Town in the foreground and the mountainous interior behind. The sight slightly soothed her frayed nerves, but the shock of nearly killing her ex-husband had yet to wear off.

'I came so close to becoming a murderer,' Anna whispered, scared to say it too loud. She now understood when people talked about the red mist descending. For a few seconds, she'd wanted nothing more than to kill, and the realisation she'd fully intended to end somebody's life shook her to the core.

'Oh, I wouldn't worry about it too much.' Irina watched as a flock of flamingos danced elegantly across the water. 'I've nearly killed Hugo twice.' Anna almost careered off the road as Irina recounted two blazing rows with her husband. The first resulted in Irina throwing a carving knife at his head and the second flooring a car straight at him. 'I deliberately missed both times.'

'Oh.' It was all Anna could manage.

Irina turned in her seat. 'What I'm trying to demonstrate is that you also deliberately chose not to kill your ex-husband by cracking his skull open like a walnut. It shows that your good sense prevailed.'

'I suppose.'

Irina nodded to show the topic of conversation was concluded. It was good riddance to Javier, but Anna squirmed in her seat as she recalled the second confrontation. 'I acted like a spoilt brat to Kristina.'

'It wouldn't be the first time, and it certainly won't be the last,' Irina half-joked. 'It'll be okay. Kristina will understand. She loves you, Anna ... but you do need to apologise.'

Beside her, Irina was the picture of cool, calm collectedness. Anna grasped her friend's hand and didn't let go. 'I will. I'm so pleased you're here.'

'So am I. You've had a lot to contend with – Javier appearing, taking in Elora and Pesce and Alex's hit-and-run. You've told me about Javier, and Elora in the hospital, what about Alex? How's he doing?'

'I spoke to his mam yesterday. The place he's in sounds amazing – the best treatment, the best experts and because of that he's coming on leaps and bounds. There's still a massive road to recovery but he'll do it. Alex is tough.'

Anna tightened her grip on the steering wheel. Pip was still in bits. The bike ride had been Pip's olive branch for weeks of arguing and barely talking but the puncture had put paid to that.

And with the secret nature of their relationship, Pip couldn't even have an open and honest conversation over the airwaves. Anna didn't know what would happen. Before the accident, Alex kept pushing Pip to disclose the truth, but he'd refused, claiming Evie was far too young to understand. It was a stalemate with no resolution. And who knew how the accident had changed Alex? However, as she negotiated the capital's streets there was someone else to worry about – Elora.

'That's good,' Irina replied, seemingly satisfied with Anna's mental state. 'I'm sorry I won't get to meet the infamous Javier. He sounds quite a character.'

'Believe me, you're not,' Anna replied bitterly. The shock was definitely subsiding because the bile rose in her throat at the very thought of him. 'You've had a lucky escape … and so have I. He suckered me in and if it hadn't been for you … anyway enough unpleasantness – we need to check on Elora.'

'Haven't you already been to the hospital today?' Anna tutted and Irina held up her hands. 'Okay, I admit I don't have a single maternal bone in my body.'

'Liar. Wait till you see Elora. She's so beautiful. You'll love her just like you love Evie who you'll see tomorrow. She's at Steffi's for a star-gazing stopover, they're all dressed up in cloaks and pointy hats.'

'Still obsessed by witches and wizards then?'

'Tell me about it! I swear my daughter is expecting a letter next year to say she's off to a Scottish boarding school. Bless her.' Anna gave her friend a sidelong glance. 'And no stoking the fire, you. I know what you're like. That wand and toy owl you sent across for her tenth birthday – she takes them everywhere with her.'

'Hey! It's good to have an active imagination. Who couldn't love Evie, she's—'

'Just like her mother. I know.'

'Anna.' It was a warning. 'Remember, you're only Elora's emergency carer. Don't get carried away.'

'I know, I know,' she replied. She didn't mention her and Pip's longing to adopt the little girl. But that seemed impossible. Elora needed to remain under the radar, so they couldn't risk going through any official channels. Apart from Anna, Pip and Inspector Marinos, nobody knew about Elora's true identity.

Irina was studying her, and the woman was phenomenal at picking up on anything untoward. Ten years on, Anna still didn't know what Irina and Hugo did. Their official line was they ran a successful security firm and undertook in-depth background checks for prospective employers. Years ago, her friend (and now brother-in-law) had tried to warn Anna off becoming friendly with the Dubois. She'd ignored him, and a decade later, he was good friends with the pair but maintained there was much more to the couple than they let on. Irina was still assessing Anna, who deliberately kept a neutral expression as she pulled into the hospital.

'I want to take care of her, that's all,' she said and quickly changed the subject. 'Have you heard anything from Hugo?'

Irina laughed. 'Yes, late last night. He could barely talk from being so shattered. I keep telling him he's an old man now, which he refuses to accept. According to my poor hubby, Filip and Andrew had taken him up the side of Everest and he finally admitted to looking forward to heading back home.'

Anna clicked the alarm and they walked towards the entrance. 'I don't know many blokes in their mid-fifties as fit as Hugo.'

Irina gave a wicked grin. 'I know. It's great.'

Chapter Fifty-Four

Anna was much calmer after visiting Elora. The little girl continued to improve, and Dr Shah was confident she'd be home tomorrow morning before Pip got back. Thoughts turned to dinner as she took the steep road down to Apokeri. They were on a particularly tight switchback section where the verge crumbled away. Rounding the bend, she screamed and slammed on the anchors. In the middle of the road lay a crumpled cyclist, ten metres from his mangled bike. It was happening again, another hit-and-run. Was it the same driver who'd left Alex for dead? Anna was out of the car instantly, ignoring Irina's instructions to wait. The man was out cold as she frantically felt for a pulse.

'He's alive,' she called over her shoulder. 'But you'd better—'

'Put your hands where I can see them, or I'll blow a hole right through the middle of your pretty little head,' the nondescript man instructed as he motioned with the gun and Anna scrambled to her feet. What was happening? One minute he appeared unconscious, and was now pointing a gun at Irina as the woman reached into the car. 'Don't even think about it, sweetheart. In the back.'

With the gun jammed in her ribs, Anna cautiously drove home. She indicated right and waited for a gap in the traffic. There was a taxi heading towards her and in the passenger seat was Javier. He saw her in the same instant as she repeatedly tucked hair behind her ear. But his impassive face turned away as the taxi passed. He wasn't coming to her rescue.

Chapter Fifty-Five

They were marched into the house as Anna ordered the dogs into their baskets. She cast her jacket over the chair before being manhandled into the living room and then pushed onto the sofa. The two women sat side by side as the gun-toting cyclist towered over them with his pistol.

'This is what we are going to do,' he calmly stated but was interrupted by excited yelps and booming barks from the kitchen.

A door slammed and a voice called out. 'Araf, Mrs Makris?'

She almost sobbed with relief. 'Araf, Jav.'

'Who the fuck is that?' the cyclist ordered as they listened to Javier's approaching footsteps.

'He's my handyman,' Anna explained.

The man's eyes were soulless. 'Get rid of him, or he's dead.'

'I was passing, so I thought I'd pop in to chat about the electrics,' Javier explained as he walked across the room and stuck out his hand. 'How you doing, mate? Always a pleasure to meet a friend of the boss.'

In an instant, Javier had their captor in an armlock on the ground but with lightning speed, the man twisted and despite the size difference threw Javier off and cracked him across the head with the gun. Javier was out cold. Anna screamed and launched herself at the man but he calmly pointed the gun at Irina.

'One more step and Princess gets it.'

Anna screeched to a halt and dropped her arms. 'You've just killed someone. What the hell do you want with us?'

'You're going to get the baby for me,' he purred and grinned wickedly.

She collapsed back on the sofa and grabbed Irina's hand. 'I can't ... sh-she's in hospital. They ... they've kept her in for breathing difficulties – r-ring if you don't believe me.'

Anna held her mobile out for him but he ignored it. 'Okay, you're both coming with me.'

'Fuck off. Where not going anywhere,' Irina snapped and leapt up to face him. 'I dare you to shoot me, you worthless shit.' He levelled the gun at her head but didn't pull the trigger and Irina laughed. 'I thought not. If I'm dead, Anna won't tell you anything, will she? Dickhead.'

The man smiled. It matched his cold, hard eyes and sweat trickled down Anna's back. 'I can do better than that, bitch. A word from me and mama bear's husband, her brother-in-law and their mate are all dead.'

Anna blanched. 'You're bluffing.'

He pulled out a mobile and punched in a number. There was an exchange in Italian and then she heard a voice and an involuntary sob escaped.

'Anna? Is that you?' his worried voice called out.

'Oh God, Pip. Are you hurt?'

'It's safe to say I'd rather be hanging off the side of a cliff right now,' he replied in that light-hearted tone she'd grown so accustomed to. It didn't matter how stressed Pip was, his voice was always upbeat. But the comment wasn't encouraging.

'Who's with you?' she asked quickly.

'Andrew and Hugo, they're both okay. Who's with you?'

But the call was disconnected before she had time to answer.

'You fucking bastard,' Anna yelled. 'I swear, once this is over, I'm going to kill you.'

It was water off a duck's back, and he merely raised an eyebrow. 'Tut, tut. Such unladylike behaviour. Now this is what's going to happen. You and Miss Freeze there will accompany me on a drive. There's somebody who wants to meet you.'

He shoved her forward and she stumbled into the kitchen and sent up a silent prayer as she fumbled in her jacket pocket. 'Shit. It's my dog, Cleo. Sh-she's hidden the car keys.'

The vein in his neck started to throb, but his voice remained calm. 'Well, you'd better find them before I put a bullet through its worthless brain.'

Chapter Fifty-Six

Jace barged into the pharmacy. Elissa had failed to return repeated calls and messages for the last two days and he'd been unable to locate her. But now she was back.

'Hello, Inspector.' There was only Rika Andino behind the counter and she greeted him with a faltering smile.

'It's time you and me had a chat, young lady.'

His voice immediately brought Elissa out of the back office. 'What's going on?'

'I believe your daughter has deliberately withheld vital information regarding the case of Mia Tovier, Mrs Andino, and I'm here to question her about that.'

The eyes hardened. This mother wasn't going to give up her child easily. 'Inspector, I really must protest—'

'I don't give a damn if you protest all day long, Mrs Andino. You and your children dropped off the face of the earth the same day a barely recognisable Tinto Zagrokis was admitted to A&E. Unbelievably the man has not sustained serious brain injuries,' Jace thundered. 'It was at the hospital I had an extremely illuminating conversation with his younger brother about the day Mia turned up on my sister's driveway. We can have a chat in your office or I'm perfectly happy to charge you and your daughter with obstruction and drag you both down to the station. Your call.'

Her glare was murderous and his was full of contempt. They both knew there'd be no more rendezvous. She'd deliberately hampered his investigations and that was unforgivable.

'Inspector—'

'Mama,' Rika forcefully intervened. 'It's okay. You don't need to protect me anymore. It's time I told the truth.'

They were all sitting in the cramped office. Jace on one side and Elissa and Rika squeezed in on the other.

Her story started the same as Petre's. They were at the house cleaning and stopped for lunch – sandwiches and orange juice. Afterwards, Rika began tidying the downstairs cinema room but started to feel weird and decided to go for a lie-down. She headed towards the guest bedroom but heard laughter coming from Petre's room. She opened the door.

The girl began to shake and tears spilt down her face as she described finding Petre and Mia. Jace held up his hand. He got the picture. Rika swallowed hard and carried on. Petre was giggling and Mia laughed at Rika and said she'd got tired of her virginal friend holding out for months and decided to step in and enjoy what Rika was too chicken to do. The girl had missed her chance. Mia then whispered something and Petre began giggling again. Mia now had a full set: Rika's boyfriend, her Uncle Giannis ... and her father. Petre laughed again, said he didn't need Rika anymore because Mia was going to make him rich. And at that, Rika fled.

'What do you mean Petre didn't need you anymore?' Jace probed the sobbing girl.

'Petre was harassing me to steal prescription drugs from the pharmacy, so he could sell them,' Rika admitted, her cheeks flushed. 'That's why I almost killed myself trying to get home the day you stopped me. I was going to put them all back before Mama found out.'

Jace glared at Elissa who defiantly met his eyes. 'That's why you were so angry when I arrived with Rika. That's why you wanted me out of the house so fast. You'd found Rika's stash, hadn't you?'

He spat out the last two words and she gave a grim smile. 'Yes.'

Had everything they shared simply been a way for Elissa Andino to protect her daughter?

'And Mia? What happened to her?'

Rika shook her head. 'I don't know. After the nice lady guided me back up to the house, I told Mr Zagrokis I felt unwell and needed to go home. I never saw Mia alive again.'

Jace sat up straight, his spider-sense on high alert. 'What nice lady?'

'The one staying in the cottage.'

'What did she look like, Rika?' Jace demanded.

The girl sat silent for a moment, thinking. 'Dark shoulder length hair, athletic build, pretty but sad. She reminded me a bit of the American actor Sandra Bullock. But the nice lady had a haunted look.'

Jace stiffened and brought out a photo of Dominique. 'Is this the woman you saw?'

'Yes.'

'Was there anyone with her?'

'I didn't see anyone, but I heard a man's voice coming from the cottage. He was singing in a soothing voice.'

Jace's pulse quickened. 'Could it have been a lullaby?'

Rika's eyes widened. 'Yes! I remember hearing a baby giggling.'

Cold sweat trickled down his armpits. That was the precious information Tinto was almost killed for. But had he given up the names of his guests and the names of Elora's new guardians? It was a nightmare scenario. He'd sworn to protect Anna and her family.

Jace was already halfway out the office door as he shouted, 'Thank you, Rika. Thank you, Mrs Andino. You've both been a great help.'

He sprinted for the car and ignored the insistent ring of his mobile. He had to get to Round the Bend, but his hands refused to cooperate. His car keys slipped from his fingers and bounced under a parked car. Frantically he dropped to his knees and began scrambling around for them. Finally, his fingers closed around the fob.

Chapter Fifty-Seven

Javier woke to the silence of an empty house. He jumped to his feet before grabbing the sofa. The floor rose and fell, he was on the deck of a ship listing at sea, and he crashed back onto the rug. Why was there so much furniture? There certainly hadn't been three overlapping flat-screen televisions on the wall earlier. And what was that weird clicking sound? It came from the corridor and was getting louder.

He wasn't alone after all, as a pack of dogs charged in. The small tan ones jumped up to lick his face, while the big white ones were under his arms trying to get him up. Most helpful. His head throbbed and he tried again but his jelly legs gave way. Crawling worked but there were three doorways. He plumped for the middle one and made steady progress to the kitchen.

He shook his head, the other dogs had vanished, and only Pesce and Cleo remained. Clinging to the bench, he dragged himself to a standing position and staggered over to the door. Good, his legs were finally cooperating. He pressed down on the door handle and cried with frustration. It was locked. Now what? Cleo barked. He ignored her. She barked again, eyes on the key hooks. He wrenched off bunches of keys and systematically worked through them all and hit luck on the eighth attempt. And throughout, Cleo and Pesce pawed at his jeans and whined.

He ruffled their fur. 'I know, guys. I'm scared too.'

He drunkenly ran across the road, thanking his lucky stars that the taxi was still waiting in the unofficial car park. Cleo and Pesce jumped in the back seat, but the ancient taxi driver shook his head and pointed to the sign of a dog with a red line through.

Javier climbed into the front. 'There's two hundred euros and not a word to anyone about this.'

The wrinkled face broke into a toothless grin. 'My lips are sealed, son.'

'Brilliant. There's a blue Golf up ahead,' Javier said as he scrolled through his phone. 'Follow it but keep your distance.'

He should have rung Marinos straightaway before charging into the house, trying to act the hero. But maybe it wouldn't have made any difference because the bloke wasn't picking up. He left a terse message and sent a text. Wasn't there some sort of rule that the police had to answer their phones? Well, if there wasn't, there should be. The taxi started up the bank as Javier continued ringing, leaving messages and texting, in the hopes of annoying the man so much he'd answer through sheer frustration. Finally, it worked.

'Marinos,' the man snapped. 'This had better be good.'

'Inspector, thank God. It's Javier Owens. I need your help. Anna Makris and Irina Dubois have just been kidnapped.'

Chapter Fifty-Eight

The taxi was long gone. Jace had intercepted it halfway up the bank. The toothless driver happily agreed to a second promise of keeping his mouth shut and even handed back Javier's two hundred euros. He liked Anna Makris. She was a damned fine domino player.

The dogs were sitting in the back of the police car listening as the two men continued arguing.

'Are you out of your fucking mind?' Jace repeated. He'd never wanted to hit someone as much as the big man sitting next to him. 'I know Anna's your ex-wife, but they'll shoot you on sight.'

'Ex-wife? I don't know what you mean.'

Jace shot a look at the distraught man. 'I've known for weeks. It's my job to investigate the background of every suspect, you fool.'

'Does … does Anna know?' he asked.

'I imagine Mrs Makris is well aware you are her ex-husband.'

'Very droll, Inspector.'

Jace sighed. 'No, I haven't informed Mrs Makris. I saw no need. However, getting back to my point.'

'Have you ever been married, Inspector?'

'No,' Jace replied sadly.

'Have you ever met somebody and known instantly they were your perfect match?'

Jace remained silent. He didn't trust himself to answer.

'Well, I have.' Javier jabbed a finger against the window. 'And that person is somewhere up there.'

Jace gripped the steering wheel. 'And that's what I'm trying to tell you. We don't have the faintest idea where the hell they've gone.' What were the chances of there being two blue Golfs on the road? It'd taken them precious minutes to realise their mistake but by that time it was too late. They now sat on a dirt track near the abandoned radar station. The views might be stunning, but Jace wanted to vomit. 'We could be in completely the wrong place. We don't even know where to start the search.'

'You're wrong, Inspector.' Javier was staring above a tangled hedge and up to Lefkada's peaks. 'Anna's close. I can sense it.'

Jace's hands twitched. He wanted to slap some sense into the Welshman. 'What a load of crap. If you think that, you've been living with Kristina too long.'

'How many times have you had a hunch, Inspector? How many times have you had a gut feeling about a case?' The policeman refused to look at him, but Javier pressed on. 'Initially, there was no hard evidence but something didn't stack up, so you kept going. Even when others scoffed at you but it didn't matter. You ignored them, went ahead regardless and eventually got the proof and made the arrest.'

Jace exhaled slowly. 'And your point is?'

'That we're in the right place,' Javier thundered. 'And the longer you dick me around, the worse it's going to be for Anna.'

'If you care for her that much why did you get divorced?' Jace snapped.

'Because I was a fucking idiot, that's why,' Javier screamed. 'I put money and greed above the best thing that ever happened to me. I abandoned the only person who saw … who saw the best in me. Who believed in me. Do you know what it's like to realise you've pissed away the last fifteen years of your life? That through sheer stupidity you've lost the only person you've ever loved and that you never stopped loving them. No matter how hard you tried to fight it.'

Owens was winding himself up into a guilt-fuelled rage, likely to get himself and who knew how many others killed. Jace had to calm him down. He firmly placed a hand on the man's quivering shoulder.

'Okay. I get it. I understand you feel the need to make amends, but this is not the best way.'

'If you think for one second I'm going to sit here after what you've just told me, think again, boyo. When are your boys and girls in blue going to show up? If at all.'

A random chicken wandered out of the undergrowth. Both dogs hurled themselves against the back windows, barking, clawing and salivating. The bird wisely shot back to safety. Jace sighed. Javier was right. And the situation was actually even worse because Jace had deliberately withheld the knowledge of Elora's parents and their connections to organised crime from his supervisors and colleagues. A shitstorm was well and truly heading his way. His police career was probably over but it didn't matter. All that mattered was Anna and Irina.

'Inspector, this is deadly serious so if you want to stop me – you'll have to shoot me yourself.'

The softly-softly approach wasn't going to work. Time to play hardball.

'Don't tempt me, Owens,' Jace growled. 'What exactly do you hope to achieve by this idiotic enterprise?'

'To buy some time, of course!' Javier replied, rolling his eyes as if his co-conspirator didn't have two brain cells to rub together. 'Like you said, we have no idea how many people we're dealing with. And you know as well as me, your bosses aren't going to sign off on any rescue mission without knowing what they're up against. That takes time, which we don't have.' Jace opened his mouth but Javier held up his hand. 'Listen to me, my whole adult life has been spent persuading people to do what I want. And I'm bloody good at it.'

'You're talking the Mafia here!' Jace cried in disbelief. 'They're not going to fall for some bloke pretending to be a handyman who's wandering in with a pet dog!'

'Maybe they will.' Javier smirked. 'Those types are so far up their own backsides they'll waste plenty of time slapping me around instead of hurting the others. And then you can charge in with the cavalry and grab all the glory.'

Jace groaned. 'You're completely delusional.'

'All you need to do is make sure Elora is kept safe in that hospital, Evie, Leyla and Steffi remain in their fortress, and track down Pip, Andrew and Hugo.'

'That's the easy bit, Owens … I don't think you should do this.'

'I don't have a choice, Inspector,' Javier said solemnly and opened the car door. 'I've got fifteen years of regret and guilt to atone for. I'm not going to fail Anna. I love her too much.'

'Alright, Owens.' There was nothing more he could do. And unfortunately, it was the best available plan. But so many things could go wrong. 'Good luck. Thanks for the laptop and the lowdown on the Andinos and Petre Zagrokis.'

'It's the least I can do. I've got plenty of my own sins to reconcile. This will help the balance sheet.' They shook hands and Javier climbed out. He opened the back door and swung a daypack over his shoulder. 'Come on, Pesce. Time to get this show on the road.'

Jace sat in the car and watched as the pair vanished from sight. He had a very bad feeling about the whole thing. Would his superiors take swift action? He could already hear their protestations and delaying tactics. Mrs Makris had negotiated the safe release of three individuals while a hostage. This was a woman who knew how to handle herself, and wasn't she in the company of the equally competent Mrs Dubois? No, Inspector Marinos, there would be no need to go charging in. Best to carefully assess the situation first.

From the back, Cleo began to whimper. It was all he could do not to join in.

Chapter Fifty-Nine

On a blazing hot late August afternoon, a well-built man and a small tan dog strode through a long-abandoned olive grove. High above the shimmering Ionian Sea, Javier thought it would have been cooler, but in the still air, the oppressive heat radiated off the ground. So, this was what a roast chicken felt like. A feral goat casually glanced up with a mouthful of grass and watched the pair's progress. As the neatly trimmed cockapoo scampered backwards and forwards, it sent up puffs of pollen from tall grasses and flowers. After watering a patch of tiny red poppy-like flowers it bounded back and with two front legs placed dusty pawprints on the man's jeans and enthusiastically licked outstretched fingers.

'Thanks, boy. I needed that.'

They set off again, flitting between shade-giving trees, gnarled and twisted sentinels that were seldom visited now. The dog easily slipped through a gap in an unkempt hedgerow but at six foot three, Javier struggled to release himself from brambles, wild roses, and honeysuckle. The thorns tore his tanned skin. He sucked at the droplets of blood springing up on the backs of his hands. Please, let it be the only blood spilt that day.

The view opened into a beautiful wildflower meadow humming with insects. He inhaled the scent of wild herbs. It seemed a bizarre moment to appreciate the splendour of nature when he was beyond terrified. Pesce appeared undaunted with his tail up and ears bobbing about, cocking a leg at every conceivable bush. How was it possible for such a small dog to pee that much? But it was a welcome distraction. Javier was a consummate planner, so flying by the seat of his pants on a reckless expedition was horrendous.

The warning voice of Marinos reverberated inside his head. 'They'll shoot you on sight ... they're not going to fall for some bloke pretending to be a handyman who's wandering in with a pet dog!' Javier took a deep breath. He believed in his outstanding gift. He believed the talent that had caused untold destruction and damage over the years could eventually be of use. He'd been an exceptional conman, tricking, defrauding, hoodwinking and betraying countless victims without a second thought. What an accolade. His genius had made him rich, but it had never been enough. There was always the next scam, and the next, and the next. He fed off the adrenaline rush. It served the trusting fools right, that's what he'd thought for too long.

The ground was steadily rising with peaks in the distance, but straight ahead, thick vegetation blocked his view. And still no sign of the hideout. But it was here somewhere. It had to be. He stopped and listened. No human activity, only incessant humming and an occasional bleat. Sweat trickled down his back and not from the heat. It was fear. He must succeed. He never lost – ever. This wasn't how he'd expected events to turn out. But against his own worse nature he'd slowly been drawn into Elora's world. He was only a bit part player, entering stage left late in the proceedings. He'd never meet some of the cast who'd dramatically exited the performance weeks ago, Marinos informed him.

And here he was, with no script but determined to play his part, whatever that turned out to be. One of the main players in the hideout had unwittingly brought him to quaint Apokeri. She continued to fight to save Elora and, in turn, Javier was fighting to save her.

He knew she was close by (despite what Marinos said), in the same way he knew when someone was watching him, even if they couldn't be seen. Or knowing someone was in the house, even if they made no sound. Maybe it was something to do with tiny changes in air pressure. Kristina would know, he'd ask her once this was all over. Stepping forward, the baking hot ground sprang back. He'd expected it, but still his heart juddered as he brushed back the dirt to reveal a pressure pad. Pesce peed on it and gave Javier an encouraging lick on the nose.

'Well, I guess they know we're coming now.' His voice betrayed no fear. His eyes were calmly determined.

After quickly messaging Marinos, he buried his only link to the outside world. The conman was ready and set off again with a confident stride, Pesce at his side. And with each step, Javier braced himself for what he hoped was the inevitable. He must be allowed to get inside the hideout and talk. To work his magic. It was the only way this hair-brained scheme stood any chance. In his head, he counted down from one hundred and prayed he and Pesce weren't on a suicide mission.

Chapter Sixty

The dilapidated barn stood in a tiny clearing where wildflowers mingled with tufts of grass. Three gleaming off-road trucks sat in a row. Behind them lay a wall of tangled hedges. As far as Anna could figure they were somewhere near the abandoned radar station, not too far from Egklouvi village. She'd visited the former military base countless times over the years. Almost smack bang in the middle of Lefkada, its elevated position afforded stunning views and the former military base was a cool place to explore. However, her current location was anything but. It was the stuff of nightmares. With hands above their heads, she and Irina were marched into a wooden building held up by sheer will. Within the set of large double doors was a smaller one. The hinges screeched in protest as she was propelled inside. Most of the barn remained in shadow and after the bright sunlight she was disorientated, only able to hear her own rapid, shallow breathing. A foot in the back shoved her into a pool of light.

'Sapete chi sono?' A male voice from the darkness asked.

Did she know who he was? Her eyes made out the silhouette of a man at a desk. Would he know she could speak Italian? It was worth the risk.

'I-I don't.' She swallowed hard and tried again. 'I don't understand Italian.'

He spread his palms on the table. 'Mrs Makris, do you know who I am?'

It was an older voice, smooth and seductive like velvet. She hadn't expected that.

She stroked her chin. 'Let me think. A cold-blooded, obsessive, paranoid psychopath, perhaps?'

He sighed with disappointment and gave a curt nod. The blow came out of nowhere and knocked her sideways onto the floor. But she managed to get an arm down to prevent her skull from cracking off the compacted earth. She was dragged back up and wrenched her arm free of a vice-like grip. This was what she needed. To get angry, so it overtook her fear.

'I'll ask you again. Do you know who I am?'

She shook her head. 'No idea. Give uz a hint?'

There was another nod but this time she jumped sideways to avoid the blow. The next moment she was spun around and belted across the face. Back on the floor, it felt as if her head was going to explode. She came onto all fours and looked up. Directly in front sat a bound Pip, Andrew and Hugo.

'Oh, hi guys. I didn't see you all there. What with being slapped around by arsehole over there.'

And down she went again after a vicious kick in the ribs. Well, it was working. She was definitely pissed off now. Pip and Andrew were staring at her as if she'd taken leave of her senses. However, Hugo slowly blinked once. She took it as a sign of encouragement and clambered to her feet again.

'Mrs Makris.' The voice adopted a reasonable tone. 'We can do this all day if you wish. However, why not save your strength? I know Elora and Pesce wouldn't have been left in your capable hands without you being made fully aware of who I am. I will ask you again. Do you know who I am? And for your sake, I suggest you give me the correct answer.'

'Fine, have it your way.' She exhaled dramatically in the same way Evie did on being forced to do a task deemed unreasonable and ridiculous. 'Your name is Francis Del Ambro Contino Junior. You are Head of the Del Ambro Contino crime family and have been for the last twenty-four years, which I suppose means you must be quite good at your job.'

'See, that wasn't too difficult,' he replied in a patronising tone. 'And yes, I'll have you know I'm extremely good at my job. And from my investigations, it would seem that you are too.'

'Yes, but I don't go around killing people to get what I want,' Anna snapped. She could see him fully now. The man paid a great deal of attention to his appearance. A vain man. A man who had an inflated ego and liked the sound of his voice. Maybe she could keep him talking. 'Did you kill Sergio and Dominique, Mr Del Ambro Contino?'

'Now, now, Mrs Makris,' he answered. 'Understand this, my orders to kill are given only when it's required. I'm not a crazed lunatic on some shooting spree.'

'I'm sure that came as great consolation to your victims and their grieving loved ones.'

'Sarcasm is the lowest form of wit I find,' he said and straightened his cuffs. 'And to answer your question, alas I have yet to kill Sergio and it has never been my intention to harm Dominique. However, be that as it may, I did not bring you up here so I could wax lyrical about myself. The reason—'

And then every electronic device burst into life and all four guards rushed out the door.

Chapter Sixty-One

Javier woke in a shadowy barn, tied to a chair. The afternoon light filtered through gaps in the wooden slatted walls and dust particles danced in the hot air. What looked to be sparrows hopped along the rafters below a metal corrugated roof and the dusty earth was carpeted with their droppings.

'Look who finally decided to wake up.'

Javier shook his head in an attempt to clear the grogginess. A sharply dressed man with a perfectly trimmed grey beard and moustache swam into view. He sat behind a desk in a large, overstuffed leather chair, completely out of keeping with the surroundings. In his late sixties, he exuded power and menace and appeared to have been accidentally transported from a boardroom meeting. Javier imagined a wizened old Greek farmer blinking his eyes in disbelief as he found himself facing an oblong table of high-powered suits.

'And who might you be?'

'I'm Mrs Makris's handyman.'

'And what are you doing here?'

Javier looked at the floor and mumbled a response.

'Speak up, man. We all need to hear this.'

The man flicked his hand, and the next instant Javier was dragged backwards and turned forty-five degrees. It enabled him to see everyone else in the room. His four burly attackers stood in a line to his right. They had charged into him like the forward line of his national rugby team. However, they were dressed in khaki T-shirts, gun belts and camouflage combat pants. Next to them stood Irina, defiant in stilettos, daring anyone to come within striking distance – even if she was handcuffed. Anna was beside her, unshackled, in dusty clothes and with hair flattened on one side. Anger coursed through his veins. And then there was Mr Beige, no longer the harmless geography teacher but an uncaged leopard ready to unleash knife-sharp claws with lethal efficiency.

In front of three doorways opening into smaller rooms sat Hugo, Andrew and Filip. The first two appeared unharmed, unlike Filip, whose face was etched with pain from a black eye and swollen lip. His clothes were ripped, and his right shoulder drooped unnaturally. He must have put up one hell of a fight before being contained. This was bad. Three more hostages. Would Marinos figure it out? Would it delay the rescue operation longer if they couldn't confirm the three men's whereabouts?

'I came to s-save Mrs Makris ... and her friend.' Javier tailed off in defeat.

'Mmmmm. So you say. But I find it hard to believe a lowly tradesman would risk his life for someone he hardly knows.' He gave a wicked grin and leered in Anna's direction. 'Unless, of course, the relationship has developed into something more ... sordid. Have you been giving her one whilst hubby's been away?'

'Don't be so disgusting,' Anna retorted.

Javier dropped his eyes and Francis laughed triumphantly. 'Ah. But you want to. That's clear enough. Is that why you came up here? Hoping your knight in shining armour act would result in a roll in the hay? I like it.'

'You bastard!' Filip screamed. 'I welcomed you into my home and the whole time you're coveting my wife.'

'My, my, Mrs Makris you do seem to stir strong emotions in members of the opposite sex. I wonder if there's more to you than your rather average looks suggest?' The room went deathly quiet as Francis gave her the once over. His lip curled with disdain. 'Perhaps not. But I'm interested to know what's in your saviour's backpack.'

Hector peered inside, smirked and handed it over. Francis chortled and pulled out bags of dried dog food, a collapsible dog bowl, dog treats, dog toys, poo bags, two bottles of water and a packet of trail mix. 'Hardly James Bond, is it? But where's your mobile?'

'I accidentally left it in the taxi when it drove off,' Javier admitted, his eyes on the floor.

Francis bellowed with laughter. 'Good grief, you are a buffoon. I find that amusing, so I'll permit you to live – for now.'

Javier exhaled slowly. So far, so good.

Francis picked up the red ball and slowly rolled it along the desk. Pesce followed it intently.

'Don't hurt him,' Anna blurted out.

'Why, Mrs Makris, I wouldn't dream of it. I love that fluff monster. After all, he was the one who finally led us to you. It's lucky for me Dominique cared so much about her pet and left it in your care because you do have loyal friends. I'm almost envious. Tinto Zagrokis didn't give you up – despite being tortured to within an inch of his life. And we would have finished the job if that idiotic inspector hadn't turned up with half the Lefkada police force.' Francis rocked backwards and forwards in his chair. It was nothing but a game to him and he flashed sharp white teeth. 'If you must know, what gave you away was a round of applause at a dog trick outside a café, and branded workwear. My esteemed colleague in the corner remembered the dog, and after that it was a straightforward internet search for your company, some tracking devices and some ambushes. However, we didn't account for your husband not drinking the drugged coffee which explains his present state. Fate is a strange thing, wouldn't you say, Mrs Makris? It would seem the gods are on my side and not yours.'

Javier stared open-mouthed at the revelation. He couldn't believe it, of all the ways to come undone. He'd been there when Pesce caught the splodge of cream, but Mr Beige hadn't turned around when everyone clapped. He must have noticed the family as he walked past with Petre. Life could be cruel and unfair. However, it didn't change the current circumstances. He still needed to buy more time for Anna.

Francis casually threw the ball and Pesce scampered after it. Squeaking it a few times, he trotted up to one of the henchmen and dropped it. The man refused to acknowledge the dog's existence, even when Pesce jumped up and pawed at his trouser leg.

'Just throw the ball, will you,' Irina spat. 'Or do you need an instruction to do even that? You probably can't take a leak without permission.'

Mr Beige rattled something off in Italian and Francis signalled for Irina to be brought forward. She didn't make it easy and stood ramrod straight. The high-pitched sound of stiletto heels being dragged across the floor was unnerving. Once in place, she turned and spat in her assailant's face and then looked down on Francis with utter contempt. He slowly rose to stand eyeball to eyeball. Even then, Irina tilted her head back to give the impression he was beneath her. Francis ran his eyes up and down her body and licked his lips.

'I like them feisty,' he said with unsuppressed lust. 'The two of us are going to have lots of fun later.'

'In your dream, little man,' Irina shot back.

In a flash, he ripped open her dress and licked her cleavage. Javier felt sick but Irina didn't flinch. Instead, she grabbed Francis's crotch and began to massage it.

'I'm ready to go if you are?' she purred. 'An audience always makes things more exciting – don't you think?'

Like Francis, Javier was transfixed by Irina – but for very different reasons. The Mafia boss was getting off on the encounter whilst Javier was filled with hope. It wasn't just him who was playing for time. Irina was bravely offering herself up as bait. The woman had immense guts. But after a few seconds, Francis stopped her hands and she was hauled backwards.

'There'll be plenty of time for that later. However, I have more important business to attend to.'

He flicked his wrist and Anna was pushed forwards again as Francis retook his seat. 'Right, Mrs Makris. You're going to get Elora for me.'

Anna frantically looked between Francis and Mr Beige. 'I can't do that,' she stuttered. 'She's in hospital. I told him that in the house.'

'What!' Filip stammered and fought to stand up. The henchmen sniggered at the hopeless gesture and one belted him across the face.

'Enough,' Francis barked at his hired thug.

'Why didn't you tell me?' Filip asked Anna.

'I didn't want to worry you. There was nothing you could do to help. She's in the best place.'

Filip slumped back.

'Well, that's what you say, Mrs Makris. But I'm an untrusting man. So you're going to ring the hospital. And you'd better be right, or we'll shoot your handyman through the head.'

Anna sobbed as she recited the telephone number and watched as a gun was placed at Javier's temple.

'Take a deep breath, Mrs Makris. You need to sound calm on the call,' Francis ordered. 'Speak in English so we can all understand. No funny business. My men understand Greek.'

Anna nodded as the speakerphone connected. 'Hello, this is Mrs Makris. Can I speak to someone regarding an update on Elora, please?'

'Hello, Mrs Makris. This is Doctor Shah. We spoke earlier.'

'Of course, but what are you still doing there? I thought you'd have left by now?' Anna replied in her usual friendly manner.

'Well as a matter of fact, Mrs Makris, you're the reason I'm still here. I've been ringing you repeatedly with no response. It's about Elora.'

'Oh my God.' Anna's hands flew to her mouth. 'What's wrong? What's the matter? My mobile is charging at home and I'm out of the house.'

The soothing voice echoed through the barn. 'Elora has taken a turn for the worse. She's stable but I've ordered more tests to be run over the next few days to determine what's causing her breathing difficulties. We need to keep her in until the end of the week. We're taking the best possible care of her, Mrs Makris.'

Anna's hands dropped to her breastbone as she tried to keep calm. 'Thank ... thank you, Doctor Shah. And please pass on my thanks – to everyone there. I know Elora's in safe hands.'

The line went dead and Francis hurled the backpack across the barn. 'Throw them into separate rooms, men. I need time to think.'

Chapter Sixty-Two

Anna shuffled uncomfortably on the cold earth. Six of them were hemmed into a space no bigger than a modest double bedroom. Hours had dragged by. It was getting dark and at the higher altitude a chill wind crept between the wooden slats. She stroked Pesce who, with his lovely fur coat, was happily curled up between her and Irina. Javier had been placed against the adjacent wall and Tweedledum and Tweedledee Junior sat on camping beds next to the door gabbling away in Italian enjoying a beer and eating pizza. Her stomach rumbled and Pesce's nose twitched. He stood up, stretched and padded over to the men. As usual, they ignored him. But this time hunger was making the dog more determined. He jumped up on his hind legs and began pawing at the pizza box. The older man shouted something in Italian and pushed the dog away. Unperturbed, Pesce jumped back up and tried again.

'He's hungry,' Anna explained. 'But don't give him any. Dogs shouldn't eat garlic or onions. Tomatoes aren't good for them either.'

The two men gave her a confused look. They didn't appear to understand much English, so she switched to Greek and they nodded. Pesce kept annoying them.

'I wonder if you could do me a favour? If one of you could go get a bag of dog food off the table out there, I can give him that and then he'll leave you alone.'

The younger one stood up.

'You wouldn't be a love and grab that packet of trail mix and those bottles of water as well?' Irina said flirtatiously and leaned forward provocatively. 'I can make it worth your while.' The lad blushed furiously and shot out of the room. But when he returned, he handed over everything they asked for. 'Thank you.

I'm ever so grateful,' Irina said breathlessly as she tenderly took his hand.

The man scuttled back to his seat as if he'd been burned and, despite everything, Anna found it extremely difficult not to laugh.

***

It was dark now and the only light came from the guards' mobile phones. They were playing some sort of game against each other and kept cursing or cheering. In the dimness, Anna could make out Javier. He was still asleep, and she was worried sick. Ever since they'd dragged him in and coshed him around the head, he kept dozing off. What if he had a concussion? But he was too far away to reach, and she didn't dare call his name. The guards were engrossed in their competition so she gently nudged Pesce awake and pointed at Javier. The little dog trotted over to him, sat down and looked back. She pointed at his face and motioned with her tongue. Pesce jumped up and started licking Javier's face until he woke up. Anna held up the leftover trail mix and a bottle of water. He shook his head.

'Are you okay?' she silently mouthed.

He glanced at the men who were oblivious and gave her a grin and a wink before closing his eyes again. Anna relaxed against the slatted wall as Irina squeezed her hand.

***

Everything was quiet as Anna lay under a scratchy wool blanket, with another one acting as the world's most uncomfortable pillow and tried to sleep. They stank of horse or maybe donkey and had been covered in cobwebs when the blushing young guard had thrown them at the women a few hours earlier. Anna had gratefully caught hers and thanked him profusely. Irina naturally flirted outrageously. The scarlet-faced youngster might have still been a teenager and appeared unused to a sexually confident woman. At least one guard wasn't a total git, as he'd even provided Javier with a blanket, much to his comrade's disgust. Anna had listened to them bickering about it for the next hour. It was much more entertaining than their earlier Champions League conversation which had gone on far longer.

The guards' mobiles burst into life. Anna tightened her grip on Irina, petrified her friend was going to be dragged away for Francis's pleasure. But the pair jumped up and ran out of the room. Anna, Irina and Javier shot up. But any thoughts of escape were short-lived as the fake cyclist nonchalantly strolled in.

'I hope you weren't thinking of going anywhere,' he asked and held up a lantern to reveal a gun directed at Anna's head. 'If anyone makes a move, the lady's dead.'

Nobody moved. Anna's heart pounded. This man couldn't be reasoned with. He would shoot them all dead without a moment's hesitation. Twenty minutes later their two guards returned in a foul mood. The older one slammed the door shut and the camp beds were once again jammed up against their only means of escape. The two men clambered into their cosy sleeping bags and began sniping about feral goats and sheep repeatedly setting off the outdoor sensors. Anna and Irina shook with silent laughter as through the wall came the sound of Filip humming 'Baa Baa Black Sheep' before being told to shut up. The rest of the night passed off peacefully.

Chapter Sixty-Three

A wet tongue and the sound of a distant cockerel woke Anna. She struggled to open dry eyes and was met with the snout of a cockapoo. Pesce stood on her chest, demanding love, attention and breakfast. After a kiss and a tickle, he squirmed between her and the wall, snuffling and scratching beneath the slats. Anna turned her head to see the legs of a much-cursed goat munching weeds. Tapping Pesce on the leg she shook her head, and with sly eyes, he stopped. Anna peeked over Irina's shoulder to find both guards fast asleep. Javier was wide awake and casually chewing on trail mix and drinking a bottle of water. He waved across the room at her. She hadn't even heard him move and neither had the guards it seemed. At the sound of munching and slurping, Pesce sped across the room for a titbit, and the older guard was instantly awake. He sheepishly glanced at his companion, who slept on. Javier cheerily waved, then mimed zipping his mouth closed and throwing away the key. Anna did likewise. A few minutes later there was banging on the door and a demand to open up for breakfast. A hand produced two hefty bacon and egg sandwiches, then two cups of coffee and two bottles of water. The older guard glanced at his captives and then called after the invisible waiter. Heated words were exchanged, and the younger guard joined in. There was a string of expletives outside the doorway but a few minutes later the same breakfast in triplicate appeared with bonus dog food. The older guard nodded to them all as he handed their food over and they all silently thanked him. He even let Pesce eat out of his hand and gave him a smile on being rewarded with a lick.

 Their room adopted a relaxed atmosphere. The guards gathered up the empty napkins and returned to enthusiastically playing their game, Pesce raced around the room with a squashed empty water bottle and Irina, Javier and Anna sat together. The situation had improved but Anna was under no illusions. If they tried anything funny, the two guards would probably shoot them. However, as long as they behaved an uneasy status quo prevailed. The warmth of the wood seeped into her bones and she closed her eyes and listened. No sound from next door and outside the munching goat had moved off. She tried to tune in to any noise but there was only silence. Nobody was coming, nobody was going to save them. But at least Evie and Elora were safe.

'There's something I've been meaning to tell you,' Javier whispered. 'It's about the night we met.' She nodded for him to continue as Irina leaned in. 'You didn't accidentally knock that pint of beer over me.'

'But I did,' Anna insisted and frowned. 'I was stone-cold sober, remember.'

He smiled, gazing past her. 'You were huddling under an umbrella in the queue, laughing with Annalise, Julia and Tom. Three groups ahead of me and my mates. I noticed your laugh first, so carefree and happy. People around grumbled about the rain but it didn't faze you. As soon as you got inside it was straight on the dancefloor.' His eyes lit up. 'You were amazing. I'd never seen anyone dance the way you did, and I still haven't. It's like, I don't know how to put it into words …'

'Pure unadulterated energy. A lifeforce. Boundless joy,' Irina supplied but shook her head. 'It's more than that. It's as if Anna *is* the music.'

'Yes, that's exactly it,' he exclaimed. 'For almost an hour I circled the dancefloor waiting for you to come off. Tom, Julia and even Annalise had gone to the bar or toilet but you remained in your own world. And I suddenly thought, what if the only time you leave it is to go home? I'd miss my chance and I couldn't let that happen. Eventually, your little group split, although the other three were still close by, keeping an eye on you. It was now or never. I weaved my way towards you. I had to get the timing just right and when you threw back your hands they connected with my glass and I threw a whole pint over myself. You should have seen your face.'

'I thought you were going to kill me,' Anna added. 'But instead—'

'I winked and said it was my fault and you agreed.'

'That sounds about right,' Irina murmured. 'And then what happened?'

'I took a massive gamble and pulled Anna to the bar and asked what she wanted to drink. And she stayed with me. I couldn't believe it. The music blared out but for an hour we chatted and laughed in this little booth and the whole time she was completely focused on me. Not glancing over my shoulder, not checking her mobile, not staring down at her glass and swirling ice cubes. Her eyes held mine and all she wanted was to know about me, which I can tell you came as a revelation, up to that point my girlfriends …'

'Had been self-centred, self-serving, high-maintenance drama queens?' Irina quipped. He nodded. 'I thought so. But please continue.'

He smiled again and caught Anna's eyes. 'And then I asked her if she wanted to dance.'

'He looked kind of nice and so I thought I might take a chance,' Anna quietly sang.

'Are those lines from a song?' Irina asked.

'Songs,' Anna wistfully replied. 'There's a male version and a female version. They were our songs and we'd each sing our version to one another.'

'Trust you to have two songs,' Irina replied.

Anna smiled at Javier and sniggered. 'But he didn't stick to the lyrics, did you?'

'Excuse me, young lady. You mean *you* didn't stick to the lyrics.' He turned to a bemused Irina. 'The lines are "And then he kissed me." Or "And then I kissed her." But on the dancefloor, Anna kissed me. And wow, it blew my socks off.'

Irina raised her left eyebrow. 'I wouldn't have had you down as the shy type, Mr Owens.'

'I'm not. I mean I wasn't.' He stumbled over his words. 'I didn't want to blow it, you see. On a dreary October evening in Newcastle, I'd found the one. Even before we kissed, even before she saw me, I loved her. My Anna. Love at first sight.'

Irina placed a hand over her heart. 'That's the most romantic thing I've ever heard.'

'Oh, Jav. Why did you never tell me that before?'

'Yes, you idiot.' Irina whacked him on the arm. 'Why the hell are you only telling us this now? Do you know how many times you could've used that as a get-out-of-jail-free card?'

He struggled to find the right words. 'The first time anyone asked us what point we fell in love, Anna immediately said it was love at first sight for her. And when they asked me, I paused. Anna laughed and said I was still thinking about it. And it got to be this joke. But the reason I'd paused was I didn't want to say "me too" as it sounded—'

'Trite,' Irina completed his sentence and again he nodded. 'Yes, I see what you mean. Who would have believed you?'

'Me,' Anna said quietly. 'I'd have believed you.'

'I know you would have, sweetheart,' Javier leaned over and kissed her cheek. 'I'm sorry, I should've told you years ago.'

Anna hugged her knees. 'I'm scared, guys. I don't think we're going to get out of this alive.' She was rocking backwards and forwards, her voice barely a whisper. 'I think Evie's going to lose both parents and Elora will end up in care.'

Her friends tucked in beside her and Javier spoke softly to them both. 'Don't be stupid. Of course you're going to get out of this. Irina and I have you covered.' Irina nodded.

It'd been a nice try but Anna felt much worse. He'd used the singular and not the plural and Irina had agreed. She didn't want freedom at the expense of her two friends' lives.

And then came another bang on the door and an order to bring all the captives out. The two guards reluctantly got to their feet. Everyone knew the dynamics would change once they left the room. Back to Us against Them. The older one nodded to Irina and Javier who stood up. All three exited, with Pesce trotting behind. Anna was the last one to stand and gave the young guard a tight smile. They were both hidden from view.

He quickly stepped forward and grasped her hand. There were tears in his eyes. 'I'm so very sorry.'

She squeezed his hand in return. 'So am I.'

Chapter Sixty-Four

Everyone was back in position. Only this time Javier wasn't tied to a chair and Francis didn't seem to mind. However, Filip, Hugo and Andrew were. And judging by their faces, things hadn't gone well in their room. The muscle in Hugo's neck pulsated with rage at being so easily snared. Andrew looked exhausted and Pip's pallor was sickly. He stuck his tongue out and licked the side of his mouth. Anna brushed her face and a flake of egg fell into her hand. Filip rolled his eyes in disbelief as she swallowed it. The exchange had not gone unnoticed. Francis flicked his wrist and Anna was dragged forwards.

'I hope you and your fellow roommates enjoyed breakfast in bed, Mrs Makris?'

Andrew's chin hit the floor. It appeared that room service had not extended to next door.

'Yes, it was lovely. Thank you for providing it and the extra food for Pesce.'

Francis studied her. 'You're welcome. And now that you are rested and refuelled you will retrieve Elora from the hospital.'

'B-but I can't. You ... you heard last night. She ... she's too ill. They're running tests.'

Francis slammed his fist down on the desk. 'I don't care how ill she is, Mrs Makris. You're going to override the doctors and bring her to me.'

Anna dug bitten fingernails into her palms. She needed to stay strong until the end. Time had finally run out. She took a deep breath and all the guards' mobiles burst into life again. Francis cursed and motioned to one of the guards from Filip's room to go check it out. The barn door banged shut and he refocused his attention on her.

'I won't do it,' she said defiantly. Let him do his worst. She could handle it.

'Mrs Makris, we're going to ring the hospital on this speakerphone and if you don't instruct them to release Elora, I'll order Hector to shoot your husband's friend in the arm.'

Her legs began to shake. It was the first time Francis had used the man's name. That wasn't a good sign.

'And if you still refuse, I'll order him to shoot your brother-in-law in the shoulder. Hector is a crack shot, but his hand might wobble, and the bullet could veer off course into the neck or heart by mistake.'

She tried so hard, but a sob slipped out.

'And if that still doesn't persuade you, Hector will fire a bullet straight through your husband's head. Is that what you want?'

The tears poured down her face. One life in exchange for another.

'I don't have all day,' Francis yelled and raised his hand.

'Make the fucking call,' Anna screamed.

'No,' yelled everyone she loved.

The rings echoed, and each chirpy trill was a nail in her coffin. It took forever to connect. 'Hello, this is Mrs Makris. I urgently need to speak to somebody about Elora.'

The calming voice of Dr Shah filled the barn. 'Good morning, Mrs Makris. I do hope you managed to get some sleep last night?'

Anna swallowed painfully. 'A little. I was with some good friends … which helped.'

Those good friends were currently out of sight, which was just as well. But she could feel their eyes boring into the back of her.

'That's good to hear. Now about Elora—'

'Yes, I was ringing—'

'For an update. But of course, she's prepped for her first batch of tests this morning.'

Francis made stabbing motions with his finger and silently ordered her to get on with it.

Pushing down tense shoulders, Anna raised her aching head and projected her steady voice so nobody could doubt her intentions. This was it. 'Excellent. I knew I could count on you,

Dr Shah, and the rest of your team. Elora is in capable hands and will be well looked after. Thank you again from both me and my husband. We will never forget what you've done for us. Goodbye.'

'Thank you, Mrs Makris. Goodbye.'

The line went dead.

'Fuck you, Francis,' Anna yelled. 'Did you really think I'd be party to Elora's execution? That I'd happily march into the hospital and extract her for you to carry out murder? That I'd forget the ultimate sacrifice of Monika, Dominique and Sergio? And the promise I made to keep Elora safe. Because if you did, you're definitely a sick, twisted psycho.'

She knew it was coming but still screamed in disbelief when the bullet tore into Hugo. Hector might have used a silencer but it didn't eliminate the horrific sound of the gun going off. It made way more noise than Hugo, who was fighting to master the pain radiating down his left arm and gave a valiant thumbs-up sign.

'Mrs Makris—'

'Boss,' Hector interrupted. 'The guard hasn't returned.'

Francis swore and signalled Filip's second guard to go and find out what was happening. 'Mrs Makris, I'm not a patient man. But I'm prepared to give you another chance. Will you take it?'

Anna quickly brushed away tears and turned to her friend of fourteen years and brother-in-law of three. What if Hector deliberately steered the bullet off course? She'd be responsible for his death. Her sister-in-law would be a widow, and her niece would lose the only man who'd ever loved her like a father. She hoped he'd understand.

'Andrew—'

He gave her a tight smile. 'Don't you dare take that second chance, Anna. Don't make the call.'

She faced Francis and shook her head. A second shot rang out and Andrew screamed. Anna hardly dared look but the shot was true. Hector had followed his instructions and hit the shoulder. Now came the kill shot. He wouldn't miss.

She smiled at the wonderful man she loved as a brother. Pip had been the very first person she'd met in Apokeri. Right from the start they'd hit it off. He was laid-back and cheeky – a perfect foil for her seriousness. Married for over ten years, they'd gone through so much and come out the other side stronger. No wonder everyone (bar Alex) thought they were a rock-solid couple. And really, they were. Apart from not being sexually attracted to one another, theirs was a perfect union. Sadness welled up. Pip was never going to openly love Alex or get to say farewell. If by some miracle she managed to make it out alive, how would she ever explain her actions to a grieving lover? Let alone her daughter and in-laws?

In typical Pip-style, he grinned. 'See you on the other side, babe.'

The gun didn't fire. Anna became aware of Francis talking but her eyes held Pip's.

'Mrs Makris. I begin to understand the unwavering loyalty you inspire. However, I grow tired of these delays, and I've come to realise that my present course of action will not change your mind. You're a remarkably stubborn woman so unfortunately, you've forced my hand and left me with no other option. If you have any last words to say to your husband, now would be the time.'

Chapter Sixty-Five

Anna refused Francis the satisfaction of a reaction but did watch the dawning realisation hit Pip, Andrew and Hugo. All three desperately tried to break free and she heard the scuffling of Irina and Javier behind. But it was useless. Nobody could save her. Two little paws pressed against her leg and Pesce nuzzled her hand. For thirty-six years she'd bumbled along, trying to do the right thing. And at last, in Apokeri she'd found her forever home and been blessed with a beautiful daughter. She loved her family and wonderful friends and had managed to cram quite a lot into a relatively short life.

She shone one final megawatt smile at her husband. 'Tell Evie that I—'

The gun went off. Anna was livid as the sound reverberated in her ears. Of all the low-level deceitful things to do. How dare Hector shoot her dead before she'd finished her goodbyes?

But hang on. How could she be thinking about being dead if she was dead? She patted her body. No pain and no blood. Her crumpled corpse wasn't lying at her feet either. And it should be, shouldn't it? I mean how did you know if you were dead, if you'd never been dead before? And Pip, Andrew and Hugo were looking at her and they must still be in the land of the living. She didn't understand what had just happened and then all hell broke loose.

Two figures burst out of a stable doorway with guns drawn. Anna froze in disbelief. She must be dead because they were Sergio and Dominique. How was that even possible otherwise? Time slowed as her two friendly guards cast down their weapons and raised their hands in surrender. Sergio, Dominique, Hector and Francis were all shouting and Pesce was yelping but to her stunned brain it was simply noise. And then Sergio called out, fired over her left shoulder and then there was a heavy thud.

Before she could turn, another shot rang out and Sergio went down.

'Vengeance is mine,' Francis triumphantly shouted, standing victorious and grasping one of the guard's guns. 'Domore, we can finally be as one.'

Dominique howled in anguish as a tan blur shot past Anna. In the place of a cute cockapoo was a quivering mass of snarling rage with its muzzle drawn. The brave soul charged onwards to avenge his fallen master. It didn't matter to Pesce that he couldn't inflict any major damage. Everybody left standing screamed at him to stop and only Francis failed to join in as with an evil grin he levelled the gun a second time and took aim at Pesce who was baring down fast.

'No,' rose Dominique's voice. 'You've killed everyone I've ever loved. But not Pesce, you won't take him.'

She aimed the gun at Francis and squeezed the trigger.

'Toni's alive,' he cried. 'Your mamma's alive.'

Dominique wrenched her arms upwards as the gun discharged, and the bullet punctured a hole in the roof, scattering the remaining birds.

And then the barn doors burst open. In swarmed an armed response unit with Inspector Marinos leading. Through all the uniformed legs pelted Cleo, straight past a confused Anna. She caught sight of Pip's horrified face and followed his eyes. First to Hector who lay dead. It was difficult to feel sorry for someone who'd intended to kill her seconds earlier. Then she saw what her husband was staring at.

He lay on the ground as if sleeping next to an expanding pool. Cleo slipped on the glistening floor and then raised a paw to gently prod him – a pure white paw slick with dark red blood. For a second, her brain refused to accept it but then she propelled herself forward and, on her knees, skidded into his blood. So much blood, too much blood and it was spreading.

'Jav,' she sobbed and cradled his head. 'Baby, you have to wake up.'

His eyes fluttered open, and he struggled to raise a hand to her face. She clamped hold of it and held on. His voice was barely a whisper. 'I didn't think it would end like this.'

The tears streamed down her face. 'You're going to be okay, sweetheart.'

She looked around wildly. At Dominique sobbing and Pesce whimpering over a dead Sergio, at Irina weeping, kissing and desperately trying to untie Hugo, her iron-clad resolve gone. At the police checking over Filip and Andrew while Francis was handcuffed and read his rights. Her two guards argued with the police and frantically pointed in her direction and, across the room, Inspector Marinos stared at her in utter dismay.

'Where are the fucking ambulances, Jace?' Anna screamed. She'd never used his first name and it cut through all the chaos.

'They're on their way,' he yelled.

'You hear that, Jav? Help is on its way. You need to hang on a bit longer, that's all.'

'At least I died saving the woman I love,' he said, but his voice gurgled and with it came a terrifying wheezing.

Anna started violently shaking him. 'Don't you dare say that. Don't you dare leave me. Not now, not when you're back to being the man I fell in love with. Not when you've got over being an absolute arsehole for the last fifteen years.'

His body started to convulse. 'Don't! It hurts when I laugh. I'm glad you know that I love you first.'

And then the guilt hit and the tears kept coming. 'I'm so sorry, Jav. I'm so sorry for being a complete bitch. I never gave you a chance—'

'Yes, you did,' he said forcefully but the once strident voice was fading. 'And it worked. I found my way back because of you. Evie told me I had to be soul-sorry and I am, Anna. Please forgive me. I threw away your love. Being married to you was the most wonderful thing that ever happened to me.'

'You're already forgiven, you stupid idiot.' Anna's eyes and nose streamed. 'I never stopped loving you. I just didn't realise it, because the hate kept it hidden for so long. But that's gone now.'

'I'm glad,' he mumbled, and Anna desperately shook him back awake. He rallied, and his eyes found hers. 'You must listen to me. I need you to do something for my family.'

'But you can—'

'Sweetheart,' he implored. 'We both know I'm not going to make it … so I need your help.'

She nodded numbly. 'I promise.'

He was speed-talking as if every word might be his last. 'Marinos has my laptop. Get it. There are bank accounts. Transfer the money into my sisters' and parents' accounts. Username BobbyW.' She broke down completely when he reeled off the password. It was the venue and date of their wedding. 'I need you to get me back home.' His voice was barely a whisper now. 'Tell my sisters I wasn't a total bastard in the end.'

She nodded and wiped her snotty nose. 'I will.'

'On the computer, there's another file. Kristina's got one. I did it. I traced her living relatives. Make sure she contacts them. Tell her she worked her magic on me. Tell Filip I wasn't—'

Anna laughed. 'Pip's not angry, Jav. He was buying time like the rest of us.'

'Good. Tell Evie she's a great kid and to keep up footie practice. You did it, Anna. You saved me. You saved Elora. You saved everyone. You always do.'

'Don't go, Jav. Please don't leave me.'

'Miracles happen, Anna. Remember that.' His voice was so quiet she had to lean right over to hear. 'My birthday wish came true. I wished for you to love me again – and you do. I love you … forever.'

'I love you too,' she whispered. He smiled that beautiful smile and his eyes closed. Against her wet cheek, his hand went limp and dropped. She kissed his lips. He was gone and then she saw a dull glint and began sobbing again. He was wearing his wedding ring.

'Noooooooooo.' A long drawn-out wail encompassed twenty years of love and hate and every other emotion they'd shared. He was never coming back. The pain was unbearable. Someone had reached deep inside her with a barbed hook and wrenched everything out. Cleo howled and Anna welcomed in the rage. It consumed her, a pressure cooker with only one release. And this time, she'd do it.

The Mafia don was being led away. How utterly perfect – no escape.

She clambered to her feet in blood-drenched clothes. She didn't have the physical strength but had the means. Unhinged laughter bubbled up because Francis was right – she did command unswerving loyalty.

'Cleo!'

The powerful dog's head snapped up, she eyed the Mafia don and began growling.

'No!' Filip screamed from across the room. He frantically fought to break free. To get past the police and reach her. But he was too far away and he knew it. 'Don't do it. Think of Evie. Think of Elora. Think of Javier. His final act will mean nothing if you issue that order.'

Pip was right. Anna collapsed over Javier's body and wept for her first love. For the man who'd taken the bullet meant for her. For the man who'd willingly sacrificed his life so she could live hers.

Epilogue

Fifteen months later.

The house on the hill looked magnificent. It was a perfect November afternoon and sunlight danced across the pool. On the terrace, Anna warmed her hands around a mug of tea and snuggled into a blanket. Reclining on a lounger beside her, Dominique did the same.

A succulent hog slowly rotated on a spit. Roast peppers, steak, halloumi and monkfish sizzled, and a team of chefs feverishly kept pace with a never-ending queue of ravenous guests. There was no chance of anyone starving. Laughter, chatter, scraping plates and clinking glasses surrounded them. They'd been invited to a fundraiser by Tinto Zagrokis. He was on a mission to raise enough money to build a specialist rehabilitation centre. And if anyone could, it would be him. The man had a programme of events lined up, and with his connections all the great and good of Lefkada had rocked up. Tinto, Alex and Anna had each given impassioned speeches and she would fulfil any request the man asked. Anna owed him an enormous debt of gratitude. He'd almost died by refusing to give up any information. He'd escaped brain injury but even extensive plastic surgery couldn't mask the physical scars – and he'd been devastated by the death of Sergio. Anna closed her eyes and, through the open doors, Tinto's beautiful violin drifted on the breeze.

'I love that piece,' Dominique murmured and shushed Hope.

Javier had been right. Miracles did happen. After years of trying, Dominique was the proud mother of a healthy seven-month-old baby. And her daughter had a doting grandmother.

However, right up to the birth, Anna had been terrified Dominique would demand Elora back. She was sure they would be locked in a custody battle – because who had the greater right? The wife of the child's dead father? Or the guardian who'd accepted the child as her own? It was needless worry. With the death of Sergio, Dominique was adamant Elora should stay with her new family. She'd immediately returned home to be reunited with Toni, taking a joyful Pesce. And that's what Anna couldn't comprehend. Dominique had risked everything for Elora when Sergio was alive, but now he was dead she'd moved on. Anna had also put her life on the line for Elora, but she'd never give the little girl up. And as of yesterday (when the final adoption papers were signed) Elora officially became a Makris and Anna could finally relax. There had been precious little relaxation over the last fifteen months.

After death and destruction in the barn, Anna had been desperate to hold Evie and Elora – it turned out the hospital had deliberately exaggerated her breathing difficulties – and then immediately set about carrying out Javier's wishes. Irina and Hugo helped set up a network of bank transfers so the Owens family were financially secure, and no awkward questions would ever be asked. And Anna sorted all the official paperwork to fly back with Javier's body. Things were made more difficult because Anna needed to take Evie. After Javier's death, the child became distraught every time Anna left her sight. There was no way Anna could go to Wales alone. However, it ended up being a godsend.

It was decided, after long consideration by the Owens, to tell Javier's father about the death of his eldest son. He'd counted down the days until Anna's arrival, believing she was still his daughter-in-law. It had been heartbreaking to find the loveable bear a shell of his former self, but Anna remained strong and answered all his questions. He'd then turned to Evie and asked who she was. Her daughter proudly said Javier had been her footballing coach and he'd been really good and she'd been his art teacher. From her backpack, Evie withdrew some of his drawings and asked if she could pin them up on his bedroom walls. Javier's dad said yes that would be nice as Anna fought back the tears.

The intimate funeral was emotion-charged. Javier's sisters were still dealing with the guilt of parting with their brother on bad terms, Javier's dad was highly distressed and his wife looked exhausted. In the tiny chapel, Evie had leaned over and whispered 'Mam, it's okay to cry. I know you loved Javier. You don't have to hold it back because of me.' It opened the floodgates and she sobbed and sobbed but afterwards, over tea and sandwiches, everyone shared happy stories that brought solace and laughter. And in what Anna thought was an incredible act of kindness, her mother, sister and brother-in-law attended the funeral, insistent on paying their respects to the man who'd saved Anna's life.

It started a strong friendship between the two mothers. And that night, when Evie had crashed out exhausted, Anna recounted the events in the barn and finally Javier's sisters understood he died loving them.

He died a hero.

On the flight home, an unusually quiet Evie blurted out a question. Who was she going to live with, when her parents divorced? Anna was horrified and it led to an explanation about different types of love. She'd been in love with Javier once and that's why they'd married, but she wasn't in love with him anymore. She loved him the way she loved Auntie Rini, Auntie Annalise and Nana Kristina. After much questioning, Evie was eventually satisfied and her distressing behaviour evaporated. The little girl had been terrified when Anna left for Wales that she'd never come back.

The small Welsh funeral had been in complete contrast to Javier's memorial service. The Apokeri villagers and more besides crammed into the church. Anna knew Javier was well-liked but was still astounded at the turnout. As well as so many residents, there were all the girls' football team with their parents and their coach, all the Benrubi Enterprises employees, and Inspector Marinos with his officers. Irina and Hugo flew in to pay their respects and Anna live-streamed the service to Javier's family who listened to readings from Kristina, Agnes, Irina and

Inspector Marinos. And then, hand in hand, Anna and Evie spoke of what Javier meant to them. It was one of the hardest and most rewarding things she'd ever done, and Evie had been unbelievable.

Sitting on the pool terrace, Anna looked towards Apokeri. Out of sight but nonetheless a comforting presence.

Alex wandered over and scooped up his goddaughter. 'Come here, my gorgeous girl.'

And there was one of the most bizarre friendships to come out of the whole affair. Anna could understand Tinto being asked to be godfather but still struggled to get her head around the rock-solid friendship between Dominique and Alex.

It started with the near-fatal clifftop collision. Dominique aborted the suicide mission at the last second. She had needed to make sure Alex hadn't died and used the last of the Castellas cash to anonymously fund his Thessaloniki rehabilitation. The couple remained in the shadows, but on hearing of Tinto's near-fatal attack, they tracked down the person who'd rung the report in. Unbeknown to Hector and Tinto, the housekeeper had slipped in to drop off a food package, overheard the horrific beating and remained hidden whilst desperately messaging Inspector Marinos. The Castellas then set about locating Hector, found the hideout and bided their time before bursting in.

Anna unwrapped the blanket and patted the sun lounger. 'You sit here, Alex. I need to catch up with Agnes. See you later, Dominique. Bye-bye, Hope.' Anna kissed the little girl's head and walked into the packed house. She'd used Agnes as an excuse.

'Hey, babe. How's it going?' Pip hugged her close. 'You look a bit lost.'

Anna gratefully accepted a mini burger from one of Benrubi Enterprises' newest waiters. He wasn't as gorgeous as Javier but still had a fine ass. 'I was outside with Alex and Dominique.'

'Oh, I see.' Filip stood for a minute staring out the window and watched Alex and Dominique chat with the cute-bum waiter. 'I need a drink.'

Anna ground her teeth. Alex's return to Apokeri had unsettled everyone. Initially, he'd appeared the same, still the same gregarious guy who had them crying with laughter. But with Francis behind bars, Anna and Pip pushed to adopt Elora and to do so meant remaining a couple for the foreseeable future. Alex supported them but was no longer content to live a total lie. Apokeri now knew he was gay. It initially caused a stir and, more importantly, changed the dynamics between the lovers. Alex no longer backed down to Pip (which Anna secretly thought was a good thing), he could harmlessly flirt and tease and had received plenty of propositions (although he wasn't interested) and was always chatting to Dominique on the phone or arranging the next visit.

It brought out a new side to Pip she didn't like. He was moody and sullen. At first, she'd let it slide but when Evie asked why her dad was so angry all the time, Anna put her foot down and told him to get his act together. Everyone had been through enough crap without his childish jealous behaviour. Alex was happy and had a new friend. Pip wasn't in the playground at school anymore. Evie needed her dad, so he'd better buck his ideas up sharpish. But her husband was still struggling to deal with his lover's new sense of freedom.

Anna nodded at Petre Zagrokis, who made a beeline straight towards her. He kissed her hand and the huge smile was infectious. 'I wanted to thank you again for agreeing to speak today, Mrs Makris. I can't tell you how grateful I am. I know how busy you are. Sorry to dash, I must catch the mayor, he's promised a donation and I don't want him to sneak off without doing so. I'll catch you at next week's footie game. Narella and Evie are a great forward line.' He kissed her hand again and was off.

'The change in the man is quite remarkable, isn't it?' said Elissa Andino. 'I don't think I'd mind him dating Rika now.'

Petre Zagrokis had been a smart lad; on the arrest of Francis, he'd immediately cut a deal and avoided prison. He agreed to testify about the drug trafficking operation and became a man reborn. He was devoted to his older brother, threw himself into the family business and the fundraising and had turned into a most dedicated uncle.

'Wow, Elissa, you look stunning.' Anna blushed furiously. 'Sorry, that sounded like—'

'I looked terrible before.' The woman laughed and it was light and carefree. Gone was the severe make-up and the tight bun. Instead, subtle eyeshadow highlighted beautiful grey-green eyes and soft curls framed a smiling face. She was a most attractive woman. 'It's amazing the effects a soon-to-be ex-husband behind bars can have on you.' Her eyes sparkled with mischief.

The Andino brothers were languishing in jail but remained tight-lipped and maintained they had no knowledge of Francis Del Ambro Contino Junior and his business affairs. They'd stuck to the same story that Mia was their contact for the drug smuggling – everything went through her. She'd played a clever game in seducing Stelios first and then Giannis. The boat was a perfect cover for the technical diver to retrieve the drugs, and pass them on to Stelios to go out on delivery trucks; it was how Nereus had survived the downturn. After Mia boasted to Petre about the operation, he wanted in, knowing that his brother's haulage business could traffic drugs all year. In the end, the death of Mia Tovier was recorded as death by misadventure.

The news of her husband's Mafia drug involvement had been the final straw and Elissa Andino filed for divorce. With her name on the business deeds, she fully intended to take her philandering husband to the cleaners. Rika went to university, Sebasti remained at Round the Bend, and both sisters chose to distance themselves from their father.

'So, no hard feelings with Petre testifying against Stelios?' Anna asked.

'Hell no. Twenty years! I'd have sentenced him to thirty at least for what he did.' Her eyes hardened but then widened slightly. 'Oh lord. Sorry, Anna. I can't stay.' And another person shot off.

The reason was pushing her way through the crowd. 'Wonderful speech, so moving. I'd love to stay and chat, but I must catch Eris and Jeremy about a job. You know … what with everything that's happened.' Anna breathed a sigh of relief as the woman continued on her way. Sarah Andino had wisely resigned her position as deputy-head because she was choosing to stand by her husband and would tell anyone who cared to listen (or couldn't get out of the way fast enough) that both Andino brothers were unwitting pawns. Privately, Anna found that stance preposterous. The brothers had smuggled drugs and lived very well off the proceedings for over three years.

In place of the huge dining table, the croupiers efficiently dealt cards and roulette wheels spun. Gambling for a good cause. Anna had so far kept Pip away from the poker table. She watched a magician point to Dr Shah's champagne flute. There was a round of applause from her colleagues when, open-mouthed, she fished out her wedding ring.

Anna jumped when a voice whispered in her ear. 'Do you fancy a stroll? I want to spy in Tinto's Japanese garden for inspiration.' Looking resplendent in a colourful kaftan and pompom hat, Kristina stuck out her arm. 'Come on, I know a shortcut.'

The pair took a flight of stairs down past the bustling kitchen where Agnes was barking orders to her team, and past a half-full cinema room glued to an action film. They stopped at the doorway of a snug den. A children's storyteller transfixed her audience with fairy tales. Completely engrossed, Pip sat cross-legged on the floor with Elora. They crept away, pushed open a door, down another flight of stairs and out into the garden. It was much quieter below the house but as they wound their way down uneven stone steps there came cheers, groans, gasps and applause. In the lengthening shadows on the lawn was an eleven-a-side walking football match. All the kids and grandkids stood on the sidelines cheering and the loudest were Leyla and Evie.

'Shoot, Nana Sofi, shoot,' they screamed, jumping up and down.

Their grandma deftly slid the ball past one of the sprightlier members of the domino club. With arms overhead, she ran the length of the pitch with her knitting club teammates yelling that grandmothers rocked. It caused the newest member of the Makris family to race across the centre line, followed by Cleo and a collection of other four-legged friends.

'Pitch invasion,' the domino club yelled. 'Disallowed goal.'

'In your dreams,' responded the knitting club as the dogs were brought under control.

Four months after Javier's death, an older gentleman with flowing robes, a pointy hat, half-moon spectacles and a long beard had entered Round the Bend. The regulars were bemused as he joined a spellbound Evie at her table with a large box. It was too bulky and heavy for the owls and even though it wasn't the typical gift for magic folk, he hoped she'd like it. Evie tore open the lid and inside was a tiny bundle of black fluff. It was love at first sight. She'd immediately rung her Auntie Rini with the news. Irina informed a wide-eyed Evie she'd met the gentleman a week ago and mentioned somebody special needed cheering up with a puppy. Evie named him Owen and every day the spaniel made her smile and laugh.

Anna and Kristina left the bickering behind. After a few minutes, they walked underneath bright red Japanese Torii Gates into a slice of heaven. They skirted an immaculate gravel garden and sat on a stone seat overlooking a tarn. Across the water stood a tiny tearoom framed by tightly clipped shrubs and fiery red Acer trees. From within came the sound of giggling and as the screen door slid open, out tumbled the newest Round the Bend recruit hastily tucking his shirt into his half-buttoned jeans, followed by Sebasti smoothing down her dress.

'Having fun, you two?' Anna called out. The pair were mortified at the sight of their boss and beat a hasty retreat. Their embarrassed laughter slowly faded.

'Love's young dream,' Kristina mused.

'So it would seem,' Anna said and watched as Koi carp rose to the surface hoping for food. 'Why don't you tell me why I'm really here.'

Kristina gave her friend a shrewd look. 'I think you're getting far too much like me, young lady. But you're quite right. I wanted to run an idea past you. I miss Javier, I miss our chats, and I miss his reassuring presence. The house is so empty with him gone. And it got me thinking. I loved helping him back on his feet and thought what if I did that on a slightly bigger scale? What if I converted the house into an up-and-coming artists' residence? Free board and lodging to develop their skills and they get to showcase their work in the gallery. In return, they help in the garden and I get some company. What do you think?'

Anna hugged her friend. 'That's a fantastic idea. When do you want to start?'

'I thought maybe in January when I get back from New York.'

'That sounds perfect.'

Kristina was remarkable. After only a little persuasion, she'd hesitantly made contact with her long-lost relations and was slowly building bridges. Earlier that year (aged ninety-three), she'd flown to Zurich for an emotional reunion with her ninety-seven-year-old sister and enormous family. And next month the pair were flying to New York State to visit their other sister's grave, spend time with the American side of the family and go back to childhood places visited by the Nilssen family so many years ago.

Arm in arm, they strolled back up to the house with Kristina taking the opportunity to enjoy the extensive grounds. Against the backdrop of a magnificent flame-red sunset, they came in via the front door to find Olivia and her brother quietly arguing in the foyer.

'Thank goodness,' Olivia cried. 'The one person Jace will listen to. He's trying to sneak off and he promised to show me how to play blackjack.'

Anna crossed her arms. 'Is that right, sir? I hope you're not breaking your word. I know you'd hate for me to get angry.'

'Fine, I'll stay,' Jace snapped, throwing daggers at his sister. 'I wanted to have a word with Mrs Makris anyway.'

'Excellent,' Olivia said brightly. 'Come on, Kristina. I want to ask you about a particular flowering shrub I know you have in your garden. I think it'll work well in my floral displays.'

'The woman's a nightmare,' Jace fumed as the two women vanished around the corner. 'She treats me like a kid, not a grown man who happens to be a police inspector I might add.'

'That's big sisters for you. At least she only teases you in front of me and Kristina and you know we'll keep quiet,' Anna quickly pointed out. 'Anyway, now that you have me, what can I do for you?'

He paused as if collecting his thoughts and Anna was struck again how, after over a decade, she still barely knew him. He was intensely private, and she sensed a tortured soul. The man never seemed truly happy. She liked to think that visiting Round the Bend most days helped. He did smile and occasionally laugh then but it was as if there was an empty void that couldn't be filled. After Javier's death, he'd avoided her at all costs. He'd stopped coming into the café and refused to return her non-police-related calls. Growing increasingly concerned, Anna had contacted Olivia.

Although they were only passing acquaintances, his sister had no scruples in revealing Jace couldn't face Anna because he held himself entirely responsible for Javier's death. On the orders of his superiors, Jace had held off bursting into the hideout until the time it was deemed right. But the gunshots of the Castellas had overridden that. Jace was guilt-ridden for following the chain of command. If he hadn't, Javier would be alive. Both women agreed the man was being completely ridiculous. Olivia, therefore, gave Anna free rein to use whatever means at her disposal to knock sense into her thick-headed brother. In the end, Anna resorted to good old-fashioned emotional bribery. The next day, Jace had opened his front door to find Evie, Elora and Cleo on the steep steps. While Anna hid around the corner, Evie handed over a letter and explained to the inspector that he must read it or she'd be in big trouble.

> Dearest Jace (sorry, but after events in the barn I can no longer call you Inspector Marinos),
> What do you think you're playing at? Olivia tells me you blame yourself for Javier's death. That's the biggest load of crap I've ever heard in my whole life. You will get your backside to Round the Bend tomorrow or else I'll drag you there myself. I dare you to defy me.
> However, that would be unwise because you know I'll do it and it would be best to save yourself the embarrassment. As an added incentive I'll allow you to order one treat off the menu each week.
> But in all seriousness. Please don't stay away. We all miss you.
> Due to the combined efforts of Javier, you and your officers I still have my darling daughters, my husband, brother-in-law, Irina and Hugo.
> You have now saved my life three times.
> I will forever be in your debt.
> Love
> Anna

He'd sheepishly turned up the next day to order the most calorie-laden meal on the menu. Two months later when Jace was awarded a special recognition for outstanding services in the line of duty he immediately handed the medal over to Anna. And she in turn presented it to Javier's family when she flew back to Wales six months later for the loveable bear's funeral. Javier's father had died peacefully, surrounded by his remaining family.

'Jace?' Anna asked gently. 'Is everything okay?'

There was nowhere to sit so he motioned to the carpeted stairs and they sat down side by side.

'I thought your speech about the benefits of bereavement counselling was compelling. Despite the fact you refused the offer from our police liaison officers.'

Anna stared at the lilies on the entrance table as a petal dropped. 'I didn't need it.'

'But you admit it worked for your daughter,' he probed. 'I happen to agree with Filip, I think you should take up the offer. It will help.'

Bereavement counselling had helped Evie. Losing Javier only a year after the unexpected death of her granda left her daughter reeling. And the counselling also uncovered other unresolved issues. Anna had felt terrible. She should have pushed Evie to take counselling after the hostage situation. But her amazing little girl had hidden her fears so well and refused help. She said everyone was safe and the bad man was locked up so there was nothing to worry about. And that was why Anna kept refusing counselling. She didn't want anyone poking around in her head, disturbing things best left alone. Deep down she hid her love for Evie's true father and carried the enormous guilt of continually lying to her daughter and choosing never to tell Daniel he had a child. Their child.

'Have you ever had bereavement counselling?' Anna asked.

'I've never needed it.'

'Because you've never lost anyone close to you?' And it was there, a tingling along her arms as he tensed. The air pressure dropped, another petal fell, and a car door slammed. 'Is that what you wanted to ask?' She deliberately changed the subject and he relaxed.

'Sorry, I was out of order. You've made your decision and I need to respect that.' He cleared his throat. 'It was only an update about the trial date, or should I say the lack of one. There's still no news. You know we're going to call upon you to testify and I'll let you know as soon as I hear anything more.'

The outlook for Francis Del Ambro Contino Junior appeared bleak. In Greece, he was awaiting trial for various charges, including murder, kidnapping and coercion. The Italian authorities were also amassing considerable evidence to charge him with kidnapping, attempted murder, historical murder and extortion. Once word of his arrest got out, everyone moved to bring him down. And an unexpected treasure trove appeared in the form of Hector's mother. She blamed Francis for her son's death and handed over a dossier on the executions of mistresses that Hector had undertaken for his boss. With her son gone, it was unlikely any posthumous charges would ever be brought. The lawyers were working through a mountain of information. And whether Francis would ever make it to court was debatable. He was in solitary confinement after two attempts on his life.

They slowly stood and Jace reluctantly glanced up the corridor to the raucous sound of partygoers.

Anna winked. 'Get yourself away, Jace. I won't say anything to Olivia.'

He smiled but looked sad. 'Thanks, Anna. You're a star.'

The front door closed, and she was left alone. When Javier turned up twenty months ago it had begun a rollercoaster of heartbreak, happiness and ultimately redemption and hope. She'd come out the other side stronger and was free to remember the wonderful times with Javier. He'd been a massive part of her life and would forever have a place in her heart. She was his legacy and through his sacrifice, she'd stuck to her promise.

They'd all played their part in saving Elora.

ACKNOWLEDGEMENTS

I poured my heart and soul into Apokeri Bay and did likewise with Saving Elora. However, the sequel was far more emotional. I think it was because I'd grown to love the characters from the first instalment and absolutely sobbed my heart out during the climactic chapter. I only hope I have managed to capture this in my writing. I sent Saving Elora to my editor before Apokeri Bay was published and I'm so glad. The weeks running up to and the months after its publication were a juggling act which I'm not entirely sure I pulled off. With that said I'm eternally grateful for the unwavering support of my family and friends. To my wonderful editor Manda Waller for helping to make my novel sing. To Debs Southwood and her team at Wigwam Studios, who worked their magic again on the book cover. Thank you to Claire Hall for the years of friendship and your proofreading expertise. To my life-long friend Nicola Huggins who provided guidance and clarification on anything medical. All errors are my own. A special mention must go to my fantastic partner, Graeme, who endures the highs and lows of a self-published author. Thank you, does not begin to cover it. And finally, massive thanks to you the readers. The wonderful feedback, reviews, shares, comments and likes make it all worthwhile.

If you enjoyed Saving Elora, please consider leaving a review on Amazon and Goodreads. It really helps us self-published authors.

It's always lovely to hear your thoughts, so get in touch on either TikTok, Facebook, Instagram or Twitter. All links are on www.jackiewatsonwrites.com, where you can sign up for my newsletter and find out what I'm up to.

Printed in Great Britain
by Amazon